Acclaim for Charlie Huston's
SKINNER

"*Skinner*'s fluency with both the world of spies and of high technology, like Olen Steinhauer by way of William Gibson, makes it a gripping read, and the humanity Skinner finds in himself is genuinely touching."
—Charles Finch, *USA Today*

"A thriller for the Edward Snowden summer.... Mr. Huston is renowned for making the fantastic believable."
—Steve Dougherty, *Wall Street Journal*

"*Skinner* is a searingly contemporary, character-driven international thriller built around a mysterious cyber attack that has parallels in today's news.... A highly complex picture of how people live at opposite ends of the economic spectrum."
—Carolyn Kellogg, *Los Angeles Times*

"This tour de force features two of the most interesting characters we've seen in years.... Huston's world is cynical, chilling, and eminently believable.... Mind-bendingly original, from the characters, to the dialogue, to the sensory-overloaded world that feels eerily like the one we're about to live in. Add Huston to the A-list." —Keir Graff, *Booklist*

"Charlie Huston writes crime fiction for a new century but does so in the tradition of the masters. Skinner specializes in 'asset protection' and his skills are tested here to their fullest." —*Playboy*

"*Skinner* is an up-to-the-second thriller, combining big ideas, gouts of blood, and a fascinating mix of damaged characters."
—Sam Thomas, *Cleveland Plain Dealer*

"Fun and inventive....An espionage thriller for the information age with echoes of John le Carré and William Gibson."

— Christian DuChateau, CNN.com

"*Skinner* doesn't just borrow from the headlines—it critiques them, in the service of a well-plotted and ultimately character-driven story. It's a hell of a book."
—Alison Hallett, *Portland Mercury*

"Taut, provocative."
—Margaret Quamme, *Columbus Dispatch*

"Guns go off. Bodies fall. And happily for him, this lonely boy from the box falls in love....All this comes to us tricked out in a blinding avalanche of twenty-first-century event-packed rhetoric that sounds like a blend of William Gibsonish future patter and Thomas Pynchonese conspiracy."
—Alan Cheuse, NPR

"*Skinner* feels remarkably current: drones, robots, cyber-surveillance, guns made from 3-D printers."
—John Wilkens, *San Diego Union-Tribune*

"Stunningly original characters, wildly surprising twists, and an ending that's both unexpected and moving make this an extraordinary genre stand-alone."
—*Publishers Weekly*

SKINNER

ALSO BY CHARLIE HUSTON

Sleepless
The Mystic Arts of Erasing All Signs of Death
The Shotgun Rule

The Henry Thompson Trilogy
Caught Stealing
Six Bad Things
A Dangerous Man

The Joe Pitt Casebooks
Already Dead
No Dominion
Half the Blood of Brooklyn
Every Last Drop
My Dead Body

SKINNER

CHARLIE HUSTON

MULHOLLAND BOOKS

LITTLE, BROWN AND COMPANY

New York Boston London

Copyright © 2013 by Charlie Huston

Mulholland Books / Little, Brown and Company
Hachette Book Group
237 Park Avenue, New York, NY 10017
mulhollandbooks.com

Originally published in hardcover by Mulholland Books / Little, Brown and Company, July 2013
First Mulholland Books trade paperback edition, April 2014

Mulholland Books is an imprint of Little, Brown and Company, a division of Hachette Book Group, Inc. The Mulholland Books name and logo are trademarks of Hachette Book Group, Inc.

The publisher is not responsible for websites (or their content) that are not owned by the publisher.

The Hachette Speakers Bureau provides a wide range of authors for speaking events. To find out more, go to hachettespeakersbureau.com or call (866) 376-6591.

Library of Congress Cataloging-in-Publication Data
Huston, Charlie.
  Skinner / Charlie Huston.—First edition.
    pages cm
  ISBN 978-0-316-13372-2 (hc) / 978-0-316-13370-8 (pb)
  1. Intelligence officers—Fiction. 2. United States. Central Intelligence Agency—Fiction. 3. Cyberterrorism—Fiction. I. Title.
  PS3608.U855S63 2013
  813'.6—dc23   2013001055

10 9 8 7 6 5 4 3 2 1

RRD-C

Printed in the United States of America

"Then it may well be that we shall by a process of sublime irony have reached a stage in this story where safety will be the sturdy child of terror, and survival the twin brother of annihilation."

—*Winston Churchill*

SKINNER

PROLOGUE

gravity of the sun

THE CIMETIÈRE MONTMARTRE.

Skinner is staring at a headstone, puzzling at the name carved there.

Reistroff Guenard Spy.

No one to hear him, he sounds the name to himself. His French spoken with the accent and affect of an advanced language tape.

With a brief pause, he adds a silent comma to the name.

"Reistroff Guenard, spy."

Changing the last syllable into a profession. Smiling.

One hundred and fifty meters away, down the Avenue de la Croix in the 28th Division, he finds the mausoleum of the Lazarous family. That name, masoned from granite, Gothic script, arched, *Lazarous.* The cuteness of it was too much for someone to resist. The designer of the op. And too easy for someone else to recognize. He hardly needs to open the door to know what he will find. A suspicion further strengthened when he reaches into the stone urn on the step and finds that the key that is meant to be there is missing. Skinner reflects on one of his favorite metaphors, all too applicable in his life, Schroedinger's cat. Until he, Skinner, opens the mausoleum door, his asset is both alive and dead inside. He is tempted to turn his back and leave, allowing for the possibility that, unobserved, the man within will remain in a suspended state of uncertainty forever. But that is not the contract. So, an unlocked gate and behind it an unlocked door, and, behind that, a corpse that will never rise. By any reasonable standard his contract is now complete. Was complete the second his asset was shot and killed. Except that Skinner has special clauses in his contracts. Invisible codicils. But known to everyone.

So he inspects the body.

Someone was direct and professional, anonymously so. First two bullets in the chest, a large target for a shot from a handgun from over twenty meters away, and the final bullet in the head, a small target that offers a level of certainty when shooting from within five meters. Two shots to bring the asset down quickly from a distance; a third shot, after closing that distance, for peace of mind.

So to speak.

Skinner looks at the rectangle of sunlight that leads out of the mausoleum. It invites observation from without, encourages a watcher. In the box himself now, neither alive nor dead. A definitive state will be arrived at on the other side of the rectangle.

A chest shooter. Conservative. Closing for the head shot.

Skinner considers, and steps through the rectangle into the sunlight, pauses on the step that leads down from the mausoleum, pulling tight the belt of the half-length khaki trench coat he chose to wear today because of the anonymity it offers in a city where the garment is ubiquitous every spring. He pushes his hands into his pockets and the first bullet hits him in the chest, pushing him back into the darkness of the mausoleum, the second bullet hitting within fifteen centimeters of the first before his upper body can quite disappear into the shadows. The shots are muffled but resonant, coughs from the throat of a large jungle cat (a cliché that Skinner knows to be accurate, having had occasion to hear a jungle cat cough). Pigeons fly from nearby horse chestnut trees, then settle again in the branches. Skinner's legs and feet, protruding from the stone mouth of the tomb, are motionless, the scuffed catspaw covering the leather soles of his dark brown oxford boots presented for inspection.

The man who emerges from the doorway of a 112-year-old maintenance hutch 27 meters down de la Croix trots with a directness that matches his methodology. Straight line, weapon held alongside his thigh so it won't be noticed by any tourists as they return from taking a rubbing of Truffaut's gravestone, eyes fixed on Skinner's feet, alert to any sudden movement.

Skinner can discern nothing specific of the man's features. Looking into the bright sun from within the tomb, all he sees is a black silhouette, its edge blurring in pulses as waves of pain continue to radiate from his chest.

Two meters from Skinner's feet, the silhouette raises its gun.

Skinner imagines that the assassin is now close enough that he can make out his own pale oval of face in the darkness. Target for one final bullet. Close enough to register also that Skinner's trench coat, while ripped open by the first two rounds, is unstained by blood. Does he, in fact, see the silhouette flinch as this revelation arrives in the assassin's brain? Doubtful. And, in any case, impossible to accurately determine, as the realization, if it exists at all, is reached at virtually the same instant that the silhouette registers the muzzle flash from the Bersa Concealed Carry pistol in Skinner's right hand, followed in an all but immeasurably short flicker of a moment by the sound of the shot as it echos from the mausoleum; any further thoughts cut short by the .380 subsonic bullet that trails the waves of light and sound.

Though tending toward conservatism in these matters himself, a fact attested to by the BAE Systems armored vest he wears under his trench coat, Skinner understands the value of taking a high-percentage, close-range head shot whenever circumstances present one. Rising to a seated position as the man is falling back, he takes a second bead on the ruined face, waits for the body to hit the ground, and squeezes off another round.

Certainty is all.

Stepping into the light, Skinner looks at the dead man. Any ID the man carries will be worse than useless; engineered to mislead. That doesn't matter. His face has been smeared by the impact of Skinner's bullet, but an ID is possible. The man's name was Lentz. Skinner has met him, a professional introduction, made by a friend. Recently.

A breeze moves the branches of a chestnut tree, sunlight flickers and tickles his ear, and Skinner knows he is being watched. He knows this, feels it as a kind of pressure, atmospheric. He looks and sees, several divisions away down de la Croix, a middle-aged man frozen in his track, ranks of gravestones between them. The man flaps his open mouth and runs. Standing near the two corpses, Skinner is painfully aware that he is in danger of playing out a scenario reminiscent of Eric Ambler. Man of mystery, fleeing through the aisles of the dead, pursued by gendarmes, his avenues of escape cut off at every turn by the flash of yet another blue uniform.

He tosses the Bersa away, skimming it over the stone floor into the mausoleum, leaving behind the dead, those entombed and those not, walking northward toward the wall that runs along the Rue Etex, stripping off the ruined trench coat as he goes, peeling the straps of Velcro that hold his armor in place, letting it drop, an audible thud that leaves him nearly two kilos lighter, a man in slacks, shirt collar peeking from the neck of his dark sweater. Against the chill he knots the scarlet scarf he'd worn tucked inside his coat, unharmed but for a burn that might easily have come from the coal of a too casually held cigarette.

As the sirens become audible, the Hôpital Bretonneau comes into view beyond the cemetery wall. A few quick steps and Skinner jumps, grabs fistfuls of green vines, the toes of his boots planted in notches between blocks of granite. He pulls, swings his legs up, lies flat atop the wall. Quiet street. After midday, high sun, the French are in the cafés, none of which are here. His chest hurts where the bullets embedded in the armor. He thinks about the gamble of having stepped into the light, trusting that the man outside the mausoleum would shoot him where he had shot the asset. Trusting that the man was as good a shot as the evidence suggested.

When did he start trusting such things? When did he start trusting anything?

To have died in the tomb of Lazarous.

That would have been foolish.

He smiles at the thought, rolls from the wall, and walks away.

Later, when detectives from the Brigade Criminelle canvass the area, a patient in the hospital, an elderly man who often spends his day peering out the window at the cemetery, as if casting into a glass of the future, will tell them that he saw a man of uncertain age, average height and weight, bland hair color, in trousers that might have been blue or brown or black, and a sweater that was similar, jump to the top of the wall and pause there, easing his head into a pillow of ivy, as if to take a nap, and then roll himself over, dropping to the sidewalk with a hesitation that suggested he might be slightly injured, before walking up the street and disappearing once he reached the corner. The only item remembered being the flash of red around his neck, streaming behind him in a sudden wind, like a trail of blood.

An account the detectives find less than helpful, but one that is, as it happens, quite accurate.

A gift of Skinner's, to cause people who view him to see only what he wants them to see. A gift cultivated during a long childhood spent on the object side of a glass pane, scrutinized by eyes that never saw, in all their years of observation, that they had bred a killer. Or caused one to be made.

A short while later, emerging from the Métro at Saint-Paul, topping the stairs next to the newsstand on the island between Rue de Rivoli and Rue Saint-Antoine, staring into the faultless blue of a Parisian afternoon crisscrossed by the vapor trails of jets on approach and departure to and from De Gaulle, Skinner experiences a memory: The infinite wall of sky that he saw for the first time when a child welfare officer, escorted by several sheriff's deputies, took him from his parents' home at the age of twelve. The shock of that vastness having swallowed in an instant more than a decade of containment and solitude. The sky. When all there had been before was Plexiglas, and beyond that the basement ceiling, unfinished, sheets of cotton candy pink insulation stapled between the joists. Skinner's heavens. In the arms of the stranger, everyone other than his mother and father a stranger, he had wrenched and squirmed, convinced he was falling upward, where that small, intensely bright ball of light would burn him.

He freezes, staring upward, face to the sun.

He is going to have to kill a great many people soon. Someone has taken his asset, and now he will have to hunt and kill any and all who were involved in that misjudgment. *Skinner's Maxim* demands it: *The only way to secure an asset is to ensure that the cost of acquiring it is greater than its value.*

Skinner has no formula to determine the value of his lost asset, the man Lentz killed in the mausoleum. He only knows that it must have exceeded any previous price he has exacted. He thinks about some of the things he has done in the past, the exertions that have firmly established his reputation in the community of asset specialists. He thinks about fingers. Scalps. Innocent family members. A thin stainless steel rod heated until it glowed white. He remembers a warehouse near the last standing panels of the Berlin Wall. The headline that ran on the cover of *Bild am Sonntag* the day after the Landespolizei found what he'd left inside. "Schlachthaus."

And he wonders why the people who engineered this bizarrely incompetent attempt on his life couldn't have left his asset alone and spared him the tedium of creating yet another slaughterhouse.

Acquisitions had been easier for him. The measures of success and failure so absolute. Either you acquired the asset or you did not. Protection is uncertainty manifest. Unless an overt acquisition is attempted you may never know if your precautions have been sufficient. If no one tries to take what you have, is it because they cannot hope to claim it or because they simply don't care?

But, in the long run, he'd failed at acquisitions. Temperament. Some nuance in his conditioning, hard to locate. A node of morality, he suspects. Over time it had come to irritate him, a pebble scraping at an obscure region of his brain. There had been consequences. Emotions. Very strong. Far outside the limits of his conditioning. He'd lacked the tools to feel these things and survive. Quitting acquisitions was the only option. But what then to do with his skills? A very specific set of abilities that fulfilled him as all talented people are fulfilled by what it is they do better than anyone else.

Protection held the answer.

He could resume the application of his trade, do those things that came to him most naturally, and do them without qualm. All that was required to ease the abraded sensitivity that the conditioning had instilled in him was to restrict the use of his talents to killing in the name of protecting others.

There were complications. The hallmarks of his work in acquisitions, corpses that appeared to materialize around bullets hovering in the air waiting for them, parties who evaporated from existence on cloudy days; these ephemeral deaths would not do. He'd had to demonstrate his commitment to the maxim. More than once. But, with time, the conditioning he impressed upon the community required only infrequent reinforcement. Still, the market forces of security guaranteed that there would always be someone willing to test the limits of the maxim. His name commanded a premium that ensured his assets would always be of great enough value that someone might be tempted to risk abomination. Skinner was not perfect; not all of his assets survived. But those who claimed the assets always lost more in the long run.

Over the years Skinner himself lost three toes from his left foot. His back had the texture of wax melted and rehardened, the result of third degree burns and only moderately successful skin grafts. The tip of a Gryphon M30A1 combat stiletto that had snapped off between the eighth and ninth ribs on his left side could not be surgically removed with any convenience. Calcium began to encase it; it grew into his rib cage. And though it caused him discomfort, he decided to leave it there. The blade in his bones. Gray appeared in his hair.

And now Montmartre.

Lentz.

Introduced to Lentz just weeks ago. By a friend.

A woman, attractive, as Parisian as the sky, comes up the stairs behind Skinner, sees the bemused look on the face turned up to the sun, and smiles as she sidles around him, hoping, a little, to catch the eye of the intriguing stranger, but failing to do so. Skinner is busy making a mental list of the future dead. Those he must kill in order to make safe those he will come to protect. The most discouraging aspect being that the people he'll have to kill are his current employers.

And his friend. Or, rather, *the friend*. Skinner's only friend.

With great suddenness, Skinner wants horribly not to kill his friend.

He loses his footing, feels the upward tug of the sky as a physical thing in his chest. All it manages to tear from him is his breath, but it is no less shocking a sensation than if his heart had been ripped free by the gravity of the sun.

Life, he thinks, *was much easier in the box.*

He blinks the sun from his eyes, mounts the final step, feels that he is unwatched, and fits himself into the flow of the sidewalks, eyes flicking upward, setting forth on a course plotted along the axis of one of the contrails that scar the otherwise perfect sky.

It is only after several days have passed and none of the people who were involved in the Montmartre Incident have died that they realize the truth.

Skinner has disappeared.

A fact that leaves none of them at ease.

PART ONE

bringer of the ball

ALL RAJ WANTS to do is go outside and play soccer with the other boys.

He kicks the ball, toes it, centimeters at a time, closer to the door. As if he is merely following where it leads. The leather shiny, new, white that reflects the brightly colored light filtering through curtains his mother has made from a sari worn too thin for decency. The color shifts as he nudges the ball again. The leather will never be this bright again. Outside it will be coated in dust in the dry months, mud in the rains, dung always. Scuffed, scratched, patched after it is inevitably kicked against an edge of sharp, rusted steel protruding from the roofline of a shanty or booted into a scatter of freshly broken glass shards that no one has yet scavenged.

Only now is it new and clean. Only now can he take it outside, trophy, to show the other boys. Shine in their eyes as bright as the ball.

The ball thumps against the open door, mahogany planks his father has cut from a tabletop salvaged in the city center, rejoined, cloth-hinged, and hung. A door. Such a luxury in Dharavi. Open now, only halfway, stopped by wall-mounted shelves, vertically slotted to hold his mother's plates and pans. In a one-room home, space allowing a door to open flush to its wall is an impossible waste.

The men and women crowded inside the single room of their home, packed around the small table, do not look up. Their conversation continues. His father is showing the others something on the screen of his laptop. An Acer Aspire with rubber guards, hand-cut from old car tires, epoxied at the corners to protect it from drops. On the screen, a diagram, electrical. Color-coded lines running in parallel, making abrupt right-angle turns, knotting themselves, unspooling, streaking to another page. His father has played games with him using diagrams like these.

Follow the green line, Rajiv, use your finger, find where it ends. Yes, yes. Oh! But now there are two green lines. Which is the right one? Follow it, follow it.

When he was five, the games became lessons. Positive, negative, erg, watt, voltage, amp. Now, at twelve, Raj can look at a diagram without knowing what it is for and determine its purpose on his first try. Or his second try, sometimes his third. And he can also rewire any of the slum's rat's-nest circuit boxes all by himself. Or with only a little help from his father. The diagram on the laptop screen is for something large. A fragment of something massive. The lines draw him almost more than the ball. Almost. But he has seen them before. Watched as his father used the software on his laptop to design that massive maze of circuits. Old hat. The ball is new.

He kicks it against the door again. And again no one looks up.

His mother kneels next to the bright orange Envirofit cookstove. Envy of the neighbors. A bed of wood-chip coals glowing in the base of the small cylinder; on the cooktop, a kettle coming to the boil. Tea soon. She arranges cups on a brass-colored tin tray.

Another kick. Thump of the ball against hardwood.

Only two eyes turn his way. The baby, Tajma, nestled in another of his mother's retired saris, at the foot of the cot that mother, father, and baby all share. Too big now to have a place on the cot, Raj has a mat and blanket. *No problem,* he says. A mat and a blanket, more than so many boys his age.

The baby's eyes are on the ball. Raj kicks it once more, her eyes dart to follow it, her mouth opening in surprise when it bounces sharply off the door.

It goes this way, and then that way!

She waits for more.

Raj kicks again, a little more force, a little backspin, a slightly different angle; the ball skips to a stop just against the door frame, half its circumference exposed to the sun.

Taji's eyes widen, her mouth an O.

Outside the door, dirt packed hard against the hump of an enormous water main running half-buried down the middle of the narrow lane between the shanties and their patchwork walls of cinderblock, corrugated steel, scrap wood, waddling, tin, and cardboard. At the far end, a scrum of filthy boys passing in and out of sight where the street opens onto a small square in front of the great shed that serves as shared factory space for the many industries of Dharavi Nagar, in the heart of Dharavi slum.

Raj's gaze travels from the boys to the ball at his feet. With his toe he scuffs the dust just inside the door on his mother's otherwise spotless floor. Fighting the dirt and mud, an endless task, like keeping her family fed. He brings his foot back; a light kick, an accident, will send the ball outside. What choice but to follow? And once outside. Well, he will deal later with the consequences of not returning immediately. When he returns, hero to the boys. Bringer of the ball.

"Rajiv."

He jerks his head around at the sound of his father's voice, his bare toe stubbing against the tile.

"Close the door."

He hops, lifting his throbbing foot from the ground.

His father snaps his fingers.

"Now, now."

On one foot, Raj bends, picks up his ball, the sun falling full on his face as he does so, the screams of the boys in the square coming to his ears clearly.

"Inside, Rajiv."

His mother, hooking the collar of his overwashed *Transformers* t-shirt, pulling him inside as she swings the door closed and seats the latch.

"Sit with your sister."

Raj, looking at the door, ball tight to his stomach.

His mother yanks his collar again.

"Later, later. Sit, sit."

Raj backs away from the door, limping slightly on his bruised toe. Eight steps to cross the room, this tiny journey an epic today because of all the guests he must edge around and squeeze between, his path taking him past the little table and its mismatch of chairs filled with the most senior and honored of their visitors.

His father grabs his arm.

"Come see."

Raj's mother, the rattling tray of tiny cups in her hands.

"Aasif."

His father looks at her.

"I want him to see."

"Let him play with Taj."

His father still with a grip on the boy's arm.

"He should see. Why else if not for him? He should see."

She sets the tray suddenly on the table, one of the men pulling the laptop out of the way.

"Yes, yes. For him."

Without serving, she takes three steps to the cot and scoops up Taj.

"And also for her."

Aasif raises a hand.

"For her also, yes, Damini. Bring her here."

One of the men at the table is staring at Raj. The one who brought him the ball. He also brought a stuffed tiger for Taj, almost as big as her. And a bag of aavakaaya for his mother. Pickled mangoes from his home to the east in Gadchiroli district, now heaped in a bowl on the tea tray. Small, dark, hair cropped close; hands calloused thick and smooth, compact muscles suggesting years swinging a hammer or an axe, but a potbelly at his middle. A voice, Hindi accented by the forests. They call him Naxalite sometimes, but Raj knows that his real name is Sudhir.

"Like the ball, little Raj, for you."

He holds up his hands, ready to catch. Raj tosses the ball and it smacks into the easterner's hard hands. He spins it between his fingers.

"Someone will tell you that it's not real. They'll say, *There's no hologram, Rajiv. How can it be real if there's no hologram.* As if the only way we know a real thing is if it has a sticker. A hologram that says FIFA. But don't believe them. The ball is real. It was made by real hands. Feel."

He throws the ball, shoving it two-handed so that it sends the boy back a step when he catches it.

"Real?"

Raj nods.

The man reaches for the teapot, using a small square of clean rag to pick it up by its wire handle so as not to be burned by the heat conducted by the cheap tin. He begins to pour, filling the cups one by one, setting the pot aside, adding the milk and sugar he also brought, making thick chai, passing the cups to the others at the table, Raj's mother first. There are some mutters from the old men of the nagar panchayat, the informal local council and arbiters of disputes: *Should they not be served first, and by the hostess rather than this jungle communist?* But Sudhir seems not to notice, pouring tea as if he were a wallah in an office, passing the cups to the women of the Social Ills Assistance Foundation, the representative of the Dharavi Business Is Booming Board, the boss of the electricity goons whom Raj's father has known for many years, a Bombay Municipal Corporation man who has something to do with water treatment, the heads of the potters' and tanners' guilds, and also men speaking for the welders and recyclers, a small-time boss from the gangwar, a woman from a Muslim microbank that loans tiny sums to women of all religions to start small businesses, and a young policeman. These, and several other dignitaries and lowlifes of the slum, are packed into Raj's home, being served tea by this outsider, Naxalite. Not here are any of the water goons or men from the Shiv Sena or the Congress party. The water goons have threatened the entire proceeding and pledged their noncooperation unless they are paid an ungodly sum. The Sena were approached, but communications broke down. And the local Congress man seems most content to pretend nothing is happening.

Raj has seen all of them here at one time or another, but never all at once. Things are happening, exciting things, but still he only wants to go play with his new ball.

Sudhir passes the last of the cups, many of them borrowed from neighbors to accommodate such a large gathering.

"People will tell you, Raj, your whole life, what is real and what is not. What you can believe in and what you can't. Don't let them say, *This is something you don't think it is. You don't understand, you couldn't understand.* It is what you think it is, you do understand it. Believe me."

He smiles.

"Or don't believe me. You decide."

He sips his chai.

"Rajiv."

A whisper.

"Rajiv, if I tell you that your father is a very rich man, do you believe me?"

Raj looks at his father, the educated outcast of Dharavi. Madman of the wires. His quest to bring the wire to every home of the nagar, safely engineered. His family lacks for nothing that can be had in the slum, but rich?

He shakes his head.

The man puts a hand on Raj's father's shoulder.

"But he is. He's rich. He owns a castle, Rajiv, in this wealthy land."

He gestures with his other arm, taking in the hut and its contents, drawing some laughter and some discontent from the gathering. This is serious business they are here for, not games.

Aasif touches Sudhir's hand with his own, brushing it off his shoulder.

"Don't confuse him."

The man stares at Raj, brown eyes, jungle green in their depths.

"I'm not teasing him. I'm telling him the future."

Raj's father looks into his teacup.

"It is *his* future. If there are riches, they are not mine. Here."

His fingers dip into the breast pocket of his loose orange short-sleeved collared shirt, coming out holding a Nokia 1100. Indestructible brick phone of the slums. He looks at the screen of his laptop, his thumb working the phone's rubberized buttons. He studies the tiny LED screen, his lips moving as he reads something, reads it over again, and once more.

"Yes. Correct."

He weighs the phone on his palm, looks around the room.

"This. And then after. I don't know."

Some of them nod, some don't move.

Raj's father looks at his wife and his baby girl, then at his son.

"Rajiv."

He offers the phone.

"Take it."

Raj tucks his ball under one arm, scooping the Nokia from his father's hand. He looks at the screen. A string of letters, numbers, and symbols. He tries to let it translate itself into something intelligible. Some lengthy equivalent to *lol* or *;(*. Sees only randomness.

He looks from the screen to the others in the room. More than one set of lips is moving in silent prayer to one of many gods. He looks at the one they call Naxalite, sees the forest in his eyes. Trees, tall and green, creaking in a breeze, footsteps muffled by layered mulch and deadfall, single-file, booted feet. Guns.

He looks at his mother and sister, his father. The family it will be his job to provide for one day when he is older.

His father touches his shoulder, light press, then gone.

"Send it, Rajiv."

Raj rests his thumb on the large select button marked with a short green horizontal line. On the screen, *SEND*, highlighted. Waiting for the button. He presses down, satisfying firm click of sturdy technology, slight give of the button's thin rubber cover. The message on the screen blinks; a little bar, empty of color, appears, quickly filling, liquid crystal gray.

MESSAGE SENT

There are many exhalations in the room, more prayers, a few laughs, someone is crying.

His father takes the phone and drops it back in his pocket.

Sudhir rubs his palms together, wood on wood.

"They will say it is not the future, Rajiv. But do not believe them. It is the future. You have touched it with your own hands. You have made it."

Aasif places a hand on his son's head, pushes him gently.

"Go play with your ball."

Raj turns, five steps to the door, snagged by his mother's finger, held as she bends and kisses his cheek.

"Play, Rajiv."

She unlatches the door, sending him sprinting into the light, ball held tight to his chest, bare feet slapping the curve of the water main, hot metal. The boys, seeing him from the square, the ball, starting to scream his name. He runs to glory, raising the ball high, as if it is the future the man they call Naxalite has said is his.

patriots

THEY KNOW WHEN they are being lied to.

Terrence reminds himself. *They are very smart. They know when they are being lied to. They've been trained for it.*

And he begins to lie.

"I'm a little lost. You asked me here for what?"

Cross allows a sigh to escape from his nostrils. The spycraft equivalent of a spit take. But he refrains from any further comment regarding Terrence's transparency. He's sitting behind a mirror-finish black desk comprised of four legs of slightly more then pencil thickness and a slab top with the profile and thinness of an iPad. No drawers, a few papers, a pen set made of the same graphite carbon material as the desk; mouse, monitor, and keyboard, no visible wires, not even a power cord. A desk meant to project the same ideas about its owner that a massive chunk of oak would have communicated in decades past.

Leaning back slightly into the black webbing of an elaborately counterweighted and cantilevered task chair, Cross looks at Haven where he sits on a long, low black leather and chrome couch against the far wall.

"He wants to know why he was *asked* here."

Haven tugs at the armpit of a jacket that Terrence recognizes as having been tailored to conceal a shoulder holster.

"Old times?"

Cross looks from Haven and back at Terrence.

"No, not for old times' sake. Haven is trying to be funny."

Terrence studies the sharp hairline that delineates the southern border of Haven's crewcut. Hair freshly clipped, the back of his neck pale. Where was Haven recently that he was wearing his hair to the collar? Where has his forehead and nose burned so deeply red-brown? Where has the skin around his eyes been raccooned so white by the constant wear of huge sunglasses? His cheeks and chin left as pale as his neck by the thick beard he'd been sporting until a recent return. So many deserts he could have been in. Shaggy, bearded, Gargoyles over his eyes. Terrence has been in those deserts himself. Khakis, a blue oxford button-down, Altama desert boots, and a sweat-stained USS *Ronald Reagan* ball cap, his Ivy League version of the local paramilitary mode. Clearly articulating that he would *not* be marshaling for an extraction in Nuristan. Judging by the deep, horizonless focus in Haven's eyes, his mind is still in the desert, while his body is here, back home, wearing a suit cut for a gun, but not wearing a gun, adapting to management, brigade tattoos hidden by navy blue wool blend.

It is unlikely that he is trying to be funny. In Terrence's experience, Haven's sense of humor is limited.

"So what you want is?"

Cross nods as if in agreement with a concept with which he is somewhat familiar.

"We're interested in exploring an avenue, Terrence."

Haven looks at the ceiling.

"An *avenue*."

Terrence touches the plastic sheathed visitor's pass clipped to the breast pocket of his houndstooth check. He'd been given it in the three-story atrium where all guests are received and cleared for entry on the Kestrel Dynamics campus. That atrium had been designed both to impress and to serve as a killbox for snipers who would ring the third-floor balcony rails should hostiles ever penetrate so far along the Dulles Corridor. Be they terrorists or budget allocators threatening cuts to the dozens of Homeland Security contractors lining the strip that runs from Loudoun to Fairfax counties.

Until seven years ago Terrence hadn't needed a visitor's pass. He'd had an office here. This office, in fact. But times change. Witness them here, together, now. An unlikely reunion.

"An avenue toward?"

Cross looks at a chronometer display mounted above the door. Analogue, vintage, salvaged from Cheyenne Mountain Directorate during a NORAD renovation. Back when Terrence had the reserved parking spot closest to the front door, he had bought it for Cross from an online auction house specializing in cold war military memorabilia. Current times in the hot spots of the nuclear age. A birthday present for his protégé.

Cross's eyes are on the clock on the far right, a small black plaque: *Moscow.*

"How far is Russia from Ukraine? Time zones, I mean, how many time zones?"

Haven looks at one of the five narrow slits of armored glass along the wall behind Cross; the Kestrel campus outside is warped by their thickness.

"Time zones."

Terrence points at the clock.

"Kiev is an hour behind Moscow. GMT plus two."

Haven's lips are compressed, the rest of his face impassive.

"Kiev. Tea. They drink tea in Kiev, right? Glasses of tea. Hacker tea time in Kiev."

"Probably they drink Starbucks."

Cross fingers a small cube of clear Lucite that is perched on his desk. Encased within, a coil of wire and a battery, the detonator from an IED that a Kestrel contractor disarmed in Anbar Province.

"If they're state actors, they get Modafinil. B-12 injections."

Haven relaxes his lips, amused.

"State actors. Ukraine state actors."

Terrence draws a squiggle in the air with his index finger.

"An incident? Ukraine origin? Is that verifiable?"

Cross stares deep into the cube, as if willing it to blow something up.

"Alarmingly so."

They will know if you lie.

"And you need an avenue."

Cross rotates the cube a few degrees, setting off rainbows instead of a bomb.

"Need. Well."

Terrence nods, touches one of the buttons of his jacket, the garment a remnant of the days when being in the CIA meant affecting the style of an Ivy League dean. Days before his own. Romanticized.

Stupid. Foolish. Romantic. Killer. Are you going to do this or not? They will know. Do they already know?

"A cyber attack. Out of Ukraine."

Cross drops the cube, letting it bounce and tumble across his desk before settling, a gambler's fixed die coming to rest.

"Bravo. How do you ever put together such apt analysis from unconnected scraps like time zones and Haven talking about hackers?"

Terrence takes a pen from the inside breast pocket of his jacket, a notebook. Terrence the note taker. And the burner. A joke at both the CIA and at Kestrel, Terrence's incessant note taking and burning of his own notes. He never met a piece of paper he wouldn't just as soon fill up with Top Secret notions and then burn. For the sake of security.

What have I forgotten? Are you doing this? They will know. They already know. They must know.

"Details?"

Haven is studying his shoes. His feet are no doubt wondering where the hell his boots are.

"It was a SCADA thing. Infrastructure attack. Kinetic. Out of Ukraine. Supposed to start a cascade of the eastern grid. We think. But all they got was blackouts in Ohio and Pennsylvania. Very small in the news cycle. But a two-hundred-megawatt generator blew. *SCADA.* The Iranian computer worm. The one the Iranians were bitching about. Went after their nuclear plant. Stuxnet worm. Looks like that. But different. Fooled a lube oil pump into shutting down. Took seconds for the turbine to grind itself out of commission. Some attributable deaths. Car accident when the traffic lights went black in Scranton. Guy fell down some stairs, broke his neck. Five dead that we know about."

Terrence clicks the button at the end of his pen. He likes the weight of it. Heft. He bought it in Stockholm a few weeks ago. Waiting for someone in a stationery store. He clicks it three times.

"Ukraine?"

Cross lifts his hand from his desk and sets it back down.

"That is what it looks like."

Terrence doodles the number five in the margin of his notebook page.

"Who else is working on it?"

Haven grins, scratches the back of his neck, shakes his head.

"Who."

Cross presses a fingertip between his eyes.

"Terrence, really. Everyone. Everyone is working on it."

Of course they are. Cyber attack. Every security contractor and agency, the military, commercial anti-virus software makers, everyone. They'll all be trying to find out who launched a cyber attack on America's power grid and caused the deaths of at least five people.

That's the point, isn't it?

Terrence scratches out the doodled number five.

"I was just thinking aloud. Yes, everyone. Kestrel. Hann-Aoki, Triple Canopy, XO, Symantec, NSA, CIA, DynCorp, Aegis, air force, army, Homeland."

He looks at Cross.

"Does anyone have an inside track?"

Cross's fingers rattle his keyboard.

"That's what we're all jostling for."

A printer across the room wakes, hums, buzzes in short bursts, smoothly spilling paper into a tray.

Cross points at the printer.

"A contract."

A last sheet of paper shushes into place, the printer goes silent.

"Freelance. Three months guaranteed, with an employer option to extend for another year."

Terrence walks to the printer, looks down at the top sheet of the stack.

"A temp contract with the company I founded. Shall I comment on the irony?"

Cross plucks a pen from the holder on his desk.

"History, Terrence. Some lingering bile to get off your mind. Is this the time for that? Now, while our country is under attack?"

Terrence pulls the top sheet of paper from the printer, looks at some of the numbers.

"Well, it has been some time since I had your balls in my hand. No telling when I might get a chance to twist them again. If not now, when?"

Cross aims his pen at Terrence, a dart looking for a target.

"You recruited me, if I recall correctly, because you wanted someone with *a robust appetite for the jugular.* Your other misjudgments aside, you got what you wanted."

Terrence looks around the office, nods.

"And so did you."

Cross points at the paper in Terrence's hand.

"Want to come out of pasture? You have the ticket right there."

Terrence looks at the contract in his hand. The logo at the head of the page. An American kestrel, the slight sparrow hawk of the falcon family, lean and swift, adaptable, stooping to its prey. A logo he designed while still working at the CIA. An embodiment of his dream for post–cold war intelligence. And, yes, that had been a lean time at Langley, but never swift or adaptable. He'd been right enough, leaving when he did, taking his legendary eye for talent into the private sector. Cut loose from the worst of the bureaucracy, he'd been free to cultivate freelancers who never would have been tolerated inside The Company. Some tremendous successes. And also Cross. A brilliantly conscienceless Beltway climber with a clear-eyed view of national security unclouded by sentiment. The perfect man to mind the details while Terrence theorized, projected, handled esoteric ops, hunted talent, and gradually, willingly, ceded authority to the young man who would sit on the couch in his office, honing his mind against the grinding wheel of Terrence's relentlessly merciless vision of the future.

Until the several follies of the Montmartre Incident made it possible for Cross to get up off the couch and bring in his evil mastermind desk.

They will know if you lie.

He looks up.

"Who do you want?"

Cross tips his head, acknowledging, it seems, Terrence's submission to the circumstances.

"I want Jae."

Terrence looks into his notebook's open pages.

"She won't work for you."

"No. But she'll work for *you*. Why else would you be here, Terrence, if not for that fact?"

Haven stretches his legs, crosses his ankles, folds his arms over his chest.

"That fact."

Terrence looks at Haven, meeting, for the first time since coming into the room, his desert-scarred eyes.

Haven blinks, deliberate closure, open.

"Late in the day, old man, for recrimination."

Terrence does not blink.

"I didn't say anything."

Haven raises a hand from the couch, drops it.

"My mistake. I thought there was a general excavation going on. Dig up the old bones and chew them."

Terrence looks back at Cross.

"Jae won't work for you. And she won't work with him. Pick another name."

Cross shakes his head.

"There are no other names. Let's not play, you don't have anyone else in your armory. They all stayed with Kestrel. You have Jae. Which is the point, don't you see? Terrence. Don't you see? Must I. Spell it out?"

Terrence doesn't move.

Cross raises and drops his shoulders.

"I must. You have Jae. She is all you have. How long would you have her if she knew you were the one who assigned Haven to Iraq?"

Terrence is remembering the first annual Conference for Securing 21st-Century Security. Year 2000. His first sight of Cross. Front row of a panel titled National Security and Climate Change, in which Terrence, overtired from an afternoon spent trolling the hospitality suites for contracts to keep Kestrel alive as it incubated, raised his voice over a modulated debate regarding the virtues of switch grass as a fossil fuel replacement: *We all know the final solution, and I'm using those words entirely conscious of what they imply—we all know that the final solution to global fucking climate change is going to be a radical reduction in global fucking population.* The hush that followed, the heads turned away, suggested that Terrence had rather embarrassingly just vomited into his own lap but that everyone would be pleased to ignore the fact if he would quietly leave and go clean himself up in the bathroom. He did, in fact, remove himself to the john, where Cross found him splashing cold water on the back of his neck and asked if he could buy him a drink. Three vodka tonics later Terrence had offered him a job, never so lucky before or since to have such a talent fall into his lap.

Haven had been there. One of the believers who had followed Terrence out of government service. His own opinion of Cross characteristically laconic. *That guy. He's got something on his mind, old man.*

Now they all have something on their mind. The past.

Terrence takes a step sideways.

"What do you have for her?"

Cross pushes his empty hands across the desk, a man all in.

"Money. I have money for her."

"She doesn't need money."

Haven touches the top of his head.

"Doesn't need money."

Cross flicks his hand westward.

"She's running around the desert in a forty-year-old Land Rover, living on a diet of amphetamines and psychedelics, playing with robots, and occasionally crawling to the edge of civilization to do whatever piecework visual analysis you manage to scrape up for her."

His face tightens, brows drawing together, lips tensed.

"She is."

He searches for the words to describe what she is and, finding them, spits them out.

"A wasted resource."

No worse sin.

He exhales, looks at the ceiling, appears about to smile but does not.

"She's what you have to offer us, Terrence."

He looks down from the ceiling.

"You got her to leave Disaster City and go to Haiti. Either you can get her to go into the field for me or you cannot."

Terrence thinks about Haiti. The Pelican Case full of cash. How heavy it was.

"There were lives to save in Haiti."

Cross allows this.

"Are there not lives to be saved now?"

Terrence knows there are. A vast number of lives that may be saved. *Do they know?*

Still holding the top page of the contract Cross has offered him, he folds it over once, a letter fold, and uses his thumb to sharpen the crease.

"If I can convince her. Security will be an issue."

Eyes shooting to Haven and back to the paper.

"As I said. She won't work with *him*. Obviously."

Cross shakes his head.

"Haven has an asset already."

Terrence doesn't look at Haven.

"You have an asset."

Haven lifts a finger.

"I have someone else for Jae."

Terrence folds the paper over again.

"Rosalind?"

Cross shakes his head.

"We don't like her for this. Too eccentric. Jae should travel with a stabilizing influence."

Haven lifts three fingers.

"I have a team."

Terrence sharpens the second crease.

"Team."

"Sloan. The new guy. Everybody wants to work with him. And two others. She'll be bracketed. Highest-value asset. Sloan and his team, they're very good."

Terrence looks at Cross.

"Jae won't want anyone from Kestrel."

Cross looks at the clocks over the door.

"You have someone new, Terrence? Looking to package this job? Take a commission on the asset *and* her protection?"

Terrence looks at the paper in his hands. It betrays no tremor, no sign of what is in his heart. *It's not too late to stop,* he tells himself. But it is too late. And he wouldn't stop even if he could.

The abyss is at his feet. He steps into it with a word.

"Skinner."

The atmosphere in the room changes with the speaking of the name. One's ears might pop.

The five clocks tick.

Cross touches a button on his keyboard, and Terrence knows that however many devices may have been recording their conversation to this point, they have all gone dead.

Cross looks at the surface of his black desk, magic mirror of an equally dark future.

"*Skinner is gone.* You said. *Never to return.* You said."

He looks up from the black desk.

"Was that not the truth?"

"I never said *dead.*"

For the first time since the conference began, Cross rises, fingertips pressing down bone-white on the black desktop.

"If he'd been dead that would have been the ideal outcome, wouldn't it have been? The list of people unsatisfied with that result would have been brief indeed. Fuck. Terrence. If he were dead, you might still own this company."

Terrence smiles.

"I doubt that very much."

Cross appears to notice for the first time that he is standing. He lifts his hands from the desk, blood returning, pinking the skin.

"It's an absurd notion. A nonstarter. No."

Terrence looks at the carpet between his toes, nodding.

"Like I said, I'll likely never have another chance to twist your balls. So. No Skinner, no Jae."

Cross looks at the bank of clock faces.

"He's not viable."

Terrence looks at the clocks, watches a few seconds of Cross's time whirl away.

"Jae can give *someone* the inside track on the West-Tebrum attackers. Once word gets out that you have her, she'll be targeted. I won't run her out there in the open without the best protection. So she gets Skinner. Or you can't have her."

Cross taps his teeth with his thumbnail, realizes what he's doing, stops.

"So strident, Terrence. So urgent."

He's looking at the clocks again.

"I would be concerned about his focus on the present."

Terrence is still holding the folded page of his contract. He opens it, glances inside, closes it.

"If he'd wanted to do something about Montmartre, he would have done it a long time ago. And you wouldn't be here now."

Cross looks at him.

"No. Neither of us would be here."

He sits, and moves a manila folder to the center of his desk. Anachronistic luxury. He flips it open. A USB drive is taped inside the cover. From his angle, standing on the opposite side of the desk, Terrence can see a heavily redacted document, 70 percent thick black censor lines.

"What will he want?"

"Money."

"Yes. And?"

Terrence is trying not to feel how carefully Haven is not looking at him. He tucks the contract away inside his jacket.

"An asset. That's all he ever wanted."

Cross closes the file.

"Such a *simple* man."

He looks at the closed file, pushes it across the desk.

"Details. An op for Jae. Now. And yes."

He looks at the clocks yet again, time the enemy.

"You can have Skinner."

Haven rises, a single movement that seems to originate somewhere above his head, a force drawing him smoothly to his feet as his ankles and arms uncross.

"Are we talking about this?"

Cross looks at him, places a finger on the keyboard button he pressed minutes before.

"We have talked about it, Haven."

He presses the button; recording resumed.

"And now we are done talking about it."

Haven touches his fresh haircut.

"Opposed."

He raises his voice slightly, speaks to the room.

"For the record."

Cross types something, rapid fire.

"Events are moving quickly, Terrence. I have to leave for Europe. Constant status reports. American lives are at risk. Let's do our best to protect them. Patriots."

Haven is looking at Terrence now, very much so.

"*Patriots,* Terrence. Remember to tell Skinner."

Exiting through the killbox atrium, Terrence squeezes the USB drive from the file between his thumb and forefinger, secure in the knowledge that Cross and Haven know he lied. But that they only know the lies he wanted them to know. The other lie, *The Lie,* they didn't catch that one, had no hope of catching it, or of catching him.

They are so smart. Such good liars themselves, they know when they are being lied to.

But I'm the one who taught them how to lie so well.

An hour later, in a Georgetown Internet café, he sends an email, calling Skinner back to the world.

The monster summoned, he starts waiting to die, and is soon on a Lufthansa flight to Cologne, speeding toward that end.

agents of taps

JAE HAS BEEN parked across the highway from the motel for nearly an hour. She doesn't want to go in. She's begun to develop sores from sleeping in the Land Rover, not to mention an intimate sweaty reek that reminds her of day-old undergraduate sex, but she does not want to go in.

Still, a bed, a shower.

She should have both before she shows up at Creech.

It's one thing to arrive two days late, another to show up reeking of road sweat, filthy from weeks of living in the desert, more than slightly wild-eyed: the residue of an admittedly ill-advised peyote experiment still wringing itself from her brain. The military expects a certain amount of eccentricity from freelance geniuses, but she suspects that she may have pushed somewhat beyond an acceptable level of quirks. Off in the desert, taking solo shamanistic journeys and playing with homemade robots. Over the border into crazy land. One of the many foreign lands where unsanctioned travel can result in one's security clearances being revoked. A trip that ends with one's file being moved from the *Watchers* drawer to the *Watched*.

Jae does not want to be watched.

A bed. A shower.

She needs the job at Creech. Whatever it is, whatever it is they want her to see and understand for them, she needs the trickle of money it will release into her accounts. Money fuels her on the road. Keeps her off the grid and away from the torrents of media and information that swamp her compulsions, dragging her into an undertow of data that never resolves into the sense her mind insists is just below the surface. She needs to top off her account, check her PO box in Barstow, pick up some parts she ordered for the robots, speak to her dealer, maybe, and get back into the sand.

She's gonna have to go in that fucking motel and look at its shitting cable TV, for fuck sake, whether she wants to or not. She raises the Nikon Prostaff 12x25 binoculars to her eyes and looks out at the motel. Battered by decades of desert sun. Parched wood. A shallow foundation perched on little more than sand and gravel. What would it take from wind or rain to turn this shit box into kindling? That's the peyote talking, backwash of paranoia at the end of any lengthy trip. Fuck it. Take a look.

The Worm will tell her if there's anything to fear.

She returns the binoculars to the case dangling off a strap looped around the glove box handle. Checklist time. She checks the laces of her trail boots, making sure they're tight. She checks the pockets of her safari vest, confirming that they hold her Garmin GPSMAP 62, Motorola Brute cell phone, a Uniden GMRS Two-Way radio with thirty-six-mile desert range, Leatherman Skeletool, three twenty-four-hundred-calorie food bars, a solar blanket, and a 3.1-liter CamelBak hydration pouch clipped to the shoulder rings. Julbo Micropores PT sunglasses on her face and jungle hat on her head. Hair and fingernails clipped to utilitarian lengths. Underwear mostly clean.

She could laugh at herself.

If a sandstorm materializes out of nowhere and blows her over the rainbow or if the Frenchman Mountain Fault becomes active and opens a crevasse beneath her feet that sends her tumbling into a buried city or if frogs rain suddenly from the sky and destroy all civilization, she'll be ready. She could really just laugh at herself. But she doesn't. Intimately aware of how the unexpected and nigh on impossible can manifest and warp the fabric of one's personal space and time.

She unbuckles her seatbelt, unlocks the door, pulls the lever, catching in her face the updraft of superheated air rising from the surface of the tarmac. She gets out, boots grinding sand into the road surface. The all-muffling silence of the desert. Standing still, disoriented by the lack of forward movement, she puts a hand on the roof of the Rover, burning her fingers. The motel, bed and shower inside, across the road.

The Worm will find the hidden dangers.

She circles around the battered Series III Lightweight, unlocks and opens the rear door, and peels the packing blanket away from the row of five black and silver Gator roadie cases. She pulls out the smallest of the cases and walks toward the motel. She walks in a jagged configuration of rights and lefts. She imagines her path viewed from above and traced by a satellite. An entirely likely proposition. The path, from that celestial viewpoint, reads as irregular biology. The EKG of a restless mind. Blood pressure under extreme duress. An erratic heart.

Twenty meters from the motel, well away from its awnings, in an area outside of the killing zone of a falling telephone pole or snapped high-tension line, she sets the case on the ground, flips, twists, unlocks two clasps, and raises the lid, revealing the coiled Worm inside. Thick as a garden hose, a black articulated whip of alloy, carbon fiber composite and Kevlar with a lidded cyclops eye at one end. Mounted into the interior of the case's lid, an iPad loaded with her own Linux hack. Restraint webbing released so that she can slip her hand into the center coil of the Worm, she tugs slightly to free it from the snug foam nest. She has to get closer to the motel. A challenge made easier with the Worm in her hand; a comfort. She walks, teased by the high-tension hum overhead, taunted, refusing to look. It's there, it wants to kill her. So what? Everything wants to kill her today. Five meters out from the motel, breathing deep, she stops.

Down on one knee, she gentles the Worm to the earth, its black coat instantly dusted with ultra-fine desert sand. She takes her Leatherman from its pocket, flips open an awl, uses the tip to slide open a tiny cover on the underside of the Worm, pokes the awl into a divot under the cover, sees a green LED come to life. She slides the cover closed, pockets the Leatherman, rises and backs away from the motel, returning to the open case. The iPad inside is already awake, roused when power tickled the Worm. She taps a squiggle icon, opens the Worm's control panel, runs down a menu of search options, chooses a simple foundation inspection routine, and flicks the Worm alive.

In the dirt, it wriggles, the lid of the eye snapping open and shut as it rises to attention, half a meter of the Worm uncoiling and arching upward, swinging the lens about, mapping, gridding the surroundings, finding the motel at hand and darting in that direction, settling into the dirt, writhing, unspooling, moving exactly like what it is: an articulated robot snake. The inspection routine itself is simple, but running it requires a complex emotional contortion. Using the Worm and its cohorts in their cases leads inevitably to the contemplation of buildings blown up, shaken to the ground, washed from their foundations. And the very specific types of bodies to be found in these variously demolished structures. The dismemberments of explosions, the paste left as residue when several floors compress into one, the sea-wrinkled skin and seaweed hair rippling in brand-new currents running across what was, until recently, dry land.

The Worm twists, seals its single eye, and begin to burrow, a tight corkscrew drilling itself into the ground to discover the hidden faults of the motel's foundations.

One of the pockets on her vest buzzes. The phone. Terrence. Why isn't she at Creech? As if he doesn't know why she's not there. She's not ready to be there. They want her eyes. They want to know what they can't see. How dangerous it might be. How can she tell them anything if she doesn't even have her eyes open yet? She's like a newborn puppy now, fresh from the desert, eyes gummed shut. Terrence knows. He taught her how to do it. Open her eyes to the world, use her compulsions, let the information in. Don't run from it, look at it.

Tell me what you see, he'd said.

And later, *Don't go to Iraq.*

But she'd gone anyway.

Shit.

If she told them, if she told them what she really sees, how truly dangerous it is, they wouldn't believe her. Or, if they did, they would cease to function. They would freeze in their tracks, paralyzed by the fear. Disaster City, her old home, that was the model. What's coming is the real thing, Disaster World.

She lets the phone vibrate, watches the telemetry of the Worm. Terrence will wait.

But he doesn't.

"You need to be at Creech in the morning."

She mutes the TV chained to a wall-mounted steel shelf above a wood-veneer chest of drawers. On the screen, a line of riot police barring a crowd of protesters from entering the Swedish World Trade Center in Stockholm. Ongoing street theater being played out as the WTO meets there at the same time as the annual Bilderberg conference. A confluence of power and money bound to draw singular rage in an era of austerity. She angles the remote toward the TV, presses the channel button, but nothing happens. The cable is pure shit, but the Wi-Fi is surprisingly solid. She's got her laptop open next to her, a browser running on her phone. She slaps the remote against her bare thigh twice and tries again. The picture blips to a fuzzy image of several large-bottomed Mexican women in short-shorts and cutoff t-shirts dancing around a man with a pencil mustache and a microphone.

"I'm not ready. Two more days. Tell them two more days. How can I tell them what I'm seeing when I don't even have my eyes open yet?"

"Could you turn on the camera?"

"I'm not dressed."

She pulls the towel tighter across her flat chest. It is her own towel. The motel's towels are hopelessly small, worn, and, like the carpet, disconcertingly stained. Her towel is a thirty-six-by-seventy-two-inch rectangle of hyperabsorbent antibacterial material that can be compressed into a pouch the size of an old-fashioned CD jewel box.

"How was the desert?"

Jae picks up the half-liter bottle of Tahitian spring water she bought from the vending machine outside the motel office. *The desert was like being in an isolation chamber, Terrence. The desert didn't force my brain to create connections between Mexican TV production and the efficacy of Wi-Fi in the Mohave. The desert felt like limbo. Same as always. It felt like waiting for the end of the world.*

She takes a sip of water.

"The desert was fine."

"Are you on anything?"

She looks at the brown pharmacy bottles and plastic baggies peeking from her unzipped duffle on the floor.

"Coming down."

"Are you secured?"

Jae slaps the remote again, presses the button, blips to a scene shot through a night-vision lens. Handheld, documentary or reality TV. Several young people, men, one woman, a law enforcement unit of some kind. Khakis, black shirts, windbreakers and caps with large yellow letters, an acronym: TAPS. An agency she's never heard of. They give the appearance of being on a night raid in some kind of underground facility, but carry no weapons. They carry cameras, infrared lamps, and several different wands and scopes cabled to various boxes strapped to their persons, everything studded with impressively glowing LEDs.

Jae looks from the TV to the screen of the Toughbook sitting next to her on the narrow bed.

Skype open, showing an active call, no video, connected to *terrenceTT*.

Is she secured?

She looks up at the ceiling. Beyond it and the warming atmosphere are three thousand or so man-made, functioning (to one degree or another) satellites. Those give her little or no pause. It is the additional dozens, perhaps hundreds, of satellites about which she knows nothing that are sometimes the focus of her ever-roving and fretful mind. She considers it unlikely that any of them is singularly dedicated to tracking her movements and monitoring her activities, but unlikely does not mean impossible. Her phone, her vehicle GPS, the Toughbook. All obvious loci for unwanted observation. Hazards of the digital age. Looking into the abyss requires, by necessity, having it also look into you.

Is she secured?

She moves her fingertip over the Toughbook's trackpad, clicks on a white icon in the shape of a cartoon spider. Eight small windows unfold, each one a square in a grid, live video feeds from the cluster of wall-crawling, eight-legged surveillance bots she released through the bathroom window as soon as she'd come into the room. Little more than camera platforms that can communicate locative data and triangulate with their clustermates, the eight spiders had scrambled away, finding roof edges, corners of walls, points equidistant and as far as possible from each other, plotting overlap between their fields of view. The parking lot, the doors of the other rooms, office, open desert behind the motel, highway, cloudless and star spackled sky above. Occasionally the camera views shift, covering gaps, rotating by minutes. Should a team of unarmed TAPS agents attempt to storm the motel and take obscure measurements, she will see them coming.

She removes her finger from the trackpad.

"There is no security, Terrence."

"Please don't tell that to our clients."

On the TV, the agents of TAPS, reacting as though they have heard a disturbing noise. They begin waving their wands and scopes, taking readings, speaking into the camera that trails them.

"Have you ever worked with TAPS?"

A silence from the computer, longer than the usual Skype delay, and then Terrence again.

"Shoes?"

"T-A-P-S. Investigative something."

"American?"

"They have a reality show. Like *COPS*. I think."

The TAPS task force, hustling down a concrete corridor that reminds Jae of a military bunker. In fact, if asked, she'd give her professional opinion that it is a bunker. Cold war era. European. Eastern.

"Weapons inspectors maybe?"

She hears a background clatter from her computer's speaker, the usually soft tapping of computer keys amplified by their proximity to the microphone built into Terrence's own laptop.

"Weapons inspectors with a reality show?"

"Looking for missing Soviet nukes. Ivory-grade plutonium. Did they get all of it from the Kazakhstan reactor? Aktau. I heard they were still trying to make the inventory come out right."

The clacking stops.

"The Atlantic Paranormal Society."

Jae is thinking about Soviet bombs, fissionable materials, vast stock-piles scattered throughout the Eastern bloc. Robots she's designed for rescue have been modified for use in potentially contaminated sites. Die-in-place units, never intended for recovery, that had been dropped through cracks in reinforced concrete caps that were never actually re-inforced. The cash margin between a proper waste depot cap and an improper one having been skimmed and split between contractors and party apparatchiks. She's seen documents, layers of redaction, but be-tween the black lines were bombs enough to blow a hole through the center of the globe, all of them unaccounted for.

Terrence raises his voice, slight distortion from the speaker.

"*Ghosthunters,* Jae."

She's opening the spider cluster windows, her perimeter is clear, but this close to Creech, the shockwave from a ten-megaton car bomb de-vice would slap this shithole to splinters with her inside.

"Jae, are you watching TV now?"

Her peyote-fatigued brain is composing scenarios for her now. A Ford F-150, parked in the lot outside the Indian Springs Casino across the road from Creech. A states' rights fanatic, unknowing puppet of a Somali al-Qaeda franchise, sitting in the driver's seat, praying to his First Testament Lord, an arming switch compressed, thumb on a detonator.

"It's a TV show, Jae. *Ghosthunters.* People who call themselves the Atlantic Paranormal Society. They look for ghosts. On TV. There's an international cast. It appears that they're broadcasting a special episode. Looking for ghosts in a decommissioned GDR command bunker near Kossa."

She picks up the remote, slaps it twice, hits the channel button as if pulling the trigger of a gun, killing the TAPS squad and resummoning the Mexican dancing girls, now clad in bikini mariachi outfits.

"Weapons inspector reality show. I should have my head examined."

Silence.

"Yes, you should."

She laughs. As the fit subsides, she has to use the end of her antimi-crobial towel to wipe a rope of snot from her upper lip.

"Thanks, Terrence, I just blew boogers all over my laptop."

"Have you even been to the east? Berlin, I mean. Former."

Jae is wiping the screen of her Toughbook.

"A conference, before I met you. Academia. *Neo-automation and design.* Something. I talked about self-assembling robots. Sounds old-fashioned now."

"I worked there in the seventies. Speaking of old-fashioned. Cultivated an asset, KGB counterintelligence agent. I don't know that I've ever met anyone else so impossibly self-serving and dirty to his core. An espionage cockroach. I was certain he'd survive World War III. The real surprise was that we never had one. Not as it was imagined, anyway."

Jae leans back into her pillows, channels flipping. She uses her left hand to surf the browser on her phone. *Mexican TV. TAPS. Kossa. World War III. Antimicrobial. Snot.* Her mind coming clear of the illusory revelations of the peyote and the blankness of the desert, reaching out through the TV and the laptop, signals, Terrence's voice, hesitant VoIP call-and-response, hunting for a configuration to weave herself into. The information around her, in the air, waves of it penetrating her body, these machines to pluck it from the atmosphere, so clumsy.

"Jae? Are you still there?"

She nods in the empty room.

"Here. Getting back online. Terrible cable here. Forty-nine channels. I can barely see anything with forty-nine channels."

"Jae, you need to be at Creech in the morning."

"Too soon."

"Too late. Very close to being too late."

Voices in the background of the call, amplified, foreign languages, she recognizes number sequences being repeated. *1099. 6766. 4320.* German, French, English.

"Where are you, Terrence? What airport? Somewhere in Germany."

"Yes. Cologne. I'm meeting someone here."

Her hands are off on their own now, receiving signals she's unaware her brain is sending. Tapping keys, launching searches. *Cologne. Flughafen. Flights. 1099. 6766. 4320.*

"Jae. Go to Creech."

"I'm not ready to look yet. I won't be able to help them. I'm still in the desert."

"No, you're not. And the pictures will be easy anyway. Something is happening. Something dangerous is happening. A disaster."

Her fingers tapping, channels flipping, scanning.

"What? I don't see anything. There are no reports. It doesn't matter. I'm not digging up more dead bodies. They can call Disaster City if they want robots to find dead people. I won't go. They need me to look at pictures at Creech."

"The disaster hasn't *happened*, Jae. It is *happening*. People are going to die. Jae."

Nothing, Terrence silent, just the flights being called in the background.

"Jae. So many people will die. But not yet. Soon. But not yet. We can. Jae. We can stop it this time. Do you remember?"

Her eyes are stinging. She blinks.

"I'm tired."

"Remember when we met. We talked about your configurations. How they all end the same."

She remembers. She cannot forget. Her search for the will of the designer. She found it. Every configuration she maps eventually shows her the same land. Land of the Dead. Where they'll all be.

"It's just what's going to happen, Terrence. The world. It's not meant to be here forever. Stop, please."

But he won't.

"I promised you something when we met."

She touches her cheek, it's wet.

"You said it all made sense. You said if I looked hard enough it would make sense. You said it doesn't have to end. The configuration doesn't have to end with everybody dead. You said if I kept looking I'd be able to see the disasters before they happened. And get there in time. You're such a liar, Terrence."

"I didn't lie. It just took a long time. Go to Creech. I'm sending someone for you."

"Who?"

"Someone with a job."

"Who with?"

A pause, and then he rushes the word to her.

"Kestrel."

"Ah, shit, Terrence. Shit."

But he just won't stop.

"What happened before, Jae, it won't happen with him. It can't. He's not like. He's not like other people. And he'll give you something at Creech, Jae. A map."

"To where?"

"To the future, Jae. It's a map to the place where the future is being made. There are lives to be saved there. You can help. Believe me."

Her cheeks are wet because she's crying. She doesn't wipe them. Her hand is going to the trackpad, clicking the call to an end before Terrence can say anything else. Her mind already caught in the tide. Awash in a dream of the future. A future that doesn't look like the desert.

The rest of the night she spends upright in bed, TV channels cycling, cable, an increasing number of infomercials, surfing her phone along a wave of links starting with the Wikipedia entry for *Weapons-grade*.

Opening her eyes.

repeat and reinforce

IT WAS HAVEN who first led Terrence to Skinner, directing his attention to a handful of scholarly articles, and more than one sensationalist account of the story in the pages of national news magazines. Back issues, old news, and forgotten. But Terrence had been unable to keep himself from wondering what had happened to the so-called *Box Boy*. The experiment might never have been completed, but he was fascinated by the idea that a child raised in such circumstances could grow into anything resembling the functioning and socialized human being that Haven claimed to have seen. If he had that capacity in him, what else might he be capable of? The vast territory of human potential, and the talents it harbored on its furthest shores, had forever been one of Terrence's obsessions.

The obsession predated the awful night when his only child had been stillborn, but Terrence would never have denied that there was a connection between that personal tragedy and his increasing preoccupation with the eccentrically gifted individuals he recruited so avidly.

His initial approach had been quite open; he had introduced himself, not inaccurately, as a CIA recruiter at a jobs fair on the MIT campus where Skinner was preparing to graduate after four years of middling academic success (by MIT standards) in the linguistics department, and tremendous athletic achievements (by MIT standards) rowing heavyweight crew and running cross-country. There had been nothing unusual in the initiation. What linguistics major at MIT did not expect to attract some interest from at least one organ of national intelligence?

Indeed, following Skinner's acquiescence to several followup interviews, events had proceeded with such irritating predictability that Terrence had pigeonholed him. *Analyst,* Terrence had thought. Without bothering to Myers-Briggs the kid, he could see the results of the personality test: ISTJ. Introverted with sensing, thinking, and judging. Not the unusual talent he'd been looking for, but a potential resource nonetheless. So the recruitment followed its course, Terrence preparing to pass Skinner off to someone, anyone, please, a bit further down the food chain, when they were mugged.

He'd have liked to take responsibility for the mugging, claim that it was a skill assessment that he'd engineered, but it was simply improbable fate manifesting in the shape of a hoodie-wearing roughneck up from Mattapan to do a loop of the darker side streets around Mass. Ave. and Western. Terrence's own reaction to having someone demand money from him on an empty block of Pearl Street under the looming bulk of the Cambridge Public Library was to reach for his wallet. His hand went into his pocket, his fingers closing on the worn leather of the billfold that he'd acquired at Yale, but before he could begin to pull it out, Skinner had stepped forward and kicked the hoodie in his left shin. The black kid's foot jumped off the ground, the hands in his pockets started to come out. Skinner pushed him, both hands, a shove with too much weight behind it. Hoodie went down on his back, Skinner stumbling forward, unbalanced. On the ground, winded, acting on instinct, the hoodie kicked Skinner's legs. The heel of one of his Nikes hammered the inside of Skinner's right knee, and down he came, on top of the hoodie. There was a flurry of limbs, unpracticed grappling, blows delivered in close quarters, lacking force. Skinner stayed on top, refused to be jarred loose, hugging the robber as much as trying to restrain him. There was very little noise; grunts, two fully clothed bodies on the pavement. Their shapes separated a bit, Skinner lifted his upper body, sat on the other man's chest, weight forward, knees planted in the inner hollows of elbows, pinning the hoodie's arms to the ground.

Hoodie talking.

"Uncle, motherfucker. You got me. Be cool. Just let me go. No one hurt. Just let me go."

Skinner grabbed the edges of the robber's sweatshirt hood, pulled it closed over the robber's face, lifted the robber's head from the ground, and slammed it down against the sidewalk. A slightly muffled scream, pain and outrage.

"Uncle, motherfucker!"

Skinner raised the head and slammed again.

Another scream, a moan, no words.

Skinner raised the head, resettled his weight, and slammed harder.

No scream, no movement.

Skinner lifted the head once more. Waited. Still no movement. He slammed it once more into the pavement and let go of the hood. Rising, favoring the knee where he'd been kicked, he stepped clear of the motionless, unsuccessful thief. His breathing was deep, rapid, but even. The breathing of a powerful endurance athlete following strenuous exercise.

Terrence looked at the man on the ground, trying to see if he was also breathing. He bent toward the man, still thinking of him as a *man* rather than a *body*.

"This was arguably self-defense."

Skinner tilted his head to the side.

"Does that matter?"

Terrence touched the man's chest with the back of his hand and reclassified him. *Body*. Without raising his face, Terrence straightened, stepped close to Skinner, and pushed him into the shadows gathered inside the entrance to the library's parking garage.

In the shadows, he lifted his face and looked up at the windows on the building opposite.

"It matters if anyone is watching us."

Skinner was still looking at the man on the ground.

"No one is watching us, Terrence. I know when I'm being watched."

Looking at him, Terrence knew it to be so. His first twelve years spent in a box, observed half his life. How could Skinner not know when he was being watched? How could he not be skilled in appearances? How could he not know just what was expected of him and how to behave in order to suit his exterior to that expectation? And with that realization Terrence knew also that Skinner was aware that his past was no secret here, that their meeting was no coincidence. And he became afraid.

He looked at the body.

"You should have given him your money."

Skinner stopped flexing his hands.

"No. He could have done anything. The safest thing was to make sure he couldn't hurt us. When he couldn't move anymore it was safe."

Terrence looked up from the body.

"Do you want to call the police, tell them what happened?"

Skinner's eyes moved over the body.

"No."

He looked at Terrence.

"I don't want to live in a box again."

Terrence hooked his elbow.

"We need to talk."

Later, in a Mass. Ave. bar that Terrence insisted they go into, mixing with the students, a crowd that could easily confuse exact times of arrival and departure, they sat across from one another in a wood-benched booth, table scarred with decades of carved initials, varnished year after year. Turning a double rocks glass of Black Label with his index finger and thumb, Terrence read his protégé's future in the half-melted ice floating in the whiskey.

"Your life will be different now. No matter what you do. How you live. Where you go. Everything will be different now. You can't change what you just did, can't take it back, and that will change you."

Skinner touched the side of his pint glass of lager.

"We are what we do. If you want to change, you have to work at it. Change what you do. You have to repeat and reinforce. Over and over. Do the same thing again and again. Until it is you."

He took a sip from his glass.

"Doing something once doesn't change you. That's just a start."

Terrence sat across from him in the bar, dozens of people packed close, jarring their table as they edged by toward the toilets.

"Do you want to change?"

Skinner ran his fingertip over the plus sign carved between two sets of initials on the surface of the table.

"Being a person."

He looked inside his glass.

"Being a person is hard."

He looked up.

"Maybe I could be something else. Something I'm good at."

Terrence drank his whiskey.

Late that night, in the furnished apartment he rented during his marriage's final deterioration, a long erosion that had begun the night he and Dorothy had watched their mercifully unnamed dead son wrapped in a small sheet and taken away from them, he would get out of bed and run to the bathroom to vomit up the alcohol. Then stay there in the harsh light of the tiny tiled chamber, afraid to return to his bedroom, where, for all he knew, Skinner was standing in plain view, willfully invisible to watching eyes.

Skinner is sitting at the coffee bar in the Terminal One concourse of the Cologne airport. The two Pakistani women behind the counter seem never to stop polishing the surfaces and appliances of the bar, rags whisking away rings of condensation that accumulate at the bases of cold glasses of Coke, or the dark speckles of espresso that splash when cubes of sugar are dropped into tiny white cups. They speak flawless Bavarian-accented German. Educated German. Terrence orders a lemonade and looks for objects that might kill him. There are many glasses at hand. A tower of them on the other side of the counter. The bar itself is round, covered in brushed stainless steel, 360 degrees of blunt object. None of the flatware is at all sharp, but the fat end of a butter knife's handle can be forced through the jelly of an eye. Terrence stops his catalogue. There is no point. Senseless Death chooses targets haphazardly; Skinner does not.

One of the Pakistani women wipes the bar in front of him and places a napkin and, upon it, a sweating glass. He wraps his hand around the glass, gets up, and walks toward Skinner, half the circumference of the round bar to be traveled. Terrence carries his drink in one hand, fingers of his other hand gliding on the smooth edge of the bar, tracing the half circle.

Am I doing this?

Terrence stops walking, one empty stool between himself and the man he's come to find. The years have weathered Skinner, but rather than making him more distinctive, they have etched him with a quality of ambiguity. His clothes have style dictated by a men's magazine rather than any real panache. Every garment will have the label of an upscale franchised brand. A businessman of means, unmarried, mindful of his appearance, an experienced traveler with a sturdy, tightly packed roll-on. A common sight in any international airport and on any flight. Camouflage for the man who exists in transit. He's drinking coffee, American, some kind of strudel on a small plate at his elbow, laptop, generic black, businessy, a news site open in the browser. Terrence notes how far Skinner's hand is from the three-tined fork resting half off the strudel plate, and sits on the stool next to him, fingers tight on the cold glass of lemonade.

Skinner drags his finger down the trackpad of his laptop.

"We never had a chance to talk about Montmartre."

And there it is, cradle of original sin, the Montmartre Incident. They should have died. Someone should have died. Either Skinner or all the rest of them. The fact that only Lentz and the asset died is one of the greatest testaments to the excellence of Terrence's gift for operational projections. Though no one knows that to be the case, and Montmartre was, ostensibly, his downfall.

He raises an eyebrow.

"Is Montmartre still relevant? Will it have to be dealt with?"

Skinner doesn't need to ponder this, having come to a decision about his response to Montmartre seven years ago.

"I'm curious about details. Have you seen it, the cemetery?"

Terrence recalls being young, a brief window of his life that closed abruptly, almost immediately, after he was himself recruited. Twenty-one, Paris, the Latin Quarter, a girl, naturally, snapping a lock closed on the Pont des Arts, their names scratched into its surface with his penknife, the key tossed into the Seine. Sex in, honestly, a garret.

"I saw it when I did my student tour."

"There's a headstone. 'Reistroff Guenard Spy.'"

"Really?"

Skinner smiles, lifting the scar on his chin.

"The comma is irresistible. Reistroff Guenard, spy."

Terrence sips his lemonade, too sweet by more than half.

"Was he?"

"I have no idea. But the sound of it."

"Eric Ambler."

For the first time Skinner turns his face from his computer and looks directly at Terrence. A look that asks if Terrence is pulling his leg in some way.

Terrence waits.

Skinner looks back at his screen.

"Yes, that's what I thought. Pure Ambler. It occurred to me a little after I'd seen the headstone."

Terrence rotates his drink, fingers smearing droplets of cold sweat on the side of the glass.

"It was a marker, the headstone?"

"Yes."

Skinner, doing a hushed voice, mysterious.

"Find the headstone. One hundred meters down the avenue."

"As if you were working for Balkans."

"Or Turks."

Terrence raises a hand.

"Don't exaggerate."

Skinner raises his own hand.

"Never that."

He lowers the hand.

"The mausoleum."

Terrence studies his lemonade.

"Mausoleum."

"There was a mausoleum."

"It's a cemetery."

"The asset was in a mausoleum."

Terrence plucks a napkin from the tray on the service side of the bar. "Christ."

Skinner looks at him again, a direct look, landing, staying on him.

"The name. Ask me."

Terrence kneads the napkin.

"What was the name on the mausoleum?"

"Lazarous. Family Lazarous."

And he looks back at his screen.

"That was over the top, don't you think?"

Terrence looks up into the web of slender girders and cables that seem too light to support the roof of the terminal.

"I never heard the details."

"My asset was killed. Yes. That was the salient detail. Yes."

Terrence pats the surface of the counter with the palm of his hand, shrugs, *assets are what they are.* There to be killed or kidnapped or stolen or sabotaged or blackmailed or turned or blown up or reverse-engineered or menaced or tortured. Their value wrung from them in whatever way is deemed most expedient to the circumstances.

Skinner is scrolling down a long page of text, blurred by speed.

"Why kill my asset first? I was the primary target. Throwing a dead body at my feet was clumsy. It couldn't have been by accident. Did you recruit Lentz?"

Terrence picks up the bit of paper wrapper that the Pakistani barmaid had left over the tip of his straw. He balls the paper between his finger-tips and drops it, as if dropping the final word on the topic at hand.

"It was a byzantine op. The snake eating its own tail. There are always inefficiencies when they try to kill one of their own."

Skinner considers this, clicks open a new tab on his screen.

"One of their own. Was I that?"

Terrence remembers the young man in the hooded sweatshirt, Skinner on his chest, pounding his head into the pavement, the expression on his face, that of a man trying to open the stubborn lid of jar.

"You were one of mine. Whatever that meant."

"But Kestrel was no longer yours."

Terrence uses his straw to stir the cubes of ice floating in his glass.

"On paper it was, but Cross had made his move, yes. The board had delivered the vote of no confidence. I was peripheral."

"Ignorant of the op until it was too late."

Terrence stops playing with his ice.

Am I doing this?

"I didn't say that."

Skinner looks at his pastry, lifts his fork.

"Ah."

"It was a protocol."

Skinner impales a wedge of strudel.

"A protocol."

"It looked for indications of alienation. Political. Social. Emotional."

Skinner contemplates the food on his fork.

"An algorithm? Behavioral?"

"Yes. It looked for emerging complexities in the behavior of a subset of field personnel. If it found those complexities, it measured them. If they tipped into the red, it triggered a set of responses. Proactive. Unilateral. Preemptive. Someone hatched a protocol meant to ameliorate a certain kind of risk. But theoretical. Until it ended up in a corporate context. Their bottom-line minds. Risk-averse in an environment that is nothing but risk. They want it to be a business. Security for profit. They miss the point that security is an end in and of itself."

Skinner smears the bite of uneaten pastry off his fork and onto the small white plate.

"A protocol."

Terrence tears a corner from the wet napkin under his glass.

"Diagramming interconnections. Projecting probable emergent threat actors within a population of highly gifted but eccentric personnel. Proposing appropriately comprehensive responses based on elimination of any possible threats."

Skinner nods understanding, he sees how such a thing would make sense. *Yes.*

"This was a white paper?"

"Pure thinkology."

"But someone activated it."

Terrence feels a great tiredness descending over him. A weary blanket of too many time zones traveled. *It is all so hard.*

Skinner pushes his plate away, food mauled but uneaten.

"How long before Montmartre was the protocol activated?"

Terrence looks at him, remembers him in MIT's Stratton Student Center, blank, rudderless, happy enough to talk about the possibility of working for the CIA. Drawing everything he could out of Terrence before revealing anything of himself.

"One week. Just after I was voted out, the protocol was activated."

"And my name popped up."

"An algorithm for measuring alienation. Your name was bound to appear."

"At the top of the list."

"I never saw a list. But yes."

"The metrics reading well into the red."

"The numbers were not in your favor."

Skinner is staring at Terrence.

"Housekeeping."

Terrence shrugs.

"If you like."

Skinner is still staring at him.

"I heard later that several of Kestrel's more exotic operations were shut down."

"There was a great deal of mainstreaming going on. Cross accelerated the process once he had the board's proxy. Moved Kestrel into more traditional territory. Improved the bottom line exponentially. He's a remarkable administrator."

"Why did he do it, Terrence?"

It is the first time Skinner has spoken his name since the conversation began. And Terrence does not know what it means that he is speaking it now.

"*Housekeeping.* As you say."

"No. Yes. I understand why he tried to kill me. My name. Not good for mainstream business. But. Terrence. If he wanted to kill me, why didn't he send Haven?"

A picture flashes across Terrence's mind, a boy, dark-haired, an absent gaze, swaddled tight in a sheet, arms and legs pinned, as one would wrap a newborn to calm it, staring in smudged black and white from the page of the magazine story that first sent Terrence looking for Skinner. That absent gaze filling Skinner's eyes now, as if it is leaching into them from the past.

"I'd sent Haven away. An operation in Iraq. A new asset, first time in the field. Tremendous potential for Kestrel. Only Haven would do for her. So I sent him."

"And Lentz got Montmartre."

Terrence lifts and drops his hands, helpless.

"He was next on the chart. I wasn't designing ops anymore, just handling details, assignments. Lentz was next."

Skinner, still staring.

"Terrence, did you recruit Lentz?"

"No."

Terrence looks up from his impotent hands and into Skinner's eyes.

"Cross did. Very impressed with him. Jumped him right up the chart behind you and Haven. Liked Lentz's *mettle* is what I recall him saying."

Skinner turns on his stool, looks out the long bay of terminal windows, past the bodies of the jetliners parked at their gates, to the sky.

"An alienation algorithm. Is there anyone other than you who would think of that?"

Terrence is looking at a duty-free shop on the far side of the coffee bar. Liter bottles of top-shelf liquor, designer perfumes, massive bars of chocolate, jewelry, tiny cameras, candy-shelled music players, noise-abating headphones. He feels an urge to vomit. The fear he's been holding in his stomach is fighting to come out.

"Cross doesn't miss the details. He's good at details. Extrapolations. He latches onto things. A small idea, you say something to him, cocktail conversation, conceptual, and you don't know what thought of yours might lodge in his head. You're emptying the garbage and he picks through it for anything he can use. So an idea like this protocol. The algorithm, it started with the numbers. Just me thinking out loud. But

Cross remembered that I'd done the work, had the program written up. When he took over he activated it."

Skinner moves a hand close to Terrence, doesn't touch him.

"And you sent Haven away. And you gave the op to Lentz."

He touches Terrence, fingers on the older man's wrist.

"I might have killed you, Terrence. I might have killed you all. I came very close to it."

Terrence closes his eyes; light is pulsing behind his lids.

Am I going to do this? It's done, old man. You did it already. Fix it. Five is a start. Billions. Fix it.

He opens his eyes.

"Cross has a job for you."

Skinner becomes still. Inanimate. No visible pulse or breathing.

There is a file, Terrence owns the only copy, that contains every known photograph of Skinner's victims. Terrence is looking at them now, a flip book in his mind, disjointed stutter of horrors.

Skinner blinks. And the young man is there for a moment, the one from MIT, an undefinable potential, untapped but for Terrence discovering it.

"What does he want me to do?"

Terrence thinks about the photos in the file and what they conceal. The extremity of violence hides a truth deeper than the sadist others believe lives in Skinner's heart, something altogether different. Something desperate and afraid. If Skinner learned, when he took up protection, that he need not be a monster in this world, then losing assets had taught him the value of still wearing a monster's mask. If anyone saw his real face, they would know what it cost him to lose those he protected. He learned that he didn't have to be a monster, Terrence believes, and then found out that he had been a person all along.

What do you think, you're going to live forever?

"They have an asset for you."

Skinner's eyes crinkle at the corners, just that much, focusing, and a vertical line creasing his forehead disappears.

"What?"

"Who."

Skinner touches the corner of his eye, rubs.

"I've been up in the sky a long time."

Terrence reaches inside his jacket.

"Welcome home."

He takes out a slightly bulging envelope the size of a business card.

"USB drive."

Skinner accepts it.

"James Bond."

"Consumer electronics."

"Everyone is James Bond now."

"Sadly, yes."

Terrence points at the envelope.

"Details. Flight numbers. Bank accounts. Frequent flier miles. Names. Dates. Details."

He reaches across the counter.

"Her name. Jae. *The Disaster Robot Lady.* The USB is for her. Beyond the job details, there's more. For *her*."

He touches the back of Skinner's hand.

"For *her*, Skinner. Yes?"

Skinner squeezes the bulge in the envelope.

"I want to be on a plane. I need to be inside something. I need to think. Plan."

He rises.

"It was sloppy, Terrence, the way Lentz killed my asset at Montmartre. A sloppy tip of the hand."

He doesn't look at Terrence, his eyes tracking an Airbus as it taxis to the top of the runway.

"Anyone paying attention would know that you let me get away."

Terrence's own eyes are studying the floor, polished concrete, their dark reflections blurred beneath their feet. He shrugs.

"They knew. And it was the last thing they needed to be able to get rid of me once and for all. So."

Skinner looks from the jet outside to the man next to him.

"That's what I thought."

Terrence tugs at his collar.

"Yes."

Skinner starts away, stops.

"It's good to see you, Terrence. I've missed our talks."

And he walks away, a man with a flight to catch, anonymous death, stopping at a kiosk for a copy of the *Financial Times*.

Terrence doesn't watch. As if some kind of distant muscle memory has been engaged from the night Skinner killed the boy in the hoodie, he feels his stomach turning. In a restroom off the concourse he vomits a few teaspoons' worth of lemonade. Tears from the strain of puking dribble from the corners of his eyes. He wants, with no warning, to see his ex. To tell her something about his work. Something he could be proud of. But he's not certain what.

I did this. I did that. This was good. That was bad. Things you don't even know you did, things you said, those are the things that can do the most harm. I said something once. Can you imagine? Words. How can words leave your mouth and become something evil? I said evil. Is it me? All the time? Is that what I was all the time? Evil. Our boy, I wish I could have met our boy. I'm most sorry about that. What a thing that would have been, to be a father.

He stops his mind's monologue, secret confession to a wife who isn't his anymore. It's done now. It's all done now. Whatever the cost, it's done. Skinner is on his way. And Terrence was the one who released him.

People die all the time. Now more will die. So.

Time to go.

When the arm loops around his neck as he steps out of the stall, he experiences a moment of relief, knowing the man who is killing him. Relief in whatever intimacy that allows him in his final moment. Relief in knowing that his death will be expert, fast, and without great pain. Then the moment is lost, with everything else, blacked out by a cloth pressed to his face, a chemical smell, a brief stab of pain in his left shoulder that shoots to his fingers and rebounds up and into his heart.

Regrets falling away as his body drops to the tile.

I did it.

arcade

THE OVERCOOLED AIR, jumbo HD screens, and testosterone laced dialogue inside Creech UAV operations always put Jae in mind of the bowling alley video game arcade back when she was an Atascadero High Greyhound. Jae had initially been dragged there by one of her girlfriends. Bolstering the other girl's self-confidence as she engaged in adolescent stalking activities centered on a weedy boy with greasy hair, a proclivity for tearing the sleeves off of his Metallica t-shirts, and all the high scores on Mortal Kombat.

Bored, Jae had dropped a quarter in one of the older games, Centipede, quintessentially deemed a *girl's game,* and promptly demolished the high score. A feat that did not go unnoticed by a boy whose initials, RAD, had been wiped from that lofty top spot. Egged on by a few comments that were perhaps a little too close in tone to her father's preferred mode of simultaneously challenging and demeaning, Jae proceeded to beat her own high score three times in a row. Then she started in on Galaga and Space Invaders.

Ranks of attackers dropping down the screen, scrolling mazes, incoming missiles. Compared with the hand-eye coordination required in the savage sets of handball she played with her father, the quick twitches on a trackball or joystick felt casual. And with no danger of a sixty-five-gram wad of hard rubber being drilled into her forehead at gun-muzzle velocity, the consequences of failure were irrelevant, but she kept playing anyway. Because each game revealed something new. Not the next level, the unlocked challenges of advancement, but rather the minds of the games' creators. The skeins of code embodied in the movements of digital aliens and insects, ostrich-mounted knights, robot warriors, frogs and plumbers. The screens became translucent, revealing a deeper stratum of play. Anticipation. Not reacting to the game but foreseeing it. Knowing where the next asteroid would pop onto the screen, what turn the ghost would take on its path to gobble you up, where the enemy saucers would zoom in from the edges of the square of known space.

The configurations, her father would tell her, were not there. The games were randomized. On his Macintosh Classic II he showed her a brief chain of Fortran code that immediately set to generating random number sequences. The video games were the same, he said; the configurations were a delusion of her own. She was mistaking adeptness at a childish pastime for an ability to perceive intentionality where it did not exist. He expected more from her. If she wanted to play games at the bowling alley she should, indeed, bowl. At least that would provide her with a modicum of physical activity. Did she know, by any chance, that he had played on his high school team and regularly broke 200? Whereupon she soon found herself back at the bowling alley, the league end, rolling frames until her elbow swelled to grapefruit size, having her form critiqued by her father as he used his terrier build to whip balls down the lane, shattering the neat triangles of pins. While, in a booth behind her, the friend who had first brought her to the arcade was busy smearing her pink-lip-glossed mouth against the neck of her greasy love interest.

The net gain of all this low comedy, as far as Jae was concerned, was that scrap of Fortran.

Nights, after her father had left for his graveyard shift minding the dials and gauges in the control room of the Diablo Canyon Power Plant, she would slip past the closed door of her auntie's bedroom, TV blaring *The Tonight Show* on the other side, despite the woman's refusal to learn a single word of English since she'd been brought here following Jae's mother's death, and into her father's office, kneeling into the ergonomic stool he used to discipline a chronic backache, switching on the Mac to run the Fortran code, watching the numbers tumble across the screen. Searching for what her father said was not there.

Reason.

Intention.

Configuration.

Will in the design. A human mind had written that bit of code. The random string of numbers had only ten digits to work with. It could only be infinitely random if one let it run into infinity. In smaller observable bursts, massive repetition was inevitable. The mind of the coder. So she knelt in the chair, watching the flickering numbers fill line after line on the screen. Anticipating, silently, what would come next. Stretching her mind, training it to see through the camouflage to the true shape hidden underneath.

Her eyes never once darted from the screen to the large framed photo ensconced on its own shelf within her father's bookcase. Surrounded on all sides by engineering and physics texts, programming manuals, histories of human achievement (movable type, agriculture, geometry, the internal combustion engine, law), and a copy of Bernath E. Phillips's 1937 bible, *Fundamental Handball.* Other than a constellation of certificates, credentials, and degrees framed on the opposite wall, the photo was the room's only decoration. There was no evidence of Jae herself. But, then again, her mother's photo had only come to grace the room following her death.

Bee sting.

Stupid way to die.

Pointless. Senseless. Random.

Sitting at the edge of the footpath that led from a parking lot to the beach at Morrow Bay. One sandal scraped from her foot as she jerked her leg back and forth in the sand of the path. Neck and face puffing and swelling until she appeared to have neither. Just a mottled purple column of flesh that grew from her torso, hair sprouting from it, a few random holes pushed into it, one of them rimmed with gnashing teeth.

Jae digging a hole in the sand, pushing her head into it, trying to bury herself.

Sitting in her father's office eight years after, looking for the next number before it could appear. Knowing there was an order. That things did not happen without being made to happen.

Feeling for the design.

The designer.

The planner.

Daring the writer of the world's code to reveal itself. So that she could smash it in its face for having killed her mom.

Standing in Creech, she feels she's looking at the dream scenario for those boys who had packed the bowling alley game room in the final years before the rise of Nintendo.

Which, she knows, is more than slightly the point.

The closer modern warfare hews to video game sensibilities, the more effectively it can be marketed to the young men who live in the demographic overlap between Call of Duty and the US Military. Unmanned aerial vehicle operations carrying the extra benefit that they don't involve being shot at.

"Do you see anything?"

She looks at the lieutenant colonel who has been escorting her since she came on base that morning. He is prototypically lean and proportioned for a cockpit, an especially idealized ratio of length concentrated in his tibia and fibula. She's long known that the cliché about fighter pilots being shorter overall than the national average is false, the more essential measurements being taken when they are seated. Measuring from the hips to the top of the head has obvious implications in an enclosed space; more interesting to Jae was learning that knees to hips tends to be critical. Too much length in the femur and you can't properly fit in an ejection seat. During a punch-out, a pilot's knees might extend an unfortunate fraction of a centimeter and clip the edge of the dashboard.

Lt. Colonel Cervantes's knees, she imagines, were never in danger when he was piloting his A-10 Warthog in Iraq.

"Ma'am, do you see anything?"

Jae folds her arms across her chest a bit more tightly. She should have brought a sweater or a jacket from the car. She knows what these buildings are like. Iceboxes in the desert. Fighting a two-front war against both nature and the ever multiplying processors, hard drives, and huge LCD screens inside the operations center. To say nothing of the BTUs produced by the human element. Behind the doors that line the long central hallway of the UAV operations center, pilots, electronic sensor operators and intelligence specialists are crammed three to a room, staring at over a dozen screens, trying to make remote sense of the situation on the ground in Afghanistan, Iraq, Libya, Pakistan, Syria, Iran, and other, more obscure locations. Or, more close to home, patrolling the southern border, searching for illegals and drug smugglers with equal fervor. Through the camera eyes of a Predator or Reaper, one desert looks much the same as another. Deserts and cities, the battlegrounds of the new century's first decades. These pilots will see much more of both. And, increasingly, they will have occasion to patrol domestic space far from the border. Though, Jae knows, it will be quadrotor drones taking on the city environments soon enough.

She looks at the screen.

Desert. High desert. Rocks, scree, scrub, time's passage revealed in the strata of a cliff face. Everything irregular but sharp-edged, even the gnarled brush that grows in the cracked surface of a fifteen-kiloton boulder. Everything irregular except for one geometrically flawless dark rectangle, three-dimensional, a shape taken directly from Euclid's forebrain.

She points.

"There's that."

He nods.

"Yeah, there seems to be a consensus that it looks a little out of place."

She stares at the shape.

"When was this?"

"Two days ago."

"Is there a closer view? Ground level?"

He shakes his head, wobbles one hand back and forth, indicating something out of balance.

"That's just a little east of Zabul. Very iffy on the ground. Many bad guys."

"It has a shadow."

He looks over his shoulder, looks back at her.

"Yeah, some of us noticed that."

She steps closer to the screen.

"So it's not a rectangle. Cuboid. Rectangular prism."

"Cargo container is what us experts have been thinking."

She drops her head to one side.

"I wish I had a robot."

"Ma'am?"

She runs her knuckles across her lips, eyes still locked on the cuboid.

"A robot on the ground. As opposed to the drone in the air. No need to send soldiers or, what do we call them now, war fighters, into iffy situations. Like to see if there are markings. Like to see if it's been unsealed. How far to the road?"

"There are a few poppy fields over that ridge. Some trails come west from there, continue about two klicks west of what we're looking at. Cuboid. And joins a road. Dirt, but well traveled. For the area."

Jae steps back, squeezes herself.

Her mental peripherals are picking up too many signals of ambient warfare. These young men and women are not playing video games, they are looking for things to blow up and/or kill. The longer she's in here, the more a vision of this work is forcing its way into her mind. Waking in the morning. A trip to the bathroom. Peeing, washing up, brushing teeth. Breakfast with the family while still in PJs. Check email. Look at a few sites. Shower. Put on the uniform. Car. Stop for coffee. Burning your tongue with the first sip. Driving out to Creech. Situation updates. Into operations. Whoever had your chair on the night patrol uses something in his or her hair that seeped into the headrest. Smells like Aquanet, but who the fuck uses Aquanet anymore? A prayer to the lord that the fucking ground crew listened to what you reported about that balky aileron. If you have to fly that crate today and keep it in the air for twelve hours it's gonna make your head split in two. And hours of boring your eyes into the screen, safe as houses, trying to give some poor fucking grunts on the ground twelve thousand kilometers away a little fucking air support that doesn't cost the taxpayers too damn much.

"I need to get out of here."

*   *   *

Exit procedures, and then the desert sunlight. Gooseflesh melted in an instant. Eyes sun-dazzled blind.

Jae puts on her sunglasses.

"Kontsern-Morinformsistema-Agat."

Cervantes is pulling his Randolph Engineering aviators from his right breast pocket. He pauses.

"Ma'am?"

"Your cuboid. It's a Club-K cruise missile system made by Kontsern-Morinformsistema-Agat. Russian. Package fits in a shipping container. Targeting, launcher, missiles. Move it on rails, ships, trucks. Prep to launch in under five minutes."

Cervantes slips the dark lenses over his eyes.

"Land to air?"

Jae extends her index finger, launches it in a short arc, finds a target, her other fingers popping open in a silent and harmless explosion.

"Yes. But the marketing videos tend to emphasize the fact that it can deploy four carrier-killers. In case you're ever attacked by four aircraft carriers, I suppose."

He touches the arm of his sunglasses.

"Shit."

"Could be bullshit. The marketing. But it's there."

"The *Lincoln* is in the Arabian Sea."

"Too far."

He tips his head at the closed door of the command center.

"Yeah, but the container isn't there anymore. That was two days ago. When we expected you."

"And now?"

He looks back at the sky.

"We lost it."

With her knuckles, she wipes sweat from her upper lip.

"Can we even do that anymore, lose things?"

"Yeah. It takes effort, but we can."

She looks at the sweat on her knuckle.

"Just about anything can get into Afghanistan from Russia using the reverse opium routes. And since Pakistan signed the APTTA, *trade agreement,* anything in Afghanistan can get across the southern border. That box could be buried fifty meters from where you saw it. Or it could be on a freighter docked at the port of Karachi, headed for a well-financed pirate enclave in Somalia."

He looks at her.

She shrugs.

"Far fetched. But possible. I get paid for the bad news."

She wipes some sweat from her forehead.

"Could we go someplace out of the sun. Where the AC is set a little higher than fifty. I'll be able to think better."

He looks at the H3 Tritium watch on his wrist.

"We can debrief in the Warren. We've got a SCIF. Where your guy is supposed to meet you."

Jae looks at her boots.

"My guy?"

Cervantes points toward the electric cart he used to ferry her here from his office.

"The one Kestrel is sending for you."

He walks to the cart and stands next to it, waiting.

"We should shake it. I have to get some details before I kick this upstairs and tell them the Haqqani Network or some Somali pirates may be able to sink the USS *Abraham* fucking *Lincoln.*"

She walks over, sits on the hot vinyl seat, and thinks about Terrence.

The place where the future is made.

Old man. Crazy old man. If he hadn't walked into her office she'd still be at Berkeley, running her own lab by now, breathing down her grad students' necks. As comfortably eccentric and doped-up as a campus will allow. *Look at this,* he'd said, handing her a satellite photo, *tell me if you see anything.* She'd seen something, alright, she'd seen a total absence of anything that suggested weapons of mass destruction. *Yes,* as he slipped the photo back into his briefcase, *but most everyone else, talented people, saw something else.* Then he'd offered her a job looking at things, part-time, paying the kind of money that could supplement her grants and actually prototype her robots.

Then came Kestrel. A chance to put her robots in the field. Then came Iraq.

And Haven.

Cervantes drives her across the base to the cluster of intelligence workstations called the Warren, and the Sensitive Compartmented Information Facility at its heart. A theoretically unsurveillable chamber that one of Kestrel's subsidiaries undoubtedly constructed. She thinks about who might be inside the SCIF, who Terrence might send to escort her on the contract he wants her to accept. She thinks about the implications of this escort.

Bodyguard.

She thinks about the implications of a bodyguard.

Threats. Acquisitions.

Terrence in her head.

So many people will die. But not yet. Soon. But not yet. We can. Jae. We can stop it this time.

the bruising world

BEING INSIDE A SCIF is always, for Skinner, more than slightly disorienting.

That they are generally very small, some no more than a moderate suburban closet, is comforting. Confinement reminds him agreeably of his early childhood. This confounded the therapists and doctors who made case studies of him after he was removed from his parents' care. The working assumption seemed to have been that his experience should have been traumatizing, so much so that he must be taking refuge behind false memories of a pleasant childhood. What could possibly lie, many of them wondered, on the other side of that wall of false memory? What terrible horrors would require the construction of a virtual fortress of lies told by the self to the self so as to keep them at bay?

Skinner, as an adult, was startled to think how completely those experts failed to put themselves into the minds of the children who were the subjects of their expertise. It was a failure not just of imagination but of basic principles. After all, what child wouldn't, given the choice, elect to be the sole focus of his or her mother's and father's entire attention for every minute of every day?

For good or ill.

Children have little notion of the consequences of the most basic actions until they are taught to consider them. How could one be expected to comprehend the consequences of obsessive scrutiny. Unflagging guidance. Untiring experimentation. How could a child, a creature so unformed that it can be conditioned to interpret a punch in the face as positive attention, be expected to understand the constant observation of his parents as anything but love? And how could that same child feel the removal from such a state as anything but a wrenching amputation of all that was warming and nurturing in the world?

That they had missed the obvious was sometimes amusing to Skinner. His parents would never have missed such a connection. Parsers of details though they were, they would still have taken a moment to survey the forest before plunging into the trees for a closer look. Perhaps the experts missed the obvious because they failed to imagine the opposite case. Never considered the consequences of total parental neglect. The obvious negative to Skinner's positive was in front of them, but they never looked to see. It seemed too banal, perhaps. Too normal to be worth investigating. Such was the case Skinner's entire life, it seemed. A boy raised in a Skinner box is so much more exotic than another of the billions raised outside of one.

So, inevitably, the tight quarters of a SCIF evoke a fraction of childhood comfort in him. Home, the close walls said. The perversity of the experience being that these rooms were constructed for the express purpose of barring any and all observation or surveillance. A SCIF was, by definition, the exact opposite of the environment he'd been raised in. The Skinner box his parents had built for him while his mother was still pregnant. The cocoon they had determined to place him in so as to better protect him from the bruising world, and to give them a perfect subject for their own work. Secretly constructed because, though both were muffled in distinct blankets of autism, they knew, even if they could not understand why, that no one would really approve of what they were doing. Indeed, they suspected, there might even be some slight legal consequences to their actions if they were discovered.

They should have had a SCIF, Skinner thinks, one to contain their lives.

Bored with ruminating on the past, he practices being invisible.

He considers the interior of the SCIF. Four by four meters, a small table at the room's center, four chairs, lighting from a sealed, battery-powered fixture over the table. The furniture is all made of a light plastic, off-white, slightly translucent, offering reassurance that it cannot conceal listening or recording devices.

There is one door. Self-closing, with a single-use internal emergency release that must be entirely replaced if it is ever employed. Ventilation is achieved via a single duct, 50 x 50 centimeters. Somewhere along the length of the duct a section of nonconductive material will have been incorporated. A firebreak to prevent anyone from using the length of the duct as an antenna or to carry the uninterrupted vibrations of conversations taking place inside. A sealed cube, designed to reveal any efforts made to subvert its integrity. He is, to a certain extent, already invisible while he is within the SCIF. But with no one to observe him, can he indeed be invisible at all?

He becomes blank. Expression leaches from his face and body, his stillness a reflection of the emptiness of the room. Invisibility. Privacy. Aloneness. He learned to construct them from within because they were not naturally available in the environment of the box. Later, he used this skill to kill people. And thinking about killing people he remains within himself a fraction of a moment beyond the point when an air force lieutenant colonel and a female civilian enter the SCIF, startling them both with his first words, neither of them having seen him until he speaks.

He looks at the colonel, eyes skimming the man's name tag.

"Thank you, Colonel Cervantes."

The officer stops short, seeing Skinner for the first time, standing with the door of the SCIF wide open, an imperative no-no.

The woman is looking past Skinner, as though trying to see the concealed trapdoor out of which he has just popped.

Skinner pulls one of the chairs from the table.

"There's a clock running."

Cervantes looks at the woman.

"I don't have clearance for whatever this is."

She nods.

"It's okay."

He looks again at Skinner, points out the open door.

"I'll be outside. If you need anything."

Skinner pulls out a chair for himself.

"Thank you."

Cervantes steps out of the open door, letting it close on the automatic mechanism, a loud clunk, as if something heavy had been dropped in an adjoining room, indicating that the bolts have shot home, sealing them in.

Skinner looks at the woman. Jae. Terrence said her name is Jae. *Disaster Robot Lady*. One of Terrence's people. And like all of Terrence's oddities, there are stories about her. The Disaster Robot Lady finds things. Bodies in rubble. Survivors in wreckage. Weapons caches in satellite imaging. Patterns in randomness. She's a finder.

His asset. If he can convince her.

"I need you to trust me."

At the word *trust* her hands begin moving from pocket to pocket, making an inventory, assuring herself that everything is in its place.

"What does Cross want?"

Skinner pictures his life aloft, the seven years of transience, sealed containers freighting him from airport to airport, hotel to hotel. An affair in Trieste, five days, his longest sustained contact in those years. Shifting his place on the globe. Dubai, yes. Moscow, yes. Also Albuquerque. Hull. Ontario, California, not Canada. Hotel fitness centers, airport business lounges, elevators with mirror-finish doors, backseats of hired cars with bottled water and copies of *USA Today*, the *Herald Tribune*, the *London Times*. Drinks presented on a tray, a selection of movies on seat-back screens, hot towel on takeoff and arrival. Cookies on pillows. A waitress in the hotel's lobby bar, she gets off at midnight, *no, that's not too late to show you some clubs, Berlin wakes up at midnight.* Her flat in the morning. Photo collage, two towels in the shower, one of them perpetually damp, ashtray full of the butts of cigarettes smoked with her last night, the empty bottles of Alsatian Riesling.

And the temptation of dark alleys, bad neighborhoods, situations that suggest danger. The opportunity to be there, present, when circumstances veer suddenly from the norm, when someone finds himself caught in a tide of abrupt violence, the possibility of stepping into that tide, altering its course, bringing someone to shore safely. The will to ignore those alleys and streets, the telltales of hazard. Knowing that to take action is to leave a signature that can be read. Aware always of faraway people in office cubicles reviewing, studying, analyzing. The possibility that they might cut across a sign of Skinner. And so practicing invisibility on a grand scale, hovering, drifting, waiting for a signal, a tug on the string of his life's balloon, pulled to earth by Terrence. Offering something, the only thing.

A job.

An asset.

To make safe.

And here she is, high-strung and exhausted, looking for any excuse to say no. He would not be surprised to find that she tastes danger in the air with the tip of her tongue. He takes the USB drive Terrence gave him from the breast pocket of his jacket, presents it between index and middle finger, and sets it on the table.

"There has been an incident of cyber sabotage. Implications of international involvement. The contract is Kestrel. You find the badguys. I go with you."

She flicks the USB with a fingernail, sets it spinning.

"And you do what?"

"I'll protect you."

She's looking at him, eyes scanning back and forth as if reading or solving. Her eyes stop moving.

"What's your name?"

"Skinner."

She gives the USB another flick, another, puts her finger on it to stop the spinning.

"I've heard about you."

"Oh."

"Are they true, the things I've heard?"

"I don't know. They might be."

She picks up the USB.

"This?"

He nods.

"The job. Details. And Terrence said there was more in there. For you."

She holds it on her palm.

"Did he."

He thinks about Cologne, Terrence touching his hand. Urgency. *For her.*

"Yes. It seemed important."

She is balancing the drive on her hand, weighing it.

"Skinner."

"Yes."

Her eyes are moving over him again, the sentience of a hunting thing is behind them, a parasite intelligence living inside her. Palpable, her brilliance.

"People are afraid of you, Skinner."

He doesn't know what she's seeing, finds himself wanting to become invisible before she discovers too much. But doesn't.

"When I do my job, yes, they are."

Her hand closes over the USB, her eyes stop looking for him.

"I like that."

She rises.

"I need things from the place I was staying."

Back in the sun, Skinner following Jae, walking toward the parking lot, beyond her, the landing strip where the winged shark silhouette of a Predator is taking flight on a training run. Practice over the deserts of home. His asset ahead of him, unsafe, drawing unrest and danger.

Seven years after he left and his heart stopped in his chest, Skinner feels it begin to beat again.

rubble

JAE MET HAVEN in post-invasion Iraq.

She was there as a rescue worker. Running her robots through mountains of man made rubble, searching for collateral survivors. A Kestrel initiative financed by cash gushing from the reconstruction pipeline. One of the hundreds of small operations meant to show the locals that the Americans were really there to help after all. As advertised by red, white, and blue flag stickers plastered over all of her equipment. That was the cover. The op, her first in the field, was concerned with mapping connections between Iran's Revolutionary Guards and al-Qaeda in Iraq's IED supply chain.

Terrence had conceived the original contract and sold it to the CIA. Jae to be set loose in a database of Top Secret files, tracing a configuration that could concretely establish the flow of explosives and weapons from Iran into Iraq. Evidence to be used in backroom negotiations with Shiite insurgents who would rather their native supporters not know how beholden they were to a foreign government. And so it had progressed for six months, fruitlessly. Yet another of Terrence's ops that seemed born to wither in the year that Cross began to challenge him for control of Kestrel. And, indeed, it was Cross, after he had wrested the company from Terrence's hands, who proposed that Jae should take the op to Iraq.

To better get a feel for the configuration on the ground, he suggested.

Eager to complete the work she had begun, to ease the pressure of the disjointed configuration in her head, Jae went to Baghdad. But the op was quickly scuttled when the CIA began feeling heat from the State Department. The newly birthed, US-backed Iraqi government would rather such connections remain suspected but unconfirmed. A reluctance to embarrass their neighbor before they could discover if they might be allies in the brave new post-Hussein world. So the op was shut down, and Jae, at loose ends in Baghdad, the incomplete configuration an unscratchable itch, was free to find some other way to focus her obsessive need to discover order.

No op, they told her. Go home. Or stay and make use of the cover story. Save people.

Haven had shown up at the site of a car bombing as she was sending one of her early Worm prototypes into a hillside of shattered brick and mortar that had been a mosque a few hours before. The prototype Worm, controlled via an umbilical cord of thickly insulated cable, range severely limited, eternally having to be dragged out by hand, was halfworking for a change when she'd felt the presence behind her, looming, looking at the murky fisheye view of small rocks on her control screen.

She was there to save people. When she'd arrived, an hour after the blast, the first thing she'd seen in the blood-slicked square was an emergency worker prying a half-dead child from the arms of a corpse. Squatting just a few yards from where she'd witnessed that tableau, using the edge of her hand to shield the screen from the sun so that she could get something resembling a clear camera image, and then looking up to find someone who was obviously in the country to kill people, had not brought out her charm. Not that Haven gave a fuck. He'd given her some room to work, and, when she thought the Worm had found something, he'd grabbed a shovel and started digging. Other men materialized, all of them wearing beards, Gargoyle sunglasses, uniforms that evoked images of mercenary forces drifting from army to army in a time of rapidly shifting fronts. They started to dig with Haven, following his jargon-laced sotto voce commands as Jae shouted directions, reading the Worm's camera eye, hunting for a safe route through the remains of the mosque, a path to a possible survivor.

The man was dead. No great shock to Jae. Her rescues consisted largely of nursing balky robots into unreachable crevasses where they could break down, while occasionally stumbling upon a flickering shadow that hinted at life, almost inevitably revealed as another tally in the final body count. Haven and his men had appeared more disappointed than she. More dismayed at the sudden reversal: one moment digging to save a life, the next moment heaving another corpse from the wreckage. If they had killed the man themselves, Jae thought, his death would have made no more impression than the satisfaction of a job well done. But for a few hours of digging, their lives had been linked to his as securely as if they had been neighbors, intimates in celebration and mourning. A connection abruptly severed when the shovels exposed him to the light of the halogen lamps that had been set up as night fell, dead flesh caked in dust, as if they had excavated a statue from an earlier era.

Jae and Haven talked about it only once. Three months later, when the war-zone affair that began after the mosque bombing was being drawn to a close by Jae's imminent return to the States. By then they had fallen into a pattern of casual intimacy. Unmentionable circumstances would take him to deeper layers of Baghdad than she had yet to penetrate. Circles of confusion and dismay that he would disappear into. Or to places where there was meant to be nothing but sand, coordinates only, where he did officially unacknowledged things involving night-vision goggles and flash suppressors. Days would pass, on one occasion weeks, and then she might return from testing a new tread on the low-profile Crawler that was meant to be unflippable but persisted in flipping at every opportunity, and find him asleep in her apartment within the Kestrel compound inside the Green Zone. His dust-covered boots near the door, sand coating the floor of her shower, face-down on her perpetually unmade bed, naked in the generator-sustained AC. She knew how lightly he must sleep, but he never seemed to wake when she entered, never until she had stripped, taken her own shower, pulled from the freezer one of the nearly impossible to obtain bottles of vodka that Haven always produced on his visits, and come to the bed with two glasses clinking between her fingers. Then he would become very much awake.

On the last night they talked about the first meeting. Both of them half-drunk but not tired, most signs of her months of residence packed into the bags near the door, Haven had told her that trying to save the dead man under the rubble had been the most unambiguously *good* thing that he had done since arriving in country. Since before arriving, for that matter. A feeling that he'd been unwilling to let go. He was telling her, he said, so she'd know that she had made it better for him, the war, more real, less theoretical. *Whatever that means,* he said.

Her own reality dissolved the next morning after her convoy was attacked on Route Irish, the long, straight highway to the airport, after the Kestrel security contractors in the lead vehicle had been blown from the road by an IED, and the engine of the follow vehicle had been sent back into the passenger compartment by the force of an exploding RPG, after the insurgents had peppered her own vehicle with small-arms fire and closed on them, looping nooses around the necks of the surviving contractors and dragging them to the base of a lamppost, reality lost as she was pulled by her hair from the vehicle.

A chatter of strobed images: the flames dancing atop the undercarriage, now the roof, of what had been the lead SUV; the feet of one of the contractors two meters off the ground, kicking; a blade cutting into her driver's wrist, sawing, a hand dropping to the pavement; the open door of the insurgents' minivan, a dark cave, as they prepared to heave her inside; the hole that appeared in the orbit of the left eye of the man carrying her feet; the mute and tongueless mouth that opened in the throat of the man with his fists twisted into her hair; and Haven, all theory removed from from his work, killing people.

Balled on the floor of one of the Humvees in which Haven and his cadre had been trailing them at a distance, Jae saw the configuration that had been camouflaged by vodka and the corona of danger that obscured everything in Iraq: Haven appearing. Haven digging. Haven seeking her out. Haven in and out of her life and her apartment like a tide. Haven watching her. Haven evoking a trust she put in no one. Haven in and out of her life, days to weeks, always returning to her quarters when she was away, as if he knew that she was away. Haven, there within moments when the insurgents tried to kidnap her. As if he was watching her, watching over her, a goat staked out for wolves.

Her last sight of Haven was of the back of his head as he ran hunched, his cheek pressed to the stock of an assault rifle that seemed to protrude from his shoulder like an organic growth, a sensing organ that pulled him toward targets of opportunity. Leading her, gun first, away from the bodies around the minivan and into the Humvee that took her to safety without him. The only words she heard spoken by him came through the Humvee's radio as possible threats were assessed in the remaining kilometers to the airport. They drove directly onto the tarmac, Haven's team passing her, hand-to-hand, out of the Humvee, surrounding her in a crouched scuttle of gun-bristling men, surrendering her care only when she was buckled into her seat in a marine-stuffed C-5 Galaxy.

Her op, it emerged, had never been dropped. Rather, it had been repurposed by Haven.

She hadn't known she was an asset. Had barely known or understood the nature of asset operations. Had never been told that she had a protector secretly watching her in Iraq. Haven. And she had certainly not known that she was the target of an especially active AQI cell. Haven had suggested deactivating Jae's existing op. Badged *Two Birds One Stone,* the new op left Jae in the open to dig in the rubble, her robots sporting American flag stickers, as attractive an asset as they could make her. A successful op. Ending with the asset secured from further threat, and the AQI cell destroyed.

Returning to the States, Jae voided her agreement with Kestrel, expressed her wish that Cross should fuck himself and die, and soon found that her previously tamable compulsion to find structure within the seemingly random had become a full-blown mania tinged with paranoia. A form of post-traumatic stress disorder that undermined her ability to read configurations as she began to forever discover hidden plots, ambushes, and trapdoors.

Years lost. Drugs. Ending up at Disaster City.

When she thought of Haven, she tried only to remember that Cross had known nothing about their affair. Whatever else she may have meant to him, Haven had kept the hours in her apartment invisible. The two of them lost in their search for the man under the rubble.

Until she returns to her motel room in the Mohave and finds him, a big man in a suit that he looks unhappy to be wearing, standing at the window, staring out at the desert, throwing just one glance at her as she opens the door. Haven.

Cross rises from the room's only chair, a sun-faded green plastic castoff from a patio set, one of Jae's spiders in his hand.

"I know this is awkward, but we really must talk."

Jae has yet to come fully into the room. She's thinking about what's in there that she would miss if she were to turn on her heels in this instant, walk back to the Land Rover, and speed away in a spray of gravel and sand.

Cross turns the spider upside down.

"What I'd like, Jae, is fifteen, perhaps twenty minutes of your time. For which I will double what you are owed for the Creech consultation. That will finance a great deal more running away and hiding."

He gestures at her open duffel on the floor, the pill bottles and baggies.

"And buy you a great deal more self-medication."

She doesn't come into the room, but she doesn't walk to the car, either.

Cross looks at the open door.

"There is some delicate information involved."

He directs his eyes at the ceiling, deep focus, beyond the ceiling to the sky.

"We've had a good look at the area, doesn't seem that anyone is on hand to peep on us, but every little bit of discretion helps."

This isn't going to end. Whatever it is, having pushed it this far, Cross isn't going to let it end until he's had his say.

And also there is this: Haven has not looked her in the eye, and she wants that.

She steps in, closes the door, takes her phone from her pocket, pushes buttons, and looks at Cross.

"Fifteen minutes. When the timer beeps, you fuck off."

He nods.

"You met Skinner."

Jae makes a point of not saying anything.

Cross is watching her face; he nods.

"I see he made an impression. Did you get the briefing?"

She nods.

"Are you planning to use me to chum for sharks again?"

Haven dips his head slightly, seems to look at his shoes.

"Chum."

Jae feels an urge to throw something at the back of his head. Something hard. She could go outside and get a rock off the ground and come back in and throw it at Haven's fucking head. And then leave.

Cross takes a half step, placing himself at the midpoint of an imaginary line running from Jae's eyes to the back of Haven's head.

"The job, Jae. Have you reviewed the file?"

She focuses on Cross, the sooner to be done and on the road.

"Espionage. Industrial. Possible foreign involvement. Travel. Danger."

Cross rubs his forehead with the back of the hand holding the spider.

"Espionage. That doesn't quite cover it. It's a cyber attack, Jae. Sabotage. The real thing. A virtually mounted, Internet-based assault on a piece of key infrastructure. The grid. They took a crack at the grid. Tried to start a cascade. We don't know, we don't know was it a feint, a test, see if their code will do what it is supposed to, but they did it. And you know how this stuff goes, routed, rerouted, bounced, reflected. We have a trail, we have our guys at the keyboards tracing, but we need, I need, someone there, the physical sites, as we trace where this thing came from. I need someone to get in there and see where they were, where they went. This is it, first shot fired, maybe it was one over the bow, but I want to know everything. Everything. And that includes the weird stuff. Whatever the weird stuff is."

He hefts the spider.

"And that's you, Jae. *Disaster Robot Lady.* Finder of lost things."

She's thinking about how many people could die if someone really crashed the grid. Thinking about stopping that from happening. Saving lives instead of digging up the bodies. *Is this what Terrence was talking about?*

"Yes."

She walks into the bathroom and starts collecting her toiletries, stowing them in a small ripstop nylon bag with a drawstring top, comes out, faces Cross, and holds out her hand.

"My spider."

"Your phone hasn't beeped."

"I said yes. What else do you want?"

"He wants you to agree to take someone besides Skinner. My people."

Haven has turned around. Gracefully blunt in his movements, a physicality that accurately suggests his vast training and experience in matters related to killing.

Jae looks at him, but her eyes fail to burn holes in his forehead. She takes her travel alarm from the bedside table, the extra water bottle she left there, the merino wool sweater she'd meant to wear at Creech.

"It's Terrence's op. I travel with his people. Terrence sent Skinner, so Skinner is my protection."

Haven touches his forehead.

"Terrence is dead."

Her phone beeps. They all listen as it pulses, then she taps a button. Silence.

"What happened?"

Cross is looking at the floor. He shakes his head.

"He was killed. Cologne. The airport."

Haven goes to her duffel on the floor, yanks the zipper, drawing it closed.

"They used a chemical agent. Looks like a heart attack. But it wasn't."

He hefts the duffel and sets it before her.

"Skinner was Terrence's choice. Not ours. He's not safe and he doesn't protect people. He doesn't have a system. We want you to use someone else."

Jae picks up the duffel, slings it over her shoulder.

"I've worked with people who have systems. I'll be happy to try something else."

"This isn't the same thing."

The spiders and the other robots are in the Land Rover. Her daypack also. Just the one mother spider in Cross's hand left to reclaim and she can get the fuck out of here.

"Terrence sent Skinner. I'll do the job with Skinner. No one else."

She looks at Cross.

"The fact that you don't want him tells me everything I need to know."

Cross is looking at the robot spider in his hand.

"Start in Kiev. I'll have more for you to go on when you get there. But start in Kiev."

He looks up.

"Excellent work this."

He offers it to her.

"Do you have a patent?"

She takes it.

"Several."

Cross nods.

"Do me a favor. Remember that Skinner isn't a robot. He has qualities that suggest automation, but he is not viable. And if you should find yourself having regrets, call us. A replacement will be sent immediately."

Jae tucks the spider into a pocket on her vest.

"Know what I like about him already?"

She starts for the door.

"I like that he scares the shit out of you."

She opens the door.

"Now I have to go. The bogeyman's waiting in my car."

"Jae."

Haven is back at the window, looking out at the parking lot through a crack in the curtains.

"The bogeyman out there might be the one who killed Terrence."

He turns from the window, looks at her.

"I could tell you to be careful who you trust, but you already know that. Don't you?"

She could spit. She could spit in his face from where she's standing. Instead she walks out. Spitting wouldn't be enough.

oddities

Skinner misses Terrence.

There is a place on the Web where he used to leave him messages. A board on vintage cycling where he could ask about frame geometries, the measurements of chainstays and seat tubes, all used to hide requests that Terrence call him. An aged recess of the Internet where the advent of social media is regarded with deep suspicion. A protocol established long before the Montmartre Incident and Skinner's subsequent banishment. Terrence used it to bring him back.

Waiting in Jae's Land Rover outside her motel, Skinner feels an urge to do something he sometimes did in the loneliest hours of his exile. Using his Wi-Fi account, he logs in to classicsteelbikes.com. The messages he left during his seven years adrift were never answered. Not until Terrence called him to Cologne. He casts yet another bottle onto the waves now, posts a question about the geometry of Eddy Merckx Leader frames. A series of measurements. A mute SOS that only his friend would understand.

Strange urge. Back in the world again. He is not himself. He will be, he hopes. After he has a chance to do those things that make him what he is.

Packing the laptop away, Skinner looks up and sees Jae coming out of her room, and, stepping into the open doorway behind her, Haven. He thinks about his box. He thinks about his parents. He thinks about his mother, and the last time they spoke, and what he did after.

Haven behind Jae, coming out of her room, and Skinner is opening the door, emerging into the heat of the waning day.

Jae walking briskly to the driver's side door, a black mountaineering duffel over her shoulder.

"Heathrow. Connecting to Kiev. That's where he wants us to go."

Skinner nods, eyes on Haven.

"Do you want me to drive?"

Jae throws the duffel inside.

"Nobody drives my car."

Cross has come out of the room now. Skinner is thinking about Montmartre. How hard it had been to leave. All that killing unresolved.

Haven is crossing the gravel lot, raising his hands, a greeting that shows they are empty. As if, his hands free of weapons, Haven is any less dangerous.

"I wanted to see for myself."

Jae climbing in.

"Let's roll."

Haven stops; hot wind stirs the dust.

"The man risen from the dead."

Skinner remembers how it felt when the knife went between his ribs, the tip breaking off.

Jae starts the engine.

"Skinner."

Haven points.

"Your asset wants you."

Skinner ducks his head and looks inside the car.

She nods at Haven and Cross.

"Stop wasting time with those cocksuckers and get the fuck in."

Another look at Haven, Cross, but he made his decision about them seven years ago. He gets in the Land Rover with his asset, his door not yet closed when she punches the gas and whips the rear end around, spraying gravel and sand. Haven emerging from the cloud behind them, visible in the wing mirror, waving.

Jae pulls her seatbelt on.

"Assholes."

Skinner pulls on his own seatbelt.

"Kiev."

She shifts into fourth, still accelerating.

"That's where he wants us to go."

He nods in the general direction of Kiev.

"Where he *wants* us to go."

"*Wants.* Yeah."

"Where *are* we going."

She runs her hands around the arc of the wheel.

"Eventually, maybe, Kiev. Right now, Miami. Maker Smith. Know him?"

Skinner remembers the slaughterhouse in Berlin.

"Yes. Work. Several years ago."

"Everyone knows Smith. He's colorful."

She twists her neck until it rewards her with a sharp crack.

"I don't want Cross to know. I don't want him to know anything until I say otherwise."

He nods.

"I go with you. Protect you. Everything else, the details, you decide."

She rubs her neck, as if she can feel something there that won't rub off.

"Okay, okay. Let's go."

Dust unsettled behind them, Haven, all the past has to offer. Skinner studies the road ahead.

PART TWO

PART TWO

energy

RAJ DOESN'T THINK they can get the truck down the alley.

In truth, he doesn't know how they got a truck this far from 90 Feet Road. Sections of Dharavi Main Road carry box lorries, but nothing so large as this. Yellow and black, colors of a Padmini cab, a diesel lorry with a flatbed trailer, common on the highways and the infinite construction sites of Bombay, unheard of here.

"Is that it, Raj?"

David presses against his back, his voice raised to be heard over the rattle of the rain falling on thousands of corrugated tin roofs, the two of them sandwiched into a rare gap where the outer walls of two shanties do not lean against one another. They are drenched by the rain, as close to submerged as one can be without drowning. Their feet are ankle deep in the muck that funnels from the alley into the space between the homes. But when are their feet not ankle deep in muck?

Raj squeezes his ball to his chest.

"Yes."

David worms closer to the mouth of the gap. If someone inside one of the two shanties leans against the inner wall the boys will either be crushed or spat into the alley like melon seeds pinched from between finger and thumb.

David is breathless.

"Bhenchod super cool."

It is super cool, of that there is no doubt. Dead of night, the truck, headlights blacked out, backing into the alley a centimeter at a time, fat tires straddling the water main that humps up from the mud, and no one out to gawk. The rains drive many indoors, equal parts shelter and the need to ensure that this morning's wall does not become this evening's floor in a sudden wash of sludge. But even in the most severe monsoon the inhabitants of Dharavi usually go about their business.

The one-room factories and textile mills churn out raw materials, the recycling centers melt plastic waste, spin it into long strings and chop it into pellets, cardboard boxes are turned inside out and stapled and sold for reuse, grills are tended in doorways, dyes mixed from toxins that would not be allowed in any other residential area of Bombay, dentistry is practiced by lamplight, bodies are sold, trinkets for the tourists are made from smelted waste lead, copper pipe scrap is beaten into plate, phone card minutes brokered, hair barbered, real estate deals closed. But just here, everyone is shut away indoors. Electric light shows behind sheet plastic windows and through the million chinks in the improvised walls; and TV voices, turned up to be heard over the river pouring from the sky. In this neighborhood, business has been all but forgotten, an unprecedented occurrence in Dharavi, let alone in Bombay, let alone in India herself. Not forgotten, then, but left unattended for a few hours. A polite gesture of respect made in response to a request that went about earlier in the day, circulated by Sudhir's men.

They came the night after he gave Raj the ball. The night after Raj pushed the button that sent the text message on the Nokia 1100. More jungle men. Riding in on mopeds and bicycles, walking, wearing the patchwork colors and filth of the slum, shorts and t-shirts, plastic sandals.

But they are not of the slum. They talk too softly, voices modulated to compete with a wind in the branches and the calls of birds and monkeys rather than the constant roaring drone and screech of the city. They cough too much, their eyes watering, bothered by the fumes of Bombay. They move in loping strides meant to cover dozens of kilometers in a day, not the quick steps required to negotiate space between millions of bodies. They walk single file, always one in their pack takes a lead several meters in front, always one straggles meters back of the others. They are out of place, almost out of this century, but they are not intimidated or overwhelmed.

And with them came the Bangladeshis. Skeleton men. A dozen of them. Dark, arms knotted with muscle that looks like knobs of bone pushing up under their skin. They went immediately to #1 Shed and began to work. Like ants hauling many times their own weight, outpacing the hardiest. Talking in cracked voices, a language that sounds like nothing but curses far worse than the commonplace bhenchod, *sister fucker*, of everyday use in Bombay. His father says they are ship breakers, and Raj imagines these men cracking the spines of freighters on the jagged ridges of coral reefs.

Now the alley is empty of people, the chug of the diesel and huff and squeal of the air brakes lost to the tinny thunder of the rain. The truck inches in the mud. Two of the Naxalites are at the end of the trailer, hands in the air, signaling the man sitting on the roof of the tractor cab, *this many centimeters right, this many left, stop, go, stop, slow, slow, slow, stop.* Their faces red in the almost constant flare of the brake lights, the men at the back of the truck hold up clenched fists, *STOP!* The truck's engine idles for a moment and then dies, red and yellow running lights still illuminated on its roofline and down the length of the trailer, outlining the shape of the faded red cargo container. The men at the front of the truck want to talk to those at the rear, but over the rain they cannot be heard. With little room to slip between the sides of the truck and the walls of the shanties edging the alley, the men climb, nimble scramblers, and meet on the roof of the trailer.

Raj squirms, trying to edge himself free of David and the wall so that he can stick his face into the alley to see more.

"Shit, Raj, stop moving, you little shit."

But Raj only squirms more fiercely. He wants to see.

"Shit!"

Raj is shoved into the wall, and the ball he has cradled to his chest all this time, protesting at last against being compressed into an unnatural shape, pops free and shoots into the alley, a sudden flash of white and red that bangs off a steel drum someone has left out to catch the rain. Raj and David freeze. Raj blinks the rain from his eyes, looking at his soccer ball half submerged in a puddle in the middle of the alley. It bobs there, rocked back and forth by the falling drops. Pulled by it, Raj edges forward, sliding his feet in the mud.

"Raj. No. Raj."

David grabs the back of his t-shirt, a fistful of Optimus Prime, but Raj reaches out, hooks his fingers on the corners of the two buildings that sandwich them, and pulls himself free, stumbling into the open, hunching, running, scooping up the ball and jumping to crouch behind the drum full of rainwater. He waits for the jungle men to appear, but no one splashes down from the top of the truck to grab him from his hiding place. He looks up. Across the alley, in the mouth of the gap where they had both been crammed a moment before, David holds his arms up in salute, a smile splitting his round face. Raj gives a thumbs-up, trying not to laugh, but his own smile suddenly stretches into something from a movie, the expression on Preity Zinta's face when the villain grabs her sari and pulls her close, as a shadow coalesces from the rain behind David, wraps its arms around the large boy and whips him away into the darkness of the gap.

Raj's scream is shoved back down his throat by the palm of a hard, smooth hand that clamps over his mouth.

"Come inside, little Shiva, before you get wet."

And Sudhir hoists him, tucking him easily under one arm, using his toe to flip the soccer ball from the puddle where it has fallen, catching it in his free hand, carrying both it and the boy toward the truck.

"Are you dry?"

Raj says nothing, rubbing the towel over his wet hair. Sudhir found it in the sleeping area behind the seats of the truck and gave it to him, keeping the ball.

A loud noise jolts the cab of the truck.

Sudhir's eyes go to Raj's window, looking through it at the big mirrors mounted outside. Angled for the driver, Raj has to shift left to see what Sudhir is seeing: several of the jungle men at the back of the tractor, uncoupling cables, preparing to free the great latch that keeps the trailer shackled.

"We'll have to push it."

Raj looks at him, and Sudhir tilts his head toward the back of the cab.

"The trailer. In the mud. Oh the many joys of this thing."

"Where is David?"

Sudhir rests his hand on the soccer ball, drums his fingers on the muddy synthetic leather.

"Home. Where he should have been. Instead of dragging his friend out into the rain to spy."

He drums his fingers again, and again, a rhythm that seems to echo the rain on the roof of the cab.

The windows are starting to fog a little. Raj sees a shadow move past his door. The figure squeezes toward the activity at the trailer hitch.

"He didn't drag me. I told him to come with me. Is he really home?"

Sudhir stops drumming on the ball.

"Where else should he be?"

Raj shrugs.

Sudhir takes his hand off the ball.

"And you also are a good friend, thinking of David. Asking first about him before anything else."

He nudges the ball toward Raj, and Raj places his own hand on it, drums his fingers once, picks it up and puts it in his lap.

"I was only curious."

"Yes, you should be. But this isn't for everyone's eyes. That's why we asked the people here to look away for a few hours. That's why I had David taken home."

The tractor shudders as the weight of the trailer is pulled free by the men in the rain.

"You did not send me home."

Sudhir wipes a droplet that has rolled from his thick hairline down his forehead and brings it to his lips, sucking the tiny bit of moisture into his mouth.

"Do you want to see?"

Raj wipes fog from the window, looks into the mirror. The men are massing at the front of the trailer. Ropes have been produced, passed up to the top of the cargo container.

"Can they move it?"

Sudhir holds up his hands.

"They must. But they will need help. There."

He wipes at the windscreen. Down the alley more men are coming, but not just jungle men. Locals, Dalits, proudly untouchable. Also the breakers. And not just men. Women. Coming through the rain, Raj's father. And there his mother is also, behind his father, her sari left at home, she is wearing her husband's shorts, and one of his t-shirts, practical.

"So we'll move the trailer."

He separates his hands.

"Will you help us move it?"

Raj's parents are edging past the tractor now, just outside the fogged window. He could touch them if he rolled it down.

"I'm supposed to be at David's, playing. They'll be mad. I should go home."

"Little Shiva."

Sudhir is whispering, a voice meant not to be heard by jungle cats and soldiers.

"Little Shiva, you are home. This is for you. This fire we will light. You are our Shiva. Bringer of wonderful change, and destroyer."

He opens his door, raises his voice to be heard over the rain.

"I have to go help. You can do as you like. It is a free world. Much to the gods' disappointment."

He swings down from the truck and slams the door closed.

Raj sits, listens to the rain, hears shouts as the jungle men and the breakers and the Dalits of his daily life prepare to move the trailer. Something is wrong. He knows it. Something is different. Too different. He wants to know what, and why. He wants to go home and see Taji, the baby, left with one of his mother's friends, no doubt.

Why has life become frightening so suddenly? These choices.

He picks up the ball, then puts it back on the seat. He won't need it in the rain.

Outside they are all wet, all in mud, pushing, hauling on the ropes tied at the end of the trailer, falling, getting up, pushing again. The trailer moves in centimeters, rolls back those same centimeters. Boards are shoved under the tires. People in the shanties along the alley worm out of the doorways blocked by the trailer and join them. Centimeter by centimeter, it moves.

Covered in mud, Raj finds his mother and father. They recognize him. Dirty and in the dark, what is that to them? They have seen him this way his whole life. They look the same now. The three look at one another. *How are we here? Why? And you, why aren't you at David's?* But nothing is said. Instead they laugh, and put their shoulders back to the work, pushing the great weight.

The fire.

memory

THERE'S NOTHING IN the USB.

Just the op files. Practical detail relating to monies they can access, travel arrangements that can be made, contact protocols for Internet dead drops. Her own dossier. A timeline on the West-Tebrum power plant attack broken down by seconds. Once the lube oil pump froze up, the turbine was doomed. No time for a response after alarms started sounding in the plant control room. Some of the code from the Stuxnet variation the attackers used. A wag at some level has named it Re-Stuxnet. Jae grunts displeasure. The tech language gets very deep very quickly, and she bails out of that particular file. Maker Smith will tell her what it all means. Better to get a gloss, feed it to her brain, get it into the new configuration that she's trying to build. Or is the configuration already there? She still doesn't know. They always feel real, external, when she discovers them. Quickly turning to sham. The big configurations will sprawl endlessly if she lets them, if she doesn't unplug her brain. Retreat to the desert or the mountains. Personal pharmacy in hand. She's feeling prickly on the plane. Raw. She makes a point of changing what she's using at any given time. But she's almost always using something. That peyote binge, trying to go deeper into the configurations instead of hiding from them, that had been atypical. Now everything is starting to feel unblunted. A necessity if she's going to find anything. Leaving herself wide open to the world. Find the future Terrence promised her.

But there is nothing in the USB. No treasure map. No clues that might lead her wherever it is Terrence thinks she should go. The place where the future is being made. Where there are lives to be saved.

Just the op. Plain Jane.

"Fuck."

Skinner looks over from the seat-back screen in front of him, shifting his earphones to the side so he can hear her more clearly.

"What?"

Jae shakes her head, closes her Toughbook, and unplugs the USB from its side.

"I can't find what I'm looking for in here."

"It looked straightforward. To me. Jargon. Nondisclosure agreement. EULA. More jargon. Plausible deniability. Money. Overview. Task assignment. Exhortation to patriotic feeling. Jargon. Vaguely worded statement that denies any and all legal responsibility for anything unfortunate that may happen related to the job. Did you expect it to self-destruct?"

She drops the USB in a pocket on her vest and zips it closed.

"Terrence said it was for me."

Skinner lets his earphones drop around his neck, tiny voices just audible.

"That's what he told me. It's not?"

She pulls her daypack from the floor, slips her Toughbook into its padded slot.

"It's missing something. It's too straightforward. Not what I do."

She presses the heels of her hands against her eyes.

"Tired. Look again later."

She uncovers her eyes.

"How long?"

"About two hours."

On the screen on his TV, a man in a suit, someone with the WTO, remarks about the European credit crisis, the protesters in Stockholm. Tiny voice from Skinner's earphones: *Venues for contraction in troubled times.*

She reclines her seat.

"Cross doesn't like you."

Skinner is taking an in-flight magazine from the seat-back pouch.

"No, he doesn't."

"He says you're not viable."

Skinner flips past ads for stereos that open and close at the wave of a hand, remote control scale replicas of Formula 1 champion cars, indoor virtual driving ranges, but says nothing.

Jae's eyes want to close. She knows she won't really sleep. Past tired now. She'll enter a fugue state populated by vivid waking dreams. Unpleasant. But she can't keep her eyes open.

She pokes Skinner with her index finger.

"What's he mean, *not viable*?"

Skinner closes the magazine, puts it back, looks at the small TV screen where a black BMW is entering the grounds of the Bilderberg conference hotel, protesters wearing vampire masks being held at bay by Swedish cops.

"He doesn't expect me to last."

He might say more, but she doesn't hear it, her eyes closing themselves on her, and the dreams beginning. Digging a hole that fills itself in again and again, someone at the bottom that needs saving. Each time, she thinks she sees the configuration, the stones that must be moved to clear a way to salvation. Each time, she chooses the wrong one and it all comes down.

No configuration.

No survivor.

She digs.

maker

MIAMI MAKES SKINNER think about cities where bombs go off with great regularity.

The intensity of the sun, the humidity, the accents, the café talk of revolution, the large amounts of cash being transferred in exchange for drugs and guns, the savage consumption of alcohol, beaches defended by uniformed men carrying assault rifles, patrol boats, and the constant trickle of sweat running down one's back.

Kabul by the Sea.

Mogadishu in pastels.

Ciudad Juárez.

In their rental, cruising the long ribbon of the Airport Expressway, eight lanes, palm trees, sweat, Jae jittery and hollow-eyed behind the wheel of the rental, Skinner reflects on the good thing about cities like this: There are always plenty of guns to be found.

The parking lot for the Oasis Condominium Towers is empty but for two overfull Dumpsters hosting a small flock of seagulls at mealtime, and a faded red Mazda Miata with peeling Clear Coat. The towers themselves, matching concrete and glass stacks making an effortful attempt to evoke midcentury style, face one another across two swimming pools. One pool scummed over with algae, the other empty, dry, and cracked. Less than four years old, the towers are in decay.

It's dim inside, no less humid than outside, an empty desk with an open guestbook, a bank of elevators, all but one wearing Out of Order signs, and sitting in the middle of a vast sectional, its hibiscus-patterned fabric still bright under the plastic it had been shipped in, Maker Smith, an oddly disproportionate pistol in his right hand aimed at an upper corner of the hockey rink–size lobby.

Skinner is about to step in front of Jae, but she keeps walking, unconcerned, and Smith doesn't look at them, let alone aim in their direction, bringing his free hand to the weapon and touching a large button on the side of its ridiculously massive grip.

"Watch."

A soft but intense buzzing draws their eyes to the corner of the room where Smith is aiming, his target, a large X of some kind of plastic hanging from the ceiling by an invisible thread, bobbing slightly in air currents. Then the X turns on its side, shoots toward the wall, ducks down and up through a toy basketball hoop suction-cupped next to a neo-impressionistic psychedelic print that depicts some kind of Aztec ruin, and returns to hover in the corner.

Skinner's eyes adjust to the light, just as his brain adjusts to the circumstances, and he sees that the gun is a remote control unit and the flying target a quadrotor helicopter drone.

Jae nods, points at the hovering gadget.

"Show me aggressive air stops."

His bulk still parked on the sectional, Smith twiddles the control, and the drone flies at Skinner's head, skimming down in a steep descent, flipping on its side at the last instant, rotors braking, halting fifteen centimeters from his nose, then buzzing back toward the wall, performing a similar maneuver, but striking a small square of Velcro and sticking there, rotors suddenly dying.

Smith pushes himself up, pulling the tail of his Hawaiian shirt over his hairy stomach.

"On full lift it will pull itself free of a patch of Velcro that size. Any bigger and it doesn't have the guts."

Jae walks closer to the wall, looks up at the quad.

"What's the material?"

He smiles.

"ABS."

She looks at him.

"You printed it?"

"The ducts, mounting plate, rotors, some of the fasteners."

Jae emits a quick burst of robotese, jargon so dense Skinner barely recognizes it as language. Smith responds in kind. This goes on for a moment or two before Jae sums up.

"Fucking cool, Smith."

"Dude, I know."

He looks at Skinner, squinting against the sunlight pouring through the open door.

"Who's your escort?"

Skinner lets the tinted glass door swing shut behind him.

"Hi, Smith. It's me."

Maker takes a half step back, hands coming up, as if he is wishing that the remote control in his hand has suddenly been transformed into the huge gun it resembles.

"Hey, I. Hey. Skinner. I."

He lowers his hands.

"Hey, Skinner."

He looks at Jae.

"Jae didn't tell me you were traveling together."

Jae looks from one to the other.

"What? Skinner said you guys worked together before."

Smith raises his eyebrows, shakes his head.

"Yeah. Worked together. Right."

He puts a hand to his heart, licks his lips, and waves a hand toward the elevator bank.

"Forgive me for being rude, you know. I'm not used to seeing ghosts. Let's just, uh, go on up, okay."

The elevator deposits them with a gentle exhortation, *Eleventh floor, have a pleasant day.*

"I had neighbors in the north tower, Oasis One, but they went Chapter Eleven and ate it. Now I'm the only one left on the property."

Down a pastel blue hallway, every third art deco reproduction lighting fixture illuminated, the rest denuded of their bulbs, they pass a door propped open with what looks like a milky white bowling ball. Smith points inside at a workshop of some kind. Carpet peeled and rolled to one end of a living room that has never been occupied, countertop converted into a tool bench, an HP desktop tower and twenty-four-inch monitor on the floor next to a large piece of machinery that makes Skinner think about Erector sets and IV bag stands. A kind of miniature steel gantry supporting a collection of tubes and hoses, all of them mounted on tracks. It's whirring and clicking, the tubes, nipples at their bottoms, zipping back and forth on the tracks, all pointed at a small object the same color as the ghostly bowling ball holding the door open.

Smith makes a gesture, hand to head, as if donning a halo.

"Fabbing up a crown for my niece's birthday. She's in a princess phase."

Again Skinner is uncertain if he speaks the local dialect.

Smith waves his hand, shifting topics.

"The developers here were overcommitted in two thousand eight. Had to finish construction no matter how much they'd been assholed by the collapse. They had fewer than a dozen contracts presold. Moving in here, it was like beach-view ghost town. Everyone looking for loopholes in their leases so they could get their money back and bail. Underwater by eighty grand. Minimum."

The corridor, like everything else they've seen so far at the Oasis Towers, feels trapped somewhere between incompletion and decommission. An open breaker panel, never-connected wires in taped bundles, surrounding wall an expanse of unpainted Sheetrock, next to a bank of fully stocked vending machines that have been pulled out, shrink-wrapped, waiting for pickup.

Maker Smith stops in front of a door plastered with bumper stickers and decals. Captain Beefheart, Frank Zappa, Brian Eno, *Evolve, The Force Is with You,* several featuring equations that, Skinner is certain, are all puns on well known formulae, a mudflap girl silhouette wearing a space helmet, an Apple sticker with a cartoon worm eating through its middle, Garbage Pail Kids, thick layers of peeling pop culture, insider geek references, tech-hipsterism, and naughty girlie pinups.

Smith shoves the door open, no key.

"Minimum security level."

He holds it for them, Jae going first, Skinner behind, entering a unit that picks up where the door decoration ended and then carries the themes on to new extremes.

Smith lets the door slam closed, spreads his arms.

"Technically I'm supposed to get permission from the board if I want to repaint, but I thought it would be cool to just go for it at this point."

One of the walls has been stripped of posters, a heap of Frazetta barbarians and slave girls in a pile, thumbtack tears at the corners. In their place a grease pencil mural layout is half filled in with air-brush. Smith, rendered honestly with his receding hairline, thick neck beard, timpani-size gut, and Day-Glo green Crocs, brandishing a battle-axe in one hand and a video game controller in the other. At his feet, arms wrapped around one of his pale, thin legs, is a swim-suit model in a ripped lab coat and librarian glasses, both of them menaced by a gang of orcs and goblins wearing blood-smeared foot-ball uniforms.

Smith holds up his hands, framing the mural for himself, a director considering the next shot.

"It's meant to be ironic. But it's also kind of based on something that happened when I was in high school."

He lowers his hands and looks at them.

"Artistic license."

Jae isn't looking at the work in progress, she's staring at Smith.

He inhales, sighs.

"I don't get a lot of people up here, Jae."

She's still not talking.

Smith pulls a rubber band from his left wrist, raises his hands, and uses it to bind his kinky, graying hair into a ponytail. As he does so, Skinner can see a large measure of antic energy drain from him as certainly as if it were being flushed down a toilet.

Ponytail in place, Smith points at a hallway.

"Come on, show you the advantages of living in a zero-occupancy development."

He leads them into a bedroom at the end of the hall, a room that has the general feel of college dropout, stoner, game designer.

"Not, for the record, my room. Just, you know, stage setting."

He opens a closet door and walks inside. Jae follows him.

Smith pushes a line of t-shirt–draped hangers down a bar and reveals another door.

"You have no idea how much a secret door with a key code lock impresses the clients. It adds fifty an hour to my billables every time I walk someone through it."

He flips up a little metal cover and reveals a keypad, enters a hex string, and the knobless steel fire door eases open with a hiss. He squeezes back away from the door, giving them room to pass through first.

"Drumroll."

Skinner follows Jae into a daisy chain of three condos with the connecting walls stripped down to their load-bearing essentials. Poured concrete slab has been exposed in the outer walls and floor, studs sheathed in dull-finish aluminum siding, windows are boxed, all light coming from fluorescent corkscrews jutting from the ceiling. Ranks of servers run down the middle of the room, well spaced to allow their heat to dissipate, cables are bundled, neatly zip-tied.

Skinner feels that he has stepped onto the set for a midbudget techno thriller featuring a second-tier star. A possible box office sleeper that is expected to make up any domestic disappointments with overseas cable rights sales.

Smith folds his arms and nods.

"Mostly it pays off on private consulting with the corporate clients. But I've snagged contracts from Customs and Border Protection, Transport Safety Admin, and Homeland. All the post–nine-elevens, they all love the shit that feels like it's the movie version of a Tom Clancy book. I have a buddy, set dresser slash aspiring art director, I gave him a concept and he did some sketches for me."

He looks around the space, nodding his head.

"It turned out nice, yeah? And it's function over form. I specced it for the real work. I'm way under load capacity on the structure. Cooling is an issue. I couldn't mess with the ducting in the building. So I bought the units above and below these, the whole plant is a nine-unit block. The extra ones, upstairs and down, all they are is insulated cubes with the AC running nonstop twenty-four-seven. Heat sinks to keep my machines comfy."

Jae toes one of the bundles of cables running along the base of the outer wall.

"Where are you drawing power?"

Smith walks to one of the server racks, pulls up the hem of his Hawaiian shirt and rubs at a smudge.

"In my dreams I scored one of those fast-breeder reactors based on Soviet-era submarine technology, but they just reached prototype phase over there. Having trouble getting them approved for field tests is what I hear. Besides, seventy-five megawatts would be a little overkill. Truth is, I'm just pulling my juice off the lines that run into Oasis Two maintenance. The wiring won't pass a code inspection at this point, but even with the cooling units, I'm not sucking up a tenth of what the designers expected the tower to consume."

Smith stops rubbing the server, drops the hem of his shirt.

"But, as I don't think you're hear to geek out on the specs of my infrastructure, what the fuck, Jae?"

She leans against a server rack, arms folded over her chest, shrugging.

"Information."

Smith glances toward Skinner.

"Uh-huh. Any special flavor?"

"West-Tebrum power plant hack."

Smith raises both hands, showing nothing up his sleeves.

"I wasn't in on that."

Jae moves her fingers soothingly, massages the air.

"We just want to know more. You're the Maker. Everyone comes to Maker Smith for knowledge. And here we are for the same thing. Knowledge about things people aren't supposed to know about."

"Whose dime?"

"Kestrel."

Smith's jaw clenches.

"You're working for Kestrel."

He looks at Skinner.

"You're both working for Kestrel?"

Jae looks at her boots.

"It's Terrence's gig. So I'm working for Kestrel."

Smith snags a task chair from his work station, rolls it back and forth on its casters.

"Cross hates me."

"Cross doesn't know we're here."

"You'd like to think."

"He doesn't know."

Smith raises his arms and spreads them far apart.

"Jae, it's a matter of scale. Do you understand vastness? Abysses that you can fall into and never get out of. Uncharted territories."

He drops his arms and speaks slowly.

"Persons unknown have attacked the USA with a modified piece of malware that was *first* discovered after it was set loose on an Iranian local area network that connected with centrifuges used to spin spent uranium as a primary step of converting it into weapons-grade. And, oh, by the way, the people who did that, the people who created that original Stuxnet worm, they were, no one doubts, US and Israeli intelligence. NSA and Mossad."

He spins the task chair.

"So now here it comes, back at us. *ReStuxnet,* aimed at a US power plant. Telling a lube oil pump to shut down. Is it a probe? Or was it meant to crash the eastern grid and hamstring the entire country? Is this some bullshit black-hat hacker proving he can do it? Is it some Anonymous remnant asshole trying to teach the US a lesson after they flipped Sabu and burned his clubhouse down? Balkan gangsters showing us what they're capable of before they begin to blackmail the country? Is it Iranian intelligence letting us know they can fuck us right back with our own dick? Most popular, is it China proving that you don't have to have a world-class military to be a world military power? Russia being peevish? Tea Party extremists trying to bring down the federal government and put us back on a gold standard? Intelligence contractors establishing a clear and present danger to keep Congress from defunding them during the next round of budget cuts? Whoever it was, every intelligence contractor in the country, from the majors like Kestrel, Mission One, and Hann-Aoki, and right down to Aegis, Triple Canopy, Xo, will be duking it out for the billions of dollars in new cyber security contracts that are going to flood the intelligence industry any second now."

He grabs the chair, stops it spinning.

"And you think Cross doesn't know you are here? Does that seem likely?"

Jae rubs her eyes.

"No. Not likely."

She takes her hands from her eyes.

"Who has *you* working on it?"

Smith shakes his head.

"Nope, not me. Hann-Aoki have been ringing the phone off the hook trying to get me under contract to trace the hackers, but I'm not playing."

"Lot of money to leave on the table."

Smith's workstation is comprised of a white-topped catering table, two printer/scanners, a bright orange adjustable Tensor lamp, four DSL modems, dozens of coiled cables hung from hooks on a pegboard mounted on the wall above the table, three power strips on the floor underneath, two carbon-mesh task chairs, an assortment of boxed laptops, most still wearing shrink-wrap, and a bucket of Red Vines.

He grabs one of the candy ropes and starts to chew.

"I'm staying on the sideline for this one."

Jae pushes herself away from the server stack.

"Biggest cyber security payday in the history of forever, and Maker Smith takes a holiday."

She looks at Skinner.

"Imagine."

Skinner blinks.

"I am."

Smith's incisors snap through his Red Vine.

"You guys. Like it's all money. Contracts. Like you, Jae, like that's what you do this for."

She takes the second task chair at the workstation, sits, eases herself close to Smith.

"What do you know, Smith? What do you already have in your head that you don't want to have to share with someone who puts you under contract?"

She smiles, bats her eyelashes.

"Please don't tell me you aren't dying to show off in front of someone who would actually understand how smart you've been."

He swallows Red Vine.

"You suck."

Jae stops smiling.

"People died. Terrence said. He said we can save lives. So. Not just money. Okay. But what? Smith. What the hell do you know?"

He looks at the half rope of Red Vine in his hand, drops it back in the bucket.

"I know that everyone knew it was coming. A little over a year after Stuxnet hit, variants started circulating. DuQu, Flame, Gauss. Undoubtedly others that were never detected. Worked up by someone who has access to the Stuxnet source code. Massive, truly massive pieces of government-engineered, customized malware. And then ReStuxnet. Someone put that one on a thumb drive with a West-Tebrum logo on it. Left it in the parking lot outside the plant. Some employee plugged it in to find out who it belonged to. Bunch of innocuous files, nothing special. But while it was plugged in, it loaded ReStuxnet from a partition on the drive. So it's inside their firewall. It spread to multiple systems within the corporate firewall, dozens, in less than a day. Spread outside, too, rode home on laptops and some portable media."

Jae closes her eyes and knocks on her forehead with her knuckles.

"So it's still spreading?"

"Yeah, but that's a good thing for us. See, every time this fucker infects a new system, it sends a data packet back home with the IP addresses and some other handy info from the infected machines. And we can track those packets. They're going to one of two domains hosted on servers located in Yemen and Kiev. Now, Yemen shows up and you can imagine how crazy they went in the Pentagon. But

Ukraine is a much more intriguing spot on the map when it comes to hackery. Hacking is practically a national industry. Tends toward credit card theft. Dwarfs what I got up to when I was a kid. Hundreds of thousands of accounts. So many that they don't know what to do with them all. Terrence had me doing some digging into credit hacks last year. Tracking some cash. Insane amounts of money. National-scale economies. I used some of the contacts I made on that gig following up this Kiev connection."

He points a finger, sends it a few inches, makes a sound like an arrow hitting its target.

"And Ukraine sounds like a real possibility for our hackers. But no, it's bullshit. Too easy. These people are smart enough to hide themselves better than that. There has to be some physical space between the badguys and their hosting."

Smith closes his eyes and rubs his temples.

"Which leaves everyone *still* trying to figure out who launched the attack. Someone with a tremendous talent pool to draw on and cash to burn. Those kinds of resources definitely point toward foreign nationals. And when you talk foreign nationals and hacking, you are always talking China."

Jae nods again.

"So the Chinese did it."

Smith blows out his cheeks and shakes his head.

"Nope. Not the Chinese."

Jae taps her head.

"Smith, I know how to hit people. When I started to get tits, my dad insisted on self-defense classes. He found a Hapkido dojang in Santa Barbara. Drove me there two evenings a week and Saturday mornings, for three years. I stuck with it for the pure pleasure of hitting people."

Smith scratches his beard, fingers disappearing into the thicket of hair.

"Yeah. Do I remember stories about you picking fights in redneck bars while you were at A&M? Classy, Jae."

"The point I'm trying to get across here is how nearly entirely out of patience I am becoming."

"Great. Stop waving your ancient Asian fighting skills in my face and I'll wrap it up."

Jae clenches her teeth but does not kick Smith's ass.

"So it's not China. So that leaves?"

Smith claps his hands once.

"Imagine, if you will, a cadre of non-state actors. Are these nebulous hackers interested in credit card accounts? No. Are they into porn? No. Are they into Nigerian four-nineteen scams? No. Are they into cracking government systems to prove their might? No. Are they interested in showing the cracks in existing systems so as to improve the overall hardiness of the Internet? No. What are their motives? What do these cyber guerrillas want? Striking invisibly across borders without regard to profit, what do they hope to gain? No one knows. We only know that they exist."

He combs the end of his beard with his fingers, a silent movie villain.

"They must!"

He stops combing.

"And these faceless agents seem to be in Sweden. Stockholm, to be exact."

Jae winces as if something has been thrown in her face.

"Swedish hackers attacked the United States of America?"

"I didn't say they were Swedish, though they do appear to speak the language. Or code in it, anyway. This French deep data diver, he caught a command packet going the other way. Written in Swedish, and, when he traced it back, not easy, he found it was coming from an IP address in Stockholm."

"So who knows this?"

Smith shrugs.

"Not too fucking many. This French guy, he's very, very *pro-Wiki-Leaks, anti-secrets, down with the Western powers, especially the USA, let anarchism rule.* I think he's torn between *information wants to be free* and *fuck you, Washington, DC.* For now he's pretending he never found it and spending his time trying to hack the Bilderberg conference. Far as I know, there's only a few of us he let in on this bit of intel.

Jae rubs her tired eyes.

"Why haven't you told anyone?"

Smith tugs at his beard.

"I'm ambivalent about these things myself, Jae. I call someone at the NSA, tell them what I know, they're not just gonna go track down whoever is on the other end of that IP address. My French friend and a lot of other people I like are going to have their doors kicked in. But someone blew something up and people died, and I don't endorse that bullshit. So. I'm telling *you*. Because you're the coolest spy I know."

Jae almost smiles.

"I'm not a spy."

Smith shakes his head.

"Tell it to the Chinese, lady, I know better."

"Where in Stockholm?"

Smith and Jae look at Skinner. Become so still as they've been speaking that they had forgotten him.

Smith finds a pen and a Post-it on his desk.

"That's the punch line."

He writes something down.

"There's a billing address for the hosting services. In Gamla Stan."

Skinner takes the slip of yellow paper from him.

"Do you have a gun?"

Maker Smith chews the end of his pen.

"Interesting conversational transition."

Jae touches the pockets of her vest.

"*Gun.*"

There's a #28 X-Acto Pen Knife on the table. Skinner picks it up, it swivels between his fingers, suddenly animate in his grasp, handle aligned with his thumb, blade jutting at an angle from the base of his palm, edge near the inside of his wrist.

Jae and Smith look at the tool in his hand, become instantly a weapon.

Skinner looks at the door, closed, having sighed shut after they entered.

"Multiple contractors, intelligence agencies, branches of the military. And it won't just be US companies and agencies. Everyone will want to know who could pull off West-Tebrum, and how. You have a great deal of very valuable information. People might want it."

Skinner holds up the X-Acto.

"May I keep this?"

Smith nods.

"Sure. Have fun."

Skinner drops the X-Acto into his jacket pocket.

"I would like to have a gun. If one is available."

Smith looks at the door.

"Do you think anyone is out there?"

"Let's see."

The door opens on a loud hiss of compressed air, but no one shoots them.

Jae exhales, expressing a depth of irritation that Skinner is certain could drown cats.

"I'm on the edge of paranoia as it is. Please don't send me tumbling over it."

She enters Smith's stage-set bedroom, stops, looks to her right, to her left, then turns around.

"Toilet?"

Smith points.

"Straight, left before the bedroom at the end. And don't go in there, it's my real room and you don't want to see what it's like."

Jae, walking down the hall away from them, muttering.

"Yeah, I need someone to tell me that."

Skinner hasn't moved, standing there as Joe walks past him, hearing the sound of the bathroom door slamming shut, then placing a hand on Smith's shoulder.

"Gun."

Smith ducks from under Skinner's hand, sidles out the door, and leads the way down the hall.

"It's not much, but it shoots. I think."

The gun is white. The same white as the doorstop bowling ball, and it is made of extruded ABS plastic.

"The barrel and the hammer are alloy. I had them machined. Spring I ordered from a catalogue. Everything else I fabbed here."

They are in the workshop unit down the hall from Smith's home. The Erector set device with its tubes and hoses is a 3-D printer, a fabricator. Homemade. Melted plastic pumped through the hoses, threadlike layers, building in 3-D plastic from digital design templates on Smith's computer.

"Industrial prototyping in your home. Cool, huh?"

Skinner is looking at the gun, wondering about the odds that it might blow up in his face should he pull the trigger.

"It's plastic."

Smith bounces his head up and down.

"Like I said, *cool, huh?*"

"Have you fired it?"

Smith scratches the back of his neck.

"Yeah. Nah. Sort of. I made a derringer, two-shot, fired that. It worked. For two shots, anyway."

The gun is bulky, big, fat. A sawed-off Desert Eagle in its proportions. But absurdly light.

Smith points at the trigger.

"It's not meant for multiples uses, you know. No disassembly and cleaning issues. So that eliminated a ton of screws and pins. But the barrel shroud, plastic. And the trigger housing assembly has dozens of tiny pieces. So, once you start shooting, I don't know how they all hold up to the heat and the recoil. Possible it melts and blows the slide off the top on round one."

Skinner looks at the bottom of the grip, presses a wedge that releases the clip.

"How did you plan to test it?"

Smith shakes his head.

"Man, I didn't. It's just a proof of concept thing. To say I did it. You know?"

Skinner pulls the clip free. For all its bulk it holds only six rounds. And it's fully loaded.

"But you put bullets in it."

"Sure. Otherwise what's the point?"

Skinner slides the clip back in. It's quite smooth, seats firmly. He pinches the slide, pulls it back, lets it go, and it snaps forward with a sound like especially large Lego pieces clicking together. He pulls it back again, checks the breech, finds a round of 9mm firmly seated.

"You won't get it back."

Smith shakes his head.

"I can make another one. Next step is making something I can put on the quadrotor. Airgun."

Skinner puts the plastic gun under his jacket at the small of his back. It is both too big and too light.

"Defense contract?"

"Fuck no. Hunt the rats that are trying to take over this place."

Skinner looks at the whirring fabricator, the object taking form.

"Terrence recruited you, right?"

Smith rakes his long beard.

"Yeah. I was serving. Time, not military. Some midnineties hacking. Credit card numbers when it still meant something to be able to get into those databases. Old darknet stuff. Ended up in one of those situations where you find out that honor among thieves is bullshit. Like that should come as a surprise. And it wouldn't have been if I'd seen anything in my life other than my mom's house. But agoraphobia, it keeps a boy in the basement."

Skinner smiles.

"I was a basement boy."

"Us introverts, some of us end up as analysts, and the rest end up in jail or with a gun in their hands."

"Have you spoken to him?"

"Terrence. Yeah. Um, two days back. Three days? Said Jae would likely be coming in for a consultation. Said she'd be traveling with someone. Someone in assets. He didn't say it was you."

Skinner counts his own heartbeats, one, two, three.

"Would that have made a difference?"

Smith touches a hose on the 3-D printer, pinches and releases it.

"Berlin. Man. That was more than I. If I'd known you were coming."

He looks at Skinner.

"I might not have been at home. You know."

He looks at his machine.

"Then again, Terrence asks for something and we all have a tendency to do it. That man is who he is."

He purses his lips.

"He okay?"

Skinner looks out the window, counting heartbeats again.

"I should have sent a robot into that bathroom before I went in. Toxic. Vile."

Smith and Skinner turn toward Jae, standing at the door.

"Skinner."

He waits.

She points at Smith.

"I need to have a private word. Off the job stuff. Yeah?"

Skinner nods, starts for the door.

"I'll wait in the apartment."

Jae holds up her hand.

"No. We'll go."

She looks at Smith.

"You still have that box?"

Smith is focused on her, *not* looking at Skinner.

"Sure. Let's go get in the box."

Skinner watches them exit. He listens to the printer buzzing, layer by layer, making the birthday crown for Smith's niece. He takes the gun from under his jacket. Too light. He aims it at the wall. Then, thinking about Terrence, he follows Smith and Jae.

burn him

MAKER SMITH'S SCIF is very small. A cube in the middle of the living room in yet another condo he owns on the seventh floor of Oasis One. The entire exterior covered in thin sheet metal that overlaps the twelve seams where the single-piece walls, floor, and ceiling were joined to one another. An excess of button rivets. Not an inch of the shell can be peeled without leaving a mark. One ventilation duct running to the condo's outer wall, also wrapped. The latch mechanism on the door is a simple mechanical lever, not unlike a walk-in freezer, locked from the inside. Lead-lined, thickly insulated, it contains no chairs or table and requires almost anyone who enters it to hunch under the low ceiling.

Smith closes the door, locks it, smiles at Jae.

"Holy what the fuck, Jae? I mean, sincerely. What the holy Jesus shitting fuck are you doing bringing fuck mother jesus hell Skinner to my fucking home? Fuck sake!"

Jae settles her back into one of the corners of the tiny room.

"What were you guys talking about Terrence?"

Smith holds up both hands, pressing his palms at her. *Halt!*

"No. See, I asked my question first, which, no matter how irrationally I may have phrased it, means I get my answer first. So. What the fuck, you know?"

"He's my protection, Smith. That's the deal. He goes where I go. Otherwise, why the fuck bother in the first place? What do you want me to tell you? It's not like I knew you had some kind of awkward past with him. He's not big on volunteering biographical details. Shit, he's not big on volunteering much of anything. Looming, he's good at. Laconic monosyllables. Jesus, he freaks me out."

Smith raises his index finger.

"Good. Very good. That is a good. Because that thing out there, that golem, he is straight out of the uncanny valley, you know. Almost human, but in a way that is creepy as hell."

Jae palms her forehead, takes a deep breath, lifts her head.

"You were talking about Berlin?"

Smith looks up, lets his jaw sag, shakes his head.

"Maaaaan. Just feel free to eavesdrop in my house."

"What happened in Berlin?"

Smith folds his arms over his chest, squeezes.

"A job happened. Like the kind of thing I can't talk about. And I was Skinner's asset. And."

He closes his eyes tight.

"Man."

He opens his eyes.

"Do you even know his deal? The Skinner Maxim?"

She shakes her head.

Smith draws a line with his finger, emphasizing a passage, something that will appear later on a test.

"*The only way to secure an asset is to make the cost of acquiring it greater than its value.* Or something like that."

Jae nods.

"So what happened in Berlin?"

Smith shrugs.

"What happened was nothing happened. I mean, as far as I knew, the gig went off slick. I was my usual rock-star self. Which mostly involved me in a hotel room doing things with a hard drive they handed me and told me they had to have back in five hours no matter what. Skinner sat on the bed and read newspapers."

Jae waits.

Smith grinds his thumb between his eyes.

"There was this big story in the papers that week. This thing had happened in this warehouse out by the Wall. Mass killing. Five people. Three were done execution-style, back of the head. Two were not. And Skinner, he had this stack of papers and magazines, all of them cover-to-cover coverage on this story, and he was reading every single word. Like, fascinated. And so, me, I'm high-strung, deep in the data on this hard drive, coming up only for Red Vines and air. Next thing I know, time's up. They come and take the hard drive, I hand them what they wanted out of it, show them what I put in it. Hells yeah, I'm awesome. And now I'm bouncing off the walls with adrenaline and, you know, whatever stress release and manic feelings of victory. So I make a joke with Skinner the cyborg. I say, I say, *Yo, Skinner, what's up with the reading material? Professional curiosity or something? Trying to figure out how it was done?* And Skinner, he folds down the corner of the paper he's reading, kind of glances at me, then flips the paper up and says, *No, Smith. I already know how it was done.*"

Smith stops grinding his thumb into his flesh and looks at her.

"And man, I knew, I knew right that fucking second. He did it. He killed those people. And he killed them because they were planning to take his asset and he found out about it. He killed them, tortured two of them, because they were planning to come after me. Jae. So. And, but, knowing it, that wasn't good enough for me, because I specialize in *knowing*. I needed to really *know*. So back home I hacked some shit. And I found out that yeah, that was a Hann-Aoki asset acquisition team. Yeah, I was the asset they wanted. And then I looked at the pictures of what he did to them."

He puts an index finger at each temple.

"So thanks for this. Bringing him here, asking for the details. 'Cause now I have that shit back up on the main screen again. Shit!"

Jae looks at the floor, she's thinking about Route Irish, the Kestrel contractor's hand dropping onto the blacktop.

"Sorry. He's what Terrence sent me. I didn't know it would be a problem."

Smith takes his fingers from his head.

"He asked if I'd seen Terrence lately. I told him a few days ago. That's all we talked about."

Jae is still looking at the floor, nodding. She stops nodding. Looks at Smith.

"Terrence is dead."

Smith opens his mouth, grabs a fistful of beard, gives it a tug, and looks at the door.

"Does he know?"

Jae shrugs.

"I don't know. Why I wanted to talk in here."

Smith is still looking at the door.

"Because you don't want him to know?"

She shakes her head.

"Because he may have done it."

Smith looks at her.

She shrugs again.

"Or that's what Cross said."

Smith grabs some hairs at the corner of his mouth, starts to chew the ends.

"Jae. You know. They tried to kill him. Back in the day. This is like, lore, yeah. Around the time you were in Iraq, before you dropped out of the game. Terrence was getting forced out of Kestrel. Cross's coup, that whole deal. Business boomed post–nine-eleven, and Cross convinced Terrence to take on investor cash so they could grow faster. The board was stacked with his people. Part of the final push, cleaning house. Cut loose my contract. Bunch of other guys like me. But Skinner. No one, no one who's ever done an asset contract with Kestrel that involved Skinner wants him going freelance. Private intelligence was getting too big, so much money. So legit. Cross did some mumbo-jumbo is the lore. Made it look like Skinner was ready to go over some line or other. Slapped an asset designation on him. And handed Terrence the paper on the gig. Said, *You created him, Dr. Frankenstein, now you burn him.* Words to that effect. I imagine."

He's staring at the locked door, chewing hair.

Jae moves from her corner for the first time since entering the SCIF.

"And?"

Smith looks at her.

"And unless that's a ghost out there, they fucked it up, didn't they?"

He stops chewing his beard, wipes his mouth with the back of his hand.

"I mean, the word, scuttlebutt, was the whole deal was blown. Someone with an interest in *knowing* things might have hacked around a little and found out that they sent a third-stringer named Lentz to do the dirty and he scored a fail. But that couldn't be because everyone knows the Skinner Maxim means that anyone involved with what they like to call the Montmartre Incident has to die horribly, but they haven't. Just Lentz. And Skinner was gone. Until now. When he's come back, and is working for the people who tried to kill him."

He wipes sweat from his brow.

"I am scaring myself shitless here."

Jae knuckles her chin, rubbing hard.

"Yeah. Me too. But. If Terrence sent the third-stringer, Lentz, to get Skinner off the hook."

"Yeah, I know."

"Then why kill Terrence now?"

Smith steps close to her, needless whisper in the box of secrets.

"Jae. His methodology is to scare people into leaving his assets alone. And he hasn't worked in years. His reputation has faded."

"I get it."

"People may not be afraid of him anymore. And they won't be until he does something to remind them how scary he is."

She shakes her head.

"I'm his asset. He won't kill me."

Smith nods.

"But he might use you to get close to the people he wants to kill. Cross. The Kestrel board. Whoever else. Terrence. Reestablish his rep and be on top of the food chain again."

She looks at the door.

"He doesn't think like that."

Smith blinks slowly.

"The sudden expert."

"It doesn't matter. He's what Terrence sent. And I have to go."

She pushes the lever, feels the lock release, the door swings open, drawing smoke into the SCIF as they register the darkness in the unoccupied condo, a muted crackle, a dancing yellow and orange glow visible in the hallway beyond the unit's open front door. The SCIF door jams half open and they look down at the corpse that has stopped it, the X-Acto blade from Smith's workstation stuck in one end of a long straight gash running across its throat.

Something moves in the hall, a shadow on the wall, long, shortening, collapsing into a man, sprinting into the frame of the doorway, two streaks of red light hit him in the upper back, and, with the sound of an immense balloon being popped, he's shoved face first into the floor.

Another shadow appears, shortening in the firelight, moving slowly. He steps into the doorway, absurd big gun in his hand, and looks into the condo at Jae and Smith frozen at the entrance of the soundproof box. He looks down at the man on the floor, raises the white plastic gun, and shoots him in the back of the head.

He looks at them, raises the pistol slightly.

"It works."

He squats and sets his gun on the floor and starts to touch the dead man.

"They didn't bring firearms."

He stands.

"That was shortsighted."

Fire sprinklers pop on and an alarm begins to sound.

Skinner raises his face, the water rinsing a spatter of blood from his cheek, then looks back at them, walks into the condo, stops just outside the SCIF door.

"We better go now."

And he offers his hand, something they can hold for balance, as they step over the dead man at their feet.

tide of a beating heart

SKINNER ENTERED THE SCIF condo just behind Jae and Maker Smith, watched the armored door swing shut and latch, and felt something like what Alice might have experienced, he thought, as she stepped through the looking glass. Outside a box, this one opaque, neither observer nor observed.

There was an experiment, in the midst of the single long experiment that was childhood, in which his parents left him alone. Forty-eight hours, unobserved. He was ten. An alien living under the eternal light of two suns, one or both always in the sky, finding itself plunged into darkness for the first time, would not have been so dismayed. He froze. As day turned to night, he began to believe that he was being watched, that something in the darkness beyond the Plexiglas, as inert as himself, was gazing into him. Watched by something unknown, he retreated to the furthest point he could find, deep within himself. For two days he stood in one spot, awake, aware, restraining all urges to urinate or defecate, willing his body to remain whole. When his parents slipped back into the basement, thinking to find him asleep, he screamed, as loud and violent a noise as he had made since infancy, drawing their attention as primally as he knew how, their gazes cementing him in the world. The following days were not without difficulty.

A potent memory; when he discovers it he has a tendency to fix in place, as if it sends an old signal through his muscles, bidding them to be still again, hold fast. Engaged in stillness, he is slow to recognize the voice from the hall that announces an arrival on the eleventh floor and encourages one to have a pleasant day.

Elevator voice, says something far inside his stillness.

People, suggests some other part of himself.

He moves.

The man who enters the condo does not have a gun in his hand, he does not wear body armor, there is no translucent earphone trailing its cable into the collar of his shirt. He's wearing white cross trainers, jeans, a royal blue t-shirt branded with the logo of the apparel company that made it, a navy blue windbreaker, and a sweat-stained Grapefruit League Yankees cap. He raps his knuckles against the frame of the open door.

"Anyone home?"

He might be lost. Repairman. Prospective tenant. One of Smith's clients.

He looks at the SCIF in the middle of the room, raises his eyebrows.

"Dude."

He has a phone in his hand, brings it to his mouth in the manner of a walkie-talkie. It chirps loudly and he speaks into it.

"Want to see something cool?"

His phone chirps again, talks back to the man.

"I don't know, do I?"

The man takes a few steps toward the SCIF, looks at something on the door, smiles.

"Yeah, you do."

"How cool?"

He walks to one corner of the SCIF and takes a look around it.

"There's a SCIF."

"Yeah, well, that was in the brief, dildo. Is there a cool part?"

The man walks back to the door, points at it, as if the man on the other end of the conversation can see the gesture.

"Cool part is the little red LED all lit up next to the lock. Says, under the LED, it says *occupied.*"

There's another chirp, a pause, chirp.

"Yeah, that's pretty cool. On my way. And call Doonan."

Chirp.

The man looks at the phone in his hand.

"*Call Doonan.* Fucking prick. Died and made you fucking king?"

Hitting a speed-dial code, pressing the phone to his ear this time.

"Doon. Fuckpants wants you. Yeah. In a box. A SCIF. It was in the brief, dildo. Middle of a condo. No shit. Come up. Because we don't need a lookout if they're in the fucking SCIF, we need bodies to handle them when they come out. Hurry your ass."

He ends the call, turns away from the door of the SCIF, begins to take a step, and, reaching down from where he has slipped himself into the cramped space between the roof of the SCIF and the ceiling of the condo, Skinner shoves several fingers into the man's mouth, hooking them into his upper palate and pulling. His other hand is already at the left side of the man's neck, shoving the curved #28 blade of the X-Acto into his jugular and raking it across his throat, a moment in which the man is double-hinged, neck and mouth both wide open, and then Skinner lets him drop to the floor. Blood pumps out, the mouth opens and closes, air whistles from the wound, he slaps the forming puddle of his own blood, splashing.

A slight squirt of blood has dappled Skinner's cheek. He leaves it to dry. Worming from the top of the SCIF, legs swinging down, he lands well clear of the blood puddle. He took off his jacket before concealing himself, rolled his shirt cuffs to his elbows, slipped off his shoes. His pants and shirtfront are covered in dust; a film of it clings to one side of Maker Smith's plastic gun where he set it on the roof of the SCIF. He rubs it on the dust-free back of his thigh. The man has stopped moving, the puddle is spreading, but slowly, seeping, no longer swelling on the tide of a beating heart. Skinner skirts it in his stocking feet, walking toward the door, silence without effort.

The man in the hallway is dressed much like his dead co-worker. Different brand of t-shirt, blue running shoes, yellow Nike swoosh on his green cap. Emerging from the door of Smith's apartment, the man is surprised to see Skinner. He stops, half out of the door, angles his head as if to see behind Skinner, looking for something.

"Where's Norton?"

Trusting in Smith's craftsmanship, Skinner shoots him twice in the chest, the second shot fired before he can register the streak of bright red light that traces the path of the first bullet, a similar tail following its partner. Smith, for reasons Skinner cannot begin to fathom, has loaded the gun with tracer rounds.

The man falls, and a fire starts on his chest, the phosphorus in the base of the bullets igniting his t-shirt. He arches his back, one arm lifts, tries to swat at the quickly spreading flames, but something has gone wrong in the nerve trunk in his shoulder, the arm won't go where he wants it to and he slaps his stomach instead of his chest. Skinner is there now. The man turns his head to the side, as if offering his ear so that he might better hear a whispered remark. The third bullet goes in his temple, and the fire consuming his torso is no longer a matter for concern, nor the sudden smell of burning hair and melting carpet fibers.

Eleventh floor. Have a pleasant day.

Skinner turns toward the sound of the elevator's voice, sparing a moment to look at the gun as he does so. There are scorch marks at the mouth of the barrel and around the edges of the ejection port but no external signs of melting. Really, it's a remarkable piece of work. A man he takes to be Doonan steps out of the elevator. Cowboy boots, slacks, and windbreaker, all black, and a white cap emblazoned with the blue star of the Dallas Cowboys. He sees Skinner, the burning corpse.

Ding.

The sound of the elevator door closing twists his head around. He tries to shove his hand inside, stop the doors, but is too late, so he turns and runs up the hall toward the red Exit sign. Skinner steps to the middle of the hallway, excellent sight line, fires twice. The man drops next to the open door of the SCIF room. No fire this time. Skinner walks to him, stops to look inside the room, and sees Jae and Maker Smith, both frozen. Their gazes upon him, he is certain that he exists, and he shoots Doonan in the back of the head.

A moment later, when Jae takes his hand as he helps her to step over the blood of the first man he's killed in over seven years, Skinner feels an urge to scream, to release what has been bottled inside for so long, and let the world know that he is here.

PART THREE

hammer

RAJ HAS SEEN dead bodies before. Several. But this is the first one he's seen with a bullet hole in its cheek. Looking at the corpse, he becomes aware that he is poking the tip of his tongue into his own cheek, just where the bullet entered the dead man's face. He stops, clenches his teeth, trapping his tongue behind them so that it will stop probing the inside of his mouth, inviting trouble.

"Do you know him?"

Raj puts a hand on top of his head, presses down, nods.

Sudhir waits.

Raj takes his hand from his head.

"Policeman."

"Thug."

Sudhir turns his attention from Raj to his mother, Taji in the crook of her left elbow, as she uses her right hand to flip the dirty oilcloth back over the dead policeman's face.

"Gangster."

She wipes her hand on her thigh, smearing a tiny spot of mud and blood onto her pink-and-orange-patterned sari.

"Gah."

She rushes to the sink, a plastic five-liter cooler strapped to the wall over a basin, and runs water over her hand, then blots the new stain.

"Filthy in death as he was in life."

Sudhir takes up the cords that had bound the oilcloth shroud before he tugged them loose to show the body to them.

"So little compassion for the dead."

Raj's mother waves a hand.

"Devils had that one from his cradle."

Sudhir measures the ends of the cord, pulling until they are even, and then begins an elaborate string of knots.

"Devils come only when they are called, and babies don't know that they exist."

She makes a noise through her nose, expressing neither agreement nor disagreement but, rather, a deep dissatisfaction with the entire notion of philosophy.

Sudhir shakes his head, as if to politely disagree with a point she has made.

"Evil is not brought to us on a platter, we discover it, early, yes, but not in the cradle. And then..."

He yanks hard on the ends of the cord, drawing the string of knots tight, securing the cocoon of oilcloth around the dead man inside. No caterpillar, he will not rise a butterfly.

"Then, we either walk away from the evil we have discovered or we pick it up."

Raj's mother plucks a bit of her sari between thumb and forefinger, shakes it back and forth, airing the wet patch where she blotted away the stain of blood.

"When he found evil he didn't pick it up, he rolled about in it; pig in a wallow."

Sudhir tucks the ends of the cord inside one of the snug loops wrapping the body.

"Still. It is terrible to die."

She raises her hand, flaps the air.

"Then you should not have shot him."

Sudhir rises.

"He was asking about the night of the rain. And then we found him poking around the Number One Shed."

He lifts his shoulders, drops them.

"It is a terrible thing to die, but I would rather it be him than thousands. Millions."

He looks at Raj.

"What is larger than millions, Raj?"

Raj doesn't have to think.

"Billions. Trillions. Many things are larger. There is a number, a googol. That is where the company took their name. Ten duotrigintillion. Ten to the hundredth power. Much bigger than a million. Many things are bigger than a million."

Sudhir is smiling.

"Billions will be enough. One dead policeman, wallowing in evil, against dead billions. One terrible death."

He fills his cheeks with air, blows.

"Light enough. I can carry his death."

He looks at the wrapped body on the floor.

"And also I'll have to carry *him*."

Taji squirms and Raj's mother shifts her to her other arm.

"Bigger and bigger, little girl."

Sudhir is still looking at the body.

"No squirming for this one."

The door opens, and Raj's father stands there looking at the shrouded dead body on his floor.

His wife begins filling a kettle.

"Tea."

He steps inside, eyes still on the body, closing the door.

"No. No time."

But she has stoked the coals in the little orange stove already.

"There is always time for tea."

He looks from the body to Raj.

"Have you found it?"

For a moment Raj thinks he is talking about evil; has Raj found evil yet. Has he? He has seen a man beaten to death for his religion. A woman disfigured by acid thrown in her face by her husband after she'd been raped by a gang. Those are almost the worst things he has ever seen. Far worse than the dead policeman with the little hole in his cheek. The worst thing that he has seen is the body of an infant, starved to death. He has seen three of those. His father says these things happen not because of evil but because of ignorance and greed. His mother makes that sound in her nose when his father talks like that. Raj doesn't know if he has found evil yet, but he wishes sometimes for a hammer, to smash the faces of ignorance and greed. Or a magic gun, to point at them, pull the trigger, and see them disappear. No more starved babies in the gutter.

But his father is not talking about evil, he is talking about the World Wide Web.

Raj turns his attention to the open laptop on the table.

"The site, yes, but there are so many posts, and you have to log in as a member to use the search function. And the bhenchod power keeps cutting off."

His father takes off his glasses, wipes them on the tail of his shirt, one of the few patches of fabric not smeared with grease from the work being done in #1 Shed.

"The power will be fixed soon."

He puts on his glasses and reaches into his back pocket and takes out a small blue notebook, sweat-stained, curved to match the shape of his bottom.

"A member account."

He thumbs through the pages of the notebook, finds what he wants.

"Try this. Member name merckxmaniac7. Spell merckx with a cee, kay, and ex at the end. All one word, all lower case, merckxmaniac7. And password helix00. No spaces, lower case."

Raj types the name and password into the appropriate boxes and hits enter.

"Yes, okay."

His father reads something else from the notebook.

"Search now for terms Merckx, Leader, geometry."

Raj types, has to delete a few letters when he misspells Merckx, retypes, hits enter.

"Yes, okay, one post, two replies."

"Okay, yes."

"The post asks if anyone knows the head tube and seat tube angles for a sixty-centimeter, nineteen ninety-two MX Leader frame. The first response asks please for no questions regarding bikes newer than nineteen eighty-three on this forum. The second response is addressed to the first responder and says that he should not take things so seriously. And that is all."

Eyes in the notebook, his father steps over the dead body, coming to the table.

"Respond."

Raj clicks a button, opens a box for responses.

"Yes."

"Reply. *No geometry charts for that year. Did my own and came up with HT: 73 degrees and ST: 72.5 on a 48cm frame with 53cm TT, 12spd. By the way, for sale, two 1948 CDF Concours.* Read it back."

Raj reads it back, his father nods, and Raj hits the post button.

His father closes his notebook and slips it into his back pocket.

"And this is how we hope to become secure."

Sudhir squats next to the dead man.

"How, perhaps, we invite the devil."

He rubs his hands together, pulls the corpse, still somewhat flexible, into a seated position, and heaves it onto his shoulder, straightening.

"If someone could get the door."

Raj's mother opens it, looks out.

"There are people."

He nods.

"There are always people in the city. Killing him was important. Hiding his death doesn't matter."

He steps to the door, stops, and looks at Raj's father.

"More police soon. And the Sena will come. And the water goons are giving much trouble."

His father looks around the room. His son at the laptop sending secret messages, his wife making tea, his daughter asleep. He takes off his glasses, tries again to clean them on his dirty shirt.

"Three more days. I think."

Sudhir adjusts his burden.

"*Our* policeman will need more money to stuff into loud mouths."

Raj's father frowns at his glasses.

"Money we have. Time we need. Takshak from the gangwar has phone cards. Prepay. Ten thousand rupees each. Tell him you want a hundred of them. For the policeman. Gifts for his friends at the station. Better than cash."

Sudhir dips his knees in Raj's mother's direction and steps out into the alley, heading toward the mire at the edge of the neighborhood, where uneatable offal and human waste are dumped. Two of his men join him; they still wear clothes meant as slum camouflage, but they have started to carry their weapons openly since Sudhir killed the policeman that morning. Machine pistols, assault rifles, bandoleers of grenades, daypacks stuffed with extra clips, ration packets, maps, and dozens of batteries for the cell phones and GPS units they all have on their belts.

Raj's father starts for the door.

"Check the bicycle site several times an hour, Raj. And move to the Number One Shed. The generators will keep you online. Soon the media center will be finished and you will need to help your friends."

"Tea, Aasif."

He looks at his wife.

"No time."

He smiles.

"Not even for tea."

She takes the dirty glasses from his hands, rubs them with her sari, places them on his face.

"I will bring you tea. But you come home for dinner."

He shrugs, neither yes nor no, kisses her, his dark wife, and leaves.

Raj gets up from the table.

"He wants me in the shed."

She looks at him, nods.

"Take this."

She pours tea into a thermos, hangs two cups from the handle.

Raj fumbles with the door latch, tea thermos in one hand, laptop in the other, and she reaches over to open it for him.

"Rajiv."

He looks up at her.

"Mom."

She frowns.

"Do not fall in the water."

He looks out the door.

"There is no water."

She shakes her head.

"It is everywhere, Rajiv."

She bends and kisses his head.

"And it is deep."

He kicks a toe against the floor.

"I know how to swim."

She straightens.

"Tea for your father. I'll come later with dinner."

He smiles and turns and runs, opposite the direction Sudhir took the dead gangster cop, away from the mire at that edge of the neighborhood, but there is more where he is running, more in every direction.

She closes the door. Taj is making noises, waking hungry, so she feeds her daughter.

remnant of the blade

SMITH WANTS TO stay and put out the fire that is growing from the burning corpse, feasting on the scattered trash inside the condo, flaring uncontrollably when it discovers the paint thinner rags near the unfinished mural. Skinner is more inclined to feed the flames and increase any chances that the entire building will be raging out of control before fire fighters can arrive. But there isn't time for either of their wishes to be granted. Smith is looping, the same illogical thought returning to its point of origin over and over, repeating. That thought leapt the gaps in his rationality when he saw the charred skin on the corpse outside the door to his apartment.

What did they want?

This originating interrogatory leading to a conclusion that he voiced himself.

They wanted to kill us.

Leading to the irrational feedback loop.

I'll just stay here and put the fire out.

Over and over until they get him to the car and Jae digs a pill bottle from her duffel and forces him to swallow a two-milligram bar of Xanax. Then, considering his bulk, makes him take another. The Xanax begins to take visible hold of Smith thirty minutes later, after Skinner has checked them into the Sleep Inn on Thirty-sixth Street along the northern edge of Miami International. With the door locked and blinds drawn, and the AC humming at full blast, Smith has settled himself into the pillows on one of the twin beds, taken his phone from his pocket, and started playing Plants vs. Zombies.

Skinner begins thinking about money.

He has two hidden accounts, one at a bank on the Bailiwick of Guernsey in the Channel Islands, the second held by a shell corporation headquartered in a small house in Cheyenne, Wyoming, that serves as the physical address for over two thousand other shells. Using the Kestrel Dynamics corporate Amex number from the USB, he books two business-class seats, a single night in the Heathrow Hilton, and a connection to Kiev. Then he uses his Cheyenne shell account to purchase two more business-class seats to Stockholm, also with a connection in Heathrow, but without an overnight stay.

Smith can't go with them. Even if his agoraphobia could be conquered to the point of getting him on a plane, his lack of a passport rules out the option. Jae wants to talk about where he can go to ground, but Smith already has a place, a safehouse. A location he will not share with them, but a protocol is agreed upon for future communications. Before saying good-bye, he accepts the rest of the Xanax and agrees to take care of Jae's robots after she unpacks just two of the spiders, encased in padded shells, and repacks them in her duffel bag.

On departure, Sinner watches as Jae hugs Smith, an apology of some kind quietly spoken. But Smith, whether by nature or because of the Xanax he has taken, waves her off. Last seen through the closing hotel room door, thumbs tapping the screen of his phone, killing zombies.

On the flight Jae seems to black out rather than fall asleep. Skinner, unable to sleep himself, makes an effort to meditate, tilting his seat back and consciously relaxing his muscles one by one, beginning in his toes. Musculature relaxed, he knows he can recover some amount of physical, if not mental, energy. Indeed, his mind circles again and again to the encounter incident in Oasis Two. At the hotel he asked Smith about the tracer rounds. *Those were the bullets I had around the place, man.* No explanation as to why he happened to have tracers rolling loose in a drawer. Skinner replays the moves he made killing the first man. He could have done better. He rehearses doing it better.

When he opens his eyes he discovers that Jae has unzipped her carry-on backpack, taken out her laptop, and is exploring the Kestrel USB.

"Partition."

Skinner rubs his eyes.

She points at the USB.

"Smith said the hackers put the ReStuxnet virus on a partition on a USB. I didn't know you could do that."

She clicks through a series of control panels for the software preinstalled on the USB.

"Asshole. There you are."

Click-click-click. And the screen begins to spool an unending list of files.

Text files in a dozen formats, spreadsheets, link dumps, JPEGs, GIFs, the contents of several email account trash files, a seemingly unending document composed of cut-and-pastes from defense industry trade collateral, technical PDFs on mil spec office furniture, the entire WikiLeaks State Department cable dump, more.

Jae points at Skinner's briefcase, tucked under the seat in front of him.

"I'll need your laptop."

She's begun to click open files, apparently at random, placing her phone on the tray table and opening a browser.

Skinner pulls out his laptop.

Jae waves fingers, vague, presence receding.

"Open a browser. Firefox if you have it. Anything if not."

He opens Explorer, and she takes the laptop from him, rests it at an angle on her thigh.

"Terrence. What did you? Everything. Okay. X marks the spot. Show me."

Clicking through files, hands dancing between phone and computers, surfing across the information, no longer, Skinner would swear, on the plane at all, silent other than the occasional grunt or mumble.

"Show me where."

*　　*　　*

Until she snaps to awareness as they stand inside Heathrow Terminal 3, trying to decide between eating at the British version of a bagel café (East Village Veggie, Harlem Nights, The Soho) or a chain sushi bar with a kimono-wearing cartoon tuna as its logo.

"Who were they?"

Skinner pictures briefly the men he killed at Oasis Two.

"Contractors. From a Kestrel rival. H-A, perhaps. Smith said they have an interest in him. They could have his home under surveillance."

"Why didn't they have guns?"

Skinner frowns at the smiling face of the tuna, the oversize chopsticks clutched somehow in one of its fins.

"Because they didn't expect to have to shoot anyone."

He looks at a nearby departures board. They have only an hour before their scheduled boarding time.

"I think these are the best options we have for now."

"How were they going to kill me? Without guns? I know there are other options. But."

Skinner nods at the Bagel Street franchise.

"This one has an espresso machine."

Jae resettles her backpack on her shoulders.

"Right."

They wait for something resembling a break in the human traffic flowing along the aisle running between the façades of the shops and the cluster of seats where they have pulled over, and then step in and dodge their way across before sidling into line behind a man speaking rapid-fire Cantonese into his phone.

Skinner turns slightly, watching the constantly shifting mosaic of faces outside.

"They weren't supposed to kill you. They were there to take you."

Jae looks at the tubs of flavored cream cheese spreads behind a sneeze glass. She shakes her head, as if denying the unnatural color spectrum of the spreads.

"Take?"

"Capture. Kidnap."

She pats her pockets.

"How do you know?"

He studies the list of paninis that are offered as dubious alternatives to the bagels.

"Because they didn't have guns."

She looks from the tubs of spreads to his face.

"I don't want any of this shit."

As she says it they come to the front of the line and Skinner orders for them.

Minutes of silence later, at their table, Jae crumples the paper around the remaining three-quarters of her bagel after she's consumed as much as she seems willing to consume.

"Why would they kidnap me?"

"They'd have kidnapped you for ransom."

"Money? From Cross?"

"Information, maybe. Or a promise to stay out of the way. In the past, nobles were taken in battle and held until the foe retired from the field."

She takes a sip of her coffee, winces at its intense bitterness, and picks through the remains of their meal until she finds an unopened sugar packet.

"They thought they could use me to get Cross to stop looking for the hackers? Leave them with one less competitor trying to get the inside track on new cyber security contracts?"

"Maybe. That's one possible motive, if it was a kidnap scenario."

She rips open the packet.

"If?"

He begins to place the paper wrappers and assorted trash onto their plastic tray.

"Kidnap was one possibility, capture was the other."

"What's the difference?"

Skinner picks up his own very small paper cup, looks at the dregs of black, unsweetened espresso at its bottom, swirls it.

"A capture scenario is usually terminal."

Jae is pouring the sugar into her cup, watching it dissolve into slush.

"I don't find euphemisms comforting. They're too ominous. I'd much rather you just say, *When they capture you they kill you.*"

"Torture. Then kill."

She watches the small pile of sugar at the bottom of her cup subside under the surface of the coffee, but she says nothing.

Skinner drinks off the last of his own double shot, places the empty cup on the tray.

"Capture and interrogation. Which almost inevitably means some form of torture."

She pushes air out between pursed lips, lets it drift back in, picks up a wooden stirrer and creates a tiny whirlpool at the bottom of her cup.

"So they were there to capture, torture, and kill me."

She drops the stirrer and drinks the last of her espresso like it's a tumbler of bourbon. Sets the cup on the tray, looks at Skinner.

"What about you?"

"They didn't know about me. Clearly."

She wipes her lips with a used napkin from the tray.

"But they know now, whoever sent them."

Skinner lifts his hands from the table, then sets them back down.

"Whoever sent them knew already, they just didn't tell the team they sent to take you."

Jae balls the napkin.

"Fucking spy shit."

Skinner draws lines on the tabletop with his fingertips, random shapes, demonstrating nothing, routes for his thoughts.

"The team was told you were a low value asset, unprotected. No reason to take the risk of carrying guns. Carrying guns in a country of laws is always a risk best avoided. Especially in a country where the police forces are armed. They were to take you, probably they had a ruse in mind. A story to tell about building safety or needing to move your car, something to get you out of the tower. The ruse failing, they had tasers. But you are not a low value asset. Anyone sending a team after you knows the stakes involved and knows your value to Cross. You are highest value. And are, therefore, protected. But they sent a poorly armed and ill prepared team to acquire you. Because they wanted to know something specific."

Jae is squeezing the balled napkin.

"Such as?"

Skinner stops drawing lines.

"Such as whether or not I'm any good anymore."

Her fist tightens around the napkin.

"And how would they know you might be protecting me in the first place?"

"They would know because Cross leaked the information."

She throws the napkin onto the table.

"That little fucker."

Skinner picks up the napkin and places it on the tray, nests it inside his empty cup.

"There are people, more than a few, who are very good at identifying threats. They can, I've seen this, they can look at a landscape, an airport terminal, and see all the viable attacks that might be mounted in that environment. So they build their security around a set of scenarios. Their opposition, the very good ones, understand this. They have a limited number of attacks in any given situation, yielding a limited number of defensive postures. The result is something like chess."

He flicks his fingers, directing her eyes down the length of the terminal.

"But this isn't a chess board."

His hand swats lazily at the air just over the plane of the table, as if knocking something invisible and slight of value onto its side.

"And you are not a piece to be surrendered when it appears the game can no longer be won."

His hand, drawn, slides across the space to where her forearm rests, stopping when the little finger of his right hand has come into scantest contact with her skin.

"You are my asset. If someone attempts to acquire you, to kill you, I will kill them. When this job is over, when I have fulfilled my contract and kept you safe, I will then find anyone who took part in planning to capture or kill you, and I will kill them all. And everyone will know that I did it because they threatened you. My asset."

He is not looking at her face, his eyes stare at the tiny patch of contact between them, where their skin presses lightly.

"When you go away for a long time, people forget who you are, what you do. I have to do my best to remind them. So I can keep you safe."

He moves his finger away, and in the instant of broken contact Jae stands, her thighs bumping the underside of the table, picks up her backpack.

"I have to use the bathroom."

And is out of the tiny café, into the flow of humanity, eyes searching for a restroom.

Skinner doesn't rush, stopping to spill the trash from their tray into a garbage can, placing it atop of stack of similar trays. A Heathrow restroom is not only bustling, but at least as observed as any other room in London. CCTV cameras, as ubiquitous here as football jerseys and tourists.

He's thinking about Terrence again. In an airport. The last place he saw his friend.

Terrence understood, from the beginning, Skinner believes, how protection might change him. How the act of hovering over another person, shielding him or her, would condition within him a new response. An emotional complexity as unsettling as the one that had driven him out of acquisitions. A palpable yearning that he studied to conceal. As with everything he did that concerned social behavior, the concealment required practice. He knows that he has exposed something to Jae. Some hint of what he feels. The irony being that she might actually recognize the emotion that is, for him, undefinable.

Terrence.

Skinner is more hungry for his friend's words than ever during his exile, these needful parts of him waking up. He can feel them tingling. Much as he still feels the tingle of contact on his skin where his pinkie touched Jae's hand. No other option, he stops at an Internet kiosk, uses a touch screen that accepts both cash and credit cards, purchases a PIN code with a ten-euro bill, and uses it to log on to the airport network at one of three terminals clustered around a narrow pillar that houses all the required hardware of Web access, a trio of screens and keyboards mounted around its circumference. Tapping in the address for classic-steelbikes, entering his screen name and password. If nothing else, he can toss a bottled message, to be lost in the digital sea. Distracted by what he sees when his account opens, it takes Skinner a moment to realize that standing at the head of the line inside Bagel Street, with a sleek young man in black, frowning at the menu in much the same way that he had a short time before, is Haven.

a robot to make her normal

As she always does, Jae has locked the stall door and then checked that the lock holds firmly before she sits down. She's done this since the age of twelve, when one of the male teachers at her elementary school walked into her stall uninvited. He'd smelled cigarette smoke, he said later, as the school nurse bandaged the bite marks on his forearm, and had gone into the bathroom to investigate. The story failed to hold water. Jae's father drew a singular lesson from the incident and outlined it for his daughter: *Always check the lock.*

And she does, always, even now in one of Heathrow's enclosed stalls, even when she is simply sitting on the toilet fully clothed, backpack in her lap, head bowed over it, practicing again her deep breathing in the face of panic.

Brain.

She's so mad at herself.

Stupid brain.

A not unusual state of affairs.

Stupid fucking brain.

She does her breathing, trying to slow her heart, calm the flush across her cheeks, the jolt of current that seems to run up her spine and over her scalp.

No, really, this is bullshit. I won't have it.

"I won't have it. Absolutely fucking not."

She folds her arms on the daypack in her lap, presses her face into them, and screams. Feeling better almost instantly.

She lifts her face, knuckling the corners of her eyes.

"Unholy bullshit."

She wants to clear her head, but instead she's thinking about Skinner. She can't help it. She's thinking about how certain she is that Skinner is somehow, disquietingly, falling in love with her.

"Shit."

His finger touching her hand.

You are my asset.

A tone she's heard usually in bed, in moments when the words feel pulled out and one is helpless to stop them.

"Insane."

And so, panic.

She'd like a robot, a tiny one, microscopic, that she could send inside her skull to deal with the disaster that is her brain. A robot to repair the wreckage left from the earthquake of her mother's death and the long drought of being raised by her father and the floods of alcoholism and the lightning strikes of bad decisions and men and the constant threat of a planet-killing asteroid. The obsessive search for the configurations that first became visible in her mental sky the day her mother was killed by a bee, and which has grown until it blots out most everything, looming over her. A robot to uncross the wires that have left her incapable of seeing anything for itself, but always in configuration.

A robot to make her normal.

She's looking at the tile floor, smaller and larger squares, and rectangles, a pattern she knows is called *corridor stacked.* She doesn't remember how she knows that. Cilantro, Blue Spice, and Arrowroot. She must have seen a webpage; the pattern and colors are lodged between the hazardous territories of her brain. The material is Corian, a DuPont product. Easy to clean, to sterilize. Popular in operating theaters and bathrooms. Prefab Corian OT and restroom setups manufactured in India. If this was an American airport the Corian would be from China, but the UK and India have a special history. She can feel the configuration of the tile, the chain of its manufacture and shipping trying to merge with her limited knowledge of the history of the Raj. A British Airways map is unfolding in her mind now, air routes blooming from Heathrow in multicolored arcs. Her brain finds a layer, a European Aviation Safety Agency report on turnaround times, minimum service schedules, levels of compliance among carriers, proposed post-Eyjafjallajökull eruption changes to air control regulations as concerned with closure of airspace, something about tephra particles per square meter and glass-rich ash. A weather map pops up, jet streams. The tiles starting to unlock from one another, floating to different altitudes, ones that remain on the floor tilting up on edge, tiny cityscapes, the floating tiles tracing the BA route map arcs, jet streams overlaid, manufacturing color-coded, the flush of a toilet in the booth next door sending a mental cloud of ash into the air around her.

She hits herself in the face, closed fist, punching her cheek, her head snapping to the side, and the layers and configurations wink out.

"Just a bathroom."

She closes her eyes.

"It's just a fucking bathroom, it's not a Rosetta stone for understanding globalization."

But the unwonted vision has let her know that her cornucopia of medications are truly flushing from her system. She's drifting closer to the nexus of her mental disasters. Coordinates unknown, found only by instinct and in inborn sense of direction that forever leads her back to her very own interior Bermuda Triangle. Stay there long enough and all lost things, real or imagined, will rise to the surface.

Something bobs up from the EASA report and into her forebrain. *Direct flights to Stockholm Arlanda are among the shortest turnarounds of all flights originating from Heathrow.*

"Shitshitshit."

She gets up, slinging her daypack over both shoulders so she can move faster, and slams into the stall door when she tries to push it open without unlocking it first. Second try and she gets it right, coming out into the hallway to find Skinner standing there, a look akin to anxiety on his face. He appears to have been on the verge of coming in after her.

"They're calling our flight."

She nods, heading for the terminal concourse.

"Something about having Sweden at the other end of the flight must make them efficient on this route."

He falls in with her, quickens his pace so that he's slightly ahead, makes subtle movements, shoulder feints, widening his stride, collapsing the handle into his bag and carrying it swinging at his side, opening a passage for them, for her, clear space. So that, following him, perched, she can feel, in his peripheral vision at all times, she is revisited by the sensation that launched her into the bathroom in the first place. The unnerving calm that fell over her when he spoke those words.

You are my asset.

The panic that dropped down on her just after, the panic of being calm. The irrationality of it. Her mind knowing, the unravaged part of it knowing, that there is nothing safe about being with Skinner. The fact of him in her life meaning that danger is pervasive; she should not be at her ease. And he may have killed Terrence.

But she can't help it.

She likes the way it feels.

in the world

SKINNER HAS BEEN among the islands of Stockholm professionally; he remembers hitting the trunk of a tree with a dead branch, causing the snow to shake free from above and fall over the dead body lying at its roots, stealing an unlocked bicycle and riding it through slush, snow melting in his shoe. He remembers Stockholm as a peaceful city. And Arlanda airport peaceful as well. Not today.

Protesters are pouring in for the WTO meeting and Bilderberg conference. Unprecedented concentration of power and wealth in an era when Western protest movements have had little luck articulating anything other than rage. Conference attendees arriving, cars plucking them from the runways as they disembark from government charters and private corporate jets.

The protesters are lining up for buses and shuttles or for rides they've arranged in advance via Skype with simpatico organizers. There are smartphones in every hand, Tweeting arrivals and calls to arms. The networks here will be straining. Then again, Sweden, they may hum along with bandwidth to spare. Scarcely any line at the taxi stand. A black Volvo V70, *Taxi Stockholm* painted in white on the door. The driver is wearing a taxi company jersey that makes him look like a Formula 1 pit crew chief. His close-shaved bullet head and etched Scandinavian features add to the impression. Skinner has never seen a cabbie look more capable of sudden decisive action. Bruce Willis would look like this if he were a Swedish cab driver. The crew chief opens the door for them, Jae opening her backpack and pulling out her laptop before they even pull from the curb, saying nothing when Skinner leans over her to grab the end of her shoulder belt, pulling it across her body and buckling her safely in. She opens the laptop and dives back into Terrence's files on the USB, as oblivious to the taxi ride as she was of the flight from London.

The E4 runs smooth, late-melt patches of snow on the sides of the road, thick stands of bare trees that had looked like piled bones when they flew in, dense, tangled, the color of stained ivory. But there is trouble after the exchange to Klarastrandsleden. Running parallel to the rail lines and Barnhusviken river, tail lights flare ahead, and their driver brakes hard enough to make Jae grab the laptop to keep it from slipping into the footwell. A train is frozen on the tracks, passengers being disembarked and led by Swedish Railways employees and police officers wearing high-viz green safety vests over their navy blue uniforms. Parked at the edge of the rail bed are a few V70s checkered in white, blue, and more of the green high-viz, *Polis* painted on the door, but otherwise easily mistaken for more cabs. A few hundred meters up the road the cause of the traffic jam is revealed. A half dozen protesters on the tracks, chains looped under the rails, wrapped around their bodies, secured with some very good locks. The cars ahead began to pick up speed as the drivers get, each in turn, their own eyeful of this distinctly un-Swedish spectacle. Accelerating away, Skinner can see a red Scania truck pulling up at the tracks. More of those high-viz squares, a theme on Swedish security and emergency vehicles, it appears. *Räddningstjänsten* emblazoned in white paint.

Skinner tries saying it aloud.

"Räddningstjänsten. Rescue Services."

Skinner nods at the driver's back.

"Who will they rescue?"

The driver waves a hand over his head. *Everyone.*

"Ach!"

Skinner looks at the driver, impressed by his ability to imbue the guttural exclamation with all the frustration and hostility of a truly great and heartfelt obscenity. At an exit marked Kungsbron, just ahead, a tall Iveco Daily panel van, unmarked rental, pulling onto the traffic island in the middle of the intersection, side door sliding open, a half dozen passengers in Gitmo-orange coveralls, surgical masks and safety goggles, jumping out to unfurl a spray painted banner that stretches across the width of the road. Their driver cuts the wheel again, perhaps more at home in an F1 cockpit than changing its tires, taking them east, two wheels bumping up on the same traffic island where the Daily has come to rest, crossing a short bridge onto Kungsholmen.

This latest maneuver finally getting at least a share of Jae's attention as she rescues the laptop again, hugging it to her chest.

"What the fuck?"

Skinner points back at the clog of vehicles forming behind them.

"Protesters."

She turns around in her seat to look.

"What did we do? We just got here."

The driver looks in his rearview, trying to see some of the chaos he's saved them from.

"World Trade Center."

Jae winces.

"Excuse me?"

Skinner raises a hand.

"Not Ground Zero, the Swedish WTC is back there."

He looks at the reflection of the driver's eyes.

"Yes?"

The driver looks back at the road.

"Yes. The WTO meeting. I had a plan to get around the police cordon, but no plan for that. We'll go this way. Longer."

He turns right, taking them back toward the river again, a street lined on both sides by anonymous office blocks, then across the bridge, a tall span over the water and the rail yards, a view to the north that includes the immobilized train, and to the south the building traffic cataclysm they just eluded.

Jae looks from one to the other.

"How long has it been like this?"

The driver tucks his chin close to his chest.

"Days. Forever."

He looks at them in the mirror again.

"Foreigners."

Said in a way that suggests he doesn't mean poor immigrants from southern climes pouring into his country in hopes of government subsidies but, rather, meddlesome, educated Westerners, fucking up his roads.

An eloquent man.

Skinner half smiles, nods, acknowledging his own foreignness here.

"We're on business."

The driver grunts, takes a left, reserving further judgment.

The office blocks have disappeared behind them. Narrow streets now, a small urban square, trees and grass starting to hint at spring lushness around the corner. Townhouses and small apartment buildings, nothing less than a hundred years old, small sleek cars parked tight along the low curbs, lean pedestrians in dark, well fitted fall attire, just the occasional flash of color, red, blue, green; true frivolity will wait until the season has definitively changed.

At the corner of Holländargatan, a middle-aged woman stands at the edge of the limestone sidewalk, out where the light streams down the narrow street, body turned to the northern sun, face tilted upward, eyes closed, basking.

Jae watches her as they pass, then closes the laptop and puts it away in her backpack.

"I like it here."

The driver runs his hands up and down the arc of his wheel.

"Spring is coming."

He smiles. Having apparently decided that Jae, at least, is worthy of his country.

austerity measures

AT THE HOTEL, some small trouble with their reservation, a bit of screwball comedy, they have only one room for them. A double to be sure, two beds, but, with many apologies, just the one room. Between the WTO attendees, protesters, Bilderberg overflow, and media, it is a wonder, frankly, that they were able to reserve a room at all. Do they need help with their bags?

The willowy Swedes behind the desk, boy and girl, impeccably well mannered, both genetically equipped to pursue successful modeling careers if they chose to do so, but neither radiating the least bit of sexuality, appear culturally tuned to a lower frequency of nonverbal communication than Jae's piercingly high bandwidth. Whether genuinely or professionally oblivious to her displeasure, they are fortunate to find the messages beamed from her eyes indecipherable. Scarring might otherwise be permanent. Unscathed, they offer further apologies accented by excellent state-supported university educations, the toots of their Swedish vowels rounded by British English lessons, consonants hardened by Hollywood movies and TV.

The building housing the Hotel Hellsten is old and European. The elevator is therefore very small, though mercifully modern. The room is on the top floor, attic, an unusually large amount of floor space rendered moot by two thick wood posts jutting into the room to support the steep angle of roof beams that even Jae must duck under.

She stands inside the door, looking at the two narrow beds pressed close together, studying the options for moving them a maximum distance apart.

"Do you snore?"

Skinner has already placed his bag on the foot of one of the beds and begun unpacking a few items, his dock kit, a clean shirt, socks, underwear.

"No."

Jae hasn't taken off her daypack. The larger duffel that she checked through from Heathrow is in her hands.

"You sure about that?"

Skinner is shaking out a blue oxford button-down with white stripes, taking a hanger from the tiny wardrobe next to the bathroom door.

"Yes."

She drops the duffel on a luggage rack that appears to have been made from a wooden frame that was once used to mount especially heavy loads on the back of a long-extinct pack animal.

Skinner hangs up his shirt.

"I'm going to shower."

And steps into the bathroom with his clean underthings and dock kit, closing the door behind himself, the sound of running water almost immediate.

Jae moves to the large windows that look out into the courtyard behind the hotel. Dozens of windows, some covered, some open to voyeurs, walls painted mustard, brick red, dark green, rooftops all steep and black, a building directly across from theirs featuring a rounded wing that extends into the shared back space like the tower of a castle. The sky is low, the light gray, one splash of sun on the top of that tower. She feels the weight of travel and time zones. But she's not ready to sleep.

Work.

She turns on the TV, cycles through the channels, finds Al Jazeera English to be most relevant to the data she wants to process, opens her laptop, plugs it into a current-adapter, sets up an account with the hotel's Wi-Fi and launches Google Earth, tapping in the Stockholm billing address Maker Smith gave her for the server account from which

Swedish commands to ReStuxnet were traced, then opens Twitter and sets up a new user, h3dcaz3, connects it to an email account she uses exclusively for crap like this, and runs searches on some terms before setting alerts for a series of established hashtags related to the protests: #bilderbergstockholm, #WTOCON, #anarchyinstockholm, #protest-stockholm, and several others of the like. The tweets in a stream in one corner of her screen. She plugs Terrence's USB into Skinner's machine and clicks it open. Sitting on the bed, a laptop on either side of her, glancing from one to the other, clicking as curiosity and random connections suggest themselves, glancing at the TV, listening to the European, American, Asian, and Middle Eastern broadcasters report stories in English every bit as educated and multicultural as that spoken by the runway model desk clerks, telling stories of a world that sound as though they might have been invented from whole cloth. So alien from what she hears at home, but she knows well that these tales are simply what is happening at the far end of the spyglass that those young airmen are viewing on their video screens back at Creech.

She clicks, deeper, more to see.

Her eyes only once flicking to the closed bathroom door, shower sounds. Once, maybe twice, then she's gone in the data, using that flaw in her own code to find the obscure.

Her back hurts, aches, and she realizes that the pain hasn't just drawn her from the data, it has woken her up. She opens her eyes. The light in the room has changed. The lamp has been switched off, both her screens gone stand-by black. Al Jazeera still plays on the TV, but the image is washed out by the bright sunlight streaming in the window. Jae scoots to the edge of her bed, straightens her back, winces as it pops at alarming volume, the noise waking Skinner, or, at least, causing him to open his eyes.

He sits up on his bed, inches from her own, where he had been stretched flat on his back, hands folded over his stomach, in knit boxer shorts and a white V-neck t-shirt. His hair is slightly mussed but looks freshly washed, and his shave is close. His skin is pale, sharp tan lines at his neck and wrists, a man rarely in the sun and never in leisure wear when he is. There's a long scar along the back of his elbow, starting half-way to his shoulder and running halfway to his wrist, it looks surgical. He curls his toes and then straightens them and they crackle. Three of them are missing.

"You fell asleep."

Jae stands, hunched, stiff, hands on hips, slowly arching, well aware how easy it is to pull a muscle on mornings like this.

"Yeah. Didn't realize it was that late when we got in. What's the day-light savings situation here?"

Skinner rises, takes a pair of gray lightweight wool trousers from a hanger; they've been ironed.

"It's a bit after twelve noon, Jae. Our flight got in at seven-thirty in the morning. Same day. We've been here about five hours."

He pulls on the flat-front pants, two buttons, zip, tucks in his t.

"Can you sleep more?"

Jae thinks about it.

"No. I'm wide awake."

Skinner has his blue-and-white oxford, also ironed.

"Get cleaned up and we'll go find food. Then the address."

Jae is already digging her own dock kit from her backpack, the magic towel, underthings, a master of her personal form of light travel.

"Ten minutes."

Jae turns on the water and begins to strip, trying not to fall back into the contents of the USB, the strata of materials Terrence dumped on the partition. The op file contains the usual mission parameters, nondisclosure agreement, meal allotments, reimbursement procedure, call-in numbers, online and physical dead drops, contact protocol, mortality benefit for next of kin. All standard. The rest of it, some seems to directly apply to the job, history of West-Tebrum, from Gilded Age robber baron mining and shipping giant to twentieth-century utility to whatever kind of global energy and information conglomerate it is trying to evolve into. But the partition consists of random pits of data. Terrence's own banking records. Expense reports for his incorporated consultancy from conventions and conferences he attended as many as fifteen years ago. PowerPoint presentations from the same events. Action assessments from Top Secret operations, scans of the original documents, postredaction, most of the text blacked out. Pages of links, a large number of them dead or broken, quickly copied and pasted into a single document, also stories and posts about Cross and Kestrel Dynamics. Traditional press coverage in the *New York Times,* hacktivist blogging following one of the WikiLeaks document dumps that included details of a Kestrel ground op in Afghanistan that resulted in thirteen collateral civilian deaths, video of Cross's testimony to more than one congressional hearing over the years, an art form that he has mastered in all of its many theatrical formalities, corporate disclosures tracing Kestrel holdings and subsidiaries, and, no favorites here in Terrence-Land, similar files on Kestrel competitors like Mission One and Hann-Aoki. Also, crushing piles of climate change data and reportage, heaps of it dating back to the quaint era when it was still referred to as global warming. Terrence appeared to have been a ground-floor believer, or at least to have taken an early interest in the national security aspects of the weather's becoming an enemy. He'd certainly written and rewritten no end of memos and briefs on the subject, all of the paper copies burned to a crisp, no doubt, but nothing that appeared, thus far in her digging, to have resulted in a budget for him to do anything, create detailed projections, draft protocols for action operations in response to climate-related security threats. More recently, very, he'd been tracking shock waves coming out of the global financial meltdown, catching up to them, trying, it looked to her, to predict where and what they would shake next.

Austerity measures.

A search term he'd been employing in an astonishing number of variations. Early hits overwhelmingly favored associations with Greece and Ireland, quickly expanding to take in Portugal, Iceland, Spain, and Italy. More recently the two words had been coming back with the initials USA in close proximity.

Other terms he'd been tracking.

Emerging economies.
Chinese Miracle.

Favela.
Urban population.
Contraction theory.
Delhi blackout.
Food shortage.
Byzantine Hades.
Renegade credit events.
IMF lending.
Arab Spring.
Occupy.
Floating armories.
Pocket reactor.
Pussy Riot.
Icepack melt.
Naxalite.
Bradley Manning.
Global Guerrillas.
Power plants online.
26/11 2008.

And, Jesus, it went on. He'd been saving the history tables from marathon online sessions, copying them and pasting them into Word docs just as he'd done with old links.

"What the fuck, Terrence?"

The words coming out of her mouth, waking her to an awareness that she's standing nude in the middle of the bathroom, steam rolling out of the top of the shower cabinet, the mirror in front of her fogged, her reflection a shadow as vague and insubstantial as Terrence's motives for dumping all that crap into what was supposed to be an operation brief.

"Seriously, Terrence, what the fuck?"

Remembering then, Terrence is dead, and she is traveling with the man who may have killed him.

gamla stan

SKINNER DIDN'T MEAN to be cheeky when he picked the restaurant. It was suggested by one of the models at the front desk, *reliable and within walking distance.* He'd focused on that, not bothering to ponder the implications of the rest of the description.

Also quite local and fun.

Sitting now at a table with a hammer-and-sickle USSR flag hanging over it, the walls, floor, and ceiling all painted scarlet, a portrait of Marx on the cover of the menus and a bust of Stalin over the bar, he is having trouble finding anything about a Soviet-themed restaurant that feels either local or fun.

But Jae is ravaging the reindeer chop on her plate, her initial hostility toward the establishment apparently diminishing as it is displaced by large mouthfuls of bloody protein.

"Gamla Stan."

For the moment the communist implications of the name *KGB Bar* seem to be attracting not a small number of distinctly nonlocal patrons favoring matted dreadlocks, anarchy t-shirts, hemp moccasins, black bandanas tied around their necks in preparation for being pulled over their mouths and noses in the event of teargas or photographers, smartphones in heavy duty construction-site-worthy cases, and backpacks that sound when they move as if they are filled with rattle cans of spray paint. Their phones have been set out on tabletops to be pondered and discussed as meals progress. An odd, though peaceful enough, scene at a place that doesn't look as though it typically does much lunch business, but there is a bit of frisson in the air as many of the protesters realize that *communist* décor does not certify *commune*-like pricing, nor does it guarantee vegan options on the menu.

Skinner swallows a bite of stew. Well-cooked meats are a habit, fewer chances of foodborne illness; vomiting and diarrhea proven to be impediments to action.

"Gamla Stan?"

Jae uses the caveman knife they'd given her, suited to sawing small limbs from trees, to carve another dripping hunk off her chop.

"Gamla Stan. That's where the address Smith gave me is. Whoever is hosting on the server that sent Swedish commands to ReStuxnet is having it billed to a Gamla Stan address. The server is somewhere outside of the city. One of the suburbs. Whatever passes for a business park in Sweden. But the billing address is Gamla Stan. We want to find who launched the West-Tebrum attack, that's our next stop."

She shoves the meat in her mouth.

"Fuck this is good."

Pink juice runs from the corner of her mouth and she wipes it with the back of her hand, making eye contact as she does so with an especially skinny young man a few tables away who seems to have twigs woven into his beard and has been looking at her and shaking his head as she devours her meal.

She smiles, teeth slicked red, a piece of gristle poking out from between her molars.

He looks away.

She swallows.

"Better look somewhere else, asshole."

Outside the restaurant, zipping her Mountain Hardware jacket, Jae nods toward the stairs that lead from Malmskillnadsgatan, dropping down a narrow block of Tunnelgatan, crossing Luntmakargatan to Sveavägen.

"This way."

She walks in that direction, starting down the stairs.

"The phones are key."

Skinner takes two steps at once, putting himself next to her. "Phones."

She waves a hand back in the direction of KGB.

"They're using them to spontaneously organize the protests."

She puts her hands in the pockets of her jacket.

"I was following some of the feeds. Twitter, mostly. Also some Facebook. Modern tools of revolution. It won't be televised, but it will be online. Until governments decide to turn it off."

Skinner is looking at a graffito on the wall next to the stairs. A single-color line drawing, cartoon, political, a vampire jabbing its fangs into the earth, WTO spelled out on its cape. He thinks of the protesters in the restaurant, the sound of spray cans clanking in their packs. Was there red paint on the fingers of the twig-bearded young man back there? Red, same shade as the drops spurting from the earth as the WTO vampire on the wall sucks away? The paint has a slight glisten in some spots, still damp.

"Like the London riots."

"Sure. Arab Spring. Occupy. Cyprus. Syria. Crowdsource protests. Classic cell structure. Radical decentralization. Anyone with a phone can play. It's about as lo-fi hi-tech as you can get, and it works insanely well."

Skinner looks back up the stairs again, KGB, the protesters inside, far from the Swedish World Trade Center, studying their phones. Far from the police lines and clashes.

"Would you say this is typical? The size and extent?"

Hands in pockets, she flaps her elbows.

"It's bigger than the typical protests for WTO and Bilderberg. But holding them in the same city at the same time. It's unprecedented. There is no typical. But."

She stops walking.

"The scale is. Unusual. Not consistent with. No, not the scale. The level of. *Organization* is the wrong word. But the news coverage I've seen, the Twitter feeds I was following at the hotel. The stuff we saw coming in from Arlanda. It feels like."

She closes her eyes.

"Like something has accelerated. Like the politicals and apoliticals who get drawn to these things have accelerated their development along some kind of evolutionary curve. Faster. Anomaly. That acceleration. But."

She opens her eyes.

"I don't know if that's important. To us."

Skinner looks west, toward the WTC nexus of unrest.

"Will they win?"

She blinks.

"Win what?"

She starts walking.

"The protesters have to have at least one central communications cell somewhere in the city, and a bunch of people freelancing for them. Aggregating TV coverage, Facebook posts, Twitter, Skype calls from the streets. They blast it back out on their own Facebook pages and Twitter streams, battlefield-quality real-time feedback. Works as long as the network can handle the traffic of a major international monetary conference, the protesters, and the old media. These guys are live-mapping on Google. Flash protests and police response."

She squints.

"Terrence was interested in the technology, how it's applied in street movements. Stuff about that in the USB partition. How it will evolve in the future."

Skinner has been walking with his hands in his pockets.

"Terrence likes the future. Thinking about it."

Jae cocks an ear, eyes on her boots, fitting, he assumes, what he is saying into whatever is happening inside her odd brain.

"He talked about the future when he called me for this gig."

Skinner nods.

"He grew up in the cold war, got his start at the CIA when Vietnam was winding down, studied at the feet of the guys who started it all. We used to talk. He said each new strategy, point of view, is built on top of what was already there. Old behaviors are never discouraged, they're encoded in the system. The community. So what we do now, all the private sector work, Homeland Security, Kestrel, fourth-generation warfare, asymmetrical threats, it's all built on top of cold war thinking. Even for terrorists, the technology has changed. But the thinking. Consistent."

He is thinking about Terrence's voice.

"I miss him."

Jae looks up from her boots.

"Do you?"

One end of Skinner's scarf has come untucked from his jacket, flapping slightly in the breeze coming up Sveavägen.

"Yes. I don't like it. Missing him."

Jae is looking at him, a look that makes him want to shift his gaze. But he doesn't.

Jae takes his scarf between her fingers and tucks it back in, back of her hand against the ironed cotton of his shirt, inside the warmth, close to him, then she pulls it out.

"I miss him, too."

Nuance is hard for Skinner. Responding accurately to verbal tones has been one of the most intensive courses of conditioning he has set for himself. It never seems to end. He makes a point of not guessing at the meaning of those obscure shifts in pitch and pace, emphasis; always responding to something specific. He decides what the other person is feeling and acts on that decision. Incapable of stinting on effort, he is often right. Which pleases him. But he must pause now, after Jae says that she, too, misses Terrence, confused by how the words have been shaped by her larynx, tongue, teeth, and lips. The air rushing through and over them, carrying the vocalization of her feelings, seems to be telling him something terribly sad.

Then he looks up the Tunnelgatan stairs and sees Twig-Beard and his friends at the top, starting down, their meal abbreviated for a hurried departure that is putting them on Skinner and Jae's heels.

His scarf flies loose again, he points southward.

"This way."

Walking, he thinks about the pressure he felt behind his face when she touched him, the physical impulse to bend, kiss her. What might have happened.

Foolish thoughts.

He tucks the scarf back. Jae has not noticed the protesters behind them. He wonders if she felt the huge serrated steak knife he dropped in his wallet pocket when he stole it from the restaurant. In his hand now, blade up the sleeve of his jacket. Cutting back to Malmskillnads-gatan, Skinner can hear the protesters closing, speeding up, breaking into a run. He is starting to spin, picturing where the sweep of his arm will draw the blade across the neck or face of the first of the charging protesters who attacks them, when Jae applies a surprisingly strong and efficient arm bar and forces him across the sidewalk and against the wall of an office building that looms over them. Skinner's intended target runs past, ignoring them both, screaming something in German and un-furling a spray painted banner from his backpack. And suddenly a flood of protesters are spontaneously erupting from the streets in all directions, filling a small park square.

Jae lets Skinner's arm go.

"It's just a flash riot. Don't kill anyone."

Skinner watches the dozens of young people as they begin to self-organize into chanting unison.

"Flash riot?"

She looks around, takes in some details of the building they're standing next to.

"Shit. The Riksbank. Fucking Swedish national bank. We should have picked a different route."

Skinner is still holding the knife, only slightly less confused, he guesses, than the office workers who appear to be the regular inhabitants of this area. Young professionals and the service economy workers who make them possible, all with no clear idea if they should fight, flee, or go about their business as the protesters, some dressed in camouflaging business attire, begin to spray-bomb the street, the sides of the Riksbank, and any cars parked at the curb. Looking at those cars, Skinner realizes that there are none moving on the street itself, that traffic disappeared just before the protesters started their action.

He grabs Jae's arm, pulls her close, starts moving them toward the protesters, but before he can take the next step, sirens echo, and half of the local spectators who have been keeping to the sidelines shuck off their coats to reveal high-viz police vests, and fully uniformed riot cops stream from the front of the bank building.

Jae nods.

"Hard to be surprised by a protest at the national bank."

Skinner is scanning the buildings that surround the park.

"They're going to use the square as a kettle. Once it's sealed they'll keep everyone inside while the city settles down. Release in small groups. Lots of photographs of everyone here."

Skinner watches as rocks are launched from a cluster of protesters, bouncing off riot shields. He can see a few protesters who have climbed a large bare tree in the square. A heavy man is jumping up and down on a bench, the slats break under him and he falls, then gets back up and starts prying one of the broken boards loose, handing it to another protester, who swings it experimentally. More benches are broken.

"Skinner."

Jae is pointing at the arcs of three flaming rocks descending toward the police line that has closed from the south end of the square.

Skinner frowns.

"Molotovs."

The three projectiles hit the street, exploding with whumps of igniting jellied gas and the tinkle of shattering glass, the police line retracting from the nearest blaze, more than a few officers swatting at small, sticky gobs of fire on their arms and legs. A large vehicle can be seen over the heads of the police now, and a second level of officers is materializing. Their horses hidden behind the front ranks, they appear giant.

Jae is on her toes.

"This is going to be a shitstorm, isn't it?"

Skinner sees a man in an Armani overcoat, shouting into his BlackBerry in English while holding up a second phone, taking pictures or shooting video.

Another Molotov flies from the trees, clears the nearest police line, ignites something other than the street. Screams. The line breaks, in the opening a flicker, rearing horse on fire, then the line closes again.

Skinner nods toward the man with two phones.

"This way."

The man is holding his second phone over his head, pointed toward the section of police line where the flaming horse appeared a moment before.

"It's out of control! I'm gonna send it. No, don't fucking put it on YouTube, sell it to someone. Fuck do I know? Talk to your guy, him, the agent. So what he's a sports agent, he fucking knows people!"

Skinner puts himself directly in the man's sight line.

"Sir."

The man's eyes move to Skinner's face.

"I'm not part of this, man. I'm just here."

Skinner points at the locked entrance to the nearby Scandic hotel.

"Sir, we're getting hotel guests inside before the police charge the square. Are you staying nearby, sir?"

He tips his head at Jae.

"I'm escorting guests safely inside. Are you a guest of one of the hotels, sir?"

The man looks at Skinner.

"You're hotel security?"

Shouts, screams, full throated bellows. They all turn to watch the vanguard of protesters charging the police line, cobbles flying up from their rear, two Molotovs, aimed at the police line, forcing a retraction as they hit and smear fire over the street. Poorly considered, the pools of fire are in the path of the charge, momentum carrying the protesters forward. Someone goes down, the mob hits the police line, and the clubs start to rise and fall.

The man has both phones up now, both shooting video, but he's started moving toward the Scandic hotel at the edge of the square.

"Okay, let's go, fucking shit, let's go, okay, move, move!"

Skinner grabs Jae's upper arm, pulls her a few feet, gets ahead of the man and in front of him.

"I need your room number and I need to see your room key, please. We're only admitting registered guests."

The protester that went down in the fire is up, running, flames streaming from the back of her head. Two more protesters run along-side and behind her, one trying to pull off her burning jacket, another trying to empty a liter bottle of Evian on her head, an officer has dropped his baton and shield, pulled off his coat, carrying it spread before him like a net, trying to tackle the girl and bring her to the ground so he can smother the flames. He leaves his feet, throws his body onto hers, and they go down, he blankets her with the coat, slapping it with flat palms, hugging her. A protester with a bench slat runs from behind and smashes it over the cop's helmet, knocking him off the girl.

The man flinches.

"Holy shit."

He puts both phones in one hand and digs in the deep outer pockets of his Armani.

"Key card, yeah, five-nineteen, shit."

The attack on the police line has disintegrated under the clubs, driven back, but several retreating protesters have stopped and formed a ring around the fallen officer, kicking him. The burning girl he extinguished is lost to view.

The man pulls a key card from his pocket.

"Key. So can we get the fuck inside now?"

Skinner knees him in the crotch twice, easing him down to the ground as he folds forward, curled on his side, mouth open wide but un-able to draw enough air to make any noise. His hands have clenched and Skinner has to pry the key card and both phones from his grip, drop-ping the phones, one each in his jacket pockets, key in hand, rising and taking Jae by the wrist.

"Let's go."

She drags her feet, looking at the man on the ground.

"Is he safe there?"

Skinner is still moving, pulling her toward the Scandic.

"No."

A new siren rises and fills the square, bouncing off the faces of the tall buildings. A warning that something large and powerful is coming. At the far end of the square the police line splits open and a towering blue and high-viz truck, unholy product of a mating between a doubledecker bus and a fully armored Humvee, rolls through, two water cannons above a high cab, windows covered by steel screens, a broad cow catcher mounted up front.

Skinner draws Jae close, his arm over her shoulder.

"Passport."

She watches Skinner take his own from inside his jacket, holding it and the key in the same hand, holding them up in clear view, as they walk briskly toward the Scandic. She unzips her jacket, unzips one of the interior pockets, pulls out her own passport, and presents it in the same manner.

Skinner is waving his passport and key at the security guards behind the locked doors, pulling Jae closer.

"We're staying in the hotel."

Skinner slaps the key card and his passport against the glass.

"Room five-nineteen."

The doors are unlocked, guards pulling them open, holding out their arms to draw Skinner and Jae inside as if pulling them from the ocean after a shipwreck. Behind them, the water cannons open fire on the square, white noise drowning the world's voice.

Someone drapes a blanket over Jae's shoulders, a man pats Skinner's back as if for a job well done. The thunder of the water cannon and continuing howl of the siren force everyone to raise their voices, Skinner can see people who have come down from the restaurant for a different perspective on events, cocktails in hand.

A man, British accent, north-something, places himself in front of Skinner and Jae.

"How is it out there? The police need to contract their lines, yes?"

Gravitas in the words.

Skinner leads Jae around him toward a bank of elevators.

A concierge crosses the carpet, meets them at the elevators, pushing the button. Her English is impeccable.

"My apologies for the situation. We, of course, have no control over something like this, but we will make every effort to see that it doesn't make your stay any less enjoyable."

*   *   *

By the time they descend in the elevator to the subfloor basement, ask a laundress with poor English for directions, lose themselves, find themselves, find the loading dock, wave off the questions of a security guard, smiles, head shakes, *sorry, we don't understand a word,* and emerge into brisk sunlight on the peaceful street of Drottninggatan, eight minutes have passed since the protesters started their flash riot a block away.

Seventeen minutes of traffic later, a taxi deposits them at the south end of Helgeandsholmen and they cross a bridge, wandering into the narrow cobbled alleys of old world charm that define the tiny island of Gamla Stan.

Postcards, cafés, historical preservationists at work. They slow down, the buildings built tall and narrow and pressed together, dense, no sound reaching them from the riot now. Sunshine on the exterior walls of the upper stories. Wooden shutters folded open. Flower boxes.

Jae checks a map on her phone, turns it this way and that, the streets a senseless tangle, points down a twisting cobbled way that appears to have been built to follow a popular goat track from some previous century.

"This way. I think."

Skinner follows a step behind, taking time to glance in the uncovered ground-floor windows, glimpses of storerooms behind businesses on parallel streets, kitchens, small domestic settings. It is an area for artists and eccentrics and families who have lived here for generations. An expensive and particular way of life, keeping house in a tourist district. But you never know what you might see. Grandpa's birding shotgun over the sink. That HK 9mm taken from a field in Bosnia while on UN peacekeeping duty during service years. Or, more likely, a well-honed boning knife. Thinking about objects he can kill with, Skinner only gradually becomes aware of how slowly they are meandering, weaving steps, their shoulders bumping from time to time.

It seems quite natural, an act that requires no thought at all, for him to take Jae's hand. And when he does, she does not take it back. Walking, hand in hand, down the streets of Gamla Stan, name like a lost province of one of the world's popular war zones, Skinner scouting for mortal weapons, Jae using him for balance as her mind drifts through the data.

Eye of the storm, winds building around them, but careless, for the moment.

pogrom

TERRENCE LIKES THE *future.*

What Skinner said before the riot. Before she tucked in the ends of his scarf and touched him.

Terrence likes the future.

That he spoke so authoritatively in the present tense means less than shit. He is, she tells herself, a killer. He's killed many people. She's watched him do it. An experienced killer must have had ample opportunities to try to hide the fact that he's killed someone. Changing the tense, from *Terrence liked the future* to *Terrence likes the future.* This is not something on which to hang your fucking hat when assessing whether the person you are traveling with has killed a friend.

I miss him.

What he also said.

Well, shit, she misses Terrence, too. And she can't stop thinking about Haiti. The satellite photos she had looked at on the plane, coming in with a team of American emergency responders. There she was, the odd lady in the window seat at the back; no one knew how she'd gotten on the flight. Most of them knew one another. Indonesian tsunami, Katrina, Brazilian favela mudslide. Regular gatherings for these specialists who operated somewhere on the border between selfless altruist and risk taking adrenaline junkie. They were pumped.

Conversation from the seats in front of hers:

Saving a life is like the most intense high ever.

There were vets. Men and women who'd left the battlefield with new scales of affect. Dulled to any scenario that did not involve screaming sirens, the unbalanced sway inside a speeding vehicle, pop of small arms, deafening shudder of helicopter blades just overhead, and blood, still wet, squelching underfoot. A plane full of creatures who had stopped feeling quite human. Stopped acting like their husbands and wives and parents. Could not see themselves in their children any longer. They'd walked or been pushed through a scrim, seen what so much of the world saw daily from birth. The limitless possibility of life ending brutally and for no reason in the next instant. Those on the plane were the crest of human evolution. The next stage. The ones who experienced calamity and learned to thrive in that environment. The age of disaster, and these its natives. For now, they could choose to visit those places where misfortune rooted deepest; soon enough everyone would be living in the shit. The end of the global configuration that she could never avoid finding. Disaster World. What was waiting for them all, around the corner.

Jae was there because Terrence stuck her on the plane. He'd found her at Texas A&M, tinkering in someone else's lab; piecework, her soldering always flawless. Assisting when municipalities would send teams of fire fighters to be accredited on new equipment in the rambling artificial catastrophe that was Disaster City. Training ground and test bed for the personnel and equipment that would try to blunt the edge of the future.

She'd stopped designing her own robots after Iraq. Stopped building them, anyway. She could never stop designing them in her head. Senseless crawling tools that could uncover lost and missing things. How could she stop? She'd blunted her own edge with Xanax and booze. The configurations were still there, but all they did was swirl around her, never resolving into anything coherent. Off the radar for Cross and Kestrel. She'd tried going back to teaching, but a room full of young people had come to look like a room full of animated corpses. Dead in waiting. Born too late. After the deluge had already begun.

So she'd walked away and found the job in Texas. And discovered that the ersatz emergencies of Disaster City dulled the constant internal hysteria that had plagued her since Iraq. Visiting fire fighters might be

impressed by the war zone verisimilitude of the street called Sniper Alley, devoted to learning fire suppression while in a crosshairs, but she
knew better. It was all so comfortingly harmless.

Then Haiti shook.

The lab emptied out. Academics only on the surface, they were men
and women building robots to save lives. They'd been at Ground Zero
for fuck sake. Their only problem was finding a plane with room for
them, and getting a landing slot at demolished Toussaint Louverture International Airport. Jae stayed behind. A day later there was Terrence
with a proposition.

Money was involved. In more than one sense. Money for her, of
course, and money on the ground. Under the rubble. In a safe. Maybe.
An office in a Hatian strip mall, lawyer's office. Someone's asset, moving
cash, lots of it, toward a political party that might have a shot at the
presidency in a country where very little was needed to give one a shot
at the presidency. The essential value of political influence in Haiti being of debatable value to Jae's mind but not, clearly, to someone else.
Someone with an interest in coastal land leases on the southern edge
of the island. An area that could serve excellently as a training ground
for both open desert combat tactics and beachhead landings. Skill sets
in much demand. There were also, in the safe, a hard drive and several
papers that could, along with the money when you got down to it, be
lost, happily, but should, most definitely, not be found by the wrong
people. *The wrong people* defined as anyone not under specific contract
to get the fucking things and destroy them. Terrence didn't need to say
Cross or *Kestrel,* she knew who she would be working for. It all sounded
terrifically fucked to Jae. Dirty and horrifying. Something she'd gladly
rather not know was happening, let alone participate in. But the money.
Soldering, though specialty work, paid no bonus for a PhD. She was
renting a room in a double-wide at a trailer park five miles from campus,
riding the bus. Long past the point where she could produce credible excuses for not visiting home a single time in the last three years. Estranged
wasn't a nuanced enough word to describe the state her relationship
with her father had reached.

Terrence put it in perspective for her.

The window of opportunity to save lives down there is closing. But, of course, the same could be said of the window on your own life.

He was the general contractor for several small and untidy jobs that people wanted done before anything could get especially organized in Haiti. Jae hadn't listened to him when he'd told her not to take Cross's contract in Iraq. Perhaps she'd listen now that he was telling her to take this one. His advice being both blunt and more than slightly surreal.

Get your robots out of storage and get your ass on the fucking plane to Haiti.

With a further guarantee that the contract would leave more than enough time for her to engage in actual rescue work. Of which there was certainly more than enough to go around.

And so the plane. And the professional disasterists. And the satellite photos.

They looked like gravel. Photos of gravel. As if, while crossing a patch of garden that had been covered in the tiny rocks, one had stopped to snap several pictures, straight down, careful to keep feet out of frame. Gravel, twigs. The impression ruined only by the presence of what could be taken for the remains of, perhaps, a few broken toys. Shattered fragments of an old train set, Matchbox cars run over by their full size brethren, crumbs of flesh-tone Play-Doh.

The safe turned out to be easily found. Large, it created a node within a rubble-filled sinkhole. They had money to pay diggers, and, natural disaster or not, money always produced cheap labor in Haiti. They'd got lucky and found the thing more or less faceup, cleared enough debris to open the door, and sent the workers back to their own searches. Families, entire lives buried. Inside the safe, plastic-wrapped bricks of hundred-dollar bills. She filled a Pelican Cube Case with them, topped it off with the hard drive and papers, sealed it, locked it, and found Terrence waiting for her at the airport when she arrived to ship it out on one of the empty relief planes heading home to reload.

Taking the case from her, loading it onto a dolly, sweating in his tweed, he'd looked at her, forty-eight hours since he saw her last, and nodded, *The world can make sense, Jae. You've just been looking in the wrong places.* The old man, again promising order in the universe. A future that could be saved from the configuration.

She watched him go, pushing the fortune in cash and potential blackmail, then she returned to the rubble. Her robots, the ones that still worked after their long layoff, were soon useless. Broken or clogged with dust. She left them where they failed, one by one, and picked up a shovel. Finding the living became almost immediately irrelevant. Impossible. There weren't any. But the dead had value. One less rotting corpse to breed disease. One less relative uncertain if she had lost her entire family or her entire family but one. One less meal to feed the feral packs of dogs. One less of God's victims abandoned and unknown.

Back home, some of the money bought a lease on workspace in a light industrial zone outside Houston. The rest of the money bought her tools and materials. Her relationships at A&M got her access to Disaster City. A year later, when the robots she needed were finished, she got her Land Rover running and started looking for Terrence's promised future. Taking his contracts for image analysis. Data diving. Finding and seeing. Her specialties. Terrence told her that they were close to the heart of things. But it would take time. And always retreating, the desert, the mountains, away, when the configuration became overwhelming. Too much detail, the particles were like fog she was lost in.

Now here she is, holding hands with a killer, liking it, very much.

Terrence likes the future.

He said. As if Terrence were still alive. As far as he knows.

She coughs, pulls her hand free of his to cover her mouth.

Skinner raises the hand that had been holding hers, looks for a moment as if he's deciding what to do with it now, then lets it go, dangling at his side, and steps to the side of the street, the open door of a gift shop, high-end, she can see reproductions of Viking swords and helmets inside, chocolate bars wrapped like jewelry, cashmere scarves, Pippi Longstocking toys made from organic cottons and merino wool.

"I'll be right back."

He goes in, nods at the proprietor, a middle aged woman with graying blonde hair and skin both weathered and robust. She looks ready for sculling or cross country skiing, whatever the weather allows.

There are also axes, leather wrapped handles.

Who buys a souvenir axe?

This is a lightly traveled street. The entry of an expensive hotel is several doors up, a man in greatcoat and braided epaulets at the curb. Cars have a special sticker on the window. Resident cars. And livery cars, Volvo sedans. She thinks of her car in Nevada, long term parking at McCarran.

Fuck, please don't be buying an axe.

She can see him at the front of the store, smiling, a tourist smile, impeccably self-effacing but expecting to be helped with the language barrier when paying these prices. Several of the larger kronor bills he exchanged for at the airport currency kiosk are passed. He accepts some change, a receipt, and comes out carrying a walking stick with a heavy brass knob at the end. He holds it in such a way that it almost disappears, not hiding it, but carrying it as an extension, as if he has always used a walking stick. *No affectation, this; just what one always has in hand.* But she can't help thinking of the way he held the X-Acto blade back in Oasis Two. Instantly weaponized by his touch.

He looks up and down the street.

"Close?"

She takes her eyes from the stick.

"This way."

Up past the hotel, brief nod from the doorman, and stepping in at an arched tunnel that cuts through the ground floor of a slightly crooked building that has been painted the color of Silly Putty. A sign above the tunnel, Lilla Hoparegränd. An especially tight alleyway beyond, the backs of town houses, locked shutters. First glance suggests a dead end, but a spill of light across the face of the last building betrays a sharp L bend to somewhere.

They look down the short tunnel. Jae checks her phone, puts it back in her pocket.

"I'm expecting an empty room. If that. More likely a mailbox. Something someone cleans out from time to time. Paper bills are safer than online billing for these guys. Probably a whole bunch of domains billed to the same address. Could even be a service someone offers. *Bill your cyber criminal enterprise's infrastructure to this address. No questions asked. Service fees payable in advance."*

Skinner nods.

"Why I got a stick instead of a broadsword."

He looks at the door, old, wood, yellow paint, a keystone above with the date it was set, chiseled, edges worn smooth. *1747.*

He puts a flat palm against the door, pushes a little.

"Good door."

He steps back from it.

"If it isn't just a mailbox we may have to leave quickly."

He points at her backpack.

"If so, it will be helpful to know if anyone is waiting for us outside."

Jae swings the pack off her shoulders.

"I have something for that."

Skinner watches as she unzips the bag, reaches into Velcroed padded pockets, and takes out two cylinders about the size of twelve-ounce beer cans, rounded at the ends, patterned in the pearlescent metallic black-and-gray checks of woven carbon fiber, a large Oakley logo on each one. Sunglass cases. The ones she took from the robot cases that were left with Maker Smith. She pushes the button on the side of one, definitive click, and it clamshells open, revealing one of her robot spiders in a custom carved nest of polyethylene closed cell foam. She gently works it loose, gives a practiced flick of her wrist, the eight carbon legs that had been folded beneath it springing out. Skinner makes a sound in his throat, and when she looks up he points to the end of the alley. She nods and continues unpacking her creations as he walks to the end of the alley, takes the L bend to the right, and disappears. Jae isn't watching. Both spiders are unpacked. She puts the Oakley cases back in her pack.

She has her Toughbook out and powered up. Control routines for the spiders open. The iPad interface she uses for the worm and some of the other robots is more elegant, more fun, but too fragile for fieldwork unless mounted in one of her travel cases. The Toughbook's Bluetooth has detected the spiders. She moves the cursor over an icon that looks like a web, clicks, enters a passcode, and windows open showing her the camera views from both spiders. One blurry, too-close view of her left boot, one hyper–low-perspective shot of the alley looking down toward the L bend as Skinner rounds the corner, walking toward her, a looming giant on the screen.

He points back at the bend.

"Empties onto one of the big streets that circle the island. Water. Ferry dock. Bridge to Södermalm. Options."

Jae clicks another icon, tiny spiders arranged in rows like tiles, and the two spiders on the ground start to skitter over the cobbles. Alarmingly fast, finding and almost instantly rejecting deep crevices between the cobbles that might upset their balance, they move at first like the jumbled plastic pieces on a Tudor brand electric football game. Vibrating haphazardly, directionless, certain to either fall or collide. But the impression is relieved a moment after it is created as the spiders learn their terrain, adjust, receive commands from the software that is interpreting the information from their cameras, and begin to move with a sudden sure-footedness that sends Skinner stepping back as one of them scampers between his feet to a drainpipe, tries several different angles of approach, then straddles it and begins to climb, a vision certain to create a new phylum of nightmares for any arachnophobe who should see it. The second spider has been moving in a zigzag between the walls of the alley, mapping, and now it scales a shutter covering street-level basement windows, balancing when it reaches the top, tiny whirs as the camera darts back and forth for new angles, then skitters and lands on the support of a decorative streetlamp that juts from the side of the building at head height, settling, and looking at a glance, clamped to the black iron, like a small bit of decoration.

Jae packs the Toughbook away, zips her pack, shoulders it, and rises.

Skinner is looking at the spider frozen on the lamp.

"Those are a little freaky."

Jae looks at her brainchild.

"Robot spiders. If there's anything missing from that concept that will freak people out, I don't know what it is."

Skinner steps to the door.

"Robot spiders with guns."

Jae tightens her shoulder straps, securing her pack for running.

"That's what Cross would like to do with them."

Skinner touches the door as he did before, palm flat, pushes, finds no give in the jamb, reaches in his jacket and comes out with the steak knife from KGB.

Jae steps back, looks up. The alley slopes downward toward the L bend, three-story buildings at the high end, four-story at the bend. Even the upper-story windows are shuttered.

"We've been here for a while. Are we being watched?"

Skinner's left hand moves, the knife rotates, finds a new comfortable place to fit, held like a chisel.

"Yes, we're being watched."

He sticks the blade into the slight crack between door and jamb, point just above the knob, angled, applies force, his weight bearing down, blade edging in another half centimeter, opens and closes his right hand, walking stick slipping down, stopping, brass knob twenty centimeters above his hand, raises it, and hammers on the hilt of the knife. Loud, echoing, three blows, and the wood splits, Skinner prying, resetting the knife tip, hammering twice more before pocketing the badly bent knife and applying the brass knob directly to the weakened doorknob, three more blows, louder, and it falls off with a clatter, Skinner stoops to pick it up, forces it back onto its stem, and pushes the door open, stepping in, looking back at her.

"Come inside where they can't see us."

She steps into the vestibule and he closes the door; crippled, it tries to swing back open, and he yanks it, grinding the twisted latch plate into the splintered jamb.

Jae is standing before an inner door. She looks at Skinner as he steps past her.

"Is there any way to do this quietly?"

Skinner puts his hand on the knob, turns it, and pushes the door open on well-oiled hinges.

"Yes."

Short hallway, one door to the left, floor of hexagonal tiles, several missing, black spots marring the otherwise uniformly dingy ivory, a tight wind of stairs, twisting left and up and out of sight, black painted iron banister. No bulbs in the ornate ceiling fixtures.

Skinner raises his hand, *hang on.*

"Which floor?"

Jae looks at the door just inside the hallway. Black letter, *C.*

"Concierge? Ours is 2B. Europe. This is ground. Then one and then two. A and B. Top floor. Yes?"

He looks at the stairs.

"Yes."

He doesn't move.

Jae looks at the broken door behind them.

"Are we still being watched?"

He points at the door marked *C.*

"That sounds empty. Sounds empty just above. Sounds not empty up top."

Jae listens. Quiet of an old building. A creak. Pop of a wood joint expanding. Her own breathing. And, yes, mumble of voices, footsteps. Could be next door, upstairs, basement, she can't tell.

"So no empty-room-mail-drop."

She resettles her pack.

"Do we go up?"

Skinner touches his earlobe, not looking at her.

"Your contract is to find things. If you need to go up to fulfill your contract, we go."

"And what about your contract?"

He stops touching his ear.

"My contract is to protect you. I'm certain I can do a better job of that by not going up there."

She steps into the hallway.

"Let's go."

Skinner's first step is never completed, becoming instead a pivot as the street door is opened behind them, squeal of protesting brass, Jae turning at the sound, seeing a man on the step outside, looking at the ruined knob that has come off in his hand. Skinner moves fast, very, between her and the man, but not before she sees his swollen red eyes, bent nose packed with wadded newspaper, oozing gash on his forehead. Though her first glimpse is brief and he's been beaten, the twigs in his beard make him easy to recognize even as Skinner grabs him by the front of his jacket, pulls him into the vestibule, drags him through the inner door, turning him, tangling the shaft of the walking stick into his arms behind his back, forcing him to the floor, a handful of throat, silencing him, looking at Jae and tipping his forehead at the street door.

"Close that."

She does, comes through the vestibule door and closes that, watching as Skinner puts his mouth close to Twig-Beard's ear, eases his grip on the man's throat, and asks his most pressing question.

"Do you have a gun?"

He doesn't. The continuing lack of easily obtainable firearms in Sweden seeming to irritate Skinner in the same way that another American might be put out by the unavailability of his favorite candy bar.

"Polizei!"

The room holds Jae the moment they go through the door. Holds her so completely that even though she hears what Twig-Beard yells when Skinner pushes him ahead of them as a human shield, she doesn't panic about the possibility that the room may very well be occupied by the kind of people who could be keeping some of Skinner's elusive guns and be looking forward to an opportunity to shoot them at supposed police officers. Guns or no, shots are not fired. A teenage boy with a mohawk and ear piercings big enough to shove a thumb through rushes them, but he's just trying to get past them and out the door. Something Skinner prevents by putting Twig-Beard in his way and letting them both fall down. Someone else, gender neutral hair, baggy jeans, and black t-shirt, seen only from behind, darts into a bathroom and locks the door. The others stay as they are, seated or standing, three of them. The many screens and radios in the room seize Jae's attention, flicker and crackle.

Skinner looks at the darkened windows, shutters closed and locked; he peers down a short hall that opens on a bedroom with a couple of cots, stacks of flattened cardboard boxes, and heaps of styrofoam packing-geometrics. Two more windows, also shuttered. One exit, and they are standing in front of it.

He uses the knob of the walking stick to point at the nearest window.

"You should have planned an escape route."

A very young man, probably no more than twenty-five (twenty-three? twenty?), with rich cocoa skin and thick black curls, stands, his traditional *bleu de travail* four-pocket work jacket worn a size too small, snug on the shoulders, short at the cuffs.

"We did not plan to run."

Good English, French accent, touch of something North African, though he's probably never seen the country his parents emigrated from.

He looks at the boy tangled with Twig-Beard on the floor, the closed and locked bathroom door.

"Until the time comes, then you find out who is a runner."

He spits on the floor, the phlegm landing indeterminately between Skinner and the boy who ran, hard to say which of them it is for, possibly both.

Jae steps further into the room, eyes moving between the three flatscreens carrying news coverage of the WTO conference and protests. SVT public channel, TV4 commercial, and CNN. At least one of the nine active laptops and desktop monitors has an Al Jazeera feed, another showing something that looks Swedishly comparable to American public access, handheld, blurry, lots of shots of the camera operator's feet. Other screens display the Google Maps of the protests and police responses that Jae had been looking at earlier, two large screens are filled with nothing but Twitter streams, packed side by side, stacked top to bottom, layered. Four Motorola two-way radios plugged into charging stations, liquid crystal screens glowing, add an air of cold war–era revolution that curiously suits the neighborhood. Smartphones have a table of their own, cabled to computers or to chargers plugged into power strips. Extension cords snake into the room from the hallway and from under the bathroom door, every effort made not to trip the circuit breakers or, more likely in a building this old, not to blow the fuses. Some of the phones are ringing and chiming. Each seems to have a distinct tone. A story to tell about who is calling or texting or emailing. A special section of BlackBerrys. Their encrypted data service having been field-tested by the looters in the London riots. A must-have for roving street battles.

Skinner puts a hand on Jae's shoulder, but she shrugs it off.

"This is very helpful. Looking at this will be very helpful."

She wants to take out her Toughbook and cable up, get online, let it be her roving eye. She wants the remotes for the three TVs, she wants to wallow in the data and see the configuration. But all she's seeing is her mother's face swollen by the bee sting.

She bends at the waist, hands on hips, and pukes on the floor.

The French boy puts his hands in the hip pockets of his blue worker's jacket.

"You are not police?"

Skinner closes the door.

"No, we're not."

He points at an open case of Etrusca spring water under one of the folding tables.

"Please."

The man who plucks a bottle from the case and offers it to Skinner is tall, looks to have been large once, but his bulk has melted away with the passing of years, skin hangs from him, sags, a deflated man-balloon with an internal superstructure keeping its hide upright. He is the only one of the protesters over thirty, and he may well be double that.

"Shpion?"

Russian.

Skinner takes the bottle.

"Lyudi, obychnye lyudi."

The old man smiles, the front four bottom teeth are gone, all the others are the brown of aged scrimshaw. He waves his hand up and down as if patting the head of a small child, *Yes, tell me another one.* Stepping back, leaning against the door frame that opens on the hallway, arms folded, waiting. He's seen all this before.

Skinner hands the water bottle to Jae.

"Okay?"

She takes it and twists off the cap, a big rinsing mouthful that she spits behind her, the only discretion allowed with the bathroom occupied.

"Yeah, okay. Little overloaded. But okay."

She takes a drink from the bottle, then points it at the protesters.

"What the fuck?"

Skinner nods.

"Yes."

He looks down at Twig-Beard and the runaway boy, Mohawk. They've untangled their limbs and scooted themselves away from Skinner's feet, half under the table that supports the cell phone collection and the three radios.

Twig-Beard is working one of the newsprint plugs from his right nostril.

"They follow us from lunch."

His English is bad, war movie Nazi.

The paper plug comes free, unspooling, red and wet, a final tug and it drops to the floor, a little drizzle of blood follows it then stops.

"Riksbank, they tell cops we are coming. I was beaten!"

Jae twists the cap back onto her water bottle, tightens it with a violence that suggests the breaking of chicken necks.

"We left the restaurant before you. The cops were waiting."

He shakes a finger at her.

"No! They knew! Yes! Knew we were coming! You! You tell them!"

"The cops knew you were coming because you tried to storm the fucking national bank during a week of WTO protests!"

The German rises a little, bangs his shoulder on the underside of the table.

"Ficken Scheisse!"

Skinner ignores him, looks at the boy with the mohawk. He has a tattoo high on his skinny shoulder, revealed by the tank top he's wearing. Warm in the room with sealed windows, several bodies, monitors and computers pumping out heat. Tattoo comprised of the letters SUF, a thin red circle behind them, off center, partially obscured by the F.

"Anarchist?"

He nods, touches the tattoo.

"Syndikalistiska Ungdomsförbundet."

Skinner gestures at the screens around them.

"Local coordinators? Your group?"

Mohawk shrugs.

"Some. Different groups."

Heavy accent, not nearly as much school as the hotel staff, and a different nuance. Not from Stockholm, and not trying to sound as if he is.

Skinner nods. He looks at the Russian, blinks, looks at the man in the blue jacket, doesn't blink, and looks at the last person in the room. Older than the boy in blue by several years, but still young, balding nonetheless, light brown skin, weathered, hard and compact, red t-shirt, round wire rim glasses, looking at the floor between his feet.

Skinner tips the knob on the end of his walking stick, a slight dip in the direction of the man in glasses, and he looks up.

Skinner shrugs.

"West-Tebrum."

Nothing changes in the room, extreme discomfort in the face of the unknown, fear and uncertainty, but no sudden glances exchanged when Skinner mentions the power plant. More phones are ringing, a voice repeats the same phrase in Swedish over one of the radios, repeats, repeats.

Skinner looks at Jae.

"I'm not good at this."

She drinks.

"That's natural."

He steps back, a move that does nothing to diminish his presence in the room, positioning himself in such a way as to be a constant threat, violence imminent, the stick in his hand.

She asks the obvious question.

"Money?"

The boy in blue frowns, looks around the room at the others, looks back at Jae.

"We have some kronor, euro. Not much."

The Russian laughs, barking seal, one loud sharp bark, then his mouth snaps shut.

Jae shakes her head.

"No. We don't want money. The money for this."

She points at all the gear, the flattened boxes and packing materials down the hall, wads of freshly stripped cellophane stuffed in corners.

"Where did you get the money for this?"

The boy takes his hands from his pocket, holding a squashed box of Marlboro Lights and a green disposable lighter. He starts to take a cigarette from the pack, realizes that everyone is looking at him, stops.

Mohawk puts two fingers held in a V at his mouth.

"We agreed to no smoking. Too small. The room. We agreed?"

Blue Jacket shrugs, flapping his arms at his sides and making a small guttural grunt deep in his throat, eloquently commenting on the absurdity of such agreements in the face of unforeseen circumstances such as these.

Mohawk nods, thinks, and repeats his own gesture, fingers to lips, an entreating tilt to his head. The boy stoops, offers him the pack, lights his cigarette. By the time the boy has straightened and lit his own, Twig-Beard has taken rolling papers and a tobacco pouch from his pocket and Red Shirt has a Fortuna in his mouth. The room is almost instantly choked with smoke. Jae and Skinner and the Russian abstain.

Jae looks at the Russian. She's never met a Russian who didn't smoke.

He seems to know this and taps the right side of his chest.

"One lung gone already. I need the other. To fight."

He smiles, the shrinkage that resulted in all that sagging flesh explained. A man who fights cancer, surrenders one lung but no more. A tough fucker.

Blue Jacket keeps the Marlboro pack and lighter in hand as if he might need another at a moment's notice. Every drag is deep, aggressive; either he or the cigarette will die.

"The money. Donations."

Jae doesn't smoke, has never smoked. Her mother did, like a dragon, a Virginia Slims 100 tucked in the corner of her mouth from morning to night. Ash always, mystically, suspended from the tip until she took the butt delicately between thumb and forefinger and tapped it against a tray. She'd been smoking when the bee stung her. The smoldering cigarette burned a small hole in the lap of her beach dress, straight through the heart of a cornflower.

Jae waves the smoke from her face, memory with it.

"The address. Other tenants?"

Blue Jacket shrugs and shakes his head at the same time.

"We are guests. We have seen no one."

On one of the TVs, SVT, live footage of a new protest outside the Riksdag, Swedish parliament. As they watch, two armored personal carriers drive onto the lawn. Soldiers. Clouds of teargas. Blue Jacket's eyes follow hers to the screen.

She points at it.

"No one's coordinating? Are you the only control cell?"

He shrugs and shakes his head again.

"We know that we are here. If there is anyone else doing this?"

He takes a drag, blows smoke, the final answer.

Jae feels something inside her head. A swelling, large, dull. Something wanting to be understood, but ill defined. All of the phones seem to be ringing now, incessant, high tones, low, ice cream truck ditties. Only lacking fingernails on blackboards. That swelling, she needs to do something with it. She steps toward the screens.

"*Guests.* Of whom?"

"Un patron."

Skinner, motionless for minutes, realigns himself, his grip on the stick.

"Protecteur?"

Blue Jacket shakes his head, no accompanying shrug on this matter.

"Patron. Um. Yes. Sponsor? Sponsor."

All three TVs are showing teargas plumes now. The cameras for SVT and TV4 have similar perspectives, high, south of the action at the Riksdag, shooting with Norrmalm in the background. CNN's shot looks like it's from a helicopter. CNN news helicopter in Stockholm? And the phones still ringing. Does no one know how to leave a fucking message?

She pulls her eyes away from the TVs, looks at Skinner.

"I need some room."

Skinner motions with his stick, inviting Blue Jacket and Red Shirt to move, come join the Russian and the others, stand, get under the table, your choice, but do it now. They move.

And Jae seats herself in front of the center of the three TVs, two laptops and a desktop machine in reach, eyes only for the screens now, the conversations just another input.

Sponsor.

"Who? A name?"

A general shuffling, feet, hands, eyes, everyone but Skinner and Jae finding something to stare at, fingernails, ceiling, ends of cigarettes.

Phones ringing. Jae has taken off her backpack, has her Toughbook out, USB plugged.

Phones. Ringing. Ringing.

"Will someone answer some of those fucking things."

Jae starts to navigate the protesters' computers away from their immediate concerns. Closing windows on one until there is only the simplicity of the Google homepage, rearranging another to show a handful of the protest Twitter streams.

Skinner turns off the phones, a glance at Blue Jacket.

"A name. Un nom. No et d'allusions. Rien de vague, s'il vous plaît. Clarity."

He silences the last phone, turns down the volume on the three radios.

"The name of whoever gave you the money for all of this, and access to the property."

He looks at the Russian.

"Can you explain to them?"

The Russian raises his shoulders high, a tired vulture, looks at his companions.

"A name. Or he will hurt us. It is not, in my opinion, an empty threat."

There are scars around his wrists, thin and white, wrapped round and round, wire that has bound him.

Blue Jacket is looking at those scars.

"Shiva."

Jae has found the remotes for the TVs, she's cycling through, finding out what channels she has available, free hand typing *Shiva* into the Google searchbar.

Blue Jacket uses the butt of his cigarette to light a new one, drops the spent one to the floor, crushes it, twisting his toe.

"Screen name Shiva. A chatroom for anarchists. Communists. Revolutionaries. He is interested in these protests. The tyranny of the WTO in developing nations. Pénible terms of debt. Onerous. Pénible terms. He is interested in seeing attention paid to this. Graphically. He wants to help. He wants to be instrumental. He talks. Invites me to a private chat. Then to a secure place. Darknet. Encrypted communications. Very difficult for me. I am not technical."

He waves his cigarette at Red Shirt.

"I need help to arrange this. My fucking browser. Shit. Shiva introduces us. Darknet again."

Jae is looking at a Wikipedia entry for the Hindu god, its many variations beyond bringer of light and destruction. She runs a new search. *Shiva anarchist.* Scrolls, eyes snagging on a word. *Naxalite.* Her mind unfolds a map of India that she has no memory of ever opening, great eastern chunks of it colored red. The Red Corridor. It's a blurry memory, and just floats in blackness, won't connect with anything. Keeps trying to merge with portraits of calm-faced, murderous Chairman Mao, but that's not what she wants it to do. The Naxalite movement in India was born out of Chinese Maoism, but she wants the fucking map to show her where she actually saw it. Just stop hopping historical associations and resolve into the page of a book or a website. She does a search on Google. Finds the map. But the context is wrong. She clicks open one of the older personal files on Terrence's USB, searching for PDFs, photos. Needle in a haystack. Unsearchable. Fucker just dropped everything in there.

"Fuck."

She opens her eyes. People are looking at her. She doesn't need to turn around to see it. For the moment she is every bit as sensitive to being watched as Skinner is. Yes, she is acting oddly; even for these circumstances, she is acting very oddly.

"When did Shiva contact you? How long ago?"

Smoke from Blue Jacket's nose, a wave of cigarette.

"I became interested in these protests when I learn it will be both WTO and Bilderberg. Announced a year ago. Less, more. Great excitement and dismay. The monster and the master in one place. Yes.

Bilderberg, these people, these politicians, these bankers, CEOs. How can it be that they meet in secret? No one is allowed. Do we believe they are playing cards? It is only social? *Merde!*"

And now a rapid explosion of French that seems to have been building in him since he began talking; too fast for Jae to distinguish the curse words, her command of the language somewhat more practical now than what she learned in two years of high school, but less complete. She opens Google Translate, keeping it ready for his next outburst. Meantime running searches on *Bilderberg*. Off the record confab of governance and finance. Post WWII creation. An effort to bring like-minded but not necessarily allied power brokers together. Transnational. Early globalism. She clicks through to some of the search hits and gets punched in the face with a fistful of paranoia. *Conspiracy. Nazi roots of. Jewish roots of.* The faceless terror of the unknown. Color it with your favorite bias and fear. She starts closing the windows.

Blue Jacket looks at Skinner, back to Jae.

"You work for them? Bilderberg. Not cops. Private security. Contractors for Bilderberg. Do not crush something, understand it. Yes. Then steal it. Own it. Subvert. These questions. Fuck you."

Skinner has moved behind her, he places a hand on her shoulder.

"I think we've been here too long."

She shrugs off his hand, shoots her eyes at Blue Jacket and then back at her screens.

"Someone is using you."

The guttural grunt again, deeper, accompanied by a slight rolling of the eyes, a quick drag and exhalation of smoke. She needs no French to understand his profound exasperation at being told what is blatantly obvious, the reason for why he is there in the first place. *Used, indeed, are we not all being used?*

"I'm not speaking generically, I'm speaking specifically. This address has been used in association with criminal activities that have resulted in deaths. There is a trail that leads here. To you."

She allows her gaze to move from the screens, to take in the accouterments of revolution all around them.

"To this."

She looks back at the screens.

"You are being used. Set up. N'est-ce pas?"

The Russian wheezes, it's another form of laughter, expressing amusement of a higher and more refined nature than his seal bark of sarcasm. Jae starts new searches, *KGB, ex-KGB, ex-KGB WTO Bilderberg*. Nothing specific, a wave of post communist gangsterism that starts knitting itself into the web of cold war dead matter from Terrence's USB. Strange Frankenstein monster, it bumps around her head, looking for a door that will take it into the big room where she is building the configuration with West-Tebrum at its center.

She frowns.

"A year ago you're online, daydreaming about protests. WTO and Bilderberg in one place. What can we do? Someone screen-named Shiva chats with you. Arranges encrypted communications on peer-to-peer darknet back channels. Then offers funding. Then offers office space in the most expensive neighborhood in Stockholm. How did he get you the money?"

Blue Jacket flicks ash, looks at the TV screens. Jae has brought them back around to the original channels. News, news, and more news. The protest outside the Riksdag has swollen, crossed the line into riot. A water cannon truck (the same one from the Riksbank protest?) is rolling over the bridge from Norrmalm. The Google Map and Twitter updates have stopped flowing from this room. After the initial flash protest struck, more protesters flooded the tiny island, no coordinating mapper showing them that an overwhelming force is waiting. Swedish soldiers are controlling the bridges now, attempting to turn the island, seat of government, into a giant kettle.

Blue Jacket watches his compatriots being bottled up, teargassed, and water-cannoned on screen.

"You will leave?"

Jae nods, she finds the protesters' Wi-Fi network password written on Post-its stuck to every computer in the room, puts the Toughbook online.

"Money, where from, how much? Details."

"Some cash. Wire transfer. Ten thousand euro."

"From?"

"Romania. And digital funds."

She starts searching *Romanian wire transfers, Romanian banking, Romanian terrorist hackers.*

Only way to reliably get money transferred in and out of Romania is through Western Union. Fucking no wonder, Romania. Does it get dirtier? Post–Soviet bloc criminality, waves of it, money laundering, black market cigarettes, sex slave trade routes. Sex slavery leads her into porn and she has to click out of a string of self-propagating windows. Finally force-quits her browser. Opens a new window. Her computer is going to need a massive virus scan and a bath after that.

She needs to know more about the money.

"What kind of digital funds? Format?"

"Bitcoins in a Dwolla account. Direct deposit from there to a BNP Paribas account, euros. Three hundred bitcoins, exchange, merde, seventy euro each, more. Eighty-seven? Over twenty thousand euro."

Searches: *Bitcoins, Dwolla, BNP Paribas.* The first leads to the infamous nexus of anarchism, uber-geek hacker techno programmer math, pure economic theory, online gaming, online drug trade, and constant calls for investigation from members of the US House of Representatives. She finds Mt.Gox, the primary trade hub for the crypto currency; bitcoins currently trading at one hundred fourteen dollars and sixty-seven cents each. Dwolla shows as e-commerce, online money transfers. Dealing primarily in cash but bitcoins as well. Layers of anonymity accreting here. She tries to find out more about the creation of bitcoins. Wall of tech-speak. Math again. And BNP Paribas? Big bank. Legit. As legit as big banks can be.

What about the Dwolla account?

"Account details, Dwolla?"

Blue Jacket leans past her, flips through some mess, scraps, empty paper cups from the Swedish coffee chain Wayne's. He finds an envelope with chickenscratch ballpoint on the back, puts it in front of her and moves away.

"Shiva gave password, security question answer, these things."

She opens the account, just a few bitcoins left. Clicks through to the profile. A name, *Courtney Cline.* Address in Montana. Dwolla users must have a US address. A cell phone number (call it later or why bother?). Gmail address. For all the many ways the Internet sprays our identities across the globe, it also gives us tools to obscure any new ones we care to create. She maps the Montana address, Bozeman. She clicks for a satellite view, street view, a small ranch house across a four-lane highway from a casino called The Cat's Paw. Globalized hacker terrorism at its best. The identity is no doubt legit, either stolen or bought. Someone living across the road from a casino is likely to have a price for just about anything.

She shakes her head.

"Montana."

Blue Jacket points at the map she's opened.

"I did not know Montana was a real thing. Just from American cowboy movies."

Her brain finally spits out some math for her, simple addition.

"That's not enough money for all this gear. Where did the rest come from?"

"Credit cards. Numbers. Expiration dates. Limits. Black market. Twenty-five euro each."

He waves his cigarette at the packaging down the hall in the bedroom.

"We buy from Amazon. The TVs, computers. Phones. This address for delivery. We are here, we will be gone. Who cares."

Jae won't open any of the black market credit card exchanges on her own machine, but she starts popping them up on the protesters' laptops. Ghostmarket.net, security-shell.ws, silverspam.net. More. Those coming from the first hits on her Google search. More than half are defunct or dead ends. The others, very inviting, *Welcome, new users.* She wishes she had on rubber gloves. She can all but feel the malware pouring out of these sites and into the poor virginal hardware the protesters have been using to irritate the power elite. The sites give off a mixed bag of hardened criminality and tutorials in hacking and the finding of lulz.

Romania.
Montana.

Ghostmarket.
KGB.
Sex trade.
Shiva.
Alpha Bank Romania S.A.
Naxalite.
Cat's Paw.
Bitcoins.
Contraction.
Wire transfer.
Dwolla.
Ex-KGB.
How did that cycle back around? Ex-KGB.

It's out of its room, Frankenstein monster in her head, lurching into the West-Tebrum configuration, tangled in the Romanian threads. The aging Russian cold warrior working with the young idealists. Shouldn't he be running a gang in St. Petersburg? She looks over her shoulder. The Russian is as before, arms folded, eyes on floor, leaning. Skinner has placed himself in a position that puts him an equal distance from everyone in the room, but the Russian may be a sliver closer to the striking range of Skinner's stick.

Sudden flicker at the corner of her eye. More like an itch. Bug bite.

What the fuck?

Eyes back to the TV screens. Nothing there to scratch the sudden itch. The water cannon is at work. Someone is clinging to a tree, then not, washed on a tide of mud that used to be the lawn in front of the Riksdag.

More French erupts from Blue Jacket. Jae gets *merde,* repeated often, and little else.

She digs a knuckle into the corner of her eye, rubs, looks again.

Nothing.
Nothing.
Nothing.

Her hand clicks, clicks, clicks, closing windows, pushing them around.

CNN still has that helicopter shot that shows nothing but smoke, the other images are increasingly jostled as the camera operators have moved toward the thick of things. The inexplicable journalistic instinct to get closer to where shit is at its most fucked up.

She looks at Skinner.

"Anything else?"

"Leaving would be good."

Leaving. Itch. Itchy itch itch. Damn.

It will come to her later and she'll wish she had the resources of the protesters' control room at her disposal. Access to this kind of media environment doesn't just fall in your lap. She should really figure out what that itch is.

Stupid fucking brain.

Enough. Time to go.

She rises, lifts her chin at Blue Jacket.

"You should go, too. Someone will be coming."

He drops another cigarette butt, not lighting a replacement this time, pocketing the packet and lighter.

"Someone to do worse than you have?"

He bats the air with the back of his hand, turns from her, sits in his folding chair, and starts clicking out of her searches, updating one of the Google Maps, planting a crop of red pins on the site of the Riksdag riot, a deterrent to protesters still at liberty elsewhere in the city. Red Shirt looks at him, looks at Jae, takes his own chair, opens Twitter and starts typing, sending out the word to stay the hell away from the Riksdag. Mohawk eases out from under the table, stretching his back as he rises, points at the phones. Skinner steps back from the table, and he starts waking them up. Twig-Beard crawls to the bathroom door and knocks.

"Lili. Ist es okay. Sie können kommen. Öffnen Sie die Tür, ich muss pissen."

The Russian doesn't move.

Jae looks at Skinner. He nods at the door. She unplugs the USB, drops in it a zip pocket in her jacket. Hot in here, she should have taken it off. Sweaty. Pack the Toughbook now.

Itch, itch, scratch.

Itch disappearing as she sees the postage stamp windows streaming video from the spider cameras. Two angles, one looking down from a steep rooftop, and one at eye level in the alley, both showing a scene taken from innumerable action movies. Men in fitted black jumpsuits and body armor, Kevlar-soled boots, urban-combat assault rifles, matching helmets, belts adangle with pouches and fittings, clasps. These stock characters featuring gold insignia on arms and chests, too small to read in the current view.

Her fingers hit two keys, windows expand.

"Säpo."

The Russian, no longer looking at the floor, looking at her computer, the men outside. He says it again.

"Säpo."

Mohawk has a phone in each hand, both starting to ring.

"Sakerhetspolisen."

The Russian, nodding, *the diagnosis is correct.*

"Security Police. Yes."

And the wheeze of laughter.

Blue Jacket rises, looks at Jae's screen, looks at the door, sits back down and starts tweeting, talking in a mixture of French and Spanish directed at Red Shirt. Twitter and Facebook open, letting the people in the streets know that broadcasts are about to cease for good. He looks at Mohawk.

"Gern?"

Mohawk looks at the door, the phones in his hands, and answers one of them, talking in Swedish.

Twig-Beard had managed to talk Lili into opening the bathroom door, but now it slams shut and he starts yelling at her, German again, maybe something about getting the fuck out now before it's too late. But it's already too late.

On the Toughbook screen, officers of Säpo are entering the building.

Skinner reaches past Jae, slaps her computer shut, shoves it in her pack, zips.

"This will happen very fast now."

She nods, slips into the straps, cinches them tight.

Blue Jacket and Red Shirt are done updating; grabbing papers now, stuffing them into a large steel wastebasket with an IKEA sticker on the side. Mohawk has gone under the phone table again, rising with a small sledgehammer. He brings it down on one of the phones. Twig-Beard has given up on Lili in the bathroom, runs into the bedroom and comes back with a duffel sack. He opens it and starts pulling out military surplus, gas masks, bright blue cylinders with pull rings on top, riot batons.

He looks at Skinner.

"Ficken sie, asshole."

Red Shirt is spraying lighter fluid on the papers in the wastebasket. Mohawk is smashing phones two at a time. Blue Jacket is putting on a mask, taking one of the smoke bombs from Twig-Beard, a baton tucked through his belt.

Jae pulls on Skinner's arm.

"Can we get the fuck out now?"

Skinner yanks her out of the way as Blue Jacket and Twig-Beard go to the door, a practiced drill, prepared anarchists. Blue Jacket counts off three on his fingers, nods, Twig-Beard opens the door, and they pull the tabs and throw smoke grenades down the stairs at the Säpo officers who have yet to come into view. Pops. Loud enough to echo. Hissing. Now Red Shirt and Mohawk are at the door, count three, pull and throw. Smoke is visible at the top of the banister. Someone falls on the stairs. Yelling from below. Smoke thickening. Blue Jacket is back at the door, one of the flatscreen TVs in his hand, awkward load, cables dragging, no countdown this time, he rushes to the banister, tips the TV over, and darts back to the open door.

Crashes from below. More yelling. Squawk of a megaphone being tested.

Red Shirt ready with another TV, out and to the banister, heaving, a pop, the TV is falling down the stairwell, Red Shirt is falling backward, flecks of blood are dotting everything, he's on the floor kicking at the banister, sliding himself on his back, a snail smear of blood following him, left hand grabbing at his right shoulder, right hand dragging at the end of a dead arm. Blue Jacket and Mohawk duck out to grab him, handfuls of his shirt, same color as before but wet now, pulling him toward the door as Skinner puts a hand in Jae's lower back and pushes. Someone steps in front of them. The Russian. Holding Mohawk's sledgehammer. He faces them, Skinner's stick is already up, angled. The Russian turns, waving for them to follow to the closed and locked bathroom door. The Russian lifts the sledgehammer, one blow and the door breaks open. Young girl, short, multicolored hair, in the tub crying, screaming now.

The Russian points up.

Over the toilet, a cutout in the ceiling. No hinges, square of painted wood resting on a lip. Skinner stands on the toilet, pushes it up and out of the way. Off the toilet, he takes Jae's pack from her shoulders, makes a stirrup of his hands, she steps into it and is hoisted up, hands grabbing the inside of the trapdoor, splinters, pulls herself up and in, squirms around, dim light from a filthy windowpane, reaches through the trap and grabs her pack as Skinner holds it up, scooting back and out of the way. Skinner's hands, his head, a smooth pull and he's next to her. The Russian forces his upper body into view, teeters, and Skinner drags him the rest of the way up. Skinner is moving toward the window, but the Russian is on his belly, looking down into the bathroom.

"Lili. Now. Now."

More crying from below. The Russian claps his hands.

"My hand."

Crying.

He says something in Russian, a curse, worms away from the trap, finds the square of wood and drops it back into place. Rising to a crouch, moving toward Skinner at the window, a little smile for Jae, bitter but genuine.

"The art of survival. All but a dead thing."

The hammer still in his hand.

Skinner is looking out the window, face well away from the glass, not satisfied with what he's seeing. He points at Jae's pack.

"Spiders."

She already has the pack off and unzipped, opens the Toughbook and wakes the screen, a moment for the processor to catch up with the video coming from the spiders. Skinner and the Russian kneeling, crowded together behind her and looking over her shoulder at the two views of the alley, packed now with Säpo.

Skinner taps the screen with his fingertip, the roof spider's POV.

"What's up there?"

Jae moves the cursor to an icon of a circle with a series of four arrow points stationed around its circumference, clicks, and the camera view from the spider on the roof starts to rotate, a little jerky, its legs not designed for smooth panning shots. The roof pitches steeply, a ramp for snow to fall from during the long winter, shelving in a few places where window boxes thrust out from the roofline. No Säpo.

Muffled screams from below, angry, sound of heavy things falling. Blue Jacket, Mohawk, and Twig-Beard coming into direct contact with the security police. The trapdoor, a thin trail of smoke starting to drift up through the crack.

The Russian grunts, rises into a crouch, all the attic space will allow his frame, and begins walking across the joists, crossing to the east-facing wall.

"Self preservation. A force of nature."

Skinner takes Jae's pack, zips, hooks her arm, and follows the Russian, towing her.

The Russian is at the east wall, he clucks his tongue against the roof of his mouth.

"There are reasons people choose a property to do secret things."

There is a small door in the wall, dwarf-scale, a hasp and a padlock.

"In Petersburg, when the apartments of the bourgeoisie were divided for the workers, sometimes a door was left. Was a time the wet nurse's room and the nursery. Now for three, four, five families. A door in an old wall. If you had such a door, into your neighbor's apartment, you kept it a secret. A bookcase in front of it. Yes. A way to get out. When they come for you. The kind of thing you look for in a new home. Amenities."

He taps the door with his forefinger.

"Someone bought this building for secret things. Police might take an interest. He looked for ways out. I came here. *I* looked for ways out. This door. So."

He lifts the hammer, smashes the lock, the hasp dangling, and tears it off with his thick-fingered hand. Standing back, looking at Skinner.

"This life. Long. And exciting. What is on the other side?"

He squats, gathers himself, puts his weathered body against the wood, and falls through into darkness as it flies open before him.

Jae unzips the long ballast pocket at the small of her back, takes out a Maglite LED flashlight, and hands it to Skinner. He twists it on, shines it through the door, down. Pinned in the beam on the floor, a two-meter drop, the Russian rising to his hands and knees, winded and wheezing, he looks up at them, a caul of thick cobweb covers his face, an aspect of something risen from dark places.

Shrill scream from below the trap. The Säpo have found Lili in the bathroom. Shrieking. A voice yelling commands in Swedish. Gunfire. Four or five pops, rapid but erratically spaced, a hole appears, punched through the ceiling from below, an arrow of light, and more smoke, and a half-dozen professionally distributed shots fired, much louder than the pops. NATO 5.56mm rounds, and no more screaming.

Skinner picks Jae up and swings her through the door, hands in her armpits, and drops her, then slides through headfirst, a slither of odd coordination, muscles she's not sure she has, hands catching his weight, elbows flexed, tuck and roll, with the pack still on. The Russian is up, jumps, slaps the bottom of the door, forcing it into place, and lands heavy, loud, even in his New Balance walking shoes. They squat, light from the Mag in Skinner's hand. Sound from the protesters' apartment limited to an occasional barked order, a small dog in the house next door. Three bleats, louder, the test button on a megaphone. Some kind of general readjustment, footfalls, en masse, and then quiet.

The Russian is peeling cobweb from his face, rubbing it from his hand onto the thick ribs of blue corduroy covering his thigh.

"Lili had a gun. Little crazy girl."

Jae looks up at the tiny door.

"The one crying in the bathroom?"

The Russian taps his chest.

"Great heart. Passion for the cause."

He taps the side of his head.

"Weak mind. A suicide bomb waiting for a detonator."

He makes a slight popping noise with his lips, shakes his head.

"Now what the fuck."

Skinner is shining the light, storage, detritus of years, file boxes, an old IBM copy machine, three broken rocking chairs, a pile of rugs, moth-eaten, material that will tear and crumble like wads of damp dead leaves.

Bleat of the megaphone. *Outside now?* Amplified Swedish. Orderly commands, firm and calm. Skinner looks at the Russian.

The Russian tilts his head, listens.

"I think something about coming out. Everyone they want out. I think."

Skinner shines the light around again.

"Door."

The Russian nods, starts shoving boxes aside, letting the upper tiers tumble where they will. Jae opens the Toughbook, a last check before they descend, and sees the image from the spider she left on the lamp in the alley. No longer an eye-level fixed view of Säpo officers cordoning off either end of the narrow lane, it's now a shot of an empty alley, a small tractor at the far end; an extendable arm folded in three sections on top, camera and another box at the end of the arm, silver, and painted in black along that folded arm, *iRobot*.

"Shitshit."

Skinner and the Russian look at the screen, look at her.

"Someone saw the spider. They think it's a bomb."

She taps the screen, the white tractor bot at the end of the alley.

"510 PackBot. They'll get a closer look with the camera. And a sniffer for explosive particulates. Operator must be around the corner."

She looks up at them.

"Evacuation."

The Russian wheezes his laugh.

"Everybody out."

Skinner is moving, shoving a way through the mess. The Russian joins him. They find a counterweighted trap with a swing-down ladder. The Russian looks at Skinner, and Skinner shrugs, uses his stick to push down on the trap, and watches it drop with a creaking of springs, ladder unfolding, ushering them downward. Russian first.

She follows, and finds an old woman standing at the end of the hallway, some kind of squat shotgun braced firmly at her hip in a practiced stance that implies it might not actually blow her off her tiny feet if she should be inspired to pull the trigger and release whatever is loaded inside the flared and gaping maw at the end of its single barrel.

Jae looks at the dragons engraved on the barrel of the weapon.

"Blunderbuss?"

"Dragon."

She doesn't look at the Russian, no idea what might set the old woman off, but clarifies nonetheless.

"The gun, not the decoration. Blunderbuss?"

Skinner behind her, feet on the bottom rungs of the ladder.

"It's called a dragon. Pistol version of a blunderbuss."

Jae feels something flutter inside herself, something giddy and eminently unstable. To find death in the personage of this woman, a gnarled piece of jerky with over eighty winters behind her, house slippers, sweatpants, and a red cardigan worn over a thick Irish cable sweater, one eye milky, the other blue and clear as the sky outside, brandishing a weapon once favored by pirate boarding parties in the time of tall ships.

The giddy thing breaks loose for a moment and a titter escapes her mouth. She covers it as if she burped in church.

"Will it fire?"

Skinner's speed, she thinks, as she watches him move suddenly past her, is a product of his decisiveness as much as his musculature. There is no hesitancy or waver in his steps or line of approach, propelled by his intention, the desire to be down the hallway and in front of the old woman makes it so, his will manifest as physical. She waits for a boom. *Blunderbuss.* Out of the Dutch. Factoids loose in her mind. Some other name before. Not currently at hand. But the translation. *Thunder pipe.*

She doesn't want to hear that particular thunder.

And she doesn't.

Skinner is there, one hand for the barrel of the museum piece, one, flat, at the end of a straight arm, propelling the old woman back, out of her braced stance, the gun staying with him as she stumbles several steps, emptyhanded.

Skinner with the gun.

"Yes. It will fire. If primed and cocked."

It's not. The hammer down on the striking plate. No flint.

The woman is talking Swedish, angry Swedish, rolling and guttural, jabbing her finger at the ceiling, at them, at the window. The Russian scratches his head through a too-small green wool watch cap that somehow finds a way to stay perched up there. Jae is starting to suspect Velcro.

"She wants to know. I think. Why we are in her attic. She is mad about that."

The woman takes a step toward Skinner.

"Mad! Yes mad!"

She points at the window, more jabbing and more Swedish.

The Russian uses his hammer to point in the same direction.

"The police want everyone in the street. But she will not go in the street. I think. I think she says, *Fuck the police.*"

She raises both hands, waves them up and down at the Russian. He shakes his head.

"No. No. She does not say, *Fuck the police.* She does not talk like that."

Skinner has his walking stick in one hand, blunderbuss in the other, looking positively ready to join an H. G. Wells expedition to forgotten lands at this very moment if the National Geographic Society should render an invitation.

"We want to evacuate her. We are here to see that everyone gets out of the building safely."

The Russian tucks a finger under his cap, pulls it forward a bit.

"She is not stupid."

Skinner doesn't say anything, and the Russian shrugs, takes his finger out from under his cap, stepping around Skinner toward the woman, picking his way through the Swedish language like a man in evening dress picking his way through a field of cow patties. Not the worst thing if he should misstep, but these are his best shoes, after all, and how did he get here in the first place?

The woman's arms cross over her slight chest, bird-boned in appearance but not likely to snap anytime soon. She listens to the Russian and then laughs in his face. A genuine laugh. Merry. He tries a few more words and she laughs harder.

He looks at Skinner and Jae.

"I told her. I think. That we are the police that she wants to fuck. In not so many words."

She stops laughing, shaking her head, a firm shake that will brook no disagreement. Then spills more Swedish, not as angry, but plenty of finger pointing, down the stairs.

The Russian nods, nods some more, smiles, wheezes his laugh, nods, scratches his head.

"She says something about the protests. She is watching on TV. She says young people should always say what they think. She says she hates Nazis, and Bilderberg was created by Nazis. She says we should leave her house and go be crazy somewhere else."

He shrugs.

"I think."

She nods, turns, and starts to march downstairs, stops, looks back at them, waving her arm, *now, now, not tomorrow, now.*

The Russian lifts the tail of his North Face parka, zipped since they first saw him, and slips the handle of his hammer through his belt, pulling the tail down over it, following the woman. Jae follows, pauses at the head of the stairs, catching Skinner studying the blunderbuss in his hands. With something like regret, he bends and sets it on the floor.

The house is clean, cluttered, cold, a TV in a first-floor bedroom is on, volume quite loud, SVT coverage of the protests. On the ground floor, a nice surprise. The old woman's house faces onto the next street over from Lilla Hoparegränd. Before she opens the door, Jae opens her Toughbook. The alley spider's camera window is filled with the camera lens mounted at the end of the PackBot's arm. Sniffing for explosives that are not there. She closes the computer and puts it in her pack, taking it from Skinner, onto her own back again. They swipe at their clothing, batting away dust and cobwebs, straightening. The old woman makes exasperated noises, watching the dust fall onto the wood floor of her vestibule, but waits until they are composed.

The door open, they walk out into the empty alley, Jae, confused for a moment, certain they have come back to Lilla Hoparegränd, but no, it is a sister street. A voice yells. Police officer at the end of the block, waving an arm at them, *this way, quickly now,* urging them to move, move move, which they do, smiling sheepishly, ushered to the other side of a sawhorse that is keeping the curious at bay while the bomb-sniffing robot does its work out of sight, intimately prodding Jae's own creation. And around a bend at the end of the alley to a highway along the waterfront: traffic. The bridges jammed with police on the other side of the island, everything backed up. People trying to turn around to take the other bridges to Södermalm, island-hop their way home. And just there, across the highway, a parking lot, for the ferry.

Twenty meters beyond the police line no one seems very much aware that there is a bomb squad at work across the highway; that a cell of protesters, possibly terrorists, has been the target of a coordinated police assault; that people have been shot. The scale of the protests has eluded most people. There is complaining, tedium, frustration. So they walk south, weaving in and out of foot traffic, a few hundred meters to the ferry, quite a bit less than that to the end of the line of passengers waiting to board. Not one line, several. There are at least half a dozen different ferries with landings here. They pick the one that seems to move fastest.

The Russian tugs his hat, adjusting its perch.

"A walk for me, I think."

Skinner picks a strand of cobwebs from his sleeve.

"Questions."

The Russian shakes his head, shrugs, *I am helpless at this sort of thing, but I will do my best.*

Skinner nods toward the mess behind them.

"You found them. Anarchist chatrooms. An old pro. Sympathetic to their cause. Yes?"

The Russian wobbles one of his hands.

"Forty years ago. Forty-five. I was trained. To do this. Be an anarchist. I was trained. These skills do not go away. The technology. Yes. Changes. But so many principles. And to bring down a government, it is much easier now."

Skinner taps the tip of his stick on the pavement.

"Trained anarchist. I see counterespionage school. Teenagers in red neckerchiefs."

The wheeze of the Russian's laugh.

"So much propaganda. No. See clubs, instead. After school. See sports. Electronics. Guns. Explosives. Girls. It was cool. To be recruited then, it was cool. No so much marching."

The post-Soviet Frankenstein monster is in Jae's head again. Part spy, part oligarch mobster. A mad scientist somewhere in the shadows. It would be funny if it wasn't her brain's way of trying to put something important together.

Skinner is tapping very rapidly now.

"And then."

The Russian clucks his tongue.

"And then the seventies. I was very popular. East bloc. I was recruited many times. So dissatisfied I was. Sullen. Military training. Valuable. Anti-Soviets loved me."

"Until they started being arrested."

The Russian holds up a finger.

"No. Very few arrests. You would be surprised. Mostly reports. Files. Mostly, one officer uses me to fuck with a rival. Then I go west."

Skinner stops tapping.

"On your own?"

The Russian wobbles his hand again.

"I am happy to go, but they are happy for me to go. Western European anarchists, communists. Blow this up. Rob this bank. Give us money. Hijack this plane. Mostly fuck and smoke marijuana and complain. Shoot bureaucrats in between fucking."

Skinner taps once, scratches the pavement with the brass cap at the tip of his stick.

"Long time ago."

The Russian nods.

"Who would think? Alive still. The devil loves me."

The Russian adjusts his cap, the tail of his parka, the collar. Preparations for leaving. Skinner raises a finger, *just one more thing*.

"The protesters, anarchists, *they* didn't find you."

The Russian is playing with the tab of his zipper, down one inch, back up.

"No. No. They found each other. Shiva found me. It was a referral from an old co-worker."

"Professional."

The Russian shrugs.

"A referral. A job. Logistics. Organization. No bombs. No guns."

"Shiva found you how?"

The Russian unzips his jacket, steps close to Skinner, holding it open, just a bit, on the left side.

"Hey. Something. Inside my jacket. For you."

Skinner doesn't move.

The Russian moves his hand just a little, widens the opening, dark inside his parka.

"For you. Take it. Not a mousetrap. Take it. You will be so happy."

The line shuffles, Skinner shuffles, stumbles, falls into the Russian, brings up his stick, clumsy, he brings it up across the Russian's throat, more clumsy, his hand whisks in and out of the older man's jacket, something in it. Balance regained, the stick withdrawn from the Russian's throat, Skinner's hand empty, something heavy in the side pocket of his jacket.

The Russian smiles, zipping his jacket.

"So happy."

He tugs his cap into place.

"He told me to give it to you. Shiva did."

The Russian's smile, ancient bones of whales, decades of the cigarettes that took his lung.

"*Give it to the killer who comes,* he said. And you came."

The Russian gone, into the tangled lines of people waiting to travel by water, the familiar land routes impassable in a city besieged by the young in revolt.

A crowded deck on the ferry. Neither of them talking. Skinner has his gun now. Jae doesn't need to peek in his pocket to know that's what the Russian had for him. Which Shiva, if the Russian is to be believed, told him to give Skinner.

"Your phone is ringing."

She looks at Skinner and he nods at the zippered vest pocket at her waist where she keeps her phone.

"Ringing."

She unzips and takes it out, looks at the screen, a blocked number. She answers anyway. More than slightly expecting to hear Terrence's voice speaking from the beyond.

"Hello."

"Yes, Jae, hello."

She looks at Skinner, mouths *Cross.* Skinner cups her elbow with his hand and does that thing he does in crowds, forcing a way through without seeming to displace anyone, leading her toward the rail. Fewer ears.

"Jae, are you there?"

She cups one hand over her left ear, reducing the wind noise.

"I'm here."

"Kiev."

She draws a blank.

"Yes?"

"Kiev, Jae. Anything in Kiev?"

Remembering where it is they are meant to be.

"Ukrainians."

A pause from Cross.

"Jae, is there some reason you can't talk?"

"No."

"Then, with respect to the fact that this is an open line, I'd like to know if you have anything in Kiev."

She leans over the rail, watches the water churn along the hull of the ferry.

"No. Nothing."

"Any details you can offer?"

"With respect to an open line, no."

Something scuffs the connection, a few muffled words, Cross covering his phone's pickup as he consults with someone, then back.

"Good. Nothing. Good. I want you out of Kiev. There are things happening in Stockholm. Have you seen the protests? Are they on TV there? We have an evolving situation, on the ground. A possible connection between the protests and your job. I want you to look at it in person."

Jae is looking at the water again.

"I know about the protests."

Another muffled word or two, and then the click of computer keys.

"One of the teams we had working on the worm, the code, they found a Stockholm connection. A physical address. Billing for hosting services. We had, with respect to an open line, we had intentions for the address, but Swedish security police are involved."

"Säpo."

The word out of her mouth before she can stop it.

A beat from Cross.

"Yes. Good, Jae, you must have already skimmed the edge of some information that will help you look into this more deeply. Säpo raid. Very recent. Active. Looking for a command cell, the protesters. Anarchists, Jae. Very promising for us."

Skinner has his back against the rail, looking at the people on deck, giving every impression that he's not the least bit concerned with her conversation. It's for the best that he has no way to listen in. If they were both hearing this Jae doubts she could make eye contact with Skinner without laughing.

"Sounds promising."

"Are the airports still open?"

Jae thinks about the time difference between Stockholm and Kiev, tries to remember how red-eye flights work going east to west. Then remembers that it doesn't fucking matter.

"Sure. We can get to Stockholm. Shouldn't take more than a few hours."

"Very good. The Swedish airports are still open. Arlanda. I don't think they'll close right away. The winds are blowing south."

"Okay. Like I said, a few hours."

More clicking from Cross's end.

"We have you booked on the next flight out of Boryspil. They go direct. Skinner?"

Jae looks at Skinner, there is still a bit of cobweb in his hair. She wants to reach up and pluck it out. But doesn't.

"You want to talk to him?"

"No."

Something in his voice, that one syllable. Unmistakable. Fear.

"I just want to know if he's working."

"That's an interesting way of putting it."

"So is he working?"

"It's fine, Cross."

And it is, she supposes. Skinner is working. But she is unwilling to discuss it with Cross.

"Good. Something has happened in the States. Nothing to be alarmed about. Tangential."

"Tangential to what?"

"To you. We approached Maker Smith, through his booking agent. Another set of eyes on the worm, the code. But he's gone to ground. Something happened at his place of business. There was, with respect to an open line, there was detritus. Three items of inert material. Material that belonged to Hann-Aoki."

Jae thinks about the dead men in Oasis Two. The corpse on fire.

"Detritus."

"With respect to an open line, yes."

Jae feels like the only fish in a very popular pond, hooks all around, twitching, baited lines. Just waiting for a nibble before being jerked taut, barbs in the mouth, pulled gasping into the air.

"But no Smith?"

"No sign. I got the impression from his agent that Smith is well but prefers to remain sequestered for the time being."

"He's a smart fucker."

"Yes."

Neither of them says anything.

Cross starts clicking again.

"So. Boryspil to Arlanda. Here soon."

"A few hours."

"A car will pick you up."

A word Cross has been using, adverb, occasional noun, finally sticks to something in Jae's brain and she stands up straight, away from the rail, drawing Skinner's eyes for the first time since the conversation began.

Here.

Here?

"Cross?"

"Yes?"

"Where are you?"

"Here. I mean, I'm sorry, Stockholm."

Jae looks around the deck of the ferry, her eyes searching for Cross, expecting him to be a few yards away, smiling at his own joke. *I'm right here. Got you!* But he's not.

"Just a coincidence. I'm here for Bilderberg. My third year. And I have to get back. It's not half as sinister as the protesters think it is, but probably more disturbing than they imagine. I'm meeting with someone from Gazprom, and a Chinese environmental minister to discuss overpopulation. We'll do a presentation. Climate decline, rogue weather events, contraction strategies. Reminds me of college. Speech and debate. Academic Olympics. Moot court. That kind of thing. Sudden exchanges of ideas, intensely brief relationships formed, and the general sense that maybe those limeys from Cambridge aren't such pricks after all. We'll come away with a ton of new connections for Kestrel. America, we still do a handful of things better than anyone else. You can buy African mercenaries by the kilo, but US-trained contractors will carry a premium as long as military spending continues to dominate the budget. Enough shop talk. We'll see you in a few hours. Things are moving very fast. There might be a bomb. European anarchists, Jae. If they're the ones, that would open an entirely new market for us."

Jae hangs up before he can say anything else.

Skinner leans on the rail, points. They're rounding a tiny island, a larger one coming into view, small enclosed harbor and another ferry landing.

"That's Djurgården. Parks. Museums. Back to the mainland next. Grand Hotel landing. Norrmalm."

Jae slips her phone back in its pocket.

"Cross is here. Stockholm. He's a Bilderberger. Doing presentations. Networking. Christ."

Skinner contemplates the deck.

"That seems reasonable."

She contemplates him.

"But you don't care for it."

He turns, leans his forearms on the rail, one hand slipping inside his jacket.

"An excess of coincidence. Or the appearance of such an excess. Serendipity. Synchronicity. No. I don't care for it."

His hand comes out holding the twisted steak knife from KGB and he drops it, lost in the water, broken tool.

"At Heathrow I saw Haven. He had someone with him. Someone dangerous, I assume."

Jae rubs her hands together. A chilly day becoming cold as the sun sinks, wind on the water.

"Not a coincidence?"

Skinner leans his walking stick against the rail.

"Not a coincidence."

Jae tucks her hands into her armpits.

"Something is happening. It's."

She closes her eyes.

"I have pieces. Lots of them. But not enough."

Skinner puts a hand in his jacket pocket.

"I think we need to find Terrence."

Jae licks her lips, the monster in her head bumps into something.

"Why?"

Skinner's hand is moving in his pocket, where he dropped the gun the Russian gave him.

"This. In my pocket. This is a .380 Bersa Concealed Carry pistol. If I take it out someone might see it, and there could be a small panic. So I need you to believe me."

Jae believes him. She is working to restrain her own small panic. Wondering if there is greater safety if she runs into the crowd or if she dives into the churning waters.

Skinner's hand moves again.

"There is no serial number on this pistol. Absolute identification would be very difficult. But there is a scuff on the grip."

He's not looking at her, his head dropped back, eyes skyward.

"It is, I think, a weapon of some personal significance to me. If I am correct, I was carrying this exact pistol when Cross tried to kill me."

He looks at her.

"And Terrence saved my life."

And, with that, the lumbering Frankenstein monster in her head smashes loose, leaving a gaping hole in the laboratory door. Following it into the daylight, emerges the mad scientist who made this thing. Distracted air of the dean of some obscure area of study, white lab coat stained with bloody handprints of all those upon whom he has performed his experiments. Terrence.

Her hand touches her cheek, crawls of its own accord over her mouth, a cartoon expression of dismay on her face.

"Oh shit. Skinner. Terrence connected those anarchist kids with the Russian. He. The Money. Fucking. That acceleration of the protests. He facilitated everything for them. He. Terrence is all over this. Oh shit."

He's looking at her, eyes carrying a spark of sunlight reflected from the waters. Hand inside the pocket that holds his meaningful gun.

I miss him.

"Skinner."

"Jae? Are you alright?"

"Skinner."

He looks at her.

She thinks about her mom.

"Terrence is dead."

He nods. His hand comes out of the pocket, empty, and he runs his fingers through his ruffled hair, looks out to the water, nods again, and looks at her.

"It's cold. You must be cold."

He takes his scarf from around his neck, places it around her neck, smooths it flat, flips the ends into a knot, eases it up under her chin, and there is no doubt at all in her mind that he wants to kiss her or that, if she were to lean just the slightest bit forward, it would happen. Nothing of her own doing, the kiss would just happen. She remembers what that was like, very young, the kiss is there, like the statue some sculptors say is already inside the uncarved block, waiting for you to chip away. Young, and finding the kiss that was always there waiting for you. Here it is, one of those.

His hands come away from the ends of the red scarf.

"Terrence is dead. Yes. I see that now."

Jae doesn't move. She doesn't lean, not one millimeter.

Skinner points at her backpack.

"Let me show you something."

They stand shoulder to shoulder on deck, backs to the rail, Skinner helping to support her laptop as she logs into the ferry's Wi-Fi network. Europe is well ahead of America when it comes to wireless. Brazenly excited about the idea of being able to access the Internet from everywhere. Neither of them is certain what payment will mean. How specifically their location might be tracked by a credit card transaction to join a wireless network on board a moving ferry. Skinner opts for using one of his regular cards, one of those he travels on, a well established identity. He tells Jae that he doesn't know if it's a bad thing for Cross to know where they are. For him to know they are lying to him. He may not care. As long as the job is done. Too much to juggle. Jae just uses the damn card.

classicsteelbikes.com.

Skinner's account. A question thread. Merckx frame geometries. Responses. A response from Terrence.

Skinner points at it, the date and time.

"When did he die?"

Jae has to think.

"I spoke to him the night before I met you at Creech. Cross and Haven told me at the hotel. Said he was killed. In Cologne."

"Yes. I was in Cologne. Well. This reply was posted after Cologne."

He looks at the reply from Terrence's account. Jae knows the numbers in it are the message or that they point to the message.

"Book code?"

Skinner is still looking at the words and numbers. As if the answer they suggest is to some question he hasn't asked. He makes a closing gesture with two fingers, snapping them down on an invisible bug that he finds irritating.

"Done."

She logs out, clears the session from history. They're already approaching the Norrmalm landing.

"Do you need to peek at your decoder ring?"

He scratches his right eyebrow.

"The numbers are coordinates. GPS."

Jae still has the laptop open, her hand moves back to the trackpad.

"Map them?"

He takes the computer from her hands, closes it, and slips the machine inside her pack, zip.

"I know where it is."

She takes the pack from him, shoulders it.

"Where?"

Skinner takes his stick from where it leans against the rail, thinks, and puts it back.

"Paris. The cimetière Montmartre."

The ferry has docked, gangway down, people are streaming off. Most of the passengers are commuters forced to improvise in the face of the day's challenges.

Jae tucks her thumbs under her pack straps.

"Why there?"

Skinner flips up the collar of his jacket, shrugs, dips his forehead toward the gangway, and they start to walk.

"It's where they tried to kill me."

She thinks about sleep, how much she'd like some.

"So Paris."

He's looking ahead, down the gangway, the flow of people.

"I think so."

Her head is humming, bubbling really. Terrence. Trails of crumbs. She's been thinking configurations, webs of causality. The treasure map. X marks the spot.

Fuck sleep.

"Paris. Yes. And to hell with Cross. We already know what's in Stockholm."

Down the gangway, Skinner's eyes still on the crowd.

"Yes, we do."

Onto steady ground, more cobbles, that crisp sun unwilling to drop the final few degrees from the sky. Energy in the press of bodies around them. Eventful day, people want to talk about it. *Have you heard? What happened? How far away? Share a taxi? Let's get drinks and wait it out.* She doesn't understand anything other than a few bursts of English, but she can translate the mood. The excitement of living through interesting times. And coming clear of the crowd, terra-cotta face of the Grand Hotel beside them, green copper roof, another of Stockholm's many park squares just ahead, she touches the soft red scarf knotted at her throat, how deftly he tied it, she stops in her tracks, turns toward him, a handful of his sleeve, and leans her body into his, pulling down on his arm until she finds the kiss right where it has been waiting for her, yes, shaped just so, everything else cleared away, just the kiss.

Skinner takes his lips from hers, one hand is in the small of her back, the other is in his pocket, she knows because her hand is in there with it, holding the Russian's gun.

He leans his forehead against hers.

"The man that was with Haven at Heathrow. He was on the ferry, following us."

He kisses her, another good one.

It might be ten seconds later that Jae starts to realize how many times she's heard the word *volcano* spoken since they first stood in line for the ferry, throughout their ride, and after they disembarked. And another word, more often, Swedish, *vulkan.* No translation necessary. Even now, still kissing, she hears it again, *vulkan*. A trending topic of general conversation. And her brain finally connects it with Cross asking if the airport was still open in Kiev, *The winds are blowing south*, and with the CNN helicopter shot that she'd thought was of the protest outside the Riksdag, that plume of smoke.

Volcano.

Iceland boiling over again. She wonders how much time they have before its particulates fill the air, grounding everything. Can they get a flight to Paris? Is it too late? She needs to stop kissing Skinner. That's very important. But she doesn't. Hand on his hand, holding the gun, traffic dividing around them, mad little city of islands, volcano erupting.

Vulkan.

She kisses him, fearless.

PART FOUR

diagram

RAJ'S FATHER WANTS him to learn how to shoot the gun.

It came from one of the water goons that the Naxalites killed last night. They killed four of them. The rest have done as he said and stopped charging people for water. The taps are open now. Everyone thought guards would be posted, Sudhir's men, but there are no guards. At most taps an old woman sits, telling off anyone who tries to take more than five liters at once. Five liters and then to the back of the line. There has been cheating in the hours since the taps were opened, graft from some of the old women, but still, the water goons are gone. Four are dead. And Raj's father has the pistol that one of them kept tucked inside his shirt.

"With no bullets."

His father holds the OFB .32 automatic on the spread palms of both hands. It is an ugly gun. Stubby, pinched at the end of the barrel. Not at all like the ones from TV and the movies. Maybe from an old movie. Black and white, that old. Guns in new movies, even in Bollywood, look like they are computerized, with many moving parts. They look like pieces of Japanese robots. This gun in his father's hand looks pitiful. Still, he wants Raj to learn how to shoot it.

Cool.

"Watch."

His father's hands turn the gun, pistol, this is a pistol, his thumb finds a catch, presses it, and the clip drops a few millimeters from the handle with a slight click. It is the first sound the gun has made. Raj expected it to make constant noise, as if it were filled with latches and bits of machinery. The sounds of guns in movies. But this gun is solid. Just the one little click of the magazine coming loose. His father pulls it free, slight effort.

He hands it to Raj.

"How many bullets?"

Raj looks at the slot that runs down the side of the clip, counts bullets.

"Seven."

His father points the pistol at the floor, pulls back the slide, revealing an eighth bullet in the chamber. It pops out and lands on the floor of the shanty and Raj chases it, getting down on his knees to scoop it from under the cot and bringing it back to the table.

His father releases the slide and it snaps into place with one of those movie noises Raj has been waiting for, though not nearly as loud.

"Cocked."

He turns the gun over, presses a tiny stud behind the trigger.

"Safety off."

He stands, extends his arm, body at an angle to the direction the pistol is pointing, aims, and pulls the trigger.

Click.

"The expanding gases released by the explosion in the chamber force the slide back, allowing the empty shell to eject, cocking the hammer, and the return spring brings the slide forward, scooping the next round from the clip and into the chamber, and ready to fire again."

He lowers his arm and places the gun on the table.

"An efficient machine."

He looks at Raj.

"Show me."

Raj puts the clip next to the single bullet on the table and picks up the pistol. The grips are made of plastic. Cheap. They might well have been manufactured from plastics recycled here in the slum. The word Ashani is stamped into the plastic. He turns the gun over. Small in his father's hands, it feels big in his own, heavier than he'd thought it would be. The safety is still off. He pinches the slide between his thumb and forefinger, starts to pull it back, but it slips loose, snaps forward; the spring is very strong.

He looks at his father, waits for the lesson. There is always a lesson. You try to do things by yourself, always, and whether you do it correctly or incorrectly there is also always a lesson to be learned. In the universe of his father you can never stop learning.

"Try it like this."

His father takes the pistol from him, places his left hand on top of the slide, heel on the forward sight, thumb and three fingers on the grooved surface of the slide, pushing it back instead of pulling. He shows it to Raj, waits until the boy nods, then points the pistol at the floor, thumb on the hammer, pulls the trigger and lowers the hammer gently.

"Try it that way, your hand covers the slide, more friction, more energy from your muscles going directly into the action."

The lesson.

He hands the gun to Raj.

"Mind the barrel."

Raj doesn't understand until he places his left hand on top of the pistol, then realizes that as he pushes, it wants to turn, aim at his belly. He stops, looks at his father, and his father nods. No need to explain this lesson. Raj points the gun at the floor, hand atop the slide, pushes it back, still harder than seems possible, hears the click of the hammer locking into place, and releases the slide, shocked at the force with which it snaps back down the length of the barrel, dragging the gun forward, almost out of his hand.

His father moves behind him, places his hands on his shoulders, steering him, until Raj stands with his feet planted at the same angle he'd adopted. Body turned away from the target of a calendar on the wall, English garden flowers. His mother likes them. Now, arm up, straight from shoulder, sighting with his right eye through the V of the rear sight, the blade at the end of the barrel caught in the middle of that angle, the heart of a purple flower waiting. He pulls the trigger.

Click.

He looks at his father, receives the nod that means this lesson is well begun. There will be practice. Nothing is perfected, his father says.

Nothing, ever. Only in science is perfection. And even then, well, his father has doubts.

He takes the gun from Raj, puts it on the table, sits. He works always since the truck came. He closes his eyes sometimes, but they open shortly after. Not even a nap. Food when it is put in front of him. There is no one else to do what he does. There are machinists and welders, mechanics, men who know how to smelt iron, men with acid burns up and down their arms who can strip corrosion, peel old chrome, burnish copper. And there are potters, Dharavi is thick with potters. The primary and historical industry of the slum. There are the Naxalites for security. There are the ship breakers, with their secret language, tireless. But no other electrical engineer. No other man with his father's knowledge. No man of his father's education chooses to live in Dharavi. For it must be a choice. In ever growing, ever modernizing Bombay, aspiring always to be *worl -class,* they must import electrical engineers to fill the need. But, still, *they* live here. Why has he been raised in a slum? Why must his mother live here? His sister? They could be living across the river, Bandra East. In an apartment. It must make sense, he knows. His father's work is here. But often it feels like his father cares only for himself and his work and not for his family at all.

His father taps a second chair.

"I have to go back."

He looks at his watch.

"Now."

But he doesn't move, waiting until Raj also sits. On the table are the remains of their lunch. A few grains of rice, samosa crumbs, empty glasses with chai dregs. Raj's mother left it for them, refusing, and not weakening her resolve, to bring food to #1 Shed. Food at home, now, *go eat it.* She herself at work with two of Sudhir's men, showing them where the border has been drawn. A place, shanties, the corridors between them, the open drains, which shops are inside the border, which ones not. They have seen the lines on maps, but Sudhir said they needed to go along the border, know where they will patrol. Soon they will live along that line, spread too thin. Three more policemen have been killed. Two of them worked for the water goons. The other refused the bribe offered him to look another way, insisted he should have more. Word is leaving the slum. Something is happening here. There are guns here.

There will be more police.

Raj's father licks the tip of his finger and presses it down on a grain of rice, brings it to his lips, and chews it delicately between his front teeth, swallows.

"Some people say we should wait for the redevelopment. *This is foolish, to do this with the DRP coming. We will all have housing. Very modern. There will be tourists. Why this? Madness.*"

Raj knows about these people. David's father believes in the Dharavi Redevelopment Project. He has a brochure pinned to the wall in their shanty. Glossy computer renderings of what the slum will look like after redevelopment. An architect, Mukesh Mehta, his renderings. His plan. But after over a decade of plans for the DRP, even David's father is ready for something else. Others say this new DRP plan *will* happen. Because Bombay is booming, and the land is too valuable for slummies to keep. Each resident with a voter card and an established legal residence that predates January 1, 2000, will get a new tenement. Twenty-one square meters. Water, electricity. Very modern. Why not wait? Stay in the transit tenements that will be provided while all this shit is torn down and new and modern housing is built. Slummies on the ground floor, wealthy on top of them, top-story apartments, views and luxury. Why not?

Raj doesn't say anything. His father isn't asking a question, he's explaining something. Something he thinks Raj needs to understand. Lesson.

His father touches the gun next to his plate, fingertip on the plastic grip, tracing the letters. Ashani.

"Your mother believes that it is simple. The DRP is all thieves. Some with hearts of gold, but thieves. Believing that they will make life better for the slummies, clean water, electricity, dignity, all these things. Believing they will bring these things to the slum cleans their conscience for anything else that happens. There will be injustices, they know, people will lose homes, livelihoods, and never reclaim them. They know.

Realists, these people. But to be modern is its own end. Yes. To improve. And to make money. For everyone, money. So out of one million slummies some tens of thousands will not have a home, others will lose their businesses. But there will be progress. So this is the price to pay. They are thieves, but they believe they are in the right. This is what your mother believes."

Raj knows very well what his mother believes. She mutters it all the day long. Her beliefs are a chant that pours out of her mouth every minute of every day. She believes that everything must be the cleanest possible. She believes that the bus you need is never the one coming next until you have given up and decided to walk five kilometers. She believes that Raj should spend less time watching soccer games at the cafés on the 90 Feet Road and more time studying the books she rides the bus to the library to get for him. She believes that her husband is more than slightly crazy. She believes that not getting enough sleep is worse than not having enough to eat. She believes that they will never get enough sleep. She believes that life is the most difficult thing. She believes that life should be a little easier and she is often very mad because it is not. She believes that she must live at least until she sees both of her children married and with children of their own. She believes that the world must be a better place for her daughter to grow into a woman than it was for her. She believes that as if she has no choice in the matter.

Yes, Raj nods, he knows what his mother believes.

His father also nods.

"I would like a modern home. We have water, electricity, a stove. Our home is well built. Our neighbors are not too loud. But I would like a modern home. Yes. Bombay will be a modern city. *World class.* But what that means, Rajiv, *world class,* is something we do not yet know. Do you know that most people in the world live in cities? Yes. It happened in two-thousand-eight. More than half the world lives in cities now. And most of those people live in slums. *World class* city. Why do we not get to decide what that is? This land was mangrove swamp. It was filled in by slummies, built by slummies, made prosperous by slummies, and now that it is worth something to the rich neighbors, they will decide how it should look. And who will own it."

He waves a hand at the door.

"This is what I hear in the street. Why so many are helping us. What they believe. This is their home and they want it this way, as it is. They will decide how modern. How *world class*. Is *world class* New York? London? Paris? Places where greatness is an old thing that is passing. Or is it Baghdad? Tripoli? Kabul? Places where no one knows what will come next."

He looks at his watch again, rubs its face with his thumb.

"What I believe. Rajiv. What I believe."

He rubs his own face, knuckles his eyes, looks at his son.

"The world does not want us. The earth. It does not want us. Too many. We are too many. And men, women, they do not need to be thieves or murderers. When the earth turns against them, they need only to care for themselves more than others, and that is enough to let the others die. And all men, all women, Rajiv, care more for themselves than for others. The few who are different, they are not enough to change anything."

He picks up the box clip and the loose bullet and hands them to his son.

"Show me."

Raj takes them, looks at the shape of the bullet and the shape of the opening at the top of the clip, how the top bullet is pressing itself upward to be released. He holds the clip in his left hand, pushes the loose bullet into the top slot, forces that top bullet down. It takes a great deal of pressure, and the two curved surfaces of the casings want to slip off one another, but he gets it in, seats the round in the clip.

Click.

His father hands him the .32. Raj looks at the underside, the hole in the pistol's butt, turns the clip so that the bullets point in the same direction as the barrel, fits it in, pushes, again it is harder than it looks in the movies where clips jump into guns by themselves, but he sets it with extra force from the heel of his hand.

Click.

His father nods, takes the gun, pushes the safety button, and holds it.

"They will let us die. Simply by looking to their own needs. They will contract into a ball and refuse to look out and they will leave us to die. Unless we take care of those needs ourselves. Force our place. Make room. We will not die for others to live. We were not born for that. But it is what they are counting on, Raj. Our willingness to quietly die."

He taps the barrel of the gun on the table, once, twice, thrice.

"I have seen their plan."

He rises, gun in hand.

"And it is not for me and my family, their future."

He offers his son the gun.

"So we will make another."

Raj looks at the gun.

His father pushes it at him.

"Take it, take it. Go to Sudhir. He will show you what comes next. I will not have the time, Raj. This little gun. You need to know how it works. That is the world now."

He looks angry. Tired and angry, his father.

Raj takes the gun.

His father covers his face, there may be tears behind his hands, Raj is not sure.

"Children with guns. That is the world now. What we made for you."

He lowers his hands.

"And now I must go and work on our big weapon. To get their attention we must be loud. We want maximum attention. *See what we can do. We do not need you. See.*"

His voice is raised, something rare. His father raises his voice for cricket matches, to tell a joke in a loud room, to call his son home. This angry loud voice, these tears, Raj has never seen them.

He looks at the gun in his hand, sets it on the table.

"I don't want a gun."

"Then I will carry it."

They both look. Raj's father, yelling, he has been so loud that they did not hear the door open. And now here is Raj's mother. Taji in her arms, picked up from David's shanty, where his big sister has been watching several of the neighborhood babies, the mothers working at #1 and #2 Sheds. Modernity, the women working. And here is his mother, coming inside, picking up the gun.

"I will carry it."

Raj's father has four fingers pressed to his cheek, as if propping up his own tired flesh.

"Damini."

But her name is the only word he can muster for whatever argument he may have wanted to mount against this new abomination. His wife with a gun in her hand. She steps near to him, presses Taj against him and lets her go. His hands come up and take her without thought, his baby daughter. He puts his face against the top of her head, thin black hair, closes his eyes.

Raj's mother looks at her son.

"Go to the shed and tell them your father is coming soon. Go, go. He needs a little rest but will be there soon."

Raj nods, goes to the door, stops to watch his father holding his baby sister, and his mother starting to clean up the plates and glasses from lunch, one-handed, the gun in her free hand, where she usually carries her child.

Outside it wants to rain. Sky bulging down over everyone's heads. A desire to stoop. There is activity everywhere. Well, every day in Dharavi is like this, full of activity, energy, the frantic scramble to survive, improve, climb. But it is different. Some people are packing their things to leave. Others are closing up the many openings in their homes, cardboard and corrugated steel over windows, tin, plastic bags. Some of the shop men, the welders and carpenters and lathe operators from the industrial sectors at the southern tip of the slum, are working on the wire, stringing it as high as they can on the walls, running it through shrouds of cut-up bicycle tires, taking it to everyone. Electricity humming.

The tires remind him that he needs to check the computer. Classicsteelbikes.com. The message he left. There has been no reply. Not yet. His father wants him to look at other things now. News sites. Indiatimes.com. Aljazeera.net. CNN. Mumbaibrunch blog. Twitter streams for President Patil, her brief messages always focused on the economy. The GOC in Chief for the Southern Command. Bombay commissioner of police. Some others. Tedious. Raj does as he's been asked, but he also looks at what Salman Khan has to say to his fans, and also Kareena Kapoor, and Kalki, whom he is a little in love with.

So he hurries to #1 Shed. It was once home to many tiny factories. Plastic recycler, potters, readymade rain ponchos, hairpins, glass tinting. Others. All shut down and moved out, making room for the truck trailer and its contents. And more, much more. There has been another truck, down the 90 Feet Road. Contents offloaded to smaller trucks, rickshaws, human backs. Crates, nothing but crates. All of them heavy. The contents. Old. So much work just to make these things work. Can it be done? Yes, his father says, yes. But in time? His father shakes his head when asked.

Raj does not believe his father.

He does not believe what his father says about people. *Only for themselves.* He does not believe that his father thinks this way. Because *he* cares for other people. He is working for the whole slum. *This* is why they are there. Living in the slum. Yes, Raj sometimes thinks his father is selfish, but he *knows* it is not true. It is just that he thinks of so many people other than his family. Planning for them.

How long?

Raj knows that his grandparents struggled to push his father from the slum and into an education. But for how long did Raj's father know he would never leave? For how long did he have this plan? Their own plan, Raj's paternal grandparents' plan for his father, began before he was born. When Grandfather made daily sojourns to the suburb of Anushakti Nagar, township home of the Bhabha Atomic Research Center. Twelve kilometers, hazards of highway traffic that must be crossed on foot while pushing his rusty Hero Roadster bike on its much-patched tires. And then, in the suburbs, the hazards of private security and police, recognizing a Dalit from the slums when they saw one and eager to send him back where he came from. A journey that ended in the dormitory kitchens that served the Atomic Energy Junior College, working in the place of his cousin Harish, whose intestine was occupied by a pork tapeworm that was revealed to be nearly four meters in length when it was finally purged. A detail in the family mythology that was always related by Grandmother with a grimace of disgusted relish. Once fit to return to work, cousin Harish kept his promise to do everything in his power to get Grandfather a job at the college or anywhere else within the Department of Atomic Energy facilities that dominated all of Anushakti Nagar. A plan that could only be faulted in that Harish, scullery boy, had no power whatsoever.

In the kitchen a blind eye had been turned to the sudden physical transformation of Harish from a skinny boy of fifteen into a stocky man of nearly twenty. These things happened. India, country of miracles. No less miraculous, when Harish transformed back into himself after several months. All that had been required for this transformation to be universally accepted was a large tithe on Harish's small wages. With the much-depleted net amount delivered dutifully by Grandfather into the hands of his aunt, Harish's mother, with none of it sticking to his own. The promise of future employment had been the only profit of his labor. A promise that could not be kept. But his hard work did not go unnoticed by the man who oversaw the kitchens and catering facilities on the DAE campus. Nor did he fail to notice Grandfather's willingness to part with a large measure of his earnings without raising a stink like so many of the filthy kitchen wallahs.

And so Grandfather and Grandmother's plan for their yet to be conceived children was advanced by Grandfather's purchase of a job cleaning the toilets in the Nilgiri Canteen on the DAE campus, bought for the price of half of all his future earnings. A price they reckoned a bargain as it included the guaranteed acceptance to the Atomic Energy Central School that was granted to the children of all DAE employees. Toilet wallahs included. And even though only one of their four children lived long enough to enjoy that privilege, Grandfather and Grandmother never voiced any regret at the years of indentured servitude that followed. When Grandfather's pay effectively doubled after the facilities manager died in the twentieth year of this arrangement, they spent a portion of the windfall on temple gifts for the man's remembrance. The rest they put in a hole in the floor of their shanty to save for their son. However, the newly inflated paychecks lasted only a few months, as Grandfather finally paid for two decades of close calls crossing the Eastern Express Highway with his Hero bicycle, when he was run over by a flatbed Tata painted in vibrant orange, blue, yellow, and red, hauling a tarp-covered load of fertilizer. Part of the cost of the job, his life. He'd never been willing to spare the price of a bus ticket for his daily commute. Tickets for his son when he began school, yes, but not for himself. Details that Grandmother considered essential to communicating the scope of God's sense of humor in these things. A man's working life spent cleaning toilets, ended by a truck loaded with shit. The reward, an educated son, electrical engineer, degree from University of Bombay, Veermata Jijabai Technological Institute. A degree her son then refused to put to work. Refused to take into the world to find a job suitable to such a well-educated young man. Refused to leave the slum at all. Married a local girl from around the corner. A dark girl! Began birthing a new generation of slummies almost instantly. And though she died in her sleep, a ripe fifty-five, one son, one grandson, cause of death, heart failure, she felt very much as if she, too, had been flattened by a truck loaded with shit. This one driven by her inexplicably ungrateful son, who had always been the light of her eye and a perfect model of obedience and effort until his great betrayal of her and of his father's memory.

Thinking of this story that Grandmother had told him, not infrequently, before her death, Raj wonders again, *How long?* How long had his father planned to keep his knowledge in the slum? To live here doing small jobs, rewiring the tiny factories for greater efficiency, bringing the current from the lines that crazed through the slum into the shanties of his neighbors, cutting deals with the electricity goons to make the haphazard exposed wiring harnesses they ran from their generators and power line taps marginally safer. He was on constant call to the goons, servicing the generators, bringing them back online when there was an outage, rerouting their taps when the Maharashtra State Electricity Board linemen found and disconnected them. Receiving, in exchange, some cooperation and extra hands as he made their infrastructure more robust and less likely to short-circuit and start fires, or fry anyone who might brush an exposed wire with his fingertip. His father, the electrician of Dharavi, handyman, appreciated for his skills and generosity by almost all, respected by those who did not account him a fool. Fool or sage, he was known throughout the slum, could talk to anyone, and he did talk. For years, his mantra of change and independence. Power was what was needed. Nothing more.

Was he planning all that time? Did he already know Sudhir? Did it begin in school when he first had access to the Internet? Slow to come to India, wholly adopted, like all modern things, once it arrived. Did he find Sudhir himself? The ship breakers? Did he begin this plan? Or did the plan find him?

Or was there no plan?

Just his father's love of the slum and desire to make it better. Safer. And the rest happening as life happens. A truck loaded with shit.

Raj is hurrying to the shed through his neighborhood, changing so fast in these few days. Populations shifting, the wires spreading. The electricity goons his father has been slowly educating over the years, slipping it into their ears like gentle poison, the safe essentials of their racket, are doing much of that work now. Plan or happenstance? And this neighborhood of his, Dharavi Nagar, a little more than six hectares of squalor and enterprise and shoddy construction and disease and color and filth and children playing in the streets and dirty water and bare feet and the stink that never goes away, Sector Six in the Redevelopment Project, home to more than two hundred thousand people. Is it plan or chance that it is just north of Sector Five, where the developers who bought the first DRP contracts have already begun to clear shanties in preparation for building the first phase?

Close to #1 Shed now, jungle men in their harnesses of weapons. More of them. Women, too. Tamil spoken with rural accents. Well schooled in walking silently, creeping around corners, sitting still in muddy ditches, waiting for days without food, sleeping on rocks, schooled also in guns and explosives. Here to bring their jungle fight to the city. The slum. They know Raj, a small shrug of acknowledgment, hands never leaving weapons. Mostly AK-47s. Jungle gun. Raj has seen them so many times in movies. Usually the gun the badguys are using.

More guards outside the shed. One of them smiles.

"Rajiv. Little engineer."

He lays out his palm and Raj slaps it, following with a fist bump.

The guard bangs on the shed door.

"Rain. We're all gonna get wet."

Raj looks up at the low sky.

"Not yet."

The guard looks up, nods.

"Not yet. But soon, little engineer. Very wet, very soon."

The door swings open, unlocked and pushed outward by one of the guards inside. Activity within, under the bright fluorescents his father installed after they covered the skylights with boards and tarps just before the truck arrived. The diesel tractor is gone, being put to other uses, but the container that was hauled by hand and rope through the rain and mud is still here, though cut down. That had been the only way to get access to the load. They didn't have the equipment or manpower to take it off the truck. It rests on now on railroad ties, waiting to be more firmly seated before it can be fired.

Soon.

It will happen soon.

Like the rain.

So much happening at once. The new machinery, rusty, seized up, liters of solvent and grease and oil are being applied. Coils of wire, great pythons of it, are being woven by hand from the cables that the electricity goons have been cutting down on nighttime raids in the suburbs. Gun classes, larger versions of the tutorial his father gave him at home. There, far end of the shed, jungle fighters, and slummies who have, almost to a man, never held a gun. David's father is there. His faith in the DRP is great, his faith in Raj's father is greater. His best friend from childhood, his educated friend who could have gone on to *such very big things* but stayed in his shanty down the street instead. How not to follow him where he is leading?

Raj goes to his seat at the new media workstation. His friends are here, too. Working. The kids all have jobs now. Tea wallah, lunch wallah, computer wallah, phone wallah, wire wallah, IT wallah, charger wallah. So much work. Under the table, where his toes can find it and roll it foot to foot, the soccer ball. He opens the laptop. He has a user account now, a password. He logs in. Last session still active. Twitter feeds. News. Classicsteelbikes.com. Still no reply to his reply. Has it been read by someone? By whoever is meant to read it? He has another message ready. Memorized, taught to him by his father who told him that he must post it the moment he sees the reply. No asking, just post it and tell him after. Speed is important in all things now. This rush of events and change. The modern racing by. *World class* is not slow. Fast. A race to be there before anyone else. What will it look like when it is reached?

This thing they are building, this fight they are starting.

Raj opens a small window, Twitter, Kalki Koechlin, it makes him wish he knew how to read French. She mostly tweets in English, but sometimes in French. Those ones look more personal. He's never tweeted anything directly to her. Or anyone else. He doesn't have an account. He'd never seen Twitter for himself until the last twenty-four hours. It's like listening to one side of a hundred different conversations being conducted with one person. He tries not to get too distracted by it, but it sounds like another world, and he wants to know what's happening inside of it. How different will it be? Sudhir says they might change everything. That nothing can be the same after they begin. The world will change, is changing. He says that they are a sign of the change. Too late to hold it back. But what will the world be like? Will the world become so different that there are no more movie stars? Raj tries to imagine that, but it doesn't seem possible, so he does an image search and looks at pictures of Kalki instead.

Rain starts to fall, hitting the tarps overhead like little bombs. When the deluge comes they have to raise their voices to be heard inside the shed, becoming louder and louder, until they are all yelling. Urgent to be heard and understood.

lonely house

NIGHT TRAIN TO Copenhagen.

First stop at the Hellsten. Jae repacks her essentials in her backpack, making room for Skinner's laptop and the two phones they took from the man outside the Scandic hotel. Skinner transfers his own necessaries into the pockets of his suit and trench coat. Chargers, pen, notebook, sunglasses, passport, an alternative set of ID, cash, phone. Slipping into the bathroom, he takes the Bersa from his pocket and looks at it for the first time since he used it to kill Lentz seven years ago. He fingers the scuffs along the barrel and the polymer grips on the left side, remembers skimming the pistol over the stone flags into the mouth of the mausoleum. Terrence's gift to him, delivered by the old man from the tomb of Lazarous.

Cross told Jae that Terrence was dead. Skinner tries to think of reasons why he would lie about such a thing. But Skinner cannot imagine Cross risking such a lie. Terrence is dead. Killed in Cologne soon after he talked to Skinner. Soon after he brought Skinner to the surface, when they were done with him at last.

He washes his face. Drying, his fingers graze his lips. The kiss. She kissed him. Dumbfounding, this world.

Checking out, a request that their luggage be stored until they can send for it. Room charged to Skinner's travel ID, nothing left to hide from anyone here. Oh, and would they happen to have a ruler he could borrow? *Yes,* a red one, translucent plastic. Skinner slips the ruler into a jacket pocket and walks out with it. A straightedge can be such a useful thing.

Stockholm Central Station, bedlam contained, society not yet crumbling, but there are runs on bottled water, snack foods, and celebrity gossip magazines. Mostly it's a matter of waiting in lines.

At the ticket counter. Swedish is not one of Skinner's languages, but English is spoken here. A stressed and tired man in his forties, loyal employee of SJ, doing his best, haggard. Skinner uses manners, impeccable, please and thank you, patient acknowledgment of these impossible circumstances, and can we possibly get to Paris? *No. Impossible.* Unfortunate. Disappointing. The people at the head of the line behind them creep closer, is it their turn yet? Urgency. So, no Paris. How close, then? *Copenhagen.* Twelve hundred kilometers short of their destination, but a volcano is erupting. Adaptation. Two for Copenhagen. There are no tickets on the night train, one assumes? One is wrong in this case. But only private compartments remain; more economical seats and berths have been taken. If the expense must be borne, it must be borne. *A private sleeping compartment?* Yes, thank you. SEK 3,200. Cash is accepted? Yes, it is. Better and better. Train departing at 2214, transfer in Lund at 0612, arrival in Copenhagen at 0728.

Your tickets, sir.

Another line for the shops. Batteries for Jae, AA, AAA, and a new pack of travel adapters. For Skinner, D batteries and a pair of long compression socks meant to reduce the probability of blood clots when seated for long periods of time. Water, bags of nuts, dried fruit, sandwiches in plastic triangles.

Cold on the platform, lines of track stretching north and south out of the yards behind the station. Shifting herds on the platform. *Do we wait here or there? Is this a ticket for a reserved seat? Dining car? I can't remember the last time I took a train.* Skinner keeps Jae away from the edge of the platform. A reserved compartment, they have no need to jockey for position. Just stand together in the cold and wait. And a realization for Skinner, she still has his scarf, inside her mountaineering jacket, red wool at her neck. Some meaning there related to the kiss, but in a code he cannot unscramble. A tether is what it feels like, his scarf around her neck, preventing either of them from falling off the mountain alone.

The train, somehow, is on time.

Night train to Copenhagen.

In their compartment Jae is immediately plugged, charging, and online. Her Toughbook and Skinner's laptop open on the surface of the tiny flip-up table at the window, her phone between them, all plugged into the socket below the table, a small bristle of adapters. The two stolen phones are dying, cableless, she ekes from them their last tendrils of connectivity to keep as many channels of information flowing as possible.

Left to his own devices, Skinner turns inward. Stretched on the lower of two bunks, he leaves the train, races ahead of it to the cemetery at Montmartre. From above, he studies the ground where he was meant to be killed years before. The design Terrence created to keep him alive. Haven should have been there. Any serious attempt on his life should have begun and ended with Haven. But only three people would truly have understood that. Terrence, Skinner, and Haven himself. Did Haven know about the attempt? Did he try to force his own involvement and find himself rebuffed? Or did he, seeing what Terrence was about, make no effort to convince Cross that the attempt would almost certainly fail? Haven was capable, quite literally, of anything.

Jae is looking at him.

Skinner sits up.

"Yes?"

She points at her laptop.

"It's on the blogs."

Skinner shakes his head.

"Blogs?"

She angles a screen in his direction, a Tumblr blog, some abstract graphics running up and down the borders, red and green lines twisting at right angles, vaguely techno, a thick column of white text on a black background in the middle. Jae scrolls up a bit.

"West-Tebrum. The attack. It started in the comments section.

Someone asking if anyone else had heard about an attack on the grid. Gets mostly pooh-poohed. But someone picks it up, says they heard about it, too. Connects it to the generator that blew at West-Tebrum. Implications of secret knowledge. *This guy I know in the "community."* So now someone does an actual post, either aggregating a bunch of comments from various other blogs or after doing some kind of half-assed research. Written up kind of like blind-item gossip. *People in the know are asking what caused that blackout in the Philadelphia suburbs.* Builds a hypothetical scenario that's not too far from the truth. It's spreading."

Skinner's eyes skim the blog entry.

"Mainstream?"

She shakes her head.

"Not yet. But between Kestrel and the other contractors and the military and intel agencies, there are a fuckload of people trying to track ReStuxnet. Hackers can be a gabby lot. Frankly, I'm surprised the lid has stayed on this long. Figure the big security blogs, Danger Room and company, they'll already have picked up at least this much and be beating the bushes for more. After that, it hits the tech blogs on mainstream news sites. Questions start coming from the *New York Times,* CNN, *Guardian,* AP. Then Homeland will have to have some kind of response, even if it's *no comment.* Once that response is in, it goes front-page. Twenty-four hours from now. Less, maybe. Probably. Soon it will break that the generator failed and people died in the blackout because of a computer worm that killed a lube oil motor. At that point the story goes from *Cyber Security Breach at Power Plant* to *Deadly Terrorist Attack on US Soil.*"

She picks up the two stolen phones.

"These are dead."

Skinner nods, rises, takes them from her. The window will only open two inches, but that's more than enough to slip the two phones out.

He closes the window.

"Did Terrence do it?"

"Run the West-Tebrum attack?"

Skinner nods.

Jae looks at the screens of the two open laptops. The blog on his and a checkerboard of open files on her Toughbook.

"Yeah. I mean no. I mean, I don't know. He was involved. He was connected to Shiva somehow. Shit, he could have been Shiva. But I doubt that. He. He was building something. A new network, maybe. A replacement for Kestrel, maybe. I don't. Shit."

She puts a hand on each open screen, pauses, and folds them both.

"Nuclear proliferation overlays."

She stands.

"Corn and wheat price indexes."

She stretches her arms over her head, her back and neck popping.

"Peak oil timetables."

She lowers her arms, shakes her hands violently, fingers slapping against one another.

"Urbanization of population."

Lifts one knee high, puts it down, lifts the other.

"Aging of population."

She takes off her jacket and drops it on the floor.

"Wi-Fi penetration in developing countries."

She walks to the door, four steps, turns, walks back to the table, bigger steps, three.

"Brazilian favelas and the global GDP, contributions to."

She raises a hand to her brow, screens her eyes as if the overhead light in its translucent white shell has suddenly begun to hurt them.

"Coal-fired power plant construction starts, China, two thousand fifteen projections."

She flicks a finger at the light switch near the door, a button that looks at though it should summon a white plastic elevator designed by Apple engineers.

"Turn that off, please."

Skinner touches the button, slightest of clicks, darkness. There are stars outside the window that come into view as their eyes adjust. Some light creeps under the door from the corridor, very little, night train, sleeper car. The screen of Jae's rugged phone gives off a dull gray glow.

Her hand appears in that graveyard corona, zombie pallor, and flips the phone screen down on the table.

"Ice cap melt rates."

She is silhouetted against the field of stars and a stutter of black shadows, leafless trees, streaming past outside.

"Critical foreign dependencies, map of."

She turns so that she is facing the window, back to Skinner.

"Black swan weather events. Somali pirate havens. Bilderberg, history of. Chinese yuan, deflation of. New American isolationism, rise of. Russian nationalism, rise of. Gray market economy and global GDP, percentage of. Gulf Stream, warming of. Mexico City slum properties, real estate value of. US health care costs and global economic growth, inhibition of."

She stops. The train rolls over the tracks. Smooth, a sound that seems more electronic than mechanical. Lights whip past, lonely house in a barren field. Summer soon. It will be green everywhere when it comes. Jae touches the window. Cold enough outside that the warmth of her fingers creates tiny halos of condensation around the tips.

"It looks like Terrence was anticipating the apocalypse. Which I guess he always was. Always looking for opportunities to put it off."

Skinner has a vision of Terrence, wild eyed, a tattered robe, raving on a street corner. But the image doesn't last, won't sustain.

"So he was funding anarchists?"

Jae's silhouette shrugs.

"It looks possible. Material he dumped in the USB about Bilderberg. The WTO. Demonstrations at the last several G8 conferences. *Twenty-first-century protest movements, viability of.* That kind of thing. He's in the middle of all this. But it doesn't look like an op gone wrong or a money grab."

She takes her hand off the window; the ghosts of her touch, illumed by traces of starlight, fade.

"Something about it is *old.*"

Skinner thinks about Terrence, a man who'd been almost entirely gray the day they met, but elastic-skinned, clear-eyed. He gave always an impression of seniority, never age. Except at their last meeting, Cologne, the airport coffee bar. But even then he'd appeared tired more than old. Tired, that eternally spry and curious mind, tired.

"Old how?"

Jae turns from the window.

"There are papers he wrote, these topics that no one was interested in ten or twenty years ago, now they're circling into vogue. Disaster politics. And it's like."

Her hands go to the sides of her head, her temples, but it's too dark for Skinner to see if she's trying to concentrate or to demonstrate something about Terrence's thoughts.

"It's like his thing with cold war strategies and mechanisms still underpinning modern intelligence work. Except it's *his* strategies and mechanisms from two decades ago, theories, really, underpinning the current work being done in crisis security. Everyone is talking about Armageddon threats. As if everything we're currently facing is comparable to nuclear war, when what we're really talking about is death from a thousand tiny cuts."

He can see a tension in her silhouette, she is squeezing her own head with her hands, trying to force something to stay inside, or to be fused from the pressure of her need. Diamonds from coal.

"Fuck. It's too. I don't have enough. Something. So fucking."

Her hands fly off her head, down, slapping her thighs.

"Too much. Not enough. I need more. Or less. I'm tired."

She stands there.

"I need to switch off now."

Skinner imagines a button, like the white plastic circle that turned off the light, on the back of her neck.

"How does that work?"

Her shoulders rise and fall.

"I need to shut down. Process. But I'm overloaded. Overtired. My brain is spinning out."

She slaps her own forehead.

"Stupid fucking brain."

Skinner thinks about meditation, the quiet rest he can summon for himself by practicing being invisible, but he's pretty sure even trying to explain something like that to Jae will just piss her off.

"Do you need quiet? White noise?"

She's looking at the wall opposite the bunks, body facing him, but features in profile, dark.

"I need some pills."

"In your bag."

She shakes her head.

"No. I left them in Stockholm, in my duffel. I didn't want to be tempted. I need to not be thinking is all."

Skinner thinks about not thinking.

Jae turns again, looking out the window behind her, dim patches of white on a low hillside, crevasses where snow has been cradled in shadow, away from the spring's cool sunlight. She turns back to him.

"Come here."

Skinner walks to the table.

Her hand comes up between them, stops, then lays itself on his chest, palm down, over his heart.

"Skinner."

"Yes."

"Not your real name."

"No."

"Why then? Something you do? That you're known for doing?"

"No."

His heartbeat hasn't changed since she touched him, some effort to keep it even.

"My parents were radical behaviorists. They raised me in a Skinner box. Until I was twelve. Then some people took me out. So. When I needed a name. Professional. Well. Skinner."

Her hand moves, angles, fingers curved over his left pectoral muscle, heel resting in the hollow of his sternum.

"Why did they do that?"

His heart is beating faster now, harder, he doesn't try to stop it.

"They were scientists. And their brain chemistry was problematic. It was an experiment. At first. And then. It was just normal. And it seemed to work. And I liked it."

Her other hand places itself inside his jacket, small, just above his waist, fingers aligned with the indentations between his ribs.

"Who took you out?"

She hasn't appeared to move, everything still, just her hands, as if entirely separate from her body or her will, touching him.

"People. They thought I was being hurt."

"Were you?"

"No."

Her right hand slips over his chest, tucks itself below his armpit, her thumb discovers the knot of scar tissue under his shirt, rubs it.

"What's this?"

"Wound. Knife."

Her hands come to the front of his shirt, collar, and begin to unbutton, to his navel, then pull the tails from his pants, the last two buttons undone, then ruck his undershirt up, and her left hand returns to its resting place, and her right hand glides up, under the shirts, leaving gooseflesh in its tracks, finds the scar, feeling its outline with one of the fingers that had touched the cold glass and created a mark with its warmth. It does the same on his skin, he can feel it.

"It didn't kill you."

"I hope not."

She smiles. He thinks she smiles.

Her left hand goes to his belt, unbuckles it.

"Skinner."

Her fingers undo the fly button and squirm inside, thumb staying out, and her hand hangs there for the moment, a slight tug toward her.

"Skinner. I want to stop thinking for a while."

She pulls on his pants, moving him closer, the hand touching the scar that hides the tip of the blade lodged between his ribs guides him, leans him down, bringing his face close, his lips. She kisses him. Pulls her lips off of his, hand finding its way inside his pants, other hand circling to the small of his back, finding the gun still tucked there, and pulling it out and setting it on the small table so that it won't fall to the floor when she undoes the final button inside his trousers.

"I want to stop thinking. I need you to help me with that."

He does his best.

On the narrow lower bunk, inside her, she tells him to stop moving, and he does. The train rocks them. He tries then to become invisible, in the dark, and her hand moves from his shoulder to the back of his neck, pulling him close, turning his head, bringing his ear to her mouth, warm breath as she whispers.

"Don't go away."

She's seen him.

Then she starts moving again, and he moves against her.

Later, when it appears that everything has worked out the way she wanted, she's stopped thinking, and she falls asleep, Skinner eases himself from the bunk, finds his pants, undershirt, and shoes, not bothering with socks, and goes out into the corridor, locking the door, walking to the bathroom at the end of the car. He urinates, washes his hands, splashes water on his face. Looking at himself in the mirror, he wishes that he'd brought the Bersa with him or the ruler he took from the Hellsten or the compression socks and D batteries he bought in Central Station. He uses a paper towel to dry his hands and face, throws it away, mentally reviews Jae's dossier for her weapons proficiency, recalls that she had been trained to use handguns.

Yes. She knows how to use a gun. Good.

Then he opens the door and finds, not unexpectedly at all, the young man he'd seen with Haven at Heathrow, and later on the ferry. He has a gun, held inconspicuously, but not casually, at his side, and he has positioned himself far enough from the bathroom door that reaction times won't be a factor if Skinner should try to attack him. A prepared young man. He's also brought two other young people with him. One looks very much like an American backpacker, her clothes composed almost entirely of bright ripstop nylon and D-rings, sun bleached short hair, nose piercing. The other looks like a British soccer hooligan, tracksuit and trainers, anorak, Liverpool colors, head stubble on a skull that appears to have been designed for butting noses in rowdy pubs. They don't have guns, and have positioned themselves in an effort to create the illusion of a line waiting to use the bathroom, witness deterrence.

The young man wears a long-sleeve pullover, technical fabric tight across the muscles of his chest, an abstract splotch of red, yellow, and orange on the otherwise black background, an exploding sun or spreading amoeba. His pants are some form of athletic semiformal wear, also black. Boots, flat black paramilitary crossed with a running shoe. His jacket is suede, a shade of brown verging on black, safari style, assuming one were to safari the fall couture shows in Milan, stalking the slender gazelles of the runways. His gun is silver, flat anodized finish, the sights, brand name, serial number, all filed off, unblemished and smooth, customized to make the carrier feel more like a badass. It is, if Skinner is honest with himself, a nice looking gun.

The young man looks at his wristwatch, black carbon fiber dial and bezel, the watch of a successful arbitrage trader who enjoys testing his limits with dark-of-moon skydiving expeditions.

"Haven wants to see you."

Skinner looks down at his own shoes, oxford boots, one of his sockless ankles visible where the cuff of his pants has snagged on the top of the boot. He pinches the fabric of his pants between thumb and forefinger, tugs upward, dropping the cuff into place, looks up at the young people.

The skydiver tips his head toward the door that leads to the next car, forward on the train.

"There."

American accent. A neutrality that suggests the Pacific Northwest. He's fought somewhere. More than one place. For more than one paymaster. Skinner can see just what he'd look like with his larynx crushed. He steps out of the bathroom, waits while the three young people rearrange themselves a bit. When they move, the backpacker leads, opening the door and stepping through, then Skinner, then the man with the skydiver style, and, lagging, the football hooligan. The next car is also a sleeper, their procession stopping next to a compartment door that the skydiver brushes with a knuckle to alert whoever is inside before turning the handle, pushing it open, and standing aside so that Skinner can pass.

It is a private sleeper with its own shower and toilet. Skinner wonders if this was the last one on the train, and, if so, how long before he and Jae bought out their three-bunk compartment Haven booked this one. Relevant to the extent that if they'd gotten it first Skinner wouldn't have had to go down the corridor to take a piss. He doesn't believe in fate, but he does believe that proximity leads to complications. Sex with an asset, for example.

Haven is perched on one of the stools that flip down from the outer wall. On the table, surface only slightly larger than the stool, is a half eaten sandwich, the same plastic triangle packaging as the ones Skinner and Jae bought in Central Station. He's chewing, wiping pale yellow mustard from his lips with a translucently thin paper napkin, mouth full. He nods at the skydiver as Skinner enters, waving, a closing gesture. The door is shut, leaving them alone. Skinner stands next to it. Haven raises an index finger, begging pardon as he chews, covers his mouth with his napkin, swallows, takes a sip of Orangina from the eternally inexplicable pear-shaped glass bottle on the table, and wipes again.

"Horrible."

He stuffs the napkin into the plastic wedge with the remaining half of the sandwich, drops it into a white plastic bag with a blue SJ logo on the side, sweeps in some crumbs from the table, and tosses the bag onto the lower bunk, where it lands next to an iPad resting screen side down on a pumpkin-orange coverlet that has been mussed by someone lying restlessly on top of it.

"Please."

He half rises, leans over the table, and flips down the stool on the other side.

"We need to talk."

Skinner sits on the stool, there is no way to be comfortable on it, but that hardly matters. The keening in his mind makes any efforts at comfort an impossibility. The high screeching tone, constant, without quaver, his nerve endings reacting to his distance from Jae. Asset unprotected.

Haven moves the Orangina bottle to the side until it is in contact with the wall, turns so that he faces Skinner squarely, half his left thigh off his stool. Neither of them will be comfortable.

"They put the private sleepers next to the bar car."

He raises his eyebrows, casts his eyes around the compartment.

"Foot traffic at all hours. Drunks. This is the measure. Swedish rail putting together a train, cars out of proper order. If you want to know how far out of joint the volcano has put things, this is the measure."

Skinner does not face him, back to the wall, the shaded window, arms folded over his chest, feet flat on floor, looking at a stain on the carpet halfway between himself and the door.

Haven puts his forearms on the table, one lying atop the other.

"They were Hann-Aoki. In Miami. Former Triple Canopy. Protective Security Specialists. Secret clearance. Did a couple Iraq contracts, on-site security at one of the refineries. Crisis response in Yemen, getting some Finnish telecom executives safely from their condos to the airport when the government started shooting protesters. Then H-A. I know a guy over there, Pence. You ever work with him? No. Pence, former Green Beret, Vietnam, Ed Harris would play him in the movie; he tells me that at H-A they have unofficial-official slang for PSS freelancers. *Cannon fodder.* Anything they want to throw a couple bodies at, see what happens, draw fire, they put out a call for guys with PSS on their resume. Secret clearance. Don't like to use their top-shelf people for that kind of thing."

Skinner nods, still looking at the stain.

"That kind of thing."

Haven shrugs.

"Poking wasps' nests. Finding out what will happen. No one is sure what to expect from you. H-A decided to get some early reconnaissance. And also Jae. The playing field is pretty even on the West-Tebrum gig. Everyone has the same resources. But you and Jae running around, that made some players nervous. H-A was interested in seeing if they could remove a variable. Cost them little. Anyway. Hard to say just what they expected. Bodies on fire. Also it's possible that they were more interested in Maker Smith."

Skinner looks up.

"Smith."

Haven is wearing a navy blue t-shirt cut for simultaneous close fit and wide range of movement, the collar rises higher than a regular crewneck, almost touching his Adam's apple. He scratches at some dark blond scruff on his jaw, a day past five o'clock shadow, rasping sound.

"He's gone to ground. The fire spread. Emergency responders. Dead bodies on the scene. Miami Dade PD. He's lost all his infrastructure. Not like he was carrying insurance. He'll have to take a contract somewhere to rebuild his finances. H-A would love to have him in-house. Could be they were looking for an opportunity to change his circumstances, put him in a position of need, more receptive to their offers. You being there with Jae. Good excuse to send in a team. Underwhelming force. Sent to deal with someone known for his ability to make a big mess. H-A can be subtle. And anyone that sanctions cannon fodder, well, that tells you what you need to know about their MO."

Skinner is wondering where Haven's gun is. The blue t-shirt is worn outside a pair of jeans dyed so black they suck the compartment's light into their fabric. Skinner saw the tail of the shirt hike up when Haven bent across the table to flip down the second seat, no gun. His shoes, supple black leather uppers with timeworn creases, black rubber soles, are on the floor next to the bunk. Haven's socks match his shirt. There could be an ankle holster. The material of the pants is so light-absorbent that it is difficult to see how narrow the cuffs are. A small black leather and nylon carry-on with a shoulder strap is on the top bunk, as is a black down jacket, thin fill, city wear. The gun could be up there. Or in the small closet, the bathroom, under one of the mattresses.

He gets tired of wondering where the gun is.

"Where's your gun?"

Haven looks at the shaded window, back at Skinner.

"I don't have one. Other people carry the guns these days."

He nods at the closest door, the trio in the corridor outside.

"If I need a gun, they have plenty."

Skinner looks again at the stain on the floor.

"You were at Heathrow."

"British deli bagels. Awful."

Skinner doesn't look up from the stain.

Haven frowns, places the tips of the fingers of his right hand firmly on the table between them, his palm arched above them, as if caging something small.

"Have you no sense of what's happening?"

The stain is old, black, shaped like an eye with some kind of bulging growth where its cornea would be.

Haven flattens his hand.

"I have a contract with Cross, personally, to protect Kestrel. With leeway. A great deal of leeway."

Skinner looks at him now.

"To protect Kestrel."

Haven drags his hand back across the table.

"Kestrel is my asset."

Haven's eyes are blue. Very dark, verging sometimes on violet. His hair is lighter than his stubble, clipped recently, conforming to the contours of his flattish skull. He has weathered since Skinner saw him last. He's been spending some time in sunny places where the wind blows hard. They have the same build, big men who carry it lightly, though Haven has always been broader in the shoulders and chest. His love of the gym and, Skinner more than suspects, of the mirrors in the gym. Skinner believes he is older than Haven by a year, maybe two, but he can't say for certain.

He can't say much of anything for certain. He looks at the stain.

"I've been away."

Haven taps at the corner of his right eye.

"Yes. I noticed."

He stops tapping.

"I argued against you for this. Bringing you back in. Throwing you into this thing cold, *Here's an asset, go!* I argued against that. You're just. You never did any research on the industry. You never kept up on who worked for who, why, when, for how much. Whatever you did know, it's all way past the sell date. You're a reputation. *Skinner's Maxim.* They teach it now. You have no idea. Those security contractors that do skills accreditation seminars. Secret clearance required. Interrogation techniques. Surveillance. They have sessions on asset operations. *Skinner's Maxim,* like a thought problem, that's how they present it. Given an operator employing such a maxim, how do you safely acquire the asset? You're not real. Not to them."

He nods at the door again.

"*They* barely have an idea that there's really someone named Skinner. They think it's like Murphy's Law. There is no Murphy. Just the law that anything that can go wrong will go wrong. I mean."

Skinner thinks about his reputation. His maxim. The things he did to establish both. A litany of fire and blood. His hand, suddenly, remembers exactly what it feels like when the blade of a flensing knife whisks an eye from its socket, a deft flourish, sucking pop, eye hanging from tendrils of nerves and arteries, until those too are cut. He imagines that, and so much more, undone by the passage of seven years, his absence erasing those actions, their meaning lost. He remembers the wasted dead, no more value left in their killing. He pictures starting over, sweat comes to his forehead, dryness to his mouth. His heart beats against the tip of the knife stuck in his ribs.

He stands.

"I'm going now. I have an asset."

Haven is looking down at the tabletop, a man trying to solve a puzzle, last few words in the crossword.

"No, you don't. Not anymore."

He looks up.

"The op is over."

Skinner doesn't move.

Haven shakes his head.

"Look, it's not a bad thing. No one is pulling the plug. But we have the badguys. Those anarchists, Gamla Stan. You and Jae sniffed them right out, went straight to them. So. Contract fulfilled. Everyone gets paid."

Skinner is standing over the stain, it's right between his feet. Looking at the eye shape, his hand feels again the whisking gesture, scrape of blade against orbital bone.

"The anarchists. For West-Tebrum. No."

"They have motive. Funding. Connections to radical and criminal networks. A stated aim of bringing down capitalist society as a whole, and American capitalist *imperialism* in specific. They look good."

"No."

Haven looks at the table again, invisible unsolved puzzle.

"This. Rigidity. In your thinking. I wonder where that comes from."

He looks at Skinner, looks at the stain Skinner is looking at.

"It's going public, the attack on West-Tebrum. Everyone is going to know. It is going to be a shitstorm. Hurricane. What is going to calm it is the fact that the badguys have already been found, caught, and are, at this moment, being loaded onto a Gulfstream that the CIA bought at auction from a former Warner studio exec when he went upside down in the collapse. Happy ending. And, thanks to you and Jae, Kestrel got to them first."

Skinner looks up from the stain. Haven's eyes, the violet shade has come into them.

"It's not them. Jae says no. It goes somewhere else. The configuration."

Haven makes blades of his hands, places them edge down on the table, defining the limits of something.

"It's like your thoughts are in a box. Like you came out of it, but your thoughts are still inside."

He lifts his hands, flicks them, shaking something off.

"Jae's contract has been fulfilled. The asset operation is over. Cross is happy with this result. Homeland is happy with this result. The investors who have heeded the trends and put their savings in private security and intelligence services stocks are *very* happy with this result. We are beginning to contract out of the op. Close it. And you, you are unemployed. You have no asset. Nothing to concern you. More activity in this area will just draw attention. More cannon fodder. The word is going out, the badguys have been caught. Everything goes still on the landscape. If you keep moving, you look like a target. H-A, the other contractors, they think there's a reason to stay in the game. Problems ensue. Difficulties for Kestrel. My asset."

He points at Skinner's feet.

"You're not wearing your socks. Do I think you were sleeping, no socks, needed to pee?"

He looks at Skinner, his eyes roam Skinner's face, the puzzle, so frustrating.

"Fucking your asset. Christ."

Something new on Haven's face; again, emotion is so hard to parse. Skinner decides that the expression indicates some form of regret on Haven's part. But he hasn't the least idea what it relates to. He wonders if Haven is still faster than him. A man that doesn't carry his own gun anymore, has he slowed?

"Is Terrence really dead?"

Haven's mouth flattens into a line crimped at both ends. He shrugs.

"Yeah. The old man is dead."

Haven looks at his bunk, scratches his earlobe.

"Cologne. After he met with you. He was a mess. All over the field. Too many freelance jobs. We tried to put him out in the cold after Montmartre. For his own good. But he couldn't stay out of the game. Working for anyone who would have him. Corporate intel, some Russian mob stuff, consulting for Venezuelan antiterrorism, for fuck sake. Anyone paying. And he got messy. Involved in too many things. Yes. *This.* He was involved. We know. I know. There was a danger that Kestrel could end up implicated in West-Tebrum if Terrence kept running around."

He stops scratching his earlobe.

"He wanted you for this because he thought he could *run* you. Poke you around the board, looking in the wrong direction. Play you off Jae. It might have worked. But he was a threat to Kestrel. So he's dead now."

Skinner remembers the night he first killed a man. His urge, never shared with anyone, to protect the man next to him. Alone, he might never have felt compelled to attack the mugger. But until the man was down, he was a danger to Terrence. Odd, these circles life runs in.

"Was it hard to kill him?"

Haven is still looking at his empty bunk, as if imagining what it would be like to actually sleep in it. He looks at Skinner.

"If you wanted to know what it feels like to kill Terrence you should have done it after Montmartre."

Skinner feels something he doesn't like.

"I have to go."

Haven rises, shorter than Skinner, but only because he's in his socks. They could change clothes and never have to visit a tailor.

"You don't have an asset. Jae doesn't have a contract and you do not have an asset."

"I have to go."

"Yes. Somewhere. But no more on this. I can't. I have to stay on my asset, Kestrel. This thing. It's a mess, this thing. Terrence. He was buying guns. Moving money. It must stop in Gamla Stan. It needs to shut down and go quiet. If you keep moving, with Jae, someone is going to take a shot at you. I can't have that noise. Bad for Kestrel."

Skinner's eyes, shaped much like Haven's, but brown, close, open.

"Kestrel. An asset. How does that work?"

"It works because I want it to. Because I can imagine what it's like. An asset, it doesn't have to be what someone else says it is. You don't have to wait for someone else to establish the value. And you don't have to wait for someone to attack it before you take action. I presented Cross with a proposition, and he saw the potential. Kestrel is my asset. I take actions to protect it. Cross went to Bilderberg. I normally would have gone with him. Instead, I stayed with a team following you and Jae. Because I still know how to watch you so that you don't know I'm there. Like I always have. And because you and she represented a greater risk to Kestrel, and greater potential for Kestrel profit than Cross understood. And I was right. You gave us the anarchists. Mission accomplished."

Skinner nods.

"Your thinking. More flexible. Yes."

He turns to the door.

"Terrence is dead. Imagine. If he'd been my asset. What would happen next."

Haven puts his hands in his pockets.

"I have. He wasn't."

Skinner nods, places his hand on the door latch.

"Joel."

His real name turns his head, the sound of it, some power, finds him like a lost thing.

Haven opens his mouth, closes it, opens it again and fills it with words.

"Go away, Joel. This isn't for you. The way it works now. Not for you. You'll only. People will get hurt."

Skinner looks around the compartment that might have been his if he'd been a little faster, nods, turns the door latch.

"They always do."

He opens the door, walks through it, past the three Personal Security Services operators and their Secret clearances and their guns. Back along the length of the misassembled train, already feeling himself drift away, tether slipping loose.

No asset at the end of the corridor, only a woman.

Not sure what that means.

when the ash leaves the sky

HER PHONE IS ringing.

Stupid fucking brain.

At least in Iraq she'd been drunk. Drunk and in a war zone.

Still ringing, light pulses around the edge of the screen that she turned face down to the tabletop before her brain went sideways and made her stick her hand down Skinner's pants.

No, really, stupid, fucking, brain.

She's so stupid it's taken her however long, however many rings of her phone, to realize that Skinner isn't in the bed with her anymore. Not in the bed. Not in the compartment. She looks at the table, the phone rings, that thin pulse of light reflecting off the gun. She tries to remember how many times her phone will ring before going to voicemail. But she's not really fooling herself. She's going to pick it up. She just wishes that she wasn't quite so naked and sticky.

It rings.

Stupid fucking phone.

She picks it up.

"What."

"You're not in Stockholm."

She pulls the top sheet up.

"No, I'm not."

She waits for more from Cross. Gets the feeling that he's looking at something on the other end of this call, something that puts her at a disadvantage.

"But you *were* in Stockholm."

"Yes. Briefly."

"Ah. There was some confusion. I thought Kiev. Left it at that. Haven, without my knowing, did not leave it at that."

Jae palms her forehead. It feels heavy, full of data, still unsorted. She needs more sleep. Much more.

"I had no idea you were there, Jae. Here. I'm still here. For the moment. Had no idea you'd been involved, witnessed what was happening on Gamla Stan."

She turns her head, easing her face into her palm, looking at the gun on the table.

"You woke me up. I'm not very clear headed just now."

A pause, Cross gathering or realigning his thoughts.

"Right. Good job finding the West-Tebrum attackers. Or the brain trust, anyway. They don't, none of them, have the technical background, but their money chain goes straight to the former Eastern bloc. Ukraine, like we thought, Romania, Hungary. There was, do you remember, there was that bank heist, prepaid ATM cards? Fidelity National Information Services. Hackers got into the database. Cloned twenty-two cards. Sent them to a network of accomplices. Countries I mentioned, but also Greece, UK, Russia, Spain. Others. Twenty-four hours, hitting ATMs for the card limits. Every time they maxed one, the hacker coordinators would go back into the FIS database and reset the limit. Twenty-two cards, twenty-four hours. They got over thirteen million, US."

He waits for a reaction, but she has none.

"The anarchists were using cloned cards from FIS. And, Jae, we have a Chinese connection."

She moves her head again, lets her hand cover her eyes.

"Chinese."

His voice is modulating into a slightly higher register, excitement that not even Cross can contain.

"Chinese. It looks good. Chinese netizens. Citizen hackers. Patriot citizen hackers. Chinese. Which is the same as the People's Liberation Army's Unit 61398. A nominally citizen hacker in Shenzhen, a member of Comment Crew, provided the anarchists with some technical support on how to set up their own Wi-Fi network, Internet in a suitcase stuff. They didn't have it operational, but the emails were right there in the trash in one of their Gmail accounts. Jae, Eastern European gangsters, Western European anarchists, and the Chinese? Very, very good job."

With her eyes covered, lights are flaring behind the closed lids, they swim, resolve, arrange themselves into a configuration, a nonsensical series of lines connecting them. She tries to move them, sort them into something like the structure that Cross is suggesting. It would be so nice, all the cyberwar bogeymen working together. Tidy package. She likes tidy things. Loose ends are irritating, unbearable. They send her to the fringes of any configuration, looking for the threads they are meant to connect, lost, never finished. No configuration is ever finished.

Nothing is complete.

"It's bullshit, Cross."

Pause. Recalibration. Words.

"It is a national security threat, Jae. One that is appearing more pervasive and imminent by the minute. And when Fox News and CNN and MSNBC and the Internet and what's left of the papers start reporting it in less than twenty hours, the heads of Homeland and the NSA and CIA and FBI and the DoD and every elected official in Washington who can get within screaming distance of a microphone will be able to assure the public that it is a threat that is being aggressively countered and that the ringleaders of the West-Tebrum attack are already in custody. I did not ask. Jae, I did not ask you to go to Stockholm when you did, but you did. You went to Smith, followed your instincts and didn't trust me, did not go to Kiev, you went to Smith instead. And as to what happened there, well, some messes are easier to clean up than others. You went to Smith and then to Stockholm. This is what you do, follow trails that no one else can see. And you found the city of gold."

He exhales, breathes deep, settles himself.

"And, well, fuck. Jae. I'm excited. I'm excited for Kestrel, and I'm excited for America. This is the kind of thing, this is how entire industries get spawned. I don't have to tell you how economically robust intelligence and security have been post–nine-eleven. It's possible, we could, with effort, see new opportunities well beyond the Beltway this time. Innovation in national security doesn't have to originate in Virginia or Delaware. And it's heartening for people to wake up, hear there was an attack, and know the perpetrators have already been captured. Morale. When a nation is heartened, when it contracts into its own concerns, you can do amazing things. I believe that. So, well done. Very well done."

He coughs.

"Now, I happen to know you're alone at the moment. Skinner is occupied. But he'll be back with you soon. And what I want you to do is check an email account. Gmail. User: ilovecats6678@gmail.com. All lower-case, no spaces. Password: kitty6678. The in-box will contain an email with some contact info and an address in Paris. A safehouse. I want you to go there. The ash cloud is blowing south at a good clip and the EU can't afford to have another two-week airspace shutdown. Not with a new hostile credit event looming every week. Bank runs in Cyprus. Airspace will open well before the ash leaves the air. Less than twenty-four hours. Meantime, you should be someplace out of the way. You should separate from Skinner. Immediately. His contract has been fulfilled. Tell him to leave you alone. That simple. He's not safe to be around anymore. Do you understand all of that?"

She uncovers her eyes, still seeing flashes, ghost configurations.

"We caught the badguys."

"Yes. We have a Kestrel product, a SCIF jail. Six cells enclosed in a SCIF. Highly portable. It can be moved on a flatbed, wide load, like a house. A flexible drop-and-deploy platform. Many applications. Anyway, they don't want to take the anarchists to Guantanamo. Too resonant of a specific era. Everyone thought the Tsarnaev brothers would characterize the next stage in the evolution of terrorism. Post-Soviet Islamists. But this is post-Islamist extremism. It needs to be defined as such. It's a market delineation. And it will make it easier for reporters to tell the story of a newly emerging threat. People will lose interest if it's not new. They have jihad fatigue. So the anarchists are going to the supermax facility at ADX Florence in Colorado, to be housed in a Kestrel SCIF Custody Unit. It's branded, the SCIF, our logo on the door. If any pictures happen to get leaked to the press."

"Cross."

"Yes."

"They're in your SCIF."

"Soon."

"Why do I need to get away from Skinner and go hide?"

Nothing.

"Because, Cross, like I said before, bullshit. You know?"

He's breathing, not dead, breathing air that everyone else breathes, same species, though Jae sometimes thinks that can't be possible. She listens to him breathe.

"Cross?"

"I have something else for you, Jae. That container you looked at when you went to Creech. Something has happened. They lost it, and now it's turned up, or one like it has turned up. Maybe. In an unlikely location. Kestrel is helping out. Lieutenant Colonel Cervantes would like you to see the new images. Some pictures. Pictures, Jae. Looking at pictures. What you like best to do. I'll send some additional contact info to that email address. Cervantes. Look at what he has to show you."

She scoots down the bunk. From here, without leaning, she can pick up the gun.

"Why do I need to get away from Skinner?"

"There's another conversation happening now. I'm listening. Well, not listening. Reading a simultaneous transcript. Nice piece of software. Kestrel developed. If I seem distracted, that's why. From what I gather, reading this conversation, Skinner may be moving into the realm of independent actions. Now that his contract has been fulfilled."

"Has it been fulfilled? Am I safe?"

"He knows that Terrence is dead. Jae. I assume you told him. Your prerogative. But it is possible that Skinner will be unable to accept the facts. Or so I'm being given to believe. Better to get away from him. Soonest."

Jae is trying to remember the last time she fired a gun. Before Iraq. The personal security course she had to take before she could be insured. She's a good shot. Her instructor had been impressed. *You've fired a gun before.* Yes. She had.

"So you don't think he might have killed Terrence anymore?"

"No. No. It appears that Terrence was cutting a swathe of late. Acquiring an ample supply of ememies. He was playing several hands at once. Had been for some time. Just recently it became too much for him. Money, it looks like. Some of that FIS money I told you about, it passed through one of his accounts. He was involved in this, Jae. West-Tebrum. More than a bit. And he pushed for Skinner's involvement. Because he thought he could influence him. Jae, if we're right, Terrence may have been brokering *materials*. It's a diffuse situation at the moment. Best to settle in somewhere until it contracts. Paris. Correspond with Cervantes. When the ash leaves the sky, come home. Or stay in Paris for a while. Job well done. Deserved rest."

"Away from Skinner."

"Soonest possible. Yes."

"Terrence was involved."

"Money. Pipeline services. Innate instability, finally manifest. He couldn't leave well enough alone. It wasn't sufficient that Kestrel has become a dominant influence in national security. He needed, I think, to see his own ideas about international security validated. His whole *a safer world for a safer nation* thing. As much as I learned from the man, he was never wholly stable. Deeply influential on my thinking, but far too radical in his own. He was trying to manipulate events. Create an outcome that would prove some of his theories. Create a market for himself. He wanted to be indispensable. Build a new Kestrel, perhaps. Very tangled. When you come back, I'd love for you to take a look. See if you can sort out how he managed it all. As it is, we'll be years discovering all the breaches he created."

"Terrence wanted money."

"That. Yes. And, I fancy, to be right. His Cassandra credentials fully established."

"So he created the attack."

"I think it will emerge that he enabled certain aspects. Not that his involvement will ever come to public light. In some ways he achieved his goal. He'll be remembered by many people as one of the few men who saw the future of security with any degree of clarity. For all his imagination he was always a great realist. Unromantic. It's what I appreciated about him from our first meeting. Clear eyed. Cold blooded. But just too perverse in the long run."

Something beeps at the other end of the line.

Jae squints.

"Are you taping this?"

Clicks, mouse clicks.

"No. The other conversation I mentioned. Which has ended. We should get off the phone."

"Who was Skinner talking to?"

"Haven."

"Haven."

"He's on the train. Keeping an eye on things. Has been. Watching."

"Skinner knows when people are watching him."

"People other than Haven. In any case. Prepare yourself. Tell him the contract is resolved. You don't need him. Physically separate from him. As soon as travel allows. In Lund if possible. Copenhagen otherwise. But avoid the boat train."

"Boat train?"

"Don't cross water with him, Jae. That will be too far. We need to shut this operation down. I'm off now. I've already got a backlog of calls from congresspeople wanting to be briefed. Someone has to tell them what to say when the camera light turns red."

Click. Dead line. Jae puts the phone down, looks at the gun. Thinks about picking it up but chooses her pants instead. She has her pants on, and her tank top, when she hears the door latch. By the time the door has opened and Skinner has begun to step into the room, she is holding the gun, at her side, pointed at the floor.

"Cross called."

She put herself very close to the wall. No room to move, run.

"He said the job is over."

Skinner nods.

"I've been told the same thing."

He steps in and closes the door.

"I'll get my things."

His eyes go to the floor, find one of his socks. He squats to pick it up, looking up when Jae speaks again.

"Am I safe?"

He holds the black sock, and looks down to find the its mate.

"Once I leave. Probably."

She can see the sock, shifts her foot so that her toes point at it.

"There."

He finds it, picks it up, drops to his bottom on the floor, and begins unlacing his boots.

"Thanks."

Jae has always wondered at the heaviness of guns. This one feels like it might pull her arm from her shoulder.

"They were following us from Nevada."

Skinner has his boots off, rucking one of the socks before slipping it on his foot.

"Yes."

"It's going to fall on the anarchists."

"That's what I've been told."

"By Haven?"

He snugs the first sock past his ankle, picks up the other.

"Yes."

Haven on this train. While she was having sex with Skinner. Her hand tightens on the gun.

"Terrence was helping them. Improving his position. Cross says."

Skinner puts on a boot, jerks the laces.

"Does Cross know about the Montmartre coordinates?"

"He seems to know we were going to Paris. I don't know if he knows specifically about Montmartre."

He double-knots his laces. It took a while, she remembers, for him to undo the knots in the dark. Two hours ago, three. Ages ago.

"So?"

He has the second boot in his hand, looks at it.

"I have no contract. No asset. They want me to go away."

He puts on the boot, laces it up, another double knot.

"You?"

"Cross has other things for me to do."

Skinner brings his knees up, loops his arms around them.

"Good."

Jae raises the gun, holding it on her hand, looking at it.

"But I don't want to work for Cross."

She steps toward him.

"I want to hire you to protect me."

She offers him the gun.

"I want to be your asset."

He's looking at the gun.

"Haven says they want me to go away. And everything will be fine."

The gun is getting heavier in her hand.

"Cross told me to get away from you. *Soonest.* Said I shouldn't *cross water* with you."

He touches his lower lip with a thumbnail.

"Yes. Well, Haven was lying to me. He has other concerns. But the people with him, they're going to try to kill me no matter what I do. I think they're probably good at it. And really, it's the only reason Cross agreed to let me protect you. To get me into the open."

"Skinner."

Brown eyes leave the gun, look up at her.

"Jae."

"Do you accept the contract?"

"I'm expensive."

"We'll deal with that later."

"I don't really care about the money."

He takes the gun from her hand.

"Where are we going?"

She scrunches her toes, standing right in front of him, looking down, as he inspects the gun, checks the safety, feels the weight, opens the breech to be certain she hasn't chambered a round in his absence.

"We're going to Montmartre to find out what the fuck Terrence wanted us to see. Find out who really attacked West-Tebrum. Find what the fuck is going on and why the old man couldn't just tell us about it and ask for our help."

Skinner leans forward, shifting his weight to rise.

"Good."

Jae places a hand on his shoulder, leans into him, pushing him back onto the floor, lowering herself.

"Don't get up."

In a hurry this time. There's a station ahead somewhere, a change of trains. She tells him not to bother with his laces, so he does little more than put the gun down and push some bits of clothing out of the way.

Pulling into Lund, her gear stowed in her backpack, all clothing back in place, something like dawn hovering below the horizon, she watches him tuck the pistol away at the small of his back, sees how his jacket and trench coat drape to hide it, a subtlety of stitching, expensive, she imagines. And, that thing still pressing from inside her mind, she asks a question that got lost while they were tangled on the floor.

"How come you don't know when Haven is watching you?"

The train is slowing, they can hear people in the corridor. The shade is up, and as they come abreast of the platform they can see that it is more densely packed than Central Station was. It looks dangerous, a few more bodies might be just enough to force people over the edge and onto the tracks. Their connection is scheduled to leave in twenty minutes. They will struggle to make it.

"Skinner?"

He turns from the window, crosses to the door, undoes the safety bolt, hand on the latch.

"He's always been able to watch me. I'm not sure why."

He turns the latch.

"But he's my brother."

He opens the door, line of people shuffling past, long wait for the exit at the end of the car, and he looks at her.

"So that might have something to do with it."

implications of the gun

IN EVERY EXPERIMENT there is a control.

Skinner is still not certain which he was. Experiment or control. Skinner in the basement, pure environment that his parents could manipulate and filter. Haven upstairs, living a normal life. Kids. Friends. School. Somehow each arrived at the same result. Not that their parents were intent on creating killers. They just wanted to know what would happen. They were scientists, mentally myopic, singularly curious about how behavior was created. Autistic.

The first pregnancy had been unexpected. They'd always used rigorous birth control. Diagnosed in an era that predated subtleties like Asperger's syndrome, neither had experienced an easy childhood. For their father, it was a minefield of social disasters and educational mismanagement typical to such cases, while, for their mother, it served as a pretext for savage physical abuse from her own mother. Knowing there was some chance they could pass their autism on to any children they might have, they chose not to have any children. Besides, even if that risk had not existed, they lacked any desire to reproduce. They had discovered an odd overlap in their stunted empathies that allowed them a mysterious degree of intimacy, but that didn't necessarily mean they could find a similar range of affection for a child. Also they enjoyed their work. Clinical radical behaviorism was a lens that focused the world. Helped them to understand why people did what they did, and equipped them to mimic some of those behaviors. A child would be a distraction. But there was a failure in the system and she became pregnant, and, as they thought about it, they began to see ways a child could fit quite seamlessly into the body of their work. Though, in a perfect world, two children would be necessary. Born in rapid succession, and of the same gender. That was the ideal scenario. Fortune favored them, to that extent.

There were details Skinner's mother was unwilling to share when he spoke with her many years later. He knows that one of the pregnancies took place in secret. His father had been pre-med, an envisioned career as a brain surgeon undermined by an inherent clumsiness. The idea of tending a pregnancy and managing a birth didn't intimidate either of them in the least. The other pregnancy was quite public, Skinner's mother suffering through the intimacies of touch and inquisition that come with bearing a child in the open. But she would not reveal which child came first.

One above. One below. One with access to playgrounds, kids from around the corner, dogs, bicycles, skinned knees, climbing trees, girls at the next desk, swimming lessons, libraries, Disney movies, the beach, after school cartoons, Keds, and whatever else his parents could divine as being essential to a normal upbringing. The other raised with sun-lamps, vitamin supplements, climbing obstacles, pictures of children and animals, shins barked on the many sharp corners of the box, books, more books, educational films and documentaries screened on his VCR, morning calisthenics, meditation, constant introduction and removal of stimulus to encourage or discourage behaviors in a precise measure meant to result in a child as observably normal as his brother upstairs.

It made perfect sense to them. Neither child was abused in any manner that their mother would have recognized from her own brutal upbringing. Both enjoyed nutritious and varied diets. Both had exercise, mental and imaginative stimulation. Their educations were, for the one, the best the public schools system could provide, and, for the other, far exceeding in variety and depth anything that could have been made available through any public resource. Though entirely different, both of their boys were afforded safe and nurturing environments in which to grow. Though, by necessity, one received more attention than the other. Much more. By orders of magnitude.

They missed it, of course, the neglect inherent in the experiment. Their autism-blunted empathy caused them to equate societal normalcy with attention. There was a physical wall between themselves and Skinner, while no such wall existed for Haven. How could they possibly be favoring the one in the box? But it was the wall, Skinner's mother told him, that created that increased attention, and, if she was to be honest, affection. He required more of their time, that much was obvious. But the wall of scratched and smudged Plexiglas was such an excellent emotional buffer, placing him at an enforced distance; it made it easier for them to be with him. When it came time to go upstairs, where they had banned for themselves use of the tools of radical behaviorism that they employed with Skinner, they found Haven's storms of utterly typical childhood emotions devastating. They were with him in immediate physical proximity, but far from present, withdrawing into the behavior shells neither of them had been able to shed in adulthood. The greatest shock of becoming parents turned out to be the extent to which it revealed themselves to themselves. How little their understanding of human behavior had actually changed them as humans.

The experiment devolved.

Putting Haven up for adoption was a difficult process. Technically difficult. Proving that they were unworthy parents was unexpectedly trying. They assumed, logically, that the simple fact that they no longer felt competent or capable of raising the boy and were willing to make him a ward of the state was sufficient evidence to prove their lack of fitness. Not so. It required months of interviews, intrusions, counseling that abraded both their symptomatic sensitivities and professional sensibilities. Had these people no understanding of why human beings act the way they do? But, in the end, they took Haven away. Surely there would be a good home for a healthy, handsome, personable boy, preadolescent or not. In any case, he'd manage. *They* had managed, after all. And Skinner was still there, in the box, thriving. So much left to learn. But no time left in which to learn it. A side effect of the prying into their lives, someone had detected an oddness that extended beyond the parents' autism-ascribed behavior. Possibly there had been some cues picked up from their own behavior, or, more probably, something seen when all those people were tramping through the house to inspect the conditions in which Haven was being raised; too many dishes in the sink, laundry, the overstuffed pantry, an unusually placed exhaust fan rising from the blacked-out basement window. In any case, someone had discovered, or at least theorized, the existence of Skinner. And they came back for him. Pulled him out from under his pink sky and hauled him out into the infinite blue.

Heartbreak, Skinner's mother said when they met again, *is a term I'm not comfortable with. Real heartbreak is a mortal condition, isn't it? So why apply it to something as ephemeral as emotion. Emotions are biological, chemical, and nothing to do with the heart. I understand why people say heartbreak, but it makes me squirm in my seat. Literally squirm. To say your father and I were heartbroken when you were taken away would be inaccurate. But we were at a great loss. I was confused for some time. Listless. I barely remember the criminal proceedings. I recall filling a paper with your names, writing it, Joel, over and over again. And, even though we'd given both of you the same name, I knew it was yours I was writing. But I can't say that I was heartbroken. When your father died, that was heartbreak. Myocardial infarction. A genuine broken heart. But just because it happened the day they told us we'd never be allowed to see you again, I don't think that means he was heartbroken because of you. He just had a flawed heart. You can inherit such a thing. You should have yours examined.*

It had been a difficult meeting.

"Your parents experimented on you."

The connecting train from Lund to Copenhagen is overfull. Seat assignments are no longer relevant. Boarding, after forcing themselves through the scrum on the platform, Skinner and Jae had been unable to determine if their reserved first-class seats existed at all. They stand close, in an aisle between the facing rows of seats along each wall of the packed commuter rail car. The mood, remarkably, is not murderous.

Skinner is looking at his shoes. A position that has not altered since he began giving an abbreviated account of his childhood to Jae.

"I *was* an experiment. Part of an experiment. Haven was the other part."

Jae has had to hunch forward to be able to hear him. They do not stand out in the car, there is a great deal of hushed conversation, attempts at privacy.

"Skinner."

He's still looking at his shoes.

She jabs him with her fingers.

"Skinner."

He looks at her, and she nods her head, slowly, acknowledging something he has not said aloud.

"That is some very fucked up shit."

He starts to nod, but it changes to a slight shake, eyes floating sideways, remembering.

"Yes, I suppose. But it just feels like normal to me."

She extends a forefinger, taps his wrist.

"Are you autistic?"

He squints, purses his lips.

"I have several symptoms that appear on the autism spectrum. But it's hard to say which of my symptoms might be genetic and which are from the box. I have trouble with affect, interpreting emotion. Understanding my own. I have intense focus. Ability to isolate interests, obsessively. My prosody, when I don't concentrate, becomes odd, flat, inflectionless. Non sequiturs slip out."

He rubs the side of his nose with his thumb.

"I also have very high visual and aural acuity. Low empathy. Helpful. With my work."

"Low empathy. I guess that would be helpful."

Her fingertip is still on his wrist, and Skinner places one of his own on top of it, brings his eyes back to her face. It's getting harder to look at her face. This is the danger of protecting things. A maxim in its own right. *The more you invest in protecting an asset, the greater its value becomes.*

He presses down on her fingertip.

"It feels like that to me, killing. When it's happening. It can be problematic later. From what I'm told, other people feel more. But that doesn't mean, Jae, that I want to do it. Not all the time. Anyway."

He looks up and down the length of the car, people beginning to rouse themselves. The landscape outside has been becoming more populated, outskirts of a city now. Copenhagen.

Jae hasn't moved.

Skinner points at the backpack on the floor between their feet, the laptops inside.

"Tickets?"

She used the Wi-Fi earlier, refreshing the Eurail website dozens of times before getting in. She picks up the pack.

"Copenhagen to Cologne, connection in Hamburg."

She takes out her phone, looks at the time display.

"With the boat train from Rødby to Puttgarden about an hour after we pull out of Copenhagen. Crossing water."

Skinner nods.

"You booked the tickets with my card?"

"Yes."

"If they didn't transfer from the night train to this one, they'll be on board for Copenhagen to Cologne."

He smiles.

Jae doesn't.

"Funny?"

"Cologne. Where Haven killed Terrence."

She fiddles with a zipper tab on her pack.

"Do you know it was him?"

Skinner's hand goes to the small of his back, touches steel, returns.

"Yes. It doesn't matter."

He smiles again.

"He found my mom for me. Terrence did. Arranged a meeting. So I could ask her. Things."

He stops smiling.

"No. It doesn't matter that Haven killed Terrence. It was bound to be one of us. And I'm happy, I think, that it wasn't me."

Copenhagen Central Station.

Skinner is being watched.

Jae has changed dollars for euros and Danish kroner and is now re-stocking their provisions, more triangle sandwiches and bottled water, some chocolate, dried fruit. Skinner waits for her. Not as packed here as it was in Stockholm or Lund, feeling of a busy travel holiday in a snow-storm. Unless you need a ticket. The lines running in and out of the ticket offices remind Skinner of Soviet era bread and toilet paper lines. They measure a length of hopelessness.

And there is Haven's backpacker standing in one of the lines, watching him, carelessly. She does bother to turn away when he looks directly at her, but that is her token gesture in the direction of covert surveillance. Skinner is tempted to shoot her. The urge is not substantial, rather like the pull of a rooftop's edge. *What would it be like to jump?* Skinner knows what it's like to shoot someone in a large public space. He doesn't need to inch closer to that particular ledge. She's there to watch and report. Fol-low blatantly, certify that Skinner and Jae board the train they ticketed for online with Skinner's eminently trackable credit card. Report any changes. Why bother trying to make a secret of it?

How far will she follow? Into what hazards? Skinner would like to know.

At the far end of the station, stairs, down, signs for luggage lockers, showers. The stairs are sparsely traveled, showers and lockers not popu-lar today.

Jae rejoins him, plastic shopping bag in hand.

"Food. Water. What now?"

Skinner looks at the large clock over the wide double doors that lead into the tunnels that feed the platforms. Analogue dial with a red digital display beneath.

"How long to our train?"

She looks at the clock.

"Fifteen minutes."

Skinner points at the stairs.

"Over there."

He starts to walk and she follows.

"So it's understood, I will reek rather than use a public shower in a train station."

"We're in Denmark."

"People are gross. No matter what country you're in, people are gross and they do gross things when they don't have to clean up after themselves."

He nods.

"Don't take a shower."

It smells like the steam room at a gym. Humidity wafts up, a miasma at the top of the stairs.

Jae groans.

"Fetid, Skinner. Fetid."

He doesn't attempt to contradict her, keeping his mouth shut, leading her down the stairs. An arched tunnel, tiled walls, luggage lockers at the end, branches to the right and left for showers and lavatories. An old woman is coming down the passage from the showers. A cane and a roller bag, her movements suggest an inertia that disdains rest. She transitions to the stairs, the bag banging up behind her a step at a time, rhythmic and distinct.

Skinner points at the lockers.

"Let's lock something up."

Jae walks toward the lockers. They line an L-shaped alcove, a converted luggage storage room from the era when human attendants would have taken your case and given you a ticket in exchange. Each locker door has a tiny window next to the lock, red or green.

Skinner walks to a locker on the bend at the far end of the L's long stem, away from the tunnel but still in view of it.

Jae unzips her pack, transferring the contents of her plastic shopping bag.

"What are we doing here?"

Skinner has swiped his credit card in the slot reader on one of the lockers on the top rank, shoulder level. He has the door open, hands inside, doing something.

"Stand in the corner."

Jae moves down in the short branch of the L, out of view of the tunnel, into the corner there, slipping the straps of her pack onto her shoulders. Skinner leans slightly, peeks down the L branch, sees that she's assumed a defensive stance, something similar to judo. He felt indications of some kind of training earlier when she arm-barred him, subtle force. Was that in her dossier? No. Good. Haven's people won't know. She is looking at his eyes. She doesn't like being scared. He has to remind himself sometimes, other people don't like feeling scared. He likes it because it makes sense to him. He knows where it comes from and why. He knows what to do when he's scared. It's like being excited, he thinks. Threatening excitement.

It sounds like weather. *Clouds, threatening excitement.*

It's not the backpacker but the football hooligan who steps into view in the tunnel, stops, looks at Skinner, turns, looks both ways, down toward the service doors where the tunnel ends, back up at the stairs. He grunts, a professional dissatisfaction with the circumstances, and walks to a locker, jiggling the locked latch up and down, just that much pretense here, staring at Skinner, as if the fact that he's been following too closely isn't his own damn fault.

Skinner finishes tying the knot he's been working on inside his locker. Turns toward the hooligan, nods at the lock he's jerking up and down, exasperated dumbshow.

"I have a gimmick for those."

Shrugging, *we're all in this ridiculous setup together.* Skinner reaches into his jacket with his right hand, and, turning, his left hand comes out of the locker, screened by the new angle of his body.

"One of these."

Taking the red plastic ruler, Hotel Hellsten logo on its side, from inside his jacket.

The hooligan has stopped moving the latch up and down, left hand still on it, right hand under his jacket, ostensibly scratching his stomach but actually caressing whatever firearm he has tucked there.

Skinner is holding up the red ruler, stepping toward the hooligan, left hand behind his thigh.

"Have you ever seen this one, the ruler gimmick?"

The hooligan doesn't move. Displeased with the turn of events. Not the kind to engage in professional chatter in awkward circumstances. Implacable deniability is his default setting for these situations. *I don't know what you're talking about. Just here to look at the roses. Lovely this time of year, yes?*

Skinner shakes the red ruler, holding it not unlike a bread knife, fingers wrapped loosely, three of its twenty centimeters sticking out near the heel of his palm.

"These are great."

The hooligan has a hand on the locker, one under his jacket, turning now to face Skinner, quick-draw angle. Quite relaxed. The relaxation that comes with knowing that one can pull his weapon and fire it from under his jacket, slight movement, very quick, and with accuracy. Something practiced a great deal. A move he's proud of. Rightfully so. Hard to be accurate with a shot like that. Skinner is certain the hooligan can make that shot count.

He points the ruler at the hooligan's locker.

"Watch."

He reaches toward the swipe slot, the hooligan lets go of the latch. Skinner's wrist snaps forward, bringing the straight edge of the ruler down on the sharp knob of the hooligan's radius where it juts slightly under the skin. The hooligan grunts, pulling his right hand toward the protection of his body as Skinner flips his own wrist backhand, bringing the corner of the ruler into the corner of the hooligan's right eye, raking, pause, flick of wrist, and the edge of the ruler comes down on the bridge of the hooligan's nose. Another grunt, both the hooligan's eyes are closed, tears welling under the lid of the left eye, tears and blood under the lid of the right eye. Movement under the hooligan's jacket. Skinner is so close, pivoting to face the hooligan squarely, any shot will tear him open. An unmissable target. But already, swinging up, over, elbow tight to his body for maximum speed if reduced force, comes his left hand, holding the large double knot he tied in the doubled-up compression socks, one tucked into the other, extra strength to keep the two D batteries swinging in the reinforced toes of the socks from ripping out and flying across the tunnel.

There is an equation for this. The speed at which Skinner's arm is moving, weight of the batteries, length of sock. A very good mathematician or engineer would factor in the material of the sock, the hooligan's own movement, humidity of the atmosphere. Torque is the relevant force here: *Foot pounds? Meter kilos? Newton meters?* Skinner doesn't remember the math, glitch in the conditioning from that period of his education, maybe, but he knows there is a number. There's a number to describe the force with which the batteries strike the right side of the hooligan's face, impact spread from his temple down across his upper cheekbone. The most fragile pieces, sphenoid bone and zygomatic process, are pulverized; the heavier zygomatic bone and supraorbital process are shattered. The hooligan's facial features are twisted, the blow snapping his neck around so sharply that his cheeks and lips flap. Skinner follows through, letting the mass of the batteries exhaust some of their residual momentum so that he won't snap his wrist trying to stop them, a whisk of blood fans the floor in a rooster tail, the hooligan's ruined face landing in its midst. His hand still under his jacket, the practiced shot never fired.

Footsteps in the tunnel.

Skinner stretches the doubled socks between his hands, wraps each fist once, batteries dangling at one end, and loops the middle length around the fallen hooligan's neck, dragging him down to the corner of the L and around it, Jae still in her defensive position, the fists at her hips coming up as he comes into view.

"Fuck."

Out of sight of the tunnel, Skinner stops, lowers the hooligan until he is sprawled on the floor face down, resets his grip on the sock, plants his knee in the hooligan's back between his shoulder blades and just below the base of his neck, and chokes him to death.

It does feel more. More than the pressure of a finger. Much more. In part, he understands, because Jae is watching and he knows this must be disturbing her greatly and he doesn't know how to change that or help her or keep her from being afraid of him or disgusted by him or any of the other sensible ways that most people feel when they see someone killing another human being in front of them. But it also feels like more because this man was following them. Working for Haven. And was a danger to Jae. It feels like more because he is protecting his asset. Doing something he has conditioned himself to do.

The hooligan is dead. Skinner drops him, leaves the bloody sock twisted deep into the tissue of his throat, and looks up at Jae. Her fists are clenched, knuckles white, and she's staring at the body, nodding.

Her eyes move to Skinner; she stops nodding.

"He wanted to kill me?"

Skinner straightens. His lower back hurts from straining to strangle the man.

"Not now. On the train. They're watching to see that I get on the train. Cross is hoping you'll leave before then. Once you board with me, you'll become dispensable. Valid collateral."

She nods, one sharp tilt of her head, then level.

"One less to worry about then."

Skinner steps clear of the body.

"Yes, that's what I was thinking."

Jae looks at the body again, at their surroundings. Skinner can see that she's starting to come back to where they are, after going to a place where people die violently before your eyes. Second time in three days. She's seen it before, and what it feels like is coming back to her. How you get used to it. That's good for some people. Not good for others. Skinner doesn't know which kind she is.

She unclenches her fists.

"We should get the fuck out of here."

Skinner offers his hand.

"Yes."

She takes it. Upstairs, the backpacker is loitering outside one of the call shops. She watches them come up the stairs and pass her. She waits. When the hooligan doesn't follow she starts toward the stairs, but the sound of a scream from below turns her around and sets her after Skinner and Jae. Skinner watches most of this pantomime in small glances over his shoulder, a stuttering kinetoscope of pursuit. He wonders if she and the hooligan were friends in any way. It might make her vulnerable if they were, unbalanced. Easier. Time will tell.

The boat train, final destination Munich, is at the platform, flip-down seats line the walls. Skinner and Jae claim two of them. People seated in the aisle rather than packed in on their feet. One hour to

Rødby. Then the crossing. Jae is still holding his hand, her index finger pulsing, just that small amount of pressure, over and over again. But what he feels is more than that. Much more.

They want everyone off the train.

It's a matter of safety. Once the train rolls onto the tracks that run directly into the lowest deck of the ferry, all passengers must disembark and climb the stairs to the upper decks before the crossing can begin. Nothing needs to be explained. All one has to do is imagine an accident, breached hull, ferry sinking, train full of people below the waterline, and just a few narrow staircases rising to the decks where life vests, dories, and rafts are to be found. But, this being Europe and not the United States, security is a relative matter. No tally of tickets is made as passengers file out of the train, along a narrow walkway, gritty nonslip tape underfoot, through a bulkhead door and up the stairs.

One flight up, an open door leading to the auto deck, also emptying. Rows of dozens of cars, hatchbacks, low station wagons, narrow vans. The small, fleet, distant cousins of the American freeways' behemoths. And then the main deck. Enclosed, shopping opportunities (duty-free!), a seafood restaurant, coffee, spiral stair to the upper deck, and doors to the exterior deck both port and starboard. The first passengers out of their cars and off the train are already emerging from the duty-free with shopping bags. Chocolate and beer seem to be the most popular items. Universal stress relievers.

"Air."

Jae is pointing to the starboard exit.

"Or are there too many potential witnesses if you want to kill someone?"

He looks through the long bank of windows at the dozen or so wind whipped smokers and sightseers outside.

"I'll adapt."

He follows her outside, the wind trying to smack them backward as soon as they open the door, both leaning into it, Jae advancing to the rail. Skinner joins her there. Sky and sea are matching gray, erasing the

horizon line, just a flat and nearly featureless background with the occasional white windmill, mounted with what looks like the propeller
blades from a massive decommissioned transport plane from the previous century, poking up from the waters.

"I was used as bait."

Jae is looking down, past the rust streaked hull, into the water.

"I was an asset, in Iraq, seven years ago. And I was bait. First we became lovers, my *protection* and I. Then he used me as bait. I didn't like
it. Am I bait now?"

Skinner touches the back of his head.

"No."

He flips up the collar of his jacket.

"Did it work?"

"What?"

"When you were used as bait."

She's looking at the deck, the sky, the sea, anywhere but Skinner.

"To the extent that someone tried to kidnap me and he killed them,
yes. Is that how these things are measured?"

Skinner wants to cup her face with his palm, wants to feel if she'll
lean into his hand. His fingers are cold, it would feel good.

"Not for me."

She forces her hands deep in the pockets of her jacket.

"It was Haven. You understand?"

It takes him a moment, but then, yes, he understands.

"That's odd."

Another complicated emotional response from her, something like
laughter, but it seems intended to express frustration or exasperation
more than delight.

She shakes her head.

"*Odd.* Yeah. I think it starts at *odd.* Then it heads straight into *freak-
ishly bizarre.*"

Skinner thinks, nods.

"It is odd. But also, for me, Haven has always been a part of my life.
Entangled. He's an influence. I see that it's odd for us both to have
been lovers with you. But it also feels like how it's always been. And you

know, as far as using you as bait, it could be said in his defense that he had a very difficult childhood."

She doesn't smile. Why would she? It's not in the least funny. But she does bring her hands out of her pockets and uses them to snap his collar back up when the wind has blown it down, tugging the wings close together in the front, releasing them, framing his face, her hands a few inches from his cheeks.

"Anyone ever tell you that you look like a spy?"

He casts an eye down at the epaulet on his left shoulder.

"I was traveling in Europe. Everyone wears these. Very good for anonymity."

"Yeah-uh?"

"If we'd stayed in the States I would have picked up something appropriate."

"Affectation, Skinner. Pure affectation."

Her hands go to his shoulders and smooth across them, down his arms, stopping at his elbows.

"But you do pull it off."

She tugs on his elbows and, watchers or not, kisses him. Their lips coming apart, she keeps him close.

"Why will they come after you on the boat?"

"I disappeared before. Cross won't want me to disappear again. So it has to be soon, while my options are limited. Before the planes start flying again. Once the sky is open I can be very gone. He doesn't want me where he can't see."

"Cross is afraid of you."

"Yes. He's not a stupid man."

She almost smiles, an appreciator of blackest humor.

"So what now?"

He puts some space between them, better to think.

"Now we choose the ground."

In the duty-free Skinner buys a very expensive bottle of perfume. Outside the shop he takes it from the bag, slips the bottle from the box, and sprays a little on the back of her hand.

She sniffs.

"Vile."

"Then you won't mind breaking it."

Down the corridor, restless people. Their journeys, already a kind of non-time between places they want to be, have become lengthy parentheticals to their lives. The ferry seemed like a romantic interlude for a moment, but now it's just one more fucking thing to deal with before they have to cram back onto the train and figure out the next leg of their travels. Tense exhaustion, even for the beer drinkers and chocolate eaters. They are massing in small numbers near the roped-off hall that leads to the stairwell door, and when Jae changes her grip on the perfume bag, upends it, grabs for the falling bottle but succeeds only in slapping it higher into the air before it falls to the deck with a crash, the resulting splash envelops them all in a dense cloud of scent named after an American pop star who is massively successful in Scandinavia, if nowhere else. Her popularity aside, no one seems happy to have their shoes doused in her perfume. By the time they are realizing that they will be smelling this woman's idea of glamour for the remainder of their trips, and by the time the purser who had been standing by the protective rope has found a crew member he can send for a mop and bucket, Skinner and Jae are inside the rope, opening the door, and stepping onto the top landing of the steep stairs.

Jae is shaking her head.

"Stuff like that works?"

Skinner pulls the door closed, takes her elbow, leads her down.

"Making people look another direction is easy enough. After that you need to move confidently. People are conditioned not to question confidence."

"And if the door was locked?"

He shrugs.

"I'm confident I would have thought of something else."

The man who steps out of the door from the auto deck surprises Skinner, as much for the Bulgarian Arcus 98 in his hand as for the fact that he isn't one of Haven's people. He opens his mouth to tell them what he wants them to do to keep him from shooting them, and Skinner's right hand comes up, the red ruler slipping out of the cuff of his jacket into his hand. Skinner shoves it into the man's open mouth, not breaking stride, pulling Jae with him. When the end of the ruler hits the back of the man's throat he gags and gasps at the same time, tries to back up, raising his hands as if to push away from the discomfort, gun a forgotten prop. He is on the brink of puking when his heels reach the edge of the landing and he falls backward down the steps, head striking the steel edges of no less than three of them as he tumbles, before sliding to a limp halt.

The ruler is broken. Skinner doesn't take time to mourn it, dropping the pieces into a pocket of the man's quilted Eddie Bauer parka before dragging him back up the steps, wiping up most of the blood from his split scalp and broken nose in so doing. On the auto deck landing, Jae is holding teh door open, waiting. From the deck, car alarms sound in discord, triggered by the rolling Baltic Sea. Every time one cycles to a stop, another two start. Skinner pulls the man through the door, waves Jae in, closes the door. It reeks of exhaust and rubber and burnt oil and gasoline. Deep thrum of the ferry's diesel engines and the wail and squawk of the alarms. Skinner is pleased.

In the second aisle of cars he finds a Skoda Superb unlocked. Pops the trunk, dumps the man inside. There's quite a bit of blood. More coming out of the open head wounds. Heart still pumping. Skinner takes the Arcus from his trench coat pocket. Jae covers her ears and turns her head, but neither precaution is necessary. Before he pulls the trigger, Skinner closes the trunk lid until he can fit only the barrel of the gun inside. The sound of the shot is a slight pop in the din of the auto deck.

He latches the trunk, points aft, takes them between rows of cars, hunched, feeling inside wheel wells as he goes car to car, moving confidently, until he finds a magnetic key box under the right quarter panel of a midnineties Saab 900. He unlocks the passenger-side door, holds the door for Jae, closes it, walks to the other side and climbs in.

Marginally quieter.

Skinner scoots down in his seat and Jae imitates him, both half in the foot wells, heads below the level of the windows.

"I thought we were choosing the ground."

Skinner is checking the Arcus's clip. It was full before he shot the man in the Eddie Bauer parka. Eighteen rounds left now.

"They beat us to it."

It's a surprisingly good gun. Not least of all because it is Bulgarian. When one thinks of Balkan guns one generally thinks of misfires and jamming. Skinner wonders if the man who owned it might have actually been Bulgarian. What that could mean. Could Eastern European gangsters really be behind the West-Tebrum attack? Are he and Jae following a wild goose of Terrence's devising?

"Skinner?"

"Sorry. Distracted by the implications of the gun."

"Skinner."

An urgent whisper. She's sunk lower in her seat, pointing in the direction of the Saab's left headlight where an unusually tall man, with a face that looks as if it has not enough skin to stretch over the massive bones underneath it, is creeping along in an awkward crouch that just allows him to peek over the rooflines of most of the cars on the deck. He has an Uzi with a sound suppressor. Venerable, reliable, very good for spraying a huge number of bullets at several clumped-up targets standing nearby. Israeli. Skinner's mind skips a beat. Could the Israelis be involved? They had a hand in the Stuxnet worm's creation. What would be their motive for attacking the US?

"Skinner."

A more urgent whisper. Warranted. The man with the Israeli submachine gun is crouching just forward to the driver's-side rearview mirror, an expression of more than slight confusion on his taut features as he tries to make sense of the fact that the two people he's looking for have suddenly appeared in front of him in positions of helplessness. Then a flat sharkish smile threatens to rip the corners of his mouth as he raises the Uzi. The smile crimps with annoyance as Skinner leans on the horn, eliciting the slightest of flinches, and then disappears entirely when Skinner opens the heavy door of the Saab (reinforced for side impacts) and slams it into the tall man's bent knees. Three shots from the Arcus, aimed through the V between the door's window frame and pillar. Chest. Chest again. Neck. The tall man falls.

The right rear window of the Kia next to the Saab explodes. Automotive safety glass, it pebbles, most of it blown inward by the bullet. Skinner slips off the seat, spinning, squatting low in the space between the two cars, trying to see whoever it is that's just come very close to killing him. To some extent he'd be happy to discover Haven's backpacker or the black-clad arbitrage skydiver. At least then he'd know who he's dealing with. On the other hand, the Eddie Bauer man and the tall man weren't very good at their jobs, and he'd be even more happy to cherry-pick someone else who hasn't been trained especially well. The missed shot is a good sign.

He flattens himself, deck plates, wet, oily, rails at regular intervals running crosswise to the parked cars. Insurance to keep them from rolling too far should anyone forget to leave an emergency brake set. He'd like to see someone faced away from him, someone he could attack from behind and kill with his hands. Hiding more bodies so that they won't be discovered until well after the ferry docks and he and Jae are under way is going to be difficult enough without more blood to mop up. To say nothing of bullet holes in the cars. Something shifts. Tone. The engines vibrate with a subtle difference. Change of course? Or are they approaching the ferry landing at Puttgarden? How long before drivers return to their cars? Feet. Boots. Military. Desert. Lightly used. Legs of expensive denim covering the laced shafts, slightly rolled at the bottom. Coming this way, other side of the Saab. There's no good way to handle this kind of thing, parking lot scenarios. You've either been in one before or you haven't. Skinner hasn't. But he doesn't think it likely that a mercenary who spent the bulk of his short career in places where one wears desert boots has handled the situation either. Common sense dictates that you can either go high or low. Unless you have a mirror on a stick you're not going to be able to effectively look under the cars and then over them. The man in the desert boots has chosen high. In a game of roshambo with rock and scissors as the only options, he has chosen scissors. Skinner is fairly certain he has a rock. He squirms under the car, setting the safety on the Arcus, reversing his grip so that he holds the barrel, hammerlike. Under the car, booted feet close, the man will see Jae any moment now. Skinner doesn't want that. Bit of a stretch from here, but he reaches, grabs for the man's ankle, misses it and gets a handful of expensive denim, pulls. Big man, a great deal of mass, well balanced, he stumbles, falls against the next car over, but that's as far as he goes. Leaning against a compact four-door Opel, Euro model not sold in the States, looking down at Skinner, head, arm, one shoulder sticking out from under the Saab. He's got another Arcus. So maybe they are Bulgarian. Or maybe the two men shop at the same store. Or maybe the procurement officer for whichever contractor they might work for got a deal on a bunch of Arcuses and their master armorer has no choice but to put them into the field on every op so the procurement guy looks good. All Skinner can say about the gun right now is that it's insanely hard to try to blindly juggle it around with one hand while you're lying on your stomach under a car, so that you can use it in the manner it was designed for rather than as an improvised club.

"Be still."

English. English from England. Urban. Working class. Not an officer and a gentleman. A soldier in her Majesty's service. Formerly. Wherever he's from, he's not shooting for the moment. Skinner assumes it's for the same reasons he was reluctant to open fire himself. Blood. Mess.

Skinner drops his gun. It makes very little noise, but the man with the desert boots appears to have very good hearing.

"What the fuck was that? What are you doing under there?"

Each question emphasized with a jab of his gun, but anything else he might ask is cut off when the Saab's passenger door flies open and Jae flies out from behind it. Low, leading with her shoulder, targeting the elbow of the arm that ends in a hand holding a gun. Done properly, she'll push the gun to the side, binding the arm against the man's body, while planting her shoulder in his gut. Tripping over Skinner's still-extended arm puts her a bit off target, sending her headlong rather than shoulder-first, but she does shove him sideways, gun pushed away from Skinner, throwing him off balance for a moment. Skinner is reaching with both hands. With his left he's straining to get the grip on the man's ankle that he wanted in the first place, with his right he's reaching for the spot where he thinks his gun fell under the Saab. Doing two things at once, he gets a bit of both. Grabs the man's jeans again, and picks up the Arcus by the barrel again.

He heaves, pulling the man's leg toward him and hauling himself further from beneath the Saab. The Englishman's good balance is compromised now, his foot and leg come toward Skinner, his body falling the other way; Jae's shove has knocked him into the aisle between the cars, the Opel won't be breaking his fall this time. But Jae is tipping as well, going down on top of the man, too close to use her fists, trying to bring a knee up into his groin, impossible when the floor is pulled out from underneath your feet. They're down, the Englishman takes the brunt but keeps his head from whacking the deck plates, sensibilities intact, his left arm is looping around Jae, right is bringing his gun back into the thick of things. When he has it pointed at her head he'll either tell everybody to stop moving or shoot her and move on to the next target. Decision making becomes simplified when you're fighting for your life. Before the Englishman has to make that decision Skinner is hammering his genitals with the butt of his own Arcus, turning the Englishman's mind into a blank white screen of pain that no thought can occupy. It stops the gun moving toward Jae, so Skinner does it again, which causes the gun to drop from the Englishman's hand, so he does it again, which causes the Englishman to let go of Jae as he tries to curl into a fetal position, so Skinner hammers him again, which is about when Jae has gotten up to her knees to deliver an elbow blow to the hinge of the Englishman's jaw and break it in two places.

"Fuck!"

She scrambles backward, between the cars, drops her bottom onto the deck plates, puts her head between her knees and hyperventilates.

"Fuckfuckfuck."

Skinner crawls out from under the car, checks to see that there are no obvious wounds on Jae, backing off when she slaps at him. He returns to the Englishman, pulls the belt from his trench coat, and uses it to strangle him.

The Saab is a hatchback, but it does have a luggage cover. The Englishman fits under it. The tall man he has to drag to the roomy trunk of the Skoda Superb. Some rearrangement is necessary to accommodate two dead men. By the end, Skinner's trench coat, grimed with oily water and mud from the deck, in no longer serviceable. He empties the pockets and leaves it with the corpses. The blood on the deck plates is blending with the slurry of oil and mud; the spatter from shooting the tall man flecked two cars that Skinner took a pass at with the trench coat before dumping it. The window that was shot out will be someone else's problem, he hopes. Chalked up to theft or the vagaries of sea travel. He peeks inside the Kia to see if there is something of relative value he can snatch to bolster any suspicions of a thief, but short of yanking out the processor mounted under the driver's seat he can't see anything that will help the cause.

The ferry's engines are most definitely slowing. Have been for some time. No one will be allowed below decks until they dock. The ferry gives a slight lurch.

"Can you get up?"

Jae stopped hyperventilating while he was cleaning up but hasn't lifted her head until now.

"Yes."

He offers his hand and she takes it, pulling herself to her feet.

"So that's it?"

Skinner leads her to the first row of cars nearest the stairwell door, crouches behind a Volkswagen Jetta.

"Sort of."

She crouches next to him.

"Elaborate."

Skinner points toward the cars with the dead bodies in them.

"I think they were Hann-Aoki."

She blinks.

"Why does H-A want to kill you?"

"They don't. I don't think they do."

"Skinner!"

His name barked with exhaustion and diminishing patience. Skinner takes note and tries to be clear, mindful of his prosody and the order of his thoughts.

"They acted like Hann-Aoki. Not very good. And not planning to kill. Here for you. I'm still with you, protecting you. They assume value. Information about West-Tebrum and the anarchists. Trying to salvage something so Kestrel doesn't control the new market."

She rubs her elbow. She did a good job delivering that blow, but bone on bone is always bad. She'll have a bruise, swelling. Skinner thinks about finding ice.

"Skinner. Haven's people?"

He shakes his head.

"I don't know."

The door opens and people start to file in. Skinner shows his palm to Jae, *Wait*. They wait, shift ground once or twice, moving to stay out of sight, the final round of alarms set off by the crossing are blipping off as drivers find their cars. Skinner thinks he hears a curse in German. The owner of the Kia seeing his broken window? Then it's time, enough people, density feels correct, he waves Jae to her feet, both of them popping up, walking with confidence around a car or two, shuffling into the foot traffic, turning, going against the stream toward the stair door. Nods of embarrassment, smiles, a few words of clumsy American-accented German. *So silly, wrong deck. We are on the train deck. Pardon. Pardon. So sorry. Pardon.*

Joining the rail travelers, down to the bottom deck, their train awaits. Remarkably, there are no conflicts over who was sitting where. In these circumstances no one seems inclined to poach seats. Really, Europe, so civilized. The train moves, pulls slowly from the open bay of the ferry onto the rails of Fehmarn. Cross the small island, then a span of bridge, then the German mainland. Then Hamburg. Then Cologne.

Packed into the train, surrounded by people, there is time to sleep. A typical reaction after stress, extreme fatigue. Jae says something about trying to get online and book their next leg from Cologne to Paris but never unzips her pack for her laptop. Instead she leans against Skinner, head on his shoulder, closes her eyes, and falls into a sleep filled with lurching starts and stops as the train trundles along.

Skinner closes his own eyes. He is watched, he knows, but cannot separate the sweep of bored and curious people-watching eyes in the car from those that might be more focused. Nor does he care to. Anyone watching him with professional intent will have some idea of what he did on the boat train, and they will be calculating the costs involved in making a similar attempt of their own. And there is also the comfort inherent in the eyes, pressure of observation, that draws him back to his childhood and the box. So he sleeps too.

Dreams of Terrence. His mentor studying the intricacies of a giant knot. Great knot experts in lab coats and monk's robes detail the impossibility of untying the knot, speak of the lessons it teaches, preach the wisdom of learning to live with the knot. Something moves in the knot. Locked in the threads, minuscule, twisted and choked, bodies, people, struggling. The knot experts tug at a thread or two, shrug, and turn their backs. Terrence reaches into the jacket pocket where his notebook is always at the ready and draws from it a sword, old, notched, but keen. He raises it and cuts, parting the threads of the knot, cleaving some of the people even as it frees the rest.

He wakes outside Hamburg. The dream slipping away.

They transfer trains in the dark. Not crowded at all on the Deutsche Bahn. Awake now. Jae diving back into Terrence's USB. The dream coming back to Skinner as she does so. The sword Terrence wielded made a noise. Sharp edge sighing as it cut through the knot. *Skinner,* the blade whispered. He doesn't need his subconscious to tell him he's being used by his dead friend. But he's interested in the detritus that washes up in there. A sword that whispers his name as it cuts. An image that may have been born when he was killing the men on the boat train. As he heard silent whispering in his mind all the while. *Jae. Jae. Jae.* For strength.

They are quiet on the Hamburg train, night again. Jae lost in the data. Skinner lost in something else, wondering how long until he will be a sword again. He feels good.

Later, in the Cologne Hauptbahnhof, things go bad.

cathedral

THE STATION IS empty.

Coming down the steps from the platforms into the echoing concrete tunnels lined with gated shops. Those for whom the station is a final stop cluster together and hustle toward the main entrance and the cab stand beyond. Jockeying for position, desperate to grab one of the few taxis that will be lingering outside in this bleak hour lodged between midnight and dawn. The others, stuck here until departures resume at 0800, follow the faint sound of a techno beat coming from a glowing storefront down one of the branching tunnels that lead to the station's concourse.

Jae looks at Skinner and he nods toward the source of the music. They walk, Jae a half step ahead, lagging just behind the gaggle of stranded travelers. The glow and the music are coming from a sandwich shop. German iteration on Subway. Rolls of dense, dark bread stuffed with assorted wursts and pale cheeses, fringed with lettuce hued an unnaturally bright green. Everyone in their group queues up, all eyes on the espresso machine manned by a slender Turk with the accent of a Westphalia native; descendant of Gasatarbeiter parents who would have come here for the abundant factory jobs of the sixties. He moves in constant rhythm, some part of his body, neck, fingers, shoulders, knees, feet, always responding to the beats coming from the small silver speakers he's cabled to the finger-smudged white case of his touch-wheel iPod. No longer supported by software updates, but serving its purpose well in this context, keeping the coffee boy in motion and awake on the graveyard shift. A staccato riff from the speakers, no midrange, bass qualities overmatched by the quantities of low end trying to pass through them, treble trying to carry all the information compressed into the MP3 file that emerges as music. Soundtrack in the modern age, tinny, slight, cranked-up, always referencing the past. The kid's wrists pick up the stutter from the speakers, responding as it slows, letting it creep up his arms into his neck and shoulders. Carrier of the beat. He even takes orders to the beat, weaving his questions and nonverbal responses into his dance. Standing near the glass counter, holding their white ceramic saucers and demitasse cups, Skinner and Jae watch him.

They are the last ones at the kiosk. Shouts come down the tunnel from where they can see it open into the concourse. A large, high-ceilinged space accustomed to the traffic of thousands, it feels haunted without them. Drunks approaching, in town from the suburbs, the party is now over, dumped here by exasperated taxi drivers. A group of five, two girls and three boys. Slight tension of uneven numbers. One of the boys is going without. Past midnight drunks drawn by the allure of junk food. Skinner finishes his coffee, takes Jae's cup and saucer, places them on the counter with his own, the dancer nods, up-down bob to the beat. Then Skinner takes her arm and leads her away from the kiosk and the music and the dancer and the drunks, away from the concourse, down one of the tunnels, rolling gates pulled closed over shopfronts, walls pierced by stairs that lead up to the platforms. Gray. Gray walls and floor and ceiling, gray light. Scuff of their own footsteps on the filthy tile, drunken debate over what to order fading behind them, music gone.

Skinner has a gun in his hand.

It's the one he took from the first man he killed on the boat train. *First man he killed. On the boat train.* Double qualifier. Skinner has killed more than one man while she has been with him, and in more than one location. Without asking it to, her mind runs a tally, comes up with the number seven. Three at Oasis Two. One at Copenhagen Central. Three on the boat train. Could there be more that she doesn't know of? Certainly there could be. Then her mind counts up the number of times they've had sex. Three times. Twice on the night train.

Two sessions. They fucked twice the first time, and once, hurried before Lund, the second. Seven divided by three is? 2.33. She doesn't know why her brain is crunching that particular number, but she feels it reaching for a memory of the number of times she had sex with Haven and shuts it down. She can do this, close an avenue of unwanted thought, by picturing her mom dying. It is more or less a mental self-destruct that obliterates the present moment, but she's unwilling to let her brain dwell on the unlikeliness of her having taken both Haven and Skinner as lovers. It will lead down too many rabbit holes of paranoia. Places she does not want to go because she so desperately wants to trust Skinner.

She comes back to the moment, the detonation of her mom's death fading, as Skinner leads her to one of the stairs, cold, very cold air flowing down from the platform. He backs her onto the first step, moves her close to the wall. Her eyes are almost level with his now. He kisses her, small kiss.

"Nothing will happen. And then everything will happen at once."

His hand moves between their bodies, finds her hand, gives her something that causes her almost to think of her mom again. She resists the urge. She needs to stay here now.

"You're too close to her, Skinner."

Man at the top of the stairs, backlit by a buzzing incandescent halo that flickers atop a pole. Dark clothes that fit him very well, rich blacks and browns, splash of red on his chest. He doesn't seem to mind the cold at all. His gun is silver, a flat finish that dully reflects the flickering light. It has the appearance of something designed self-consciously to look retro. Circa WWII, but with all the modern comforts and efficiencies. Like a Wurlitzer housing an Internet connection to a vast digital catalogue of pop hits. His vanity is tangible. She'd be happy to shoot him. Or to watch Skinner do the shooting.

He makes a vague gesture with the barrel of his ostentatious weapon, a short arc to his right, angled toward the ground.

"Caren is going to shoot you in the head. Standing that close to your friend, Caren could miss and hit her. I doubt it, but things happen. Haven says not to kill her if we can avoid it. If you take a step back, that would make it a sure thing."

Jae looks over Skinner's shoulder in the direction the man waved his gun, up the tunnel, where the stairs drop from the opposite platform. Holding her own pistol in the practiced manner of a target shooter, braced, one third of her body concealed by the corner of the wall, steady, two hands, a young woman dressed for a long hike. Short hair, nose piercing. The woman is over thirty meters away, but looking at the eyes sighting down the barrel of her gun, the aesthetic opposite of the fetish object the man at the top of the stairs carries, Jae believes she can see the clarity of their blueness.

When she shoots at the woman, Jae aims for her torso. Impossible shot, bringing from between their bodies the pistol Skinner pressed into her hands when they were kissing, firing from the hip. It's a blind shot, and it misses the woman by several meters, hitting the wall, spraying concrete chips that cause her to blink as she pulls the trigger of her own weapon. Her shot is also off target, just over their heads, close enough to hear the impact, feel their faces peppered with concrete dust and slivers. Jae's gun bucks harder than she expected, years removed from the last time she pulled a trigger, nearly jumps from her hand, her other hand tries to help out, coming away from the warmth between their bodies into the cold, managing to keep the gun from dropping to the ground just as Skinner shoves her and she starts to fall against the steps. Another gunshot, she doesn't know who has fired (not her), and there is blood now, in her left eye, and she feels the trigger under her finger again and holds tighter and squeezes it three times, pointed, she thinks, in the direction of the young woman named Caren, then she hits the steps hard and the gun is out of her hand, bouncing onto the tile floor of the tunnel. She looks for Skinner. There he is, moving away from her, gun in his hand, the one Terrence sent to him, firing, down the tunnel, evenly spaced shots, very professional, walking briskly to the opposite wall. Jae wants to pick up her gun. Skinner is shooting at Caren, someone needs to shoot at the asshole at the top of the stairs. She looks for the gun, sees it, lunges for it. She'll look for the asshole when she has the gun. But before she has the gun, the asshole's body comes down the steps, a slow, boneless slide, face down, forehead hitting each step with a sound that is lost in the constant gunfire being exchanged by Skinner and Caren.

Jae thinks she must have missed something, a phase in the gun battle when Skinner shot the fancy-pistol-asshole. Her brain wants to rebuild the sequence, find the missed beat, somehow relate it to the coffee kid's spontaneous choreography. It takes a wrenching mental twist to force her brain in another direction, toward the gun on the floor. But is it the asshole's blood in her left eye? He was on her right. Whose blood is in her eye? Her hand is on the gun. Funny that it feels so familiar already, fits her grasp, finger snakes around trigger. It's in her hand. Something to shoot at? But the shooting has stopped.

Skinner is gone. Caren is gone.

Jae turns and crawls up the stairs to the platform, into the flickering light. Drizzle, barely falling, a density just greater than mist. The lights up and down the platforms glow vaguely. Jae stretches over the top stairs, edges of concrete digging into her shins, thighs, stomach, breasts; arms outstretched, hands together, holding the gun. Shadows and lights on the opposite platform. Dark shelters plastered with ads for kitchenware and video games and calling cards. She wonders how long the German police take to respond to reports of shots fired. Her brain takes this as an invitation and summons a comparison of violent crimes in the EU in the years before and after the economic collapse. Connects that to cash for cars programs in Germany. Somewhere in there, a section covering replacement of vehicles in government motor fleets. Rüsselsheim is less than two hundred kilometers away; Opel corporate headquarters. Cologne police mostly drive Opels. Souped-up Opels painted green and something. No. Silver and blue. No more regional police colors in Germany, they all use silver and blue.

Gunshot.

She never wiped the blood from her left eye and now it's crusted shut and she can't scrape it clean without taking a hand off the gun and that shot came from her left side and she can't see shit over there. She turns her head. Mist and darkness between the platform lights.

Gunshot.

A spray of gunshots. Flare of muzzle flash, burr of a machine pistol, bullet impacts, shattering glass. One of the shelters on the opposite platform disintegrates. Jae aims at the ghost images the flare left on the vision of her right eye and starts firing before it can begin to float, before she can think about what a person looks like when she is shot and what it will mean if she makes someone look that way. She shoots before she can remember if Skinner took the Uzi the tall man was carrying on the boat train and whether or not he might have somehow been carrying it since then. Before any of that she empties the remaining rounds in her pistol, waiting for Caren to draw a bead on her own muzzle flashes, return fire, and take off the top of her head, and only stops shooting when the slide locks back on the empty clip. She drops the gun and writhes back down the steps, wiping at the crust of blood over her eye, realizing that it is coming from a deep cut on her forehead.

"Fräulein?"

The dancer from the sandwich shop, descendant of Turkish immigrant workers, peeking around the corner of the tunnel. Looking from her to the corpse of the asshole and back to her.

"Sie okay, fräulein?"

Footsteps on tile, the dancer turns, sticks his hands into the air. Jae thinks about doing the same but decides to wait until the police actually tell her to do so. Arms too heavy to lift unless someone forces the issue.

Skinner comes into view at the foot of the stairs, gun in hand, suit damp, hair a mess. He looks at Jae, touches his forehead over his left eye.

"Okay?"

She nods.

He holds out his empty hand.

"Let's go."

The dancer still has his hands in the air, eyes only for Skinner's gun. Jae comes down the steps, stops.

"Polizei?"

The dancer shrugs.

"Yah."

Jae nods, turns to Skinner.

"The police are coming."

Skinner bends and picks up the asshole's silver pistol, frowns at it, sets it back down as if rejecting it as an unsound premise, not bothering with the shtick of wiping fingerprints. The station is filled with CC cameras.

Jae remembers the Israeli hit squad in Dubai. The local police used security camera records from across the city to track their steps from the moment they entered the country until they left it after assassinating Mahmoud al-Mabhouh. With a modicum of international help the German police will have little trouble tracing them back to Stockholm, the flight from Miami. Jae traveled on her real passport. She imagines a tectonic event, something like the one that demolished Haiti, shaking her life into rubble and dust.

She looks at Skinner.

"Can we run now?"

He tucks his gun under his jacket.

"Yes."

They do. Down the tunnel, past the gaping drunks, through the concourse, under the giant clock, out onto a vast plaza of gray slabs, light pillars casting pools of greenish light, drizzle falling heavier now. Cologne Cathedral, Gothic spires and arches, spiny and ominous in the dark, looming. The cab stand, three drivers clustered, smoking, one turning toward them, Middle Eastern, bundled against the alien cold and damp. He points at the first cab in line and Skinner nods at him.

"Flughafen Köln."

Said loud enough for all the drivers to hear.

But two blocks from the station, sirens in the air, Skinner shows his gun to the driver. An expression of extreme displeasure, he slaps the side of the wheel, pulls over, starts to say something about how little money he has. Skinner points his gun at the door. The driver slaps the wheel again, once more, shakes his head, zips his jacket to his chin, pulls on the hood, and gets out as Skinner and Jae both open their own doors and move to the front seats. The driver last seen in the mirror, hands in pockets, stamping his feet on the pavement. A kilometer away, on a tree lined street of apartment buildings, Skinner pulls up next to a man just about to unlock the door of his Mercedes, briefcase under one arm, travel mug in hand. They interrupt his morning commute ritual, leaving him in a state not unlike that of the taxi driver.

Only once they are in the Mercedes and under way does Jae look at her backpack and see the large hole in it, edges melted. She unzips it and finds that the hole continues through Skinner's laptop, enters her Toughbook, and stops somewhere inside of it.

"Who shot me?"

Skinner glances at the Toughbook in her hands.

"I don't know. You went down on the steps."

She makes certain Terrence's USB is in an inner jacket pocket, looks through the pack. Nothing important. She doesn't want to carry anything.

"I thought you pushed me down."

"No. The bullet."

She touches the scabbing cut on her forehead.

"How did I?"

"I don't know."

He's driving back toward the center of Cologne, they cross the Rhine. Jae thinks about the bullet that almost found its way into her back.

"Did I shoot Caren?"

He takes them around a traffic circle.

"No. You got her attention. But you didn't shoot her."

"Did you?"

"I killed her."

"Oh."

He stops on a bridge and they dump the contents of the backpack into the river and the backpack itself and their phones and Skinner's old ID and credit cards, and then they get in the car and drive southwest.

Paris. The cimetière Montmartre. Destination.

Hoping for a message left by the dead.

PART FIVE

politics

THE SENA MEN have come.

No one is surprised. Something is happening in the slum. There are no secrets from the Shiv Sena in the slums. Even now, after the death of the patriarch Bal Thackeray, as their hold on power in Bombay (*Mumbai,* insist the Sena) has finally eroded after over fifty years, they cannot be ignored. You do not ignore the bully and his friends at the end of the alley. You can only hope they do not see you. The Sena need the slums, the votes of the slums. Dharavi with its Muslims and immigrants, this was once where the Sena came to run riot with swords and lathis, cutting and beating. And with jars of gasoline. A favorite gesture of the Sena, dousing a man or woman in gasoline and burning him or her alive. David's father tells the story of a Sena in the '93 riots setting fire to a Muslim news agent, undoing his fly and pissing on the burning man, laughing at the hissing sound it made.

So now, here are the Sena men. *What is happening here? What is in this shed? Who are all these new people? There are complaints and we want to know.*

The biggest one has a gun in his pants.

A column of one hundred Sena men weaving through the tight alleys and lanes of the slum. Few of them are much older than thirty. Young, jobless, uneducated; the Thackeray dynasty has a way with these materials. They stomp and scream, wave their swords and long bamboo sticks. They push and shove until they are at the doors of #1 Shed, where Raj's father stands with his arms folded, looking up at the night sky.

The big one, his head looks like it was caught in a vise when he was a baby. Big dents on either side and strange tip poking up. Like a condom, Raj thinks. Condom Head.

Condom Head is slapping the door of the shed.

"What is this, then, eh? This is a factory, eh bhenchod? Open always in the bhenchod heat. Closed now, eh? And what is this people, eh? New people. Congress, eh bhenchod? Bhenchod Congress men coming here and stealing votes, eh? What did they bhenchod promise you, eh bhenchod? We hear they bhenchod promise to stop redevelopment and this is a new bhenchod tune they are singing. Eh bhenchod, you listening to me, eh bhenchod?"

His thick hand flies from his hip and smacks Raj's father on the side of the head. He takes a half step, finds his balance, stands, arms folded. He's been hit before.

Condom Head raises his lathi, waves the length of bamboo in Raj's father's face.

"Bhenchod next time you get this, eh. Bhenchod and after that, you bhenchod get this bhenchod."

He touches the gun tucked in his pants.

Raj's father looks up at the sky.

"Where have all my neighbors gone, eh?"

From his spot overhead, peeking out through a split seam in the corrugated facing of the shed's loft, Raj looks at the alleys around the shed. Only the Sena men are left. The real people have disappeared into their hutments.

Condom Head raises his lathi, puts his other hand on his gun.

"Eh?"

A mob of Congress men is what he's thinking. Political foes, street forces of the Congress party. Swords and lathis, he's thinking. *Ambush, eh?* That is what he's thinking. And he is correct, but it is not Congress thugs come to riot over who will reap the windfall votes in Dharavi in the coming open election. Not another battle in the endless saga of *lafda,* strife. Controlling Dharavi will be like plugging a tap into the great pipeline of money that is going to flow through Redevelopment. Of course there must be *lafda.* But that is not what is happening now.

Condom Head dies first. A single bullet that perhaps goes in one ear and out the other, like a complicated idea quickly dismissed for the effort it requires. Then more Sena men die. Raj is surprised that only eight of the fighters from the jungle can do this so easily. On the second floors and roofs of hutments, shooting down into the column. Single rounds. He thought they would rock 'n' roll on full auto. Like a movie. No. They choose targets and shoot, one bullet at a time, some working the edges of the column, some the middle. Dismay in the ranks. There is flight, but, if Raj understood Sudhir's plans, men will be waiting for them at every turn in the alleys. Dharavi men. Lathis and swords. Waiting for the panicked Shiv Sena. Raj will not be surprised to hear later that there were jars of gasoline. More than one Sena burned.

The gunfire slows. Stops.

He crawls back from his view, turns, moves to the edge of the loft and looks down at the shed floor.

Progress.

The jackhammers are silent after opening the foundation. The Hitachi 66MW steam turbine generator has been lowered in, dropped the final half meter when one of the winches gave out under the weight. The ship breakers have been pouring concrete, hand mixed by the potters, a pre-welded cage of rebar will reinforce the new foundation. The welders have been at work on the steam fittings. A web of pipes and catwalk rises from the floor of the shed to the roof, consumes more than half the space, arc torches flaring from its depths. Outside, more pipe, running from the shed, through hutments, to #2 Shed. Under the roof of that shed, the cooling towers have been raised over the water basin. The entire #2 Shed is a swimming pool now, with giant smokestacks mounted on a low steel gantry. Raj has not been to see it since they flooded the pool, but David says all the boys and girls have been swimming. Now is the time to get wet, before the water boils at 82 degrees Celsius.

The PHRS tank here in #1 Shed is not nearly so big but much deeper. The sappers dug a ramp into the earth, just wide enough for the trailer, opening into a wide, deep pool. The trailer was rolled down the ramp, the motor on the repaired winch complaining as it played out cable, easing its load into the empty pool. Once it was on level ground, rolled into place, it was jacked several centimeters into the air before being allowed to rest on stacked railroad ties. Then the welders crawled underneath with their torches and cut away the axles, everything except for the truck bed itself. Jacks again, lift the load, removing ties, lowering, settling, lifting, removing ties, lowering again. Until it rested on the freshly poured concrete floor of the PHRS tank. Then more concrete was poured, locking the trailer's load in place, the ramp filled in, a pre-poured slab used to close the final notch in the wall of the tank.

There it is now, the primary module, in the dry tank, set in concrete mixed in fifty-gallon drums by the potters and their wives and their children. The secondary module has been connected above it, and soon the web of pipes filling the rest of #1 Shed will be hooked up. Then the water.

Then, his father says, it will be ready to be fired.

"Raj."

His father, down on the floor, waving him out of the loft.

Raj climbs down the ladder. His father will want to talk about why he is up there. Already knowing that Raj must have watched the massacre of the Sena men. He will have a lesson to impart. Raj is so full of lessons these days. The change is constant. First his father starts holding meetings in their house, meetings with men from all castes, all regions, all religions. Then they start looking at plans. Buying buildings like the shed, hutments, streets. No one but his father seems to know where the money comes from. Then Sudhir appears. Then his Naxalite fighters. The ship breakers arrive. The truck comes. All the work in the sheds. First it is only people from their chowk. Then from all over Dharavi people are coming to work even as many old neighbors leave the chowk. Then the other trucks, and #2 Shed. And Raj must work and never play. And lessons with a gun. His mother with a gun. Now the Sena men are killed in the streets. And Raj is not where he is supposed to be, watching the Internet and waiting for a message that never comes on classicsteelbikes.com. And all he wants now is to play with his soccer ball.

"Raj."

His father has broken his glasses. Was it the slap from Condom Head? As he talks, he is wrapping black tape to attach the left arm where the hinge has been ruined.

"The Sena men."

"Yes?"

His father bites the tape, it tears, and he inspects the repair.

"We tried to talk with them weeks ago."

Satisfied, he tucks the roll of tape in the breast pocket of his filthy, sweat-stained workshirt, takes a handkerchief from his hip pocket, and rubs the lenses of the glasses.

"They didn't understand. I spoke to them about independence. The cost of it. Power. They didn't understand. They wanted to know what I was asking for. They thought I wanted a toilet, hookups to the water, electricity, a TV. They wanted to know how many votes I could bring them."

He stuffs the handkerchief away and puts on his glasses.

"Then here they come, as I knew they would. Because something they do not understand is happening. So it must be a threat. And they are very dangerous, Raj. More dangerous than the police or the army or the United Nations. Because they are here. So many of them live here. Our neighbors. What they could see, tell. The secret is too big here. Number One Shed. Everyone will know. Very soon. And then we will see. But what if they saw? Yes. Number *Two* Shed. So now it is too late for some secrets. The policemen have died. The water goons have died. Now the Sena men have died. Next, we will start to die. But here in Dharavi, everyone knows now we will fight. And fighting, we will protect our secret until it is too late for anyone to stop us."

The lights flicker in the shed, go dark, come back on, go dark again.

Raj looks up.

"How much longer?"

His father rubs his thumb on the smeared face of his Timex.

"The transformer is done, I hope. Soon. Then the tap."

Lights flutter.

"We will balance the load in an hour."

Raj nods.

"India Standard Time?"

His father smiles, wobbles his head on his neck, shakes his finger; suddenly a bureaucrat booster of all things Bombay.

"No and no, we are most modern and extra up-to-date in this operation. All things regular and in the businessway. On time means on time and no other thing. We must not be waiting always for these lazy wallahs to fix things up and making the toilets to flush after the shit is on the floor."

He lowers his finger, looks again at his watch.

"One hour. I will see to it."

He turns, stops.

"I will never be clean of those deaths, Raj. I did not pull the trigger, but they are all mine."

He shrugs.

"Destroy to create. I did not come into the world thinking this was the law. But it is. All the same."

He puts a hand on Raj's shoulder, pushes softly.

"You should be at the computer. Yes. When the tap is finished, you will have no excuses. *Oh, there was no power. I had to reboot again.*"

He pinches Raj's earlobe.

"And there will be more help after the tap. Turn on the lights, and many will come to help. I know."

He looks at the floor.

"Where is your ball?"

Raj points toward the far end of the shed, the computer stations where he works with the other kids.

"Under the table."

His father scratches the growing bald spot on top of his head.

"Do not lose it. I want to have a game later. When we take a break."

He looks at the watch again, doesn't like what he sees, and hurries off.

Raj sees two of the jungle fighters join his father, walking just ahead and behind him, watches as the welders and the potters and tanners, wallahs of every kind, tinkers, vendors, barbers, all nod to him as he passes. Under guard, his father walks into the street where the dead are being cleared away in his name.

At the computer there is still no reply. But there is something new. On the blogs for the *Times of India.* Comments section. People asking about what is happening in Dharavi. Rumors circulating. And now, as he refreshes the screen, a report of gunfire. Twitter. He searches #Dharavi. There, yes, a new rumor. Someone asking if anyone has heard about a terrorist attack. *26/11 again?* And someone laughing. *LOL! ISI terrorists attckng slums. Mks sens. ;).*

Terrorists.

Raj thinks about his father and Sudhir and the jungle fighters and his neighbors and David and his mother and Taji and himself. Then he thinks about the bullets hitting the Sena men. Funny that it didn't bother him watching it. But thinking about it now he can't stop crying.

inevitable

THE CEMETERY AT Montmartre.

Skinner and Jae are standing in front of the mausoleum of the Lazarous family. Skinner kicks a rock.

"Terrence."

Jae is rubbing the back of her neck.

"Skinner. Is there any chance?"

"No."

Skinner turns his back to the mausoleum gate.

"Terrence is dead."

He sits on the top step of the mausoleum, thinks about Lentz, the man he shot in the face on these steps seven years ago, and begins picking at the double knot on his right boot.

"It was Terrence's idea that I should meet my mom. Talk to her. After all those years. He told me that he knew where she was. On faculty. A girls' school in Canada. Outside Thunder Bay. Her office walls were covered in drawings by her students. An exercise she did every term with every class. *Draw yourself alone.* She pinned them to the walls, layers of them. She cracked the window to smoke and the wind came through the crack and rustled the drawings."

Skinner knows that he has lost his prosody. He's talking like a robot programmed to mimic human conversation. To make himself sound like everyone else he has to think about conversations he's overheard, or movies or TV. Everyone tries to talk like movies or TV. When they talk about important things, they use the tones of one-hour dramas. Just as they use the inflections of sitcoms when trying to be light. Skinner doesn't sound like TV, he sounds like Morse code.

"I had been acquiring assets. Do you know what that means?

Jae nods. She knows what it means.

Skinner studies the knot in his laces.

"I was good at it. Which was a surprise. For me. Not Terrence. He'd recruited me, scouted me, thinking I'd be an unusual analyst. Not unlike you. An eye for data. Side effect of the box, I think he assumed. But Terrence saw me kill the first time. It was. Not as big a surprise. For him. He'd already met Haven. Recruited Haven. And Haven was good at killing. Some talents do run in families."

He's having trouble with the knot. Trouble talking and undoing the knot at the same time, and Jae sits next to him, moves his hands, and starts to work the laces herself.

"Haven."

Skinner thinks about her gift for seeing the next thing, the connection. And wonders if she sees through him.

"Haven. He'd gone into the military. Marines. Very traditional. Foster children and the military. Many orphans fight our wars. And he was good at it. Force Recon. Fleet Antiterrorism Security Team. Signed with Aegis Private Security. Where Terrence found him. And recruited him for the CIA. Terrence knew one of his *kind* when he saw us. He saw something in Haven's work that suggested gifts. And then Haven told him about me."

The knot comes undone. Jae starts working on the other one.

"Haven knew about you? That you were his brother?"

Skinner's eyes skip back and forth, find the middle distance, tombstones blurring in his vision.

"We'd never met. But he knew I existed. When the experiment was in progress. He discovered it. Me. In the basement. And he watched me. On the monitors my parents had upstairs. A locked cabinet. He was curious. Found the key. Saw what was on the monitors. A boy in a box in the basement. Then sneaking into the basement when I was asleep. But my parents never knew. He never told them."

Jae has the second knot untied.

"Who did he think you were?"

Skinner doesn't move.

"I was the boy in the basement. The one his mom and dad spent all their time with. I don't know what he thought. But he was a child. So it probably scared him and made him angry. And it struck me, when I did finally speak with Mom, how naïve, ignorant it was of her, never to have realized that it was Haven who told the people about me. After Mom and Dad gave him over for adoption. It never occurred to them that he knew. And that he told someone. But it seems very obvious to me that he did it. And then they came and took me away, too."

He takes off his right boot, turns it upside down and shakes a pebble from it and then puts it back on. When he shakes the left shoe no pebble falls out.

"Childhood is a fraught time."

He puts the left shoe on. Jae begins retying them.

"And he told Terrence about you?"

"Yes. He directed Terrence's attention to me. Thought my history would interest him. And of course it did. If not for Haven. I would never have found out. What I'm good at. As I said before. His life entangled with mine. He was the one who told Terrence where our mother was."

"Terrence wanted you to talk to your mom?"

"*Wanted.* Yes. Put that way. I think he did. It had become apparent that my gift for acquisitions was limited. I was. Eroding. Unhappy in my work, someone might say. I didn't feel any different about the killing itself, but it was making me feel something different as a whole. I started using certain conditioning techniques on myself. Negative reinforcements in the manner they are popularly misunderstood. Punishing myself for inefficiencies. There were levels of empathy, unexpected, creeping into my work. I used a taser. On myself. When I felt those things. Poor technique. My parents would have been horrified. Something complicated was happening. I didn't understand it. I still don't. I wasn't human. Raised in a box. Copying behavior. Inhuman. Inhumane. Very little differentiation. Killing people. Well. I was a monster. That made sense. More sense than pretending to be like other people.

The Thing Under the House. That made sense. Every day it made more sense, but I couldn't seem to live with it anymore. I don't know why. I was very close, I think, to killing myself. That was when Terrence told me about Haven. I knew I had a brother. I had been told sometime after I was taken from the box. I had never met him. And I knew of Haven, as a professional. And now he was my brother. I *felt,* if I can use that word, like I was in a Dickens novel. A modern adaptation. My secret brother was the asset specialist Haven. Terrence said that I should try protection. Like Haven. Maybe that would work. I did. But I wasn't good at it. It was. Passive. I'm not. My, *talents,* are specific. Not applicable to the care needed to protect. Terrence told me about my mom. Suggested she might help. And. Going to visit Mom in Thunder Bay seemed logical enough in the circumstances. Who else might understand what was happening to me?"

He turns his head and looks at the door of the mausoleum, thinks about going in, but doesn't get up.

"I told her. Everything. It was. Easy. And. Comforting."

Jae has finished retying his laces. She moves on the step, into a patch of sun filtering through the branches of the horse chestnuts.

"My mom was killed by a bee."

Skinner brushes his hands along his thighs, pats his knees once.

"I'm sorry. Is what people say."

"Yes. I know."

Skinner nods.

"I'm sorry."

"It was a long time ago."

"Does that make a difference?"

Jae thinks about it, her face turned to the sunlight.

"No. Long time ago. Yesterday. It doesn't matter. She's dead and I wish she wasn't."

Skinner scratches his chin.

"That's what I thought."

Jae rubs the back of her neck.

"What did your mom say?"

Skinner closes his eyes, remembers the sound of the drawings on the walls of his mom's office as they were rifled by the cold blade of air slicing in through the crack under the window. The smell of cigarette smoke. Trues. Blue package, plastic filter. He'd not known she was a smoker. She never smoked in the basement. And he never smelled her. Not that he would have recognized the smell of stale tobacco smoke in her hair and on her clothes. She chain-smoked one after another in the office. Overflowing ashtray. Disheveled. Hair more gray than black, twirled on top of her head and held in place by an arrangement of what looked like white enameled chopsticks. She was, her assistant had told him while he waited for her to return from a lecture, a wonderful teacher. *She says things no one else says.* That was easy for him to imagine. The lack of a verbal governor, typical of some autistics. And her knowledge was deep and wide. *If you ask her about something she doesn't know about, she goes and finds out about it and always has an opinion. She's kind of awesome. You're super lucky to have her for a mom.* Then she'd come in from her class and told Skinner that she only had an hour and closed the office door and opened the window wider and started smoking.

He opens his eyes.

"She told me the results of the experiment. That in both cases. Control and experimental. The results were the same. The subjects became killers."

Skinner pulls his jacket tighter. It's cold in the shadows of the trees.

"She said that she was uncertain if this would have been the case if the experiment had not been interrupted. But it had been. She said she thought it was a good thing that my dad didn't ever find out. About Haven and me. She said he would have blamed himself. But *she* didn't. She said she was *no longer a behaviorist.* It explained too little. But she knew that conditioning worked. She said, *If Haven can protect people, so can you. You're not that different from one another,* she said. She asked me about assets, how their value is set. I told her the contract sets the value. And she said I was wrong. She said the effort to destroy the asset dictates the value. *The market,* she said, *sets the value.* And she outlined a possible experiment. Behaviorist. In which one could condition others to recalibrate their value assessments. By making them horrified.

Horrified. Was her word. Horror implies a strong and visceral reaction that cannot be controlled. I needed to make the cost of acquiring my assets horrifying to contemplate. *If you feel like a monster, Skinner,* she said, *it is possible that you are one. Capitalize on that,* she said. *In your work.* So I did."

He flicks a piece of gravel from the step.

"And then. She told me. What she had learned. *From raising two boys.*"

Skinner remembers her dragging hard on the butt of a True, her cheeks drawn in by the suction, smoking-wrinkles radiating from her lips as they puckered around that plastic filter tip that would not save her from the cancer that was growing already in her lungs. *What I learned from raising two boys,* she'd said, and then crushed out the butt.

Jae leans forward slightly, looks at him, squinting against a flare of sunlight in her eyes.

"What did she say?"

Skinner shrugs.

"Boys will be boys, she said."

Then she'd pulled up the cuff of her hooded fleece jacket, checked her watch, and stood up. Time for another lecture. Classroom of girls. Fathomable, somehow, in ways that her own children never had been. Perhaps because they were someone else's. Or because her interactions were not skewed by the act of observing. No experiment. Just life. From a drawer in her desk she'd taken out a prescription bottle and swallowed two capsules, using the cold dregs from a coffee mug that read *World's Greatest Tenured Professor* on its side. Circling the desk, she stood next to Skinner and looked at him. Frowned. Kissed the top of his head. And walked out the door. Leaving him in her office by himself, surrounded by the rustle of the drawings, hundreds of them. Stick figures, collages, watercolors, Crayola, pastels, an oil painting, several charcoals, ballpoint, felt marker, #2 pencil. Girls, as they pictured themselves, alone. All of them, bound by the edges of the pieces of paper, looking as if they were contained each in their own box.

Skinner left the office. On the flight home he wrote out the maxim.

And began to horrify people. Until he knew he could keep someone safe within the walls of that horror. The box of safety that only he could create.

On the steps of the mausoleum, he looks at Jae in her patch of sunlight.

"Boys will be boys."

Jae pulls up her knees, wraps her arms around them, rests her chin on top.

"I know I've said this before, Skinner. But that is some seriously fucked up shit."

Skinner nods.

"I recognize that fact."

Jae rubs her chin on her knees.

"Where is she now?"

"Dead. Cancer. Lungs. Everywhere, really. Ugly death. I didn't go. But that's what I hear. That's what Haven told me. After he saw her."

Jae lifts her chin.

"She talked to him, too?"

Skinner looks at the door of the mausoleum.

"Often. Haven says. But he's a liar."

He stands, offers Jae his hand.

"Take a look?"

She pulls herself up.

"If he's in there, Skinner."

"He's not."

"If he's in there alive, I'm going to kill him."

"He's dead, Jae."

She puts her hands in her jacket pockets.

"Well fuck."

The key is inside the urn where it was meant to be seven years ago. Skinner expects nothing less than this. Terrence's sense of humor showing. Little grace notes to be expected. The key opens the mausoleum door. Skinner pushes it open, wondering if he's wrong, if he will find Terrence sprawled on the floor in grim imitation of that long-dead asset. *Surprise!* A rambling and marvelous joke. Shaggy-dog story for the spy set.

Terrence is not inside. But his remains are.

chemotherapy agents

IN THE MAUSOLEUM Jae starts flipping through the five file boxes. On the cover pages of more than half the documents inside, stamped in translucent red ink, TOP SECRET. Nothing redacted. Terrence, the burner of all things paper, had been burning his employers for years. Saving, hoarding, filing, amassing. While she looks through the documents, Skinner is inspecting the rest of the contents of the mausoleum.

Two passports in the names of people neither of them has ever heard of but who look exactly like themselves. Two sets of state-issued ID from Illinois. Credit and bank cards in the same names. Two fully charged BlackBerrys on prepaid accounts. Two fully charged laptops with pre-paid Wi-Fi contracts. Rollaway carry-on bags prepacked for a business trip. Several changes of clothes in vacuum-sealed plastic bags. Similarly packed trail mix, dried fruit, nuts, salami, crackers. A Leatherman and a small toolbox. A Garmin GPS unit. And packing materials in the form of tape, shipping labels, and Sharpies. A hand truck.

Terrence, it seems, intended for them to travel.

Flipping through the files, many of them the originals of material that is in the USB dump, Jae finds Skinner's continuing verbal inventory of their supplies beginning to manifest in the configuration. Business cards, included in the ID packets, for a systems engineering firm. Perigee Systems Consulting Inc. The clothes in the bags, lightweight, stain resistant. The hardy, practical phones favored by professionals everywhere. Maps start flipping open in her head as she flips the files. Warm climates, developing, boom economies, mud. Locations to suit the identities and supplies left for them. A limited number of candidates if China is eliminated. To the background now, those maps. Open the Critical Foreign Dependencies map from the USB surfaces. Brazil highlighted, underseas telecom cable landings and several mineral resources. Battery-grade manganese, niobium, etc. India. Chromite mines. Pharmaceuticals manufacturing, chemotherapy agents. All of it, cables, minerals, drugmakers, deemed essential elements in American security. Tenuous outposts of national interest. Strange borders.

Favelas.

Slums.

Urban density.

Her mind flings those at her. Something obvious. She's missing it.

Back to the beginning. West-Tebrum. Cyber attack. Modified Stuxnet worm telling a lube oil motor that it was circulating thirty gallons per minute when it was pumping nothing. Launched from servers in Ukraine and Yemen. Western European anarchists backed with money sourced from Eastern European gangsters and hackers. Chinese connection. Wet dream come true for private security companies that have been beating the drum on cyber warfare.

Cross.

Cross in Stockholm. Bilderberg. WTO. Cross the patriot. Terrence's protégé. Cross on Terrence: *deeply influential on my thinking.* Terrence shaping Cross, and Cross maneuvering Kestrel out from under Terrence. The slight and swift bird of prey that was Terrence's tool for shaping global security in the twenty-first century becoming Cross's lobbyist-driven Beltway engine of profit. Terrence and Cross. Shaping. World. Cross and Terrence shaping the world? Numbers. A ledger. A very long string of digits on Cross's bottom line. She balances on that long thin line. Her fingers still walking through the documents, flip, flip, flip, her brain wobbling its arms up and down trying not to fall from its perch. *Fall now and start again.* Something just ahead.

A crime has been committed. First question. Who stands to gain?

"Skinner."

He's using the blade on the Leatherman to cut open a packet of trail mix. He stops. Looks at her.

"Are you okay?"

"Skinner. Cross."

"Jae."

Her fingers are flipping pages, eyes scanning, brain sifting, skipping, returning to *Cross*.

"But. Cross."

"You sound funny."

"How?"

"You sound like me."

She can't stop flipping through the pages. TOP SECRET. Words, a few on each page, flickering by. Like flipbook animation. But telling a story in words. *War. Inlet. Penultimate. Cause. Contraction. Tides. Resources. Extreme. Reliance. Population. Weaponized. Crater. Stockpile. Alternative. Satellite. Economies. Contraction. Drone. Urban.*

"Jae?"

She starts to flip more slowly. Words accumulating.

"Would it be paranoid of me to suggest. Not Terrence. But Cross? West-Tebrum. He has. Motive. Means. Opportunity. If it was a murder, he'd be convicted on that much."

Absorbing a bit more of each page now.

Bio-disaster event horizon. Liquid metal fast-breeder reactor. Orbital mirror array. Al-Qaeda franchise structure. Black start. Neutron poison. Contraction operations. Open source prototyping. Population contraction. Foundational new-isolationism. Nonsupport as national security. Humanitarian overreach. Systemic contraction. Critical infrastructure garrisons. Corpse load.

"Corpse load."

Skinner is looking into his bag of trail mix.

"What?"

"Nothing."

He frowns at the nuts and raisins.

"You like Cross for West-Tebrum?"

She's pulling a document from the box.

"No. Sorry. Wrong. About that. I'll be back soon. Wait here."

But she doesn't leave the mausoleum, just walks to the corner, turns, plants her back there, slides down until she's sitting on the floor. Eyes never leaving the papers in her hands. Reading the message Terrence left for her.

The title of the conjecture is *Hostile Climate Abatement: Endgame Strategies.*

It was on the USB, but Jae had skimmed past the title. One of many hundreds of references to disaster scenarios, her mind had touched on it and woven it into the configuration as a part of the background environment. It was, after all, just dumped in there with everything else. No hierarchy. Once past the Kestrel operation file and into the partition, it all looked like dead storage. A basement where your eccentric uncle tossed everything he didn't use but couldn't throw away. Opening the door after he dies (no surviving spouse or children), all you can think is, *How the fuck am I going to sort through this shit?* She knew, could feel, there was something in there that Terrence wanted her to find, but she couldn't find it.

Which was the point.

If she couldn't find it, neither could anyone else. And the only way even she could find it would be to follow Terrence's directions. Secret directions. Whispered silently from beyond the grave. Slowly building the West-Tebrum configuration until only this piece could finish it. Until, picking it up and reading the title, with a click she can feel in her head, she finds the piece around which the entire configuration has been building. An absence that didn't know its own shape until it comes into her hands.

Go here. Now do that. See this. Ask. Look there. Up. Higher. There! Now back up. Further. Look out for the cliff! Oops. You fell. Start again.

Until you end up in a mausoleum in a Paris cemetery looking through the dead man's treasure of treasonously collected documents charting seminal thinking and strategies in regard to cataclysmic threats to national security.

Hostile Climate Abatement: Endgame Strategies.

Misleadingly titled, it turns out, as the conjecture puts forth only one endgame strategy. The essence of that strategy: *contraction.* The repeated word. So innocuous that she missed how frequently it was appearing. A simplistic metaphor is proposed in the body of the conjecture. A turtle. A clutch of eggs. In the face of a storm, a rising tide. The eggs cannot be moved. So the turtle buries them, moves to high ground, and contracts into its shell. The tide rises. Some of the eggs, tremendously valuable but not necessary to the turtle's survival, are swept away. The turtle, high and dry and within the defenses of its shell, is unscathed. As for any other turtles on the beach, well, they're none of the turtle's business anyway. And if many of them should be lost in the tide, that's just a few less turtles going after the same resources.

So.

Contraction.

It's a conjecture. Based on thinking. Not a formal strategy. Or proposal. Not a plan or a set of recommendations. Just a conjecture. Some thoughts, each page marked TOP SECRET, ruminating as to how the duly noted catastrophic effects of climate change (these things are not denied when the lights are out and all cats are gray regardless of political affiliation) could best be mitigated.

Neglectful population reduction.

The seas will rise. The storms will worsen. Drought and flood and famine. And with them, disease. Warfare. The worst of it regional. Isolated. Undeveloped. Just developing. Poor. Poorly resourced. The places where exposure to the world is greatest. Where food and clothing and shelter are daily challenges. The shitty places. Disaster World.

In the end, the conjecture sums up, *having already failed to take decisive and timely action to avert a hostile climate, nation-states with the means to contract and to harbor their own essential populations and critical infrastructures will find that it is further inaction that will save them until such time that the demands and burdens of the global population have been reduced and put back in balance with the available natural resources.*

A timeline for this happy outcome is proposed. A framework of two centuries. Within which the reader is asked to imagine, yes, burdens put upon their children, grandchildren, and great grandchildren, but a very real possibility that their fourth generation of descendants will reap the rewards generously bequeathed them once a not unstartlingly large number of people, in places they will never have to look at, are dead.

When Jae does finally move she walks to the door of the mausoleum, pries it open, and stands crying in the fading sunlight.

"It's a meme."

She blows her nose into a tissue from a travel pack Skinner has found in one of the bags.

"Terrence created a genocide meme."

Back in her corner, the conjecture where she dropped it, open on the floor. She flicks a finger at it. Something to be abhorred.

"He wasn't trying to. It was Terrence. You know. No thought is so terrible that you can't say it out loud. The specific thinking shows up in a bunch of stuff in the USB. But it's old. That's one of the reasons I couldn't quite get it. It's old thinking. Old for Terrence. As far as he was concerned, climate change was a hot topic in the seventies and eighties. He was sounding that trumpet when he was still at the CIA. By the nineties, he had moved it to The Land of Foregone Conclusions. Too late to fight climate change, time to start thinking about what to do *when* it happens, how to survive. When he first brought up contraction theory, everyone thought it was grotesque. Can you imagine? Suggesting that the most realistic way to deal with climate change was just to embrace the fact that billions would die and the earth would sort itself out. He was Doctor Strangelove."

Skinner has one of the laptops open. Online. In its case he found a large envelope. Still unopened.

"But he wrote the conjecture."

Jae nods.

"For Kestrel. Cross encouraged him. He was always encouraging Terrence to codify his ideas. He was creating a database of intellectual property for Kestrel. Preparing for the day when he would take over and Terrence wouldn't be there anymore. No more in-house visionary, but his thinking was locked up in the vaults to be pillaged for years to come. Hell, Terrence was predicting a new cyber security front in nineteen eighty-five."

Skinner picks up the closed Leatherman, deploys the blade.

"Cyber security."

Jae tosses her hands in the air.

"A paper about it in the box, right there, written in eighty-five, updated fifteen years later for Kestrel. Cross has been waiting for something like West-Tebrum. Priming the pump. Taking Terrence's ideas, fears, whatever, thinning them to acceptable levels, and talking about them over lunch with Senator Pork Barrel from Ways and Means. Major General Future Defense Industry Consultant from the Pentagon. Former Governor I Took the Money from the anti-virus-software lobby. He's been taking Terrence's thinking and finding ways to articulate it and spread it at a policy level. And he's good at it."

Skinner picks up the envelope.

"Cross is good at talking."

Jae rolls her eyes.

"And selling. And. But Muslim extremist terrorism. Cyber security. These are difficult concepts to get across until they are blowing something up. The threats and the responses to them. There wasn't a meme. An idea or concept that snagged people's subconscious and became a part of their thinking. Cross did enough to establish Kestrel as a cyber security leader before West-Tebrum, but his real interest is to shape the conversation. He wants to create the policy that will allow Kestrel to own the market. He's never had something as catchy as, say, *Shock and Awe* that he could sell. The Iraq War bombing campaign. That was a doctrine that came out of the National Defense University. Ullman and Wade. It entered the popular culture. So hokey. Like a pop song. Shock and Awe. It became a meme, replicating and mutating in other forms. T-shirts, movies, repeated on talk shows, comic strips. Until it becomes a late-night monologue punch line."

Skinner slips the blade under the flap of the envelope.

"Meme."

Jae picks up the conjecture, flips the pages.

"*Contraction.* The name of the strategy. Radical isolationism sounds, well, radical. *Contraction.* So easy to communicate. Eloquent, but untainted by any negative connotation. It could be talked about. Just a conjecture. So Cross talked about it."

She leans her head against the wall, looking up at the ceiling, low, stone, cold.

"*It's a matter of contraction policy, Congressman. Do you see any room for contraction advancement in that, Secretary? We're curious about contraction territories, Ms. Vice President.*"

She drops the conjecture on the floor.

"People start asking for the source material. Terrence's conjecture. *Hostile Climate Abatement: Endgame Strategies.* They have staffers do coverage on it, half-page digests, and, after reading them during their morning crap, they walk away with an easily communicated concept of national security. *Contraction theory.*"

She pulls her head from the wall and looks at Skinner.

"At first it's just Cross talking, lunch, drinks. *Hey, have you seen our new SCIF design? Come in and take a look. While I have you in here, can we talk contraction?*"

She points at the file boxes.

"It's all over the place in there. Used in dozens of contexts. *Contraction.* It communicated itself. Security wonks love it. So theoretical. You can build models. Using fictional countries, of course. But Skinner."

She shakes her head.

"Terrence *didn't write* most of those documents. Contraction caught on. It's like what Terrence used to say about current intelligence policy being built over cold war policy. Contraction is in the new foundation. *He* meant it as a worst-case scenario. The only option we'd be left with if we didn't do something aggressive about climate change. And even then it was a conjecture, meant to spur thought, incite new ideas and solutions. But it's been picked up as a strategy for *all global national security threats.* Moving forward. The problems. The things Terrence has been worried about in the last few years: Gray market economies undermining the financial markets. Food shortages. Asymmetrical warfare. Cyber terrorism. Neo-nationalism. The threats that are on the doorstep *now,* US policy reaction to them is being built on contraction theory. Without anyone explicitly saying anything about it, it's being assumed that *not* doing anything will be a key element in response to all global threats. As long as the main weight of the threats falls outside the US. And Terrence."

She's crying, tears that seem to scorch her eyes as she sheds them without a quaver in her voice, lachrymal rage.

"He was already on to the next big threat. What he saw as the emergent hazard in the second half of the twenty-first century. What to do with all the dead bodies. *Corpse load.*"

She wipes at the tears, grinding them from her eyes with the heels of her hands.

"Cross has a mobile jail built inside a SCIF. Prototype technology for drop-and-deploy intelligence stations. Anticipating a security market based on contraction. Halliburton can set up a military base in a few days. Kestrel will be able to set up an intel ops hard point, SCIF-certified, near any piece of critical foreign infrastructure in the world. And man it with their personnel. Advance work for contraction. Making sure as many of the eggs survive the storm tides as possible."

Skinner draws the sharp edge of the blade across the envelope's flap, sound of paper being cut.

"Cross spoke. At Bilderberg."

Jae wipes her hands on her thighs.

"Cross has been speaking at Bilderberg for *years*. Some of the documents in the files are diplomatic cables. Some of the ones WikiLeaks published. No one was looking for a word like *contraction,* were they? But it's in there. Referenced by diplomats. Over tea, *What's the prime minister's thinking on contraction?*"

Skinner nods, folds away the blade, and sets the Leatherman on the floor.

"Genocide meme."

She puts her hands together, pulls them apart, spreading her fingers.

"Self-replicating. Spreading in an environment in which it can thrive."

"High level politics and finance."

Jae shrugs.

"You don't have to do anything. No one is to blame. It's just the way the world is. Let it work itself out. Like the markets."

She spits on the floor.

Skinner tips the envelope, spills its paper contents into his hand.

"Terrence was dead."

Small, brightly colored folders, he opens them and looks inside.

"When I got the answer to the question I posted on the bicycle message board. The coordinates for this place. Terrence was already dead."

He rises from the floor, sets the papers neatly on top of the sarcophagus where one of the charged laptops is open. He turns it, shows Jae the screen: classicsteelbikes.com.

Jae stands, comes over and looks at the screen.

"Right."

Skinner puts a fingertip on the trackpad, bringing the screen out of power save mode, fully illuminating.

"My first communication was a simple ping. Here I am. Where are you? I need to talk. The response was coordinates. Coordinates Terrence gave to someone. To bring us here."

She looks at the boxes of documents, the travel packages and miscellaneous gear.

"And now."

He shrugs.

"My asset has never been my employer before. We're well equipped to run and hide. Or find out what Terrence wanted us to do. With all."

He lifts a hand, takes in the files.

"This."

She's rubbing the back of her neck.

"I don't think Cross is trying to kill us for this. For knowing about contraction. Maybe if he knew what Terrence left here. But I don't think he knows."

Skinner is shaking his head.

"No. Cross isn't trying to kill anyone. Haven is. Kestrel is his asset. It's a test, I think, of contraction. Cross has pulled back decision-making authority on matters like this. It's all up to Haven. Terrence was a threat to Kestrel because he was doing something outside the lines. You're a threat because you're following Terrence's lead. And I'm a threat because I'm alive. Cross is contracting. He doesn't have to do anything to protect his company. He just has to look the other way and let Haven do it."

Jae looks at the laptop screen.

"I want to know what Terrence was doing. I still want to know why he'd engineer an attack on West-Tebrum."

Skinner puts his hands on the keys.

"If he did."

He types, a quick chicken-peck style. *Do you happen to know anything about serial numbers for that period?*

And posts the question. Hits refresh. Refresh. Refresh. And again. Again.

Jae eats some trail mix. Looks at the vacuum-packed clothes and starts opening the seals. Outdoor casual. Technical fabrics meant to be worn in an informal workplace on the side of a mountain. She picks out fresh cargo pants, sports bra, t-shirt. Dark, sweat- and dirt-concealing colors. She keeps her desert boots, jacket. Skinner changes his suit for one that is almost identical in cut but made of a lighter material. A polo shirt. There's a trench coat. Terrence knowing his man. He keeps his boots. Returning to the laptop every minute or so to hit refresh.

Jae is putting the lids back on the boxes. She can't look at the papers again. She'll fall down that hole and into the still-spreading configuration.

"There might not be a reply, Skinner. This may be what he wanted. No next stop. He funded the anarchists, tried to make some gesture toward opposing the powers that be, and left these papers here. Our decision what to do with them. WikiLeaks. *Rolling Stone. New York Times.* Anonymous. That kind of thing."

Skinner hits refresh. Nothing.

"Yes. That might be."

He's still talking robot-voiced. Jae suspects that he's close to some kind of emotional overload. His brother. The story of his mom. Terrence dead. Whatever it is he's feeling for her. And the rest of it. The contemplation of genocide. Jae has switched over to automatic pilot. Unwilling to collapse, and lacking anyone to hit, autopilot is the best she can do. Who the hell knows what passes for emotional shelter inside Skinner's head? She remembers him in the dark on the train. He'd not spoken, but his engagement had been total. Or it had felt that way to her. This Skinner, flat-voiced, unable to hold eye contact, unable to put complete sentences back-to-back, this might be the truest Skinner she's seen. The lover in the dark may well have been more of his adaptation. Behavior he's conditioned in himself.

She gets out the other laptop and logs into the Gmail account Cross told her about. One email from a Kestrel account. Paris safehouse details. One email from angel.cervantes@creech.af.mil.

Related to your visit, would like you to have a look at this. Our missing box? I don't think so, but it could be a similar item.

And a link to an encrypted air force file share. A log-in ID, and a password hint. *Can't send this in the clear. Password is the geometric shape you mentioned. If you can't remember, bounce me an email and I'll try something else. Already breaking security on this. Safe travels.* She hits the link, enters the log-in ID. The password: *cuboid.*

The files, a series of three satellite photos. Night. Taken as fast-moving weather passed through the area. Partially obscured by clouds. Chunks of time separating each photo, gaps while the storm system masked activity on the ground. Dense urban area. Hyper-dense. Low build quality. Very little ground light for the density. Slum. The primary element in each photo has been circled. Stages of movement. Turning from what looks like the only street on the landscape that an object that big should be able to traverse. Squeezing into a crack between shacks, impossible to see how that was achieved on the ground. Then half concealed, one end inside a building much larger than the card houses dominating the area. She looks at that last one again. Dots swarming the object. People. Pushing it. A cargo container, unmarked. Reddish-brown paint. A brother to the one Cervantes showed her in Afghanistan.

Carrier-killer.

Her brain is opening the configuration, ripping backward, unfolding maps again. The destinations suggested by the wardrobe Terrence left behind, cross-referenced to an urban slumscape and massive fast-moving storm systems. Heat, rugged, dirt, Western business concerns. The reduction. Brazil. India. She looks at the flatness of the landscape in the satellite photo. Compares it to images of Brazilian favelas her mind digs up. Hillside slums stacked in rising tiers. But there could be others. Right? No. Yes, there could. But, no. The satellite. Slum. Something she's seen in the past. In the USB? Doesn't matter.

The cargo container in the satellite photo is in India.

"Jae. Mumbai."

She looks at Skinner.

"What did you say?"

He shows her the screen of his laptop. He has a reply. No words this time, just a string of numbers. Coordinates. In his hand, the GPS unit Terrence left for them. Coordinates entered and searched. Mumbai. Slum.

Dharavi.

She rubs the back of her neck.

"How do we get there?"

Skinner picks up the small colorful folders next to his laptop. Opens them. Air charter tickets. De Gaulle to Mumbai. A private carrier. Specializing in highly perishable pharmaceuticals and high-paying long-distance business commuters. Nearly infinite flexibility built into the stratospheric cost. And, in their passports, how convenient, six-month Indian visas courtesy of Travisa Visa Outsourcing.

"So. A next step. Final. I think. Mumbai. Find out what Terrence did there."

Jae bends, picks up the conjecture that she'd left on the floor, stuffs it into a jacket pocket, and zips it closed.

"He gave them something, Skinner."

She turns her laptop, shows him the satellite photos. Circled container and its route to concealment.

"He gave them a weapon. And while he was giving it to them he made everybody look the other way so they wouldn't see what was being aimed at the backs of their heads. He set up West-Tebrum to hide *this*."

Skinner is looking at his own laptop, the message board. He frowns, taps a few keys, shows her what he has written.

Thank you, Shiva. See you soon.

Jae nods, and Skinner hits the enter key.

Refresh. Refresh. Refresh.

You are very welcome. -Little Shiva

Jae looks at the screen name.

"Little Shiva. Same contact as the Russian and the anarchists?"

Skinner closes the laptop and packs it away.

"Let's go find out."

From under his jacket he takes the Bersa .380 and sets it on the sarcophagus. Its final resting place.

Jae could almost laugh at the expression on the face of the caretaker when they come out the gates of the cemetery. She is rolling the two bags behind her. Skinner is pushing the hand truck loaded with file boxes. Unsure of what to do in these circumstances, he watches them as they hail a taxi and tell the driver where they wish to go.

The winds have been blowing south, and the EU ministers, still reeling from the battering the euro zone has taken from repeated Greek, Italian, and Spanish credit events, Cyprus banks runs, have exerted backstage pressure to see that airspace be reopened promptly once the air quality has returned to its new, and lower, standards. The ash has left the sky, and planes are flying, and De Gaulle is excellently equipped. They are made quite comfortable waiting until their charter service departs on their night flight to Mumbai. Some of the time they pass at the shipping desk for FedEx France. The rest of the time they pass in the Air France lounge. Private showers, dining, workstations, a bar. Perks of the frequent flier status enjoyed by their cover identities.

Terrence, so thoughtful.

Jae drinks tea, an elaborate service. Skinner drinks a beer. He's more himself again. Or not. More animated. But his presence is brittle. She feels she might shatter him with the wrong word. And doesn't know what she would find behind the broken façade. So she doesn't talk. Unsure what words could expose a sudden flaw. And looks where his eyes look. At the planes taxiing to and from the gates. Launching themselves skyward. Beacons flashing as the night deepens. She remembers Terrence in Haiti. Taking the Pelican Cube Case she'd retrieved from the buried safe. Great chunks of cash inside. She wonders what that money bought. And how far back he must have begun. This great engine of regret he set into motion. Violent atonement for his callous thoughts and dismal regard for the potential of humanity to do something better.

Montmartre. As least that far back. Undermining the op with two results in mind. First, save Skinner, put him out of play until needed. And second, get himself finally and absolutely discredited. A man on the outside, with the freedom to move, light and lethal. A true sparrow hawk in his last seven years. And she sees it then, how she also was moved on the board. Terrence saved Skinner, and he did it by sending Haven to Iraq. Knowing Haven's methods, approving the changes to her op in order to keep him there, with her. Was she also meant to be shifted to the edge of things? Emotionally incapacitated and moved from the center until he could use her erratically jumping mind? She could cry again. Reaching, instead, across the small table in the hushed lounge, and taking Skinner's hand.

He looks down at their entangled fingers, squeezes, and nods in the direction of the fifty-two-inch LCD TV mounted over the bar, BBC World News, volume off in deference to the American jazz standards and French synth pop that play softly over the lounge's excellent sound system. Closed captions are set to English. Still the language of internationalism, even in France (give China a few more years on that). Blonde newscaster, brisk manner, the kind of cold beauty that the English cultivate in their news media personalities. The still image off her left shoulder shows the Raj Hotel in Bombay, flames and smoke pouring from several windows. Seeing this, it takes Jae a moment to realize that it is a stock photo from the November 26 attack in 2008 and has nothing to do with the events being described in halting, and sometimes misspelled text scrolling in fits over a black background at the bottom of the screen. Something has happened in Bombay, a spate of killings by terrorists. An incursion by Naxalite extremists from the eastern provinces. Unprecedented urban guerrilla warfare from rural fighters, but seemingly isolated from the seats of Bombay governance and power. Attacks restricted entirely within the confines of the Dharavi slum. A story of relatively little international interest, coming as it does from a city where extremist activity has become at least a monthly occurrence. The Brits, with their special regard for their former colony, can be expected to prick up their ears at such goings-on, but, for the rest of the world, the news would typically receive only passing coverage the following day. Except for a last twist on the traditional models of gunfire and bomb blasts in far off cities. According to the closed captioning, one of the *terrorists,* captured by a Quick Response Team from the Riot Control Police, has claimed that the Naxalites have *nuclear capacity.*

Summing up, the cool blonde characterizes it as *an unsettling development, if true.*

Jae and Skinner are both on their feet, several euros dropped on the table, bags collected, and on their way out of the lounge and onto the busy concourse. On their way to encourage their charter to take flight as scheduled before events in India can progress and the airports be shut down under the possible threat of a cloud altogether more ominous than mere ash.

The Dassault Falcon 7X is full.

Jae, Skinner, a flight deck crew of three, attendant, and six other passengers who give the appearance of being exceptionally accustomed to flying in this manner. All of the others are Indian, or of Indian descent, anyway; two of them speak Cambridge-quality English. There is a familiarity among the regular passengers. This is a commuter flight for them, something they do at least twice a week; leaving home on Monday mornings to go to the office before returning on Friday. Occasional midweek trips home for special occasions. None of them, other than the attendant, does more than nod at Jae and Skinner. A form of caste politics at work even in this environment.

The jet is Aircell-equipped for broadband, voice, and satellite TV. Each seat graced with its own media screen. Skinner and Jae have one between their facing seats, tuned to the BBC. Coverage of international events, cycling back regularly to the earlier reports of what are now being called *potentially nuclear-armed terrorists.* The sound is off, but no closed captions. Just the ticker scroll of updates at the bottom of the screen. Anyone interested in sound can plug the gold-tipped cable of the luxuriously padded Bose headphones into a seat arm socket.

The mood in-flight, as it had been on the ground when they made their way to the charters gate, uncertain if the jet would be taking off at all, is mildly nonplussed. No one is inclined to react in a manner that might be perceived as outsized. This has happened before, after all, and it turned out to be nothing. *Hasn't it? Didn't it?* Some confusion on this point. It seems as though it must have happened, an air of familiarity pervades the discourse both in the media coverage and in the reactions of the experts and officials who have been dredged up to comment. Most of these being American, as Europe was generally abed when the news struck, and the Indians themselves are avoiding anything but the most neutrally toned statements informing the public that they will not comment on unsubstantiated rumors that might foment panic if acknowledged officially.

Yes, it all seems very much as though it has happened before. Recently and regularly.

But Jae knows that it has not. Terrorists are not in the habit of claiming nuclear capability. Such a claim would be counter to the nature of any true extremist. Self-respecting terrorists don't make statements about their offensive capabilities in advance of using them, they just blow things up.

No, this has not happened before.

What has happened before are any number of things that feel similar.

9/11. The invasions of Iraq and Afghanistan. London subway bombings. Bombay attack. Madrid bombings. Asian tsunami. European heat wave. Darfur. Somali pirates. Hurricane Katrina. Bird flu. SARS. H1N1. The July war in Lebanon. Fiscal cliff. South Ossetia war. Kashmir earthquake. North Korean nuclear tests. Batman gunman. Global economic recession. Occupy Wall Street. Superstorm Sandy. Deepwater Horizon oil spill. WikiLeaks diplomatic cable release. Sandy Hook Elementary massacre. Haitian earthquake. China floods. Pakistan floods. Indian blackout. Boston Marathon bombers. Midwest drought. *Innocence of Muslims* riots. Queensland floods. Euro zone destabilization.

Mexican drug wars. Arab Spring. Japanese tsunami. Highest recorded temperatures. Syrian civil war. Death of Steve Jobs.

All against a constant background of bombings and reprisals, decreasing probability of economic recovery, energy crises, YouTube atrocities, increasingly massive cyber security breakdowns, rising food cost panics, universal political intransigence, radicalized weather events, collateral casualties, systemic unemployment, and the rising awareness that the presence of men with guns in public spaces is becoming a status quo feature for all countries.

It isn't, Jae is thinking as she watches BBC, that potentially nuclear terrorists are common, but rather that, conceptually, they suit the times. Of course some group of extremists or another has perhaps gotten its hands on a nuke. *Haven't we been talking about this kind of thing positively forever?* Also the resulting sequence of reactions, subsequent responses, paramilitary ops, and what have you. Calls to increase security. Warnings about threats to personal freedom. What it all *means*. Realignment of world powers to deal with these threats. *Yes, we've gone through this, we know how to behave. Now if you'll excuse me, I have a call.* And there is quite a lot of phone calling on the flight. Business and family, reassurances that both will progress as normal. Until otherwise informed. After all, life on the brink can only jar one's peace of mind so often before it becomes the natural environment. *These times in which we live, private jets to shuttle you back and forth between a Paris office and a Malabar Hill villa, wondrous, yes?* Everything with a cost.

Skinner has been watching the other people on the jet. Several of them have lapsed into naps following the in-flight meal. He looks across the small table between their facing seats, over the remains of the excellent cassoulet they'd been served.

"Conditioning. They've panicked before. Bad news. Events that feel momentous. But the world is still here. Their world is still here. Positive conditioning. An emergency introduced to the environment over and over. Until they react as if there is no emergency."

Jae runs the tip of her spoon around the inner edge of a white ramekin, scraping up the last of her crème brûlée.

"Yes. That's what I was thinking."

"Everyone is in neutral on an airplane."

She licks the custard from the spoon.

"Until it starts to go down."

Skinner nods.

Jae's phone rings. Generic pulsing tone. Factory setting.

She has to find it in her laptop bag. The volume is maxed and she fumbles with it a little trying to answer quickly before she wakes any of the sleeping rich people around her. Not realizing that she has no idea who might have this number until she is already holding the phone to her ear and speaking.

"Hello? Yes. I'm here."

"Jae. It's Cross. You're not at the Paris safehouse."

She hangs up and drops the phone on the table.

Skinner looks at it.

"Not, I'm assuming, a wrong number."

She folds her arms over her chest.

"Cross."

The phone starts to ring again, still at top volume, vibrating loudly on the hard surface.

Skinner picks it up, presses the power stud, and the ring mutes. He holds the phone on his flat palm as it trembles like a frightened thing.

"It would be helpful to know how he got the number."

Jae is feeling like hitting him. She wonders how many more times she can experience that feeling before she finally acts on it.

She takes the phone from his hand. There is something judgmental entering the serene atmosphere of the jet. Passengers disturbed in their repose, projecting their displeasure into her space. More impulses to hit people run through her. Then she remembers the feeling of the man's jaw breaking under her elbow on the auto deck of the boat train, and the urges diminish. She inhales, exhales. Answers the buzzing phone.

"How did you get this number?"

Silence.

Cross clears his throat.

"It was emailed to me. To my personal account. My most personal account. The one I use for family. Sent several hours ago from a Gmail account. I chose not to act on the information until I knew more about the source. I've been told, after some investigation, that it originated in Mumbai. Assuming that you've seen something of the most recent news, you'll understand why I'm very interested to know exactly where *you* are right this moment."

Jae is mouthing the word *email* to Skinner. A brief pantomime of typing gets her meaning across. Skinner rolls his index finger in the air. *Get more.*

"Jae, that wasn't a statement, I'm asking, with a great deal of concern, just where the hell are you right now?"

Jae wishes there were some way around explosive decompression at forty-five thousand feet. Some loophole that would allow her to open the cabin door and fling the phone into the troposphere.

"People tried to kill us."

A long exhale from Cross, exasperation physicalized.

"You stayed with Skinner."

"People. Who work for you. Tried to kill us."

"I'm uncomfortable, Jae, talking about that kind of bizarre accusation on an open line."

Jae attempts to rephrase.

"Fuck you."

A burble on the line, possible ghost voice evoked by the great distance between them, the near-mach speed of Jae's flight, and their signal's journey into orbit and back to earth; communication haunted by the technology that makes it possible.

Cross taps something, computer keys, thumbnail on teeth, a brief tattoo of frustration.

"We've been finding things. The anarchists are forthcoming. We have computer forensics. Terrence was doing more than profiteering. He was engaged in something dangerous. Not just dangerous to Kestrel but to America. Jae, I've checked that Gmail account I opened for you. I see that the email from Cervantes was read. Did you look at what he had to show you?"

Jae thinks about the satellite photos. Cargo container. The payload it could carry. Thinks about *nuclear capacity*.

"I looked."

"It's possible. I know you know that it's possible. The claims on the ground *are possible*. We've done a very good job so far, the community, NGOs, even the governments themselves, tracking these kinds of *materials*. Making sure they don't go places we don't want them to go. But there's just so much of it. The cold warriors made so damn much of it. And the goddamn Soviets did a piss-poor job of securing it all while their pants were falling down. So we don't know."

"What *do* you know?"

"We know that there has been shooting. Organized. Not suicidal. Concentrated in a hard point. Defensive. We know that the source of the nuclear claim comes from a native of the area in Dharavi. Someone that is not, as reported, likely to be a terrorist. We know that the same claim has been made by more than one such person. We do not know if the corroborating claims were made under duress. Torture. We know that the Indians are not inviting foreign involvement at this time."

"But there is foreign involvement."

Cross clucks his tongue.

"Undoubtedly. Every embassy on foreign soil has someone tasked with intelligence duties. Some countries have several someones. Some countries are riddled with such personnel inside and outside of their embassies."

"India is popular."

"India is a nuclear power at constant odds with another nuclear power that happens to share a border with a country where the United States is currently trying to withdraw from a war that is both constantly drifting over that border and increasingly under the auspices of the fucking CIA, Jae. Yes, there are spies all over the goddamn place, and many of them are no doubt trying to find out if these people really have nukes."

"And if they do?"

"If they do, India will be relieved of the burden of asking for foreign involvement."

Jae imagines a room in an aircraft carrier somewhere. A SCIF-certified room with very comfortable chairs. Large men with buzzed hair and intensely focused eyes. SEAL Team 6 veterans of the Operation Neptune Spear killing of Osama bin Laden. Looking at the same satellite photos she has seen. Being briefed on the possibility of a Club-K carrier-killer system armed with nuclear warheads. Intelligence on the topic, including her own determination about the container in Afghanistan.

She rubs the back of her neck.

"People tried to kill us, Cross."

"I've heard that several bodies have been found in Germany. Assorted locations. Unless he is among them, I don't know where Haven is. And, if I did, I am not in a position to change his contract. There were terms I agreed to. He wanted to define parameters. Do you understand?"

She looks at Skinner.

"Yes."

The attendant is hovering, he wants to clear their plates, Skinner smiles at him. *Another moment, please.*

Jae looks at her thumbnail. Dirty. Far longer than she likes. With a very sharp knife she could shave it to the quick.

Cross clears his throat again.

"Where are you?"

Jae mouths to Skinner, *Where are we?*

He looks out the porthole window at the lights flashing on the tip of the wing, looks back at her, and nods.

She purses her lips, unsure. But it seems events have moved beyond the point of caring who has been trying to kill whom. Details.

"We're on our way to Bombay."

"Mumbai."

"Nobody calls it that, Cross. Nobody who lives in Bombay calls it Mumbai."

"Whatever it's called, I don't have anyone there. No one reliable. I need someone reliable."

"Good luck with that."

"Jae."

She looks out the porthole herself, hoping the stars might tell her something. What to do. But she can't see past the beacon on the wing.

"We're going. I don't know what we're going to do there. Find out what Terrence was trying to do. I don't know. But we're not going there to keep Kestrel's name out of anything."

Cross, a silence, gaping, and then a laugh.

"Kestrel. Out of anything. Jae. *Nuclear capacity.* I have a sense of proportion."

Jae doesn't laugh.

"Want to know what I think?"

"If it's helpful."

Jae spreads the fingers of her left hand, hears the knuckles crack.

"I think you're experiencing firsthand the potential drawbacks of *contraction theory.*

She makes a fist.

"This is the real endgame of withdrawing from the concerns of the world. This is what can happen in those lost corners. And your watcher against the chaos is off interpreting his mandate however he pleases. While you sit at home with your dick in your hands. Asshole."

Again she hangs up. This time he doesn't call back.

Skinner takes the phone from her and looks at the call log.

"He used an unscreened number."

She shrugs.

"He wants us to be able to call him."

Skinner hands her the phone, nods to the attendant, and they are silent as the plates and silver are cleared. Real silver. A perk of traveling in rarefied air. When they are alone again, their illusory bubble of privacy, Jae puts both her hands on the table, palms down.

"Someone emailed him the number from Bombay. A few hours ago."

It's dark in the cabin. All but one of the other passengers have switched off their lamps; all of those attempting sleep have left their media screens on. Low flickering light, and the flashes from the wings. One passenger sharing the late hour with them, eating a second helping of crème brûlée and drinking port from a double rocks glass. One of the English speakers with the elite accents, he is watching rugby highlights, occasionally flipping to BBC World or Al Jazeera English, Bose head-phones clamped over his ears.

Skinner touches the edge of the table, resting a fingertip.

"The number was emailed about the time I responded to the last bi-cycle post?"

She turns her head, rubs her chin on her shoulder.

"That fits, yes."

"So then. Shiva."

"Little Shiva."

"Terrence left behind some very detailed protocols for someone. Once he, whoever has been posting in Terrence's place, *Little Shiva,* once he or she sent the Bombay coordinates, he or she also sent an email to Cross with the number of one of our new phones. Or both numbers."

"Terrence wanted Cross to be able to communicate with us. Or us with him."

"Yes."

She squeezes her eyes shut.

"I'm tired."

Skinner eases a hand onto the table, close to hers but not touching.

"Sleep."

"I should be online. Watching TV. It will help when we're on the ground."

"Sleep."

She opens her eyes.

"When we get there, Skinner, I don't know what I'm going to do. I don't know. Terrence, whatever he expected of us, help this *plan* of his, whatever. I don't know if I'm going to do that. Or something else. *Nuclear capacity.* Cross said he has a sense of proportion when it comes to stuff like that. But I don't. A nuke in Bombay? Whatever Ter-rence wanted to do, expose contraction theory, make up for creating the meme, I won't let people die. Thousands and thousands. I won't. I don't know what I am going to do, but I won't help blow up a city or an aircraft carrier so Terrence can make a point from beyond the grave. I just."

She curls her fingers, tight, small fists on the table.

"This is a weird conversation."

Skinner looks at her hands, scars on her knuckles.

"Yes, it is. Undiscovered country. The place where you find yourself talking about the unknown."

She uncurls her fists.

"What will you do?"

He looks up from her hands to her eyes.

"I'll protect my asset. I'll protect you, Jae. Everything else is just the world."

Not moving his hand forward, he extends a finger, and Jae does the same, until they touch. In her head, those three words, *I'll protect you*. She lets them repeat themselves over and over as she closes her eyes, sleep, finally; the chairs, on the sixty-million-dollar jet, uncommonly comfortable.

Everything else is just the world.

It and its troubles will still be there when they land.

She hopes.

constantly upon her person

THE DRONES HAVE come.

Herons, say the Naxalites.

Sudhir squats next to Raj in Media Control. A few hours ago it was his home, but now it is Media Control. All the computers and TVs and phones they had been using in #1 Shed have been moved here. Raj's father says they need to *decentralize*. Besides, now that the electricity has leveled, there is no need to stay close to the gas-powered generators in #1 Shed. Here will do. Anywhere with a tap to the wire will do. And everywhere is on the wire now. Their chowk is lit up, humming, regular and smooth. As he promised, Raj's father has brought the wire to everyone.

Now, they are joking, *if only we had a place to shit.*

The wire and the water first. Toilets next. One thing at a time, Raj's father is saying.

Raj wants to believe. Toilets next. But what if there is no *next?* The drones have come. What if there is no more time for next?

Sudhir squats, his INSAS assault rifle rested horizontally across his knees, potbelly pressing against it.

"They don't shoot, the Herons. Just for looking. In Gadchiroli, they tried flying them over the forest. Heat vision. Stupid. The forest, everything is alive. What will they see? No. Nothing to be afraid of, the Herons. The helicopters. Be afraid of the helicopters. If they want to kill us from the sky, it will be with the helicopters. The Americans are not here. Predators. Not yet. So now be afraid of the bhenchod helicopters."

Raj understands this. The HAL Light Combat Helicopters, new pride of the Indian army and air force, have been buzzing overhead for hours now. They shake the corrugated roofs of hutments and both #1 and #2 Sheds. Everyone flinched and ducked at first, but now they are becoming numb to the noise. Numb and also very tired.

Sudhir said they could shoot one of them down, maybe. But not yet. Not until the work has been finished. Even with the rumors that have reached the Internet and TV, shooting down a helicopter might bring the army and police crashing through the slum behind the column of bulldozers and APCs that has been massing on 90 Feet Road.

Too soon.

For now, the Naxalites have created a perimeter around the chowk. There has been talk of *fields of fire.* And there are mines. Trip wires. Slummies who live along the perimeter have either left the chowk or moved themselves and their favored possessions into the hutments of friends. As a result, many hutments now have two TVs! And, thanks to Raj's father, plenty of electricity to run both. Also on the perimeter, natives of the chowk, standing watch with the Naxalites. For every slummie leaving the chowk, there are two who want in. They have heard that the wire is finally humming! They want to see. Some of this electricity is surely too. All these new vacancies, someone must occupy these hutments. *A cousin of mine. See! See! He will live here. Help your cause.* Even with the helicopters and the army and the police, the notorious occupancy and squatting laws of Bombay draw slumlords to empty hovels like flies to shit. Both buzz throughout Dharavi.

The locals who sit in watch with the Naxalites give thumbs-up and thumbs-down.

Yes, yes, this one I know and he is a bhenchod good man. There was no food at home for me and I knocked on his door and he fed me. And I him. That one? No. A bastard, a real bastard bhenchod. Bhenchod he sells iPhones, you see. But with no insides! Then says that you did not ask about the inside! A real bastard. Make him go away. Shoot him, maybe.

Some who want to come in change their minds when the Naxalites say they must leave their phones. Each one with a piece of paper taped to it, the name of the owner written in black ink by the daughter of a courtroom clerk, a young woman often praised for her remarkable penmanship. The phones will be returned, soon. Probably. But no phones now. It is too easy for the police to put their people in here. Impossible to keep them out. Informants, yes, those are certain. But also some actual policemen. Somewhere in the chowk, poking, they must be here. Talk to your friends and your family. No need to be rude, but speak of general things with the new people. Safety first! And no phones.

They cannot control the perimeter for long. Not once the army and the police decide it is time to come in. So the rumors. Raj's father said he would have liked not to start them, but they need more time. Once the Shiv Sena men were massacred, they could no longer hope to hide what is happening. Too many guns. Too much gunfire. Could there have been a different way to deal with the Sena? Perhaps. But it set a tone of seriousness. To the outside world, it will appear to be nothing but a slaughter of fellow citizens. But to Indians, to Maharashtrians especially, and Bombayites most especially, it signals something very specific. An absolute line. A confession. *We will die.* No one shoots down the Sena and lives. Whatever is left unsettled by the army and the police, the Sena will settle with the citizens of the chowk. Lathis will swing, as will swords, and the jars of petrol will break and burn. So. Everyone in India understands. The people, slummies, Naxalites from the east, whatever craziness it is they want if they will ever open their mouths and say it, they are very ready to die, and to kill.

And now, the rumor says, they have a bomb.

Maybe it is best for the army and the police to wait and see what is to be seen. These people inside that bhenchod chowk, these Sena-killing madmen, they will blow up the whole damn fucking slum. And much of the city. If they have this bomb.

So the drones have come, and the helicopters. And Sudhir is right, the helicopters are more dangerous. A threat just over their roofs. But Raj cannot help being afraid of the drones. So high, invisible, looking down at them on the ground. What do they see? How much? If they see too much, it will be over. The helicopters will have their way, and the soldiers and the cops behind the bulldozers. And then the Sena. He wishes he could blind the Herons. Stab their eyes as if they were actual birds.

Sudhir is rising, lifting the assault rifle over his head as he stretches.

"So now you know better than to worry, okay?"

He lowers his arms and the weapon and wiggles the stock at the half-dozen boys and girls, none older than thirteen, sitting at the media stations in the shack.

"And you have responsibilities. A cadre. Eh, kids? Your leader should be fearless?"

The kids have known Raj all their lives. So they laugh. Because they have seen him run from bullies. Run from his mother. Run from some of them when they have fought with him. But they do not laugh long or very hard. Because Raj never leaves anyone behind when he runs, and, once they are safe from the threat, he always has a plan for what to do next. There is nothing wrong with being afraid. In the slum, you are afraid or you are foolish. Raj is not foolish.

Sudhir laughs, too.

"Okay, so now we all got to go back to work, yeah? I got to go out to Number One Shed and see what is happening, and I got to check with my fighters on the perimeter. We got to talk on our radios and our phones so the army and the police can listen in, yeah? Hear what we say to each other. *Disinformation.* And you kids got to be careful, the TV news, what they say on their blogs, Twitter. How they are talking to each other, some of that is for you. Same thing. *Disinformation.* So don't panic if you read some bhenchod Twitter that they just captured your leader or similar lying bullshit. They know we're listening. Everyone listens to everything now. They just want to scare us. Make some panic. So don't panic. Listen to Raj. Stay cool, you know. Unless he says you got to run. When Raj says you got to run, you got to run. Yeah?"

The kids are laughing and nodding; Sudhir, stern-faced, acting out how they should run, potbelly bouncing as he trots in place with his weapon held at port arms, pretending that something horrible is chasing him. A helicopter thunders overhead, each turn of the rotors slapping the roof and making it jump, some of the kids covering their ears so that they are the last to hear the series of pops that become audible after the copter has passed. Gunfire on the perimeter.

Sudhir is at the door when the pops stop, followed by a bang. New sound. Land mine. He stops, points at their screens.

"Look, look. Find out what they are saying on TV."

He taps the two-way radio attached to the shoulder of his body armor by a Velcro strap.

"Call me and say. Okay."

When he runs he does not do it with the high-kneed trot he used to make them laugh, but becomes something sure-footed and elegant in movement, disappearing between two shanties, running toward a rising column of smoke and dust just now glimpsed in a sliver of sky between crowded rooftops.

The other kids are looking at Raj.

An urge to run, but there is nowhere to run to. He is in his home.

He has known them his whole life. David. Chiman. Khadim. Khajit. Rani. Avinashi. They run in the same alleys. Fall in the same mud. They all love Kalki. They also like Priyanka, but everyone likes Priyanka. Kalki is not so much older than them and she doesn't act like a star. They have eaten in each other's homes. They shit in the same holes at the outhouse. He has scars, one on his elbow and one above his right eye from fights with David and with Rani. He is a little bit in love with Rani, he thinks. But he also likes Avinashi. Khajit has no parents, lazy-eyed boy with only his grandmother, and they rent some floor in Khadim's house. Chiman is the best cricket player. He can bowl and hit. He is holding his willow-bladed bat now, squeezing the cane handle.

How can they be looking at him for what to do? Sudhir has already told them. What can he say that will change anything? He rubs his nose, almost dips his finger inside his nostril, but Rani is watching and she hates it when he picks his nose.

"You know, Priyanka and Kalki, they must know about what is happening here. Do you think they will maybe Twitter about it?"

Rani looks at the ceiling, rolling her eyes.

"Bhenchod no. Piggy Chop is so stuck up anyway and why would she care about the slum. And Kalki only uses Twitter to answer questions from her fans."

Raj rubs his nose harder.

"We can maybe ask her what she thinks, yeah?"

More pops from the perimeter.

Raj points at the screens.

"But we got to work also. David, the TVs are saying what now? 24x7NDTV.com. Okay. Chiman, don't look so much at the bhenchod cricket scores at the bottom of the screen. Okay. Avinashi, please, Breakfast News From Bombay is live-blogging what? Okay. We are not running yet so we are working. Khadim, Khajit, new hashtags to create. This is the list."

Dropping a list of Twitter topics to create. Conversations to start. Places where news might come to them.

#dharaviuprising. #dharavirevolt. #dharavirevolution. #dharavinuclear. #dharavispring.

There are many more. A list his father has been preparing for weeks.

They are all sitting at the screens now. Raj can see that the 24x7NDTV online news stream is showing live video. From a rooftop west of the slum. A blurry zoom shot on the smoke and dust raised by the land mine's detonation. He looks at the list of email accounts, dozens and dozens, opened by himself and the other kids over the last few days. Matching Twitter accounts. Google accounts. Facebook. That is what is next. Now that the rumor is out, he needs to prepare for his father's statement. So, Facebook pages are created.

Official Facebook Page of Dharavi. Dharavi Official Page. Dharavi Independent. Independent Dharavi. Dharavi State. Dharavi City. Official Page of the independent City-State of Dharavi.

"Raj, Raj."

He turns and looks at Rani; her desktop is covered in Twitter windows. Official feeds from government, police, and military offices. Also US government. UN. UK. Pakistan. One of the windows is pulled center.

"Raj. What do I ask Kalki?"

Everyone stops clicking.

Raj rubs his nose.

"Ask her if she has ever come to Dharavi."

Khadim shoves Khajit with his elbow.

"Like maybe on the tour."

Khajit holds out his hands and makes his eyes big and sad.

"You got money, lady? My mom and dad are dead. You got money, lady?"

The wonderful scam they like to do when the people come for the Dharavi tour, rarely leaving 90 Feet Road or the 13th Compound.

They all laugh.

Raj raises his hands.

"Bhenchod you ask her then if you know."

Rani is already typing.

"No. I want to know if she's ever come. It's a good question."

Chiman turns back to his Dell monitor, one corner of the screen covered in duct tape where it is cracked.

"She won't answer."

He taps a key, turns back to Rani.

"But also tell her we are her biggest bhenchod fans ever."

Rani nods, typing.

"Okay, yeah, good."

A helicopter passes overhead again, not as low as before, but the roof and parts of the walls rattle. No more gunfire heard from the perimeter. Raj doesn't know what that means. He doesn't know what any of it means. His mother will be back soon. She took lunch to his father. She carries the gun with her always now. Tucked somewhere inside her sari. As constantly upon her person as Taji. Raj wants her to come home. If he cannot work in #1 Shed any longer, he wants at least one of his parents nearby. If one of them is at hand, he knows that he cannot be left alone. They will either live together or die together.

Something changes on the screen of his computer. Something not connected to the mindless work of opening Facebook accounts. An alert. classicsteelbikes.com. A message alert. He clicks the icon and the message board appears. New box of text. Private message.

Very close, Little Shiva. Where are you?

POPOPOPOPOP.

Short burst, rapid fire. Closer than the perimeter? What does he know about the sound of gunfire? Nothing until these last few days. Everyone working, talking about Kalki.

Very close, Little Shiva. Where are you?

That is wrong. Why does this person want to know where he is? Raj sent the coordinates. Why does this person not simply go to the coordinates? Where the two water mains run past #2 Shed, the space between them glutted with garbage, open space on all sides. That is where this person should be. And if there, then quickly surrounded by the Naxalites. They will take this person where he is meant to go. This is not Raj's job. Not any longer.

Bhenchod.

Why is this happening? Now, when there is gunfire outside and his father is at #1 Shed.

Bhenchod.

What will happen if he gets up now and runs to his father? Will his friends become nervous without him? He is meant to be here. Where is his mom?

Another message.

Quickly, please.

Quickly. So urgent? Why are you so urgent? Go to the coordinates. Enough. He types.

Go to the coordinates.

Hits the enter key. Trying to solve the problem on his own before asking help. As his father would want him to.

Men with guns, Little Shiva.

He can use the radio, call his father. Call Sudhir. Wait for his mom to come home. *Men with guns, Little Shiva.* Yes. We have sent messages to you, brought you here, and there are men with guns waiting for you. Okay. They won't hurt you. But will this person believe him? No.

Bhenchod.

The helicopter passes again. Somewhere above, Herons circling. Naxalite fighters on the perimeter. Army on 90 Feet Road. Sitting here in his home, watching what the world is saying about his neighborhood, always ignored, until now. Because of guns and the promise of a bomb, now they are talking about his home.

Bhenchod.

All he wants to do *bhenchod* is go outside and play with his *bhenchod* soccer ball *bhenchod*.

Instead he types a string of coordinates, easy enough. Open the GPS on the phone on his little tippy computer table and ask it where it is. Nothing else to do but hit enter and this person will know exactly where Raj is. Okay.

Bhenchod come here and I will bhenchod take you where you are supposed to bhenchod be.

He hits enter.

He turns his head to look at his friends. David leaning to push his shoulder against Avinashi no matter how many times she tells him to stop. Chiman clicking away from 24x7 for cricket highlights. Khadim and Khajit playing a word game only they know the rules to, finishing a sentence the other starts, the last word always a curse. Rani clicking through the Twitter feeds, returning second by second to see if Kalki has responded to them.

He suddenly sees with great clarity that some of them will die because of what his father has done. All of them may die. Has he done something to speed them to their graves by sending his last message, inviting this itinerant ghost into his home?

Where is his mom? Where is she with her gun?

encounter killings

SKINNER THINKS ABOUT the Bombay police force and their reputation for unsanctioned executions. *Encounter killings* is the term of
choice. Suggestive of a scenario in which a police officer just happens
to be there when a dangerous criminal attempts to do something of an
unlawful nature, requiring a response in deadly force. In practice it is
a euphemism for *ambush*. The thought is certainly relevant to his current situation, though he knows that none of the men hidden nearby,
apparently waiting for him to arrive, have any affiliation with law enforcement.

They are very good at hiding, but their skills have limits. They cannot, for example, make themselves invisible. Skinner is invisible. In any
case, they haven't seen him yet, and because they haven't seen him yet
he's been able to stay on his uncertain perch atop a flimsy scrap wood
awning shading the front of some kind of workshop that reeks of caustic
fluids. Heaps of filthy rectangular fifteen-kilo cans made of tin plate fill
a tiny yard behind the shop and hint at the recycling industry housed
within. One of the gunmen is in that yard, wormed onto a corner of the
roof at the rear wall of the shop, eyes poking up just high enough to see
the garbage dump that matches the coordinates Skinner received in the
Lazarous family tomb.

The distance between the two men is no more than four meters. The
rooftop of the shop less than half a meter above Skinner's perch. He has
no idea of its structural integrity. Assuming that it's made of something
he can navigate without crashing through and landing in a vat of acid

underneath, he feels quite certain that he can maneuver himself into position without being heard by the man or seen by any of the other men with guns concealed nearby. Whether or not he can kill the man while remaining undetectable to the others is quite another matter. A matter he hopes can be offset by taking possession of the man's assault rifle. After that, everything rests on whether or not he has indeed identified the hiding places of all the men or, rather, fighters (some of them appear to be women) waiting to ambush him. Six is the number he's arrived at. Kill the man in the backyard and that would leave five to quickly pick off before they've ascertained where the gunfire is coming from. It is, he thinks, a highly idealized scenario.

Preferable, by far, will be if Jae can successfully contact Little Shiva and get an alternative meeting place. More than likely this ambush is Little Shiva's work, but requesting a new meeting place will at least force improvisation on the other side. Improvisation inevitably leads to mistakes. Skinner is very happy to play a little chess on this occasion. The opaqueness of the circumstances aren't likely to reward blunt action. And, truly, his greatest wish at the moment is that he'd thought to take a piss before climbing up onto the awning. More than one man has been killed because a full bladder led to impatient action.

To distract himself, he counts the fighters again. The number is still six. They are exceptionally good at being still. Perhaps less so at camouflage in this environment. They are, judging by appearance, members of the force that is holding the slum's perimeter against the Indian army and Bombay police. Same equipment, similar garb. Well-equipped, excellent commercial-grade communications, newer body armor, favoring AK-47s, street clothes, and jungle boots. But however skilled they may be as soldiers, they are spread impossibly thin. The only things more porous than their perimeter is the supposed no-man's-land the army has tried to establish around the entire slum.

Expecting the possibility that any egress from Chhatrapati Shivaji International Airport might be restricted in light of the current events, Skinner and Jae had been more than slightly surprised to find that not only were they not hindered, but there was no indication of heightened security anywhere near the airport. Arranging a cab to take them to within close proximity of Dharavi had been rather more difficult, but primarily because of the intense competition involved in taking possession of a taxi in the first place. After that, their final destination was entirely a matter of negotiation. The cabbie giving every indication that he would happily drive them through the police lines and directly to the heart of Dharavi, provided the compensation was above market rate. Having declined his offer to take them closer than Mahim Junction railway station, they did accept his suggestion that they leave a small amount on deposit with him, in consideration of which he would wait some vaguely defined number of hours and keep watch on their bags.

It had been difficult to determine whether the bustling crowd surrounding the slum was more a product of curious onlookers eager to get a peek at an antiterrorist operation, or inhabitants of the slum who were equally eager to decrease their proximity to the mad goings-on in their neighborhoods. As for the prospects of a nuclear device, that was little, if any, great concern. While the world media were beginning to foam at the mouth over the prospect that such a thing might be true, the local angle on the story seemed to be that it was likely all a great deal of hoo-ha dreamed up by these terrorist people to increase their news coverage. Obviously incompetent, these people, because otherwise why would they be attacking Dharavi, where everyone knows nobody in government gives a shit what happens unless there is an election. An alternate reading of the events had been offered by their cabbie, one in which the real estate developers were behind the whole thing and this was how they were going to finally clear out Dharavi and begin Redevelopment in earnest. *You simply look at the money and it tells you who is guilty all the time. Blood on the hands is good, yes, but look for the money is better.*

Skinner could hardly disagree.

Having made their way through the crowds, paid a bribe to a police officer under the pretense of being members of the foreign press hoping to get closer to the action, and passed into the no-man's-land, Skinner and Jae found it densely populated with Dharavi residents who had no intention of leaving. The general sentiment being that, if they walked away, the government and the developers would swoop from the sky, demolish their hutments, and drop an apartment block in their place. Only as they approached the center of the slum had the population thinned. The streets taking on the character of a troubled frontier town in a western. The helicopters becoming louder, everything else drawing to silence.

When gunfire erupted some distance away, they were holding a position twenty meters from the defensive perimeter. As Skinner was taking a GPS reading and contemplating an approach that would minimize the danger of tripping a land mine, they'd watched a family of locals (mother, grandmother, four daughters) pop out of the window of a home on the near side of the perimeter, walk two meters and through the doorway of another hutment on the far side of the perimeter. And so there the path was clear of mines. Skinner saw no reason to complicate things. The hut on their side of the perimeter was unoccupied. Entering by the doorway and exiting by the window, they crossed the alley and walked through the door that the family of women had taken, and found that clan had already moved on. But the space was occupied by another grandmother and eight young men who were either her grandsons or her tenants. There was some confusion at their appearance, but Jae was able to use some of the rupees Terrence had left for them to ease their passage.

Through the lines, it has become easy to see that the balance between the defenders of the perimeter and the forces of the Indian army and Bombay police is quite the work of fiction. The only thing that will keep the attackers from overwhelming the slum will be if they choose to rush the defenses on foot and horseback. Scattered, these jungle fighters would be more than able to cut multiple paths of destruction and death across Bombay. They are armed and equipped for just such a task, but, entrenched as they are, it will take only the most modest of armored forces to slaughter them and overrun the slum.

Nuclear capacity.

The cornerstone of their defense is a rumor. No wonder the authorities are only moderately troubled by the prospect. The situation on the ground speaks volumes about the great possibility that the claim is purest bullshit. In a room somewhere, several rooms, Dharavi natives believed to have ties to the fighters will be undergoing close scrutiny. Asked to illuminate the nature of the *capacity*. Encouraged to elaborate on what the fighters actually have in their possession. Beatings and blood, electricity, the knife, nothing spared in the circumstances. Disinformation breeds distrust, anger. Interrogation so often takes on the character of revenge. Skinner has seen this.

The center cannot hold. Collapse will come soon. Whatever it is Jae will learn or do here, it will have to be accomplished quickly. The violence will be indiscriminate and wholesale. Pitiless.

Minutes have passed. The gunfire stopped before Skinner and Jae arrived at the dump. She is hunkered in an empty hutment, working to reestablish contact with Little Shiva while Skinner perches on his awning. There is nothing for him to do here. His skills won't shift the odds in their favor. With immense slowness and care he slithers backward off the awning, making the boldest of his movements when the loop of a helicopter brings its noise closest. Success and failure are easily judged in situations like this. No one shoots him, so he knows he has succeeded. A pause some meters away to piss on a wall, and then back to Jae's hut.

She squats with her back to the wall, laptop on her knees, looks up as he comes through the door, a panel of rippled green fiberglass that is lifted to the side and then replaced.

"Little Shiva sent new coordinates. A few streets away. Or alleys. Or whatever."

Skinner looks around the interior of the shack. It takes only a moment to mentally superimpose a grid over the space and then inspect each square in sequence. Tiny home. Nothing of value. TV. Every hutment he's seen has a TV, but no toilet or water taps. Utilities are a live wire running from one of the tangles of cable outside, and a hose running from a gas cannister to a single ring burner. No knives here. The utensils are all wood.

"Do we know if it's really Little Shiva?"

Jae is closing her laptop.

"You know who really wrote Shakespeare's plays?"

"No."

She slips the laptop into her daypack. All their other luggage still in their waiting taxi, if not rummaged and sold off by now.

"They were either written by Shakespeare or by someone calling himself Shakespeare."

She rises.

"I have a set of coordinates from someone who either is Little Shiva or is calling himself Little Shiva. For all we know, the person Terrence wanted us to meet was killed before any of this started and we've been played all along."

Skinner looks again for a weapon, a matter of habit.

"There's going to be a great deal of killing here. Soon."

Jae, putting her arms through the straps of her pack, pauses.

"Yes. That seems. Yes."

Skinner stops looking. There are weapons outside. He'll have one soon enough.

"Aside from the imminent danger of being caught in the middle of that killing. There is also the prospect of seeing it."

She yanks the pack straps tight.

"I've seen it before."

He dips his head.

"Yes. That's why I thought you might want to avoid it this time."

She rubs the back of her neck.

"The bee that killed my mom. I didn't like that. The senselessness of it. So I tried to figure out why it happened. I started doing bee research. The area was not a natural bee habitat. Where did that bee come from? Allergy research. My mom hadn't always been allergic to stings. So where did that come from? What I found out was that the bee colonies had been displaced by housing developments that had been displaced when a nuclear power plant was built nearby. And I learned that allergies are linked to a genetic mutation. Radiation, mutation. Nuclear power plant. I was young, suffering from PTSD after watching my mom die from anaphylactic shock. Not terribly rational. I saw a configuration connecting the Diablo Canyon Power Plant to her death. My dad worked at the plant. Blame seemed easy to place. But there was no configuration. What was happening was changes in my brain chemistry as I entered puberty. Obsessive behaviors that I learned how to focus over the years. Sometimes. But, even when they're focused, I can't really stop myself from finishing these connections. Configurations. Whatever *finishing* means in a given situation."

She stops rubbing the back of her neck.

"It's not like I want to be this way, Skinner. I just am."

She walks to him.

"I need to finish this configuration. Terrence was counting on that. So let's go see what he built for me."

She puts her hand on the back of his neck.

"And maybe after that."

Kiss.

"You can take me someplace safe."

Part of the myth of himself that Skinner created, part of the horror he instilled in others, was the idea that he couldn't be surprised. But he can be. There is always something new and unexpected. The trick is to not be put off guard by the surprises. Jae has been a surprise, but he has kept his feet. Arms twirling wildly from time to time, but still upright. However, after they walk the empty alleys, twists, and cutbacks, guided by the glowing red dot on the GPS, and find the hutment they are looking for, careful to not be seen by the guards posted outside a large warehouse just up the wide main road, he is surprised to find that the hut is filled with children. Stepping inside, there are more surprises. For instance, the kids are manning a media center almost identical to the one the anarchists had in Gamla Stan. Surprised a third time to see a beautiful young woman tending a squat bright orange stove, a baby in the crook of her arm. And again surprised when a boy of ten in a muddy *Transformers* t-shirt stands up and tells them that he is Little Shiva. All other surprises eclipsed when Haven steps from behind the still open door (oldest of traps), aims with swift and deliberate care, and shoots Jae.

Making it, improvised or not, a very good ambush indeed.

a child in his home

IT HURTS LIKE hell.

The wound hurts in an otherworldly manner. Like something literally brought to her from another dimension. An alien sensation that it is not possible to comprehend until thrust upon you. Here now, occupying her body, colonizing it. Seed of future distress. And still, still she cannot let go of the configuration.

Stupid fucking brain!

She missed it. So lost in the configuration Terrence built, she missed how obviously backward and exposed their line of communication had been. A public message board? Skinner's great fucking blind spot. His own brother. Heathrow. If Skinner saw Haven, then Haven most certainly saw Skinner using the public terminal to get online. Log on at the same terminal, the search registries are notoriously never erased. classicsteelbikes.com. Scanning over the most recent posts, how long would it take him to recognize his brother's messages? Skinner trying to communicate with dead Terrence. Shit, imagine how he felt when he saw that the man he'd killed was messaging to Skinner from the grave. All Haven had to do was keep looking back at the board to see if there were any new messages. Supposed frame geometries that were GPS coordinates? How sly. Hack the account? Hack a message-board account and send your own private messages? Fucking who can't do that? And Skinner. His password is probably something like skinner101. The elite protector. Fuck.

Fuck it hurts.

Haven is the smart brother. Clearly. Hacked the account. *He* contacted Little Shiva after he arrived at the original coordinates and saw the ambush waiting at the dump. *He* came here. He did everything they did, but *he* did it first. Then waited for Skinner to see the ambush and do the same thing. Already here, telling the kid how to respond.

Played by Haven again. Used to pull his real target into the open. And then the asshole goes and shoots *her*.

Fuck! It hurts!

And that kid! Little Shiva the destroyer and bringer of light. Fucking kid. Terrence. Kill Terrence. If he was here, just fucking kill Terrence.

Fuck! It! Hurts!

Who knew a bullet could hurt so much.

She can smell the blood. Route Irish again, blood and burning in the air. There's so much blood that she can smell it. Shit. The shack is so small they probably all smell it. Two of the kids are crying. The one with the cricket bat (cricket bat?) and the one with the lazy eye. The girl next to them is shushing. The tallest boy is putting an arm around the lazy eye kid, hugging him. Jae would like to cry. Shit, tears are all over her face, but it isn't real crying, just pain and anger. But she'd like to cry. Dying like this, she really wants to cry.

Haven is still pointing his gun at her and she doesn't know if she has time to cry.

He's pointing the gun at her on the floor, but looking at Skinner a meter away.

"Do I have your attention, Joel?"

Skinner hasn't moved. Still frozen, half turned toward Haven, as if the gunshot has disconnected some wire in his head, immobilizing him. He hasn't turned to look at Jae on the floor, poised on an internal cusp. Still deciding, Jae thinks, whether to try to kill his brother.

Haven, pointing that tiny gun at her.

"It's a good wound, Joel. Outside thigh, away from the femur, full metal jacket. Close range, small caliber. As long as you don't move toward me, the only thing she has to worry about is bleeding to death. And you can stop that with a tourniquet. Look at it. I'm not lying. It's a good wound. Trust me. I don't want to kill Jae. I think you know that.

Do something now. Give yourself a task. It will help you calm down. I know you don't like being upset like this. I know how uncomfortable and confusing all those emotions must be. Focus. Just look at the wound. She's not dead. Look at the wound and bind it."

His voice soft, coaxing, but authoritative. Man to child. To dog.

Skinner looks at her.

When he kneels, unbuckling his belt to wrap it around her upper thigh, she almost writhes away. An animal instinct to distance herself from a touch that will cause pain. His hands are shaking as he cinches the belt tight a few inches above the wound, cutting off the flow of blood. He looks only at the wound.

The baby starts to cry. Haven looks up and the mother opens a gap in her sari, sticks the baby's face inside and the crying stops as the tiny thing latches on and starts nursing. Still crouching by the stove, she lowers her bottom to the floor, leans against the side of the cot next to it. The boy, Little Shiva, is looking at her. The other kids look at him.

Skinner is done with the tourniquet. His hands no longer shaking.

Haven looks at the back of Skinner's head.

"Do you have a gun?"

Skinner shakes his head.

Haven nods.

"On the cot."

Skinner rises, takes a few steps, turns and sits on the cot, careful not to let his legs brush the arm of the nursing mother at his feet. Jae's blood is on his fingers and he rests his wrists on his knees with his hands palm up. A man come inside with greasy fingers, unsure what he can touch.

Haven looks at Little Shiva and tilts his head in the direction of the guarded shed at the end of the lane.

"What is it?"

The boy looks from Haven to the woman with the baby. His mother, Jae now sees. Resemblance in the eyes and nose, point of delicate chin. A child in his home. Man with a gun. Bleeding woman on the floor. As scared as Jae is, the boy is far more scared.

Jae's mind does something to her. The part of her that is uncontrollable, the part that *needs* the configurations, it tells her to stop hurting so much, and the pain goes far away, becomes small. In its place, the configuration, pushing up against the interior of her skull, filling it with those arcing international flights, cargo carriers, opium routes, ice flow retraction, free-trade agreements, oil pipelines, urban growth and rural shrinkage, IMF bailout terms, Chinese auto industry orders, Terrence's file boxes, ash concentrations in the sky, Club-K carrier-killer promo video, contraction meme adoption cues, Naxalite, West-Tebrum peak consumption charts, load-balancing fluctuations, critical dependencies, energy dependencies.

The boy's mother nods at him. Jae looks at him. And behind him, on one of the laptop screens, she sees an open Facebook page for *The Independent City-State of Dharavi.*

And she knows, before the words come out of his mouth, what is in the building at the end of the lane. What came here in a cargo container that the people of Dharavi crowded around to push inside and out of sight.

Little Shiva speaks.

"A seventy-five-megawatt Atomenergoproekt VVER-TOI liquid-lead-cooled fast-breeder reactor connected to a Hitachi steam turbine generator power plant."

The Independent City-State of Dharavi. Its nuclear capacity. Power for its people.

Jae laughs, but has to stop because it hurts her leg so fucking much.

afraid to find out

SKINNER IS IN the box.

He had no choice but to put himself inside. It was almost too late. When he turned and looked at Jae on the floor, her blood. It was almost too late to get in the box and slam the door closed behind himself.

So simple, everyone thinks, to figure Skinner out. A kid raised in a box. Doesn't know how people feel. Doesn't even understand that people are real. Zero socialization. Ipso facto, the box made him a killer. He's a weirdo, but there's no big mystery.

So simple.

But they never saw his face. When the strangers came into his box, strangers, the first humans he'd ever seen other than his parents. Came in to take him out. And couldn't see him at all at first. Invisible. Corner. Making them not look at him. Stiller than the air. Looked and looked. Then saw him. He knew it before they did, their eyes starting to focus, saw their pupils sharpen, and he went after their eyes with his nails and his teeth.

It's really much simpler than anyone knows.

See that boy being dragged from the box. Taken from his home. Stolen from his parents. See that creature twisting and clawing and biting until they wrapped him in a wet sheet and put a needle in him and took him into the daylight for the first time to cringe away from the sun. See that terrified child being ripped from everything he knows and loves, and any mystery you think may hide the secret of his killing nature will be instantly solved.

Killing is hard. Until you find the part of you that wants to do it. That twelve-year-old boy would have dragged the sun from the sky and cracked it open with his hands to get what he wanted. To remain in his parents' regard always. He never got it.

And the person who took his life away just shot Jae.

So back inside the box, little boy. Get in your corner. Be invisible. No sheet and no needle this time. Haven has a gun. And he's still pointing it at Jae. And you don't want to lose everything again. Break like that again.

Family, he thinks, *is very complicated.*

"Joel."

Haven is talking to him. From inside the box, he can hear his brother's voice. He doesn't answer, staring at Jae's blood on his fingers.

"They have a reactor, Joel."

A helicopter circles, passes. The kids are still crying, but quieter. A two-way radio emits a burst of static from time to time. There's a tapping noise, nervous, light, plastic on plastic.

"Kestrel is my asset."

Skinner looks up. Nothing has changed. Kids are afraid. Mother is nursing next to him. Little Shiva is tapping the tip of a pen on the edge of his computer's keyboard next to the two-way. Jae is on the floor, periodically easing the tension on the tourniquet made from his belt. Haven has a gun pointed at her. And Skinner is still in the box, looking at his brother from very far away.

"You're carrying a gun this time."

Haven lifts and drops his eyebrows.

"Yeah. Well. Time to get dirty. So. So they have a reactor. Terrence. That guy. I thought it would be Kestrel-specific. Something targeting the company and Cross. This is on an unexpected scale. I thought he was leaving a trail. Bunch of red herrings with a shaggy dog at the end. I thought he got you involved to make sure it would get messy. Draw a great deal of attention. Maybe let some anarchists get their hands on something non-weapons-grade. Scare everyone shitless and put Kestrel's fingerprints all over the mess."

"Terrence wasn't petty."

Haven thinks about that, nods.

"No. He wasn't. But he was dangerous. I'd decided, before he even mentioned your name, I'd decided to kill him. But I wanted to know where you were. Loose end. So I followed him. Terrence in the field. Never a good thing. And watching you. Well. I won't pretend it's easy, but I manage."

He smiles.

"You're in there right now, aren't you? Jesus, you are. You're inside your goddamn box right now. You are so. Predictable."

He stops smiling.

"A nuclear reactor. I have to."

He stops talking. Shakes his head.

"Did Mom and Dad ever talk to you about free will?"

Skinner remembers humanism. Locke. Hume.

"No. I found it in books."

Haven's smile comes back.

"Is that where they keep it, free will? In books? They told me we were born with it. But. They were lying. They didn't believe what they were telling me. Just part of the experiment. Trying to make me believe I could choose. And it worked. For a long time. But you can't. Not really. Look at us. Used by a dead man. Terrence put us all here in this room. From Montmartre down the line."

He bares his teeth, half smile, half grimace.

"I was so mad when I got back from Iraq. Sending Lentz to kill you. I was so mad."

He looks at Jae.

"Sorry about shooting you, Jae. I didn't plan it this way. I didn't, you know, I didn't plan Iraq. Terrence sent me to you. And I didn't plan for anything to happen with you. But it did. I had to do something to make you safe before I got called back to the States. That's all. But I didn't plan it like that. Terrence, he was the planner."

His teeth are all grimace now, looking at Skinner.

"Free will. Shit. Inside the mind, it's just a hamster wheel going around and around. Same thoughts, ideas, memories. And now this. A nuclear reactor. And what am I supposed to do? Am I supposed to *not* kill you, Joel? Suddenly decide it doesn't matter what you do if you live? Who *you* kill? And *her*. She has it all in her head. Every little piece that Terrence used to make this happen. She can put it all together and write it up and show everyone how it connects to Kestrel."

Skinner looks at his bloody fingers.

Haven outside the box watching him.

"Joel."

Skinner is wondering, listening. Little Shiva has stopped tapping.

"Joel!"

Wondering, looking down, the nursing mother by his side. No more static from the radio.

"Joel, look at me."

Does Haven see all of me?

"Come out of there and look at me."

If I make my hand invisible, will he see it moving?

"Do you know why, Joel?"

And this woman with her baby.

"I just sat there."

Did she mean for me to see?

"Why I never even tried."

What is it like for that boy called Little Shiva, to be so smart?

"I watched you."

And his mother so brave?

"In your box."

To hold her baby so close.

"And I thought about it."

So close to that gun inside her sari.

"Every time I went down to the basement to watch you, I thought about it. But I never did it."

Time to come out now.

Skinner looks up and into his brother's eyes.

"Why you never did what?"

Haven's eyes look tired, like they'd just as soon shut and never open, but he keeps them open.

"Why I never let you out, brother?"

Skinner smiles, shakes his head.

"No. No, I never did."

Haven smiles.

"Well, I *wanted* to let you out."

"Okay."

Haven raises his gun.

"But I was afraid to find out what would happen if I did."

He aims at Jae.

"So there's your free will."

He doesn't pull the trigger.

He points at Skinner's hand, moving toward the nursing mother.

"Joel. What are you doing?"

Nothing happens. Nothing happens. Nothing happens.

"Joel. I can see you moving."

Until everything happens.

Haven blinks, looks at Little Shiva.

"Is that radio sending?"

Skinner, his hand not invisible at all, is reaching for the gun inside the woman's sari. Shiva's finger comes off the talk button on the side of the two-way and a blast of static squawks from the speaker as a jungle fighter with a potbelly rips the door from its fabric hinges and throws it into the muddy lane and Haven pulls the trigger of his gun as the bullet the nursing woman has just fired, blowing a hole through her sari, free hand covering the infant's ears, hits Haven in the chin and knocks his jaw sideways on his face, the full metal jacket round from his pistol popping the screen of an already much-abused Gateway monitor, and Skinner is stepping across the tiny room and over Jae, the drying blood on his fingers smearing over what's left of Haven's face as he covers his brother's eyes with his thumbs and forces them to stop looking at him and the children are screaming and the potbellied man is using the butt of his rifle to try to pry him off as he pounds Haven's skull against the hard floor until he hears Jae talking to the wild boy inside him, the boy whose brother finally opened the door of the box and found out what would happen.

Joel, she's saying to the boy, *it's not safe here,* she's saying to him, *protect me.*

*   *   *

When they leave Raj's home Skinner is carrying Jae through the rain that has started to fall. All of them walking toward the shed, the helicopters and the Herons in the sky. Little Shiva is holding his mother's hand, the one that shot the gun. And his friends are all around him and none of them have died.

very special education

THE BOY'S REAL name is Raj, and his father, some kind of insane fucking maniac genius, is wearing a very clean, dark blue engineer's smock with pens sticking from the pockets, over a white collared shirt and dark tie. His thin hair is combed and his tape-repaired glasses polished, and he stands in front of the reactor containment vessel submerged in the deep pool behind him, a gantry of pipes filling the shed, his voice raised to a near shout to be heard over the high-pitched roar of the turbine.

"With the control rods at half throw we are currently producing over thirty megawatts. We have most gradually increased our production since our transformer was installed some twenty-four hours ago and we connected to the Bombay Municipal Corporation grid in order to balance our load. Engineers for the BMC will notice, I am certain, that current consumption via our transformer shows no more than two megawatts. Yet all of Dharavi is alight. This is with great thanks to many years of effort myself and my team have invested in improving infrastructure in the newly independent City-State of Dharavi in preparation for this great day."

He pauses, looks down at the notes in his hand, walks a few feet so that a bank of computer monitors helmed by men and women in smocks that match his own are now behind him, and the man shooting him on a compact Canon 5D camera gives a thumbs-up.

Raj's father clears his throat, glances again at his script.

"Our excellent DeltaV software by Emerson is the most up-to-date and ensures that our system runs evenly and without risk. Our Hitachi generator, while surplus indeed, is in top condition and operating well under spec. At three-quarters throw we will produce its full sixty-six megawatt output. Well beyond the needs of the ICSD. Allowing us to make our excess energy available to the citizens of the BMC. Beyond the industrious and varied people that live here, raw energy is our greatest resource."

He shifts again, putting the reactor in the background once more, and the potbellied fighter, wearing something that looks like a police uniform, khaki shirt, epaulets, peaked cap, joins him.

"We will build no walls or fences to define our territory. Our desire is to exist as a civic sister to glorious Bombay. Our friends from the eastern forests have joined us as a peacekeeping force. Unrest is not our friend. Dharavi has long thrived on diversity and openness. The ICSD continues those traditions. Émigrés of all races and religions are welcome to visit and apply for citizenship."

He and the Naxalite revolutionary dressed like a cop shake hands, and the Naxalite smiles at the camera and steps out of frame.

Raj's father looks at his script, then assumes a somber countenance.

"For those of you who are thinking that we are idealists and fools, I say you are half right in this. Yes, we are idealists, but no, we are not fools."

He folds his script away.

"We will not allow our rights as citizens of the world, our very humanity, the dreams we have for our children, to be contracted. We will not stand by, impotent, while great powers absolve themselves of great responsibility. We will not wait in blind faith for eyes and ears to be turned our way when we are in greatest distress. Silence and invisibility are the enemies of survival. If we are not known, we can be allowed to die."

He tips his head toward the reactor.

"So we have made a great noise."

He steps slightly closer to the camera.

"With our load balanced across the BMC grid, there is no danger of overload on our generator and no risk that our reactor can go critical. If we are disconnected from the grid, our load will unbalance and there will be unfortunate consequences. Likewise, as long as water pours from the water mains we have breached and into our cooling tank, we can safely maintain core temperature."

He points west.

"In our next video I will take you on a tour of our Number Two Shed and show you the cooling towers. We will also soon publish online the full specifications for our equipment and infrastructure so that the people of the world can be certain that we are operating a first-class power plant. Once we are certain of our political stability, we will invite observers to inspect our facilities and confirm their operational capacity and fitness."

He stops talking. The cameraman rolls a finger in the air.

Raj's father takes off his glasses, rubs his eyes, puts the glasses back on.

"This will be hard. We are not fools. This will be very hard. We have taken on a great responsibility. We will not abuse it. Peace is a treasure, and treasure is hard to find, always. We will dig for it. Hidden wherever it is. We have children, you see. So we must find whatever there is."

He smiles.

"Jewels of the future, yes? Our children. All of our children. It will be hard. But we'll sort it out. Okay. Bye-bye."

He smiles. The cameraman turns off the camera. Thumbs-up.

Raj's father brushes a hand at him.

"Go post it now. Quick, quick. And you kids, Twitter it everywhere. All our Facebook pages. Email to everyone. Hard copies. Everything."

The cameraman and the kids who had been working in the media center are already trotting out the door into the rain, an escort of three fighters with them.

Raj's father rubs his face, fingers under the lenses of his glasses.

"We must be quick."

He walks over to them now, his wife and his baby and his son, raising his arms and wrapping them around his family. Too loud in the shed to hear what they are saying. Jae knows she wouldn't understand anyway. Now that he is done giving his message to the world, Raj's father can speak in his own language. He is asking questions. His wife and Raj explaining. There had been no time when they first arrived here. The video was about to be shot. No need more urgent. If they're going to have a chance here, it will only be possible if their true nuclear capacity is known, understood, and believed.

He's looking at them now, Skinner and Jae. He steps away from his family.

"You are hurt."

Jae nods.

He looks at the scratched face of his watch.

"We have a doctor. And a little time."

He leads them, Skinner, Jae, his family, out of #1 Shed. Yet another of Terrence's oddities, this one bent on changing the world.

"He found me on the Internet. This is natural today, I think. Where we find everything. Lost toys. Education. Songs we hear. Guns. We found our generator on the Internet. So why not me?"

The doctor is very young. Jae doesn't ask where he got his schooling or how in-depth it may have been. His office is a cinderblock cube, interior painted white, and it is very clean. His instruments and supplies are stored in small, brightly colored plastic tubs. Jae lies on a table, handmade, wood, sanded and painted white, a clean sheet beneath her. Raj's father, his name is Aasif, sits on very small chair, something for a child, Skinner stands at the curtained doorway. Raj and his mother and the baby are on the other side of the curtain in the doctor's home with his wife and children and in-laws. A TV is playing in there, a Hindi station. It was a soap opera when they came in, but now it has been changed to news. They are waiting.

The doctor prods her legs with his finger.

"Okay?"

She can feel the pain deep inside her leg, but not on the skin. She doubts it's going to get any better so she nods yes.

He also nods, picks up scalpel.

"Okay."

He did his initial examination without painkillers, listening to the pulse in both femoral arteries, feeling the extent and tightness of the swelling in her thigh, asking her to extend her leg; but cleaning the entrance and exit wounds requires a series of lidocaine injections. The exit wound is ragged, but none of the tissue appears to be necrotic, so he doesn't trim it. The entrance wound shows black flecks of gunpowder. Result of being shot at such close range. He'll use the scalpel to scrape them away.

Aasif talks throughout. Using what little time he has, and helping to distract Jae.

"I was at school, you know. And Terrence was looking for someone educated. Someone from the slums, but educated. Very special education. I was interested mostly in chatting with engineers. Other places. Western. Classes at the university were quite good, but slow. I am the son, you see. And in my family, the only son. You know how this works?"

He is looking at the curtain next to Skinner, his own son beyond.

"Everything for the sons. This is our culture. Right, wrong. This is what it is. What he wants, the boy gets. Eats first, plays first. Birthdays, oh my. Everything. Rich family, poor family, everything for the son. Especially poor family. My father cleaned shit. To raise his son's caste, he lowered his own. So his son could be educated and raise the family's caste. This is what I understand irony to be. *I will clean shit for my son to be an engineer so I will no longer clean shit.* Also so that *I* do not have to clean shit. So I wanted to work harder at school. I am not unusual in this. You ask what men are afraid of here, they are afraid they cannot support their families. Afraid. Not *concerned, worried, stressed out.* They live in fear of this. Because if they cannot, the next step is the slum. And if you are already in the slum, the next step is living on the street. And then the garbage dump. And then you are dying and your whole family is dying with you. I was not special wanting to work harder. Simply I was very good at it."

The doctor is done scraping the wound. He cleans it again with a mild soap, rinses it with saline. Blood is still welling from inside, but very slowly. He makes a sound in his throat, the deep contentment of a well-fed cat. He likes how the wound looks, and starts unwrapping sterile gauze pads.

Aasif is touching the pens in his smock pocket.

"There was a small financial award I found out about from an online friend in Texas. Very obscure, an energy company in the US. This was not something I knew how to investigate. Who they were or what they did. An energy company searching for new markets. So they were asking engineers, electrical, civil, nuclear, practical people, students, what were the concerns of their developing nation areas. Slums especially. And what kinds of solutions would we see moving forward into the brave new twenty-first century. A contest sort of thing. My proposal was one that was selected. So much talk about suitcase nukes. I said, *Why not a suitcase reactor?* The technology from submarines, okay? One such reactor to power a slum like Dharavi for forty years and still extra power to use for other things. Modular, you know. When it has been used up, the fuel is removed in a module and a new fuel module put in. You can do this many times. So I got some money for my idea and thank you and this man from the company started to talk to me in chats and messaging."

The doctor is done bandaging Jae's wound. He looks at her bare legs and nods. The pants he scissored off of her are in a waste bin in the corner along with her socks and underwear. Her boots are bloody, but usable. A sheet is draped over her lap. He raises a finger, *wait,* and slips out through the curtain.

Aasif looks at his watch, frowns.

"I thought there was a job for me with this company. But that was not so. This man, he wanted to talk about my home. Dharavi. The practical. If there was a reactor, how would it work? Not just design theory. Wires. Cooling water. Infrastructure for such a thing. And he asked me about the future and what I wanted. And then we were becoming friends."

He winds his watch.

"And then again one day he wants to show me some things. In person. He is here, unexpected, at the university he finds me so that he can show some things to me. That is how I find out that my friend has created an idea that lets people think about letting everyone I have ever known die. *Contraction.*"

He taps the face of his watch.

"And then he asked me what I was going to do to stop this from happening. How I was going to stop the world from ignoring my home so that when they started saying, *Oh, things are so bad now it is too late for us to help you and we can only help ourselves,* so that when they started saying those things, we could say, *Okay, we will help ourselves. We have power to help ourselves.* It was stupid, though. The money was impossible. The reactor did not exist."

He looks up from his watch.

"But you know my father died run over by a truck full of shit on his way to clean shit. The job he took so that I could raise our caste. And I was the son. It was my job to make it better. Things are stupid, you know. I cannot tell you how stupid. I am stupid. So I became *Shiva.* I reached out into the world and began to talk to the people Terrence introduced me to. And I started to rewire Dharavi. I brought my degree back to the slum. My mother was not happy. She was betrayed by the son she had sacrificed for. Her husband had cleaned shit and died in shit. And I came back here to make the wires better for everyone else, but she had to live in the same shitty hut she had always lived in and then I married a little dark girl from around the corner. So my mother died. And I rewired Dharavi. And I built a network of people to go with my network of wires. You have to know everyone. The ones living in the gangwar, the cops, the Sena, Congress, water goons, electricity goons, the old men in the panchayat assemblies, Hindus, Muslims, Christians, local bureaucrats from the BMC, and all the people in their homes when I came to change their wires and they thought I was there to steal their electricity. I did it because if I did not do it then I would be contracting, too. Looking only at how I could protect what was already mine. *It's not there, the world. Do something else and be normal.* That bullshit. So I went outside my hut and wired as much of the world as I could. For everything else there was Terrence."

The doctor comes back with a pair of deeply stained but recently laundered green cotton shorts. His own. He holds them open and helps Jae to slip them up her legs and past the bandaged wound. He is slender but they are still too big for her. He has a solution, a length of twine for a belt. She ties it around her waist.

Aasif is pushing himself up from his tiny seat.

"Everything else was money. Terrence said getting money was only hard if you did not want to get caught. And he said that getting caught would be what happened no matter what."

He smooths the front of his smock.

"He was very good at using people, Terrence. Putting them together in combinations that produced what he wanted. Criminals, spies, politicians, businessmen, revolutionaries."

He points in the direction of #1 Shed.

"Some of the investors in Atomenergoproekt's reactor project, they are not legal and aboveboard. You know? The prototype cannot get approved. Even in Russia. So much money being lost every day. A field test is needed. Terrence was vague when speaking to them, I am certain. But he had money from the credit card scams he had set up. And he had sold weapons to insurgents and sold the insurgents to governments. And he had blackmailed United States government officials and sold the blackmail evidence to lobbyists. Oil lobbies. He had millions and millions and millions because he did not care who caught him. As long as he did not get caught until just in time. So he gave money to the Atomenergoproekt investors, men of shady type, oligarchs, cash-loving, and they helped to see that the reactor would be moved to someplace where it could be stolen and taken away for a field test where regulations would not interfere and there would be tremendous publicity for their product."

He shrugs.

"But if you want to steal a nuclear reactor and its fuel rods you must also create a distraction to cover the noise that will make. The computer worm he bought for West-Tebrum was almost as expensive as the reactor. So much noise and confusion was needed to hide the stolen reactor. To hide that it *had* been stolen. Secret chatter in Russia, coded messages about a missing reactor. Imagine if the world knew it was missing? Everyone would have looked. But because of West-Tebrum, the lookers were too busy to be bothered. When *your* country starts hearings on how such a thing could happen, a nuclear reactor slipping across borders, across a war zone, and no one in your security knew about it, they will see how obvious it was. If they had only looked. But too late now. Too late."

Jae has pushed herself up on her elbows, the change in her heart rate starting a new throb in her leg. She and Skinner still are not looking at one another. Too much. No time for that now. When will there be time? Never? She swings her legs over the edge of the table and the flash of pain almost blacks her out but she shakes it off and holds up a hand.

"And what's the plan when everyone finds out the reactor doesn't work?"

Aasif smiles, nods.

"Yes. Yes, that is good. Terrence said, he said you see everything. Good. Well. When they find out the reactor does not work, they will kill us then."

He steps to the curtain.

"Come with me, please. I will show you our real secret."

As they pass through the living quarters, they pause for a moment to watch the TV, where Aasif can be seen standing in front of the reactor and delivering his message. The doctor's family look from the TV to Aasif and point, *Look, look, you're on TV!*

They're hanging by a thread, these people, and most of them have no idea.

In #2 Shed, Aasif shows them the secret that makes the big lie possible.

"General Electric makes them, 747 engines. That is what it is, inside. More complicated than that, but at its heart it is a fifty-megawatt generator run off the power from a 747 engine. GE LM6000. Brilliant engineering. Excellent product. Horribly inefficient."

It's small, smaller than the cargo container that brought Dharavi its reactor. If they had the proper filters mounted on the air intakes, and scrubbers for the exhaust, it would be at least twice as large, but stripped bare it's no larger than a motor home, mounted on a firm cement foundation, a cluster of a dozen thick cables running out of one side to a junction box that spews a hundred thinner cables through an opening into a hut next door, where they begin their journey of patching and repatching throughout the slum. The entire unit is dwarfed by the fake cooling towers that stand next to it, exposed to the sky now that the shed's tin roof has been peeled away to allow steam to escape. The steam itself is in part the product of the LM6000's exhaust being pumped into the water tank below the sham towers, and in part created by the heating elements also inside the tank.

"Heat is a tremendous difficulty."

Aasif is pointing up at the steam rising from the towers.

"They will look to see if we're generating enough heat from the reactor. At Number One Shed we can heat the underside of the tin roof and that will be enough to hide that we are in fact safely at full throw, no reaction under way at all. But cooling towers must be exposed. So they will look here. The LM6000 stays hidden under a section of roof, but its own heat helps with the illusion. And it produces the power they see balanced over the BMC grid. Very good solution. I am proud."

He waves them to the door and away from the noise of the generator.

"We didn't have time. The window to receive delivery on the reactor was so small. We could not hide it here, keep it a secret. And our foundations. The LM6000 can stand on a housing foundation, but the Hitachi would rip itself out of the ground. Our cooling tank, also not ready. We were not prepared for the water flow we need to cool the reactor. The towers were not finished. Very little was ready, but the reactor was coming. And the software is very hard to run. We used video capture of screenshots to display while we made the video. And inside Number One Shed, a recording of a generator running, played back over a PA. Very loud."

As they walk down the lane, Raj and his mother and sister rejoining them, Jae leans on Skinner and on an old rattan cane the doctor gave her.

"What about spectroscopy? What happens when they analyze the chemical contents of the exhaust plume? They will."

Aasif nods.

"And what if they analyze the sound of the generator in the video recording and realize that it is a loop? And what if our man in the water department cannot hide the fact that we are not diverting enough water to cool a reactor? And what if they find the taps we have on the gas lines to feed the LM6000? These are our vulnerabilities. We have only a little time, however long it is, before our contrivances are discovered. We must bring the reactor online in earnest before then. Or they will come in and they will kill us."

There is a liveliness in the lane. Shops have opened in the evening air. The helicopters have gone, and, while the soldiers and police are still on 90 Feet Road, no one feels as threatened. Spices are on display, meat is being cooked on small grills, families have come out. From open storefronts and homes on the lane, every TV can be seen showing Aasif in the reactor shed or someone talking about what it means and what must be done. The world talking about Dharavi. They wave at him, point, as if he is a Bollywood star and not the crazy boy who always was changing the wires. Bushels of bright vegetables, incense bundles, open sewage ducts running into the alleys, kids playing, animal heads on display at the butcher. Lit up, despite the current flowing from the LM6000, by the soft glow of oil lamps.

It is a beautiful evening, and Jae leans against Skinner more than she needs to.

Aasif says a few words in Tamil to someone and then leads their small party down one of the alleys toward #1 Shed.

"Weeks. We need at least four weeks before they find out. Six weeks would be better. Two months would be best. The LM6000 has been running for over a month. We've been able to power Dharavi that long, fine tuning the wiring, but it was erratic until we balanced the load, hiding it on a factory transformer at the edge of the slum. Now it is perfect."

He stops walking.

"I have a lot of work to do. So now is the time to talk."

He looks at his watch.

"How will you get us more time?"

It is a dull shock to perceive this final checkmate of Terrence's. Pushed all over the board, square to square, one instant a pawn, the next instant queened on the back rank, free to ravage from behind the lines. But suddenly her knight is being taken.

Terrence. You son of a bitch.

She shakes her head.

"No. Terrence was wrong about this part."

Aasif taps the face of his watch.

"He said someone would come. A list of message boards and mail drops. A protocol for what messages to look for. How to respond. What Raj was doing, my Little Shiva. Terrence said someone would answer and then come. There was more than one point to the West-Tebrum attack. A distraction, we needed that. Obviously. But Terrence said we needed more, *A catalyst,* he said. To begin a reaction that would bring *you* here."

Jae feels stupid.

"No."

But Aasif is not looking at her. He is not talking to her.

Aasif is talking to Skinner.

"Terrence said that you could get us more time."

He puts a hand on his Raj's shoulder.

"He told me what to do."

He presents his son.

"Skinner, this is my son, Rajiv. Will you make him your asset?"

wonderful scam

THEY GO BACK to the shopkeepers' street.

Oil lamps. Darkness coming on. It smells like faraway places. There are red stains everywhere on the ground and the walls, it's only paan juice, spit up by chewers, but Skinner thinks about Haven's blood on the wall of the hutment.

Outside their family home, Skinner and Jae stood with Raj and his mother and baby sister. Haven's body was gone from inside. Skinner's own clothes, ruined by his brother's blood. He washed his hands at the doctor's office, but it is there under his thumbnails, reddish black. At the broken door, he looked at the young mother and her baby. The bullet hole in her sari. She doesn't know that she shot his brother. There was a man with a gun in her home, and there were children. Some problems are uncomplicated. He wanted to tell her what a marvelous shot it was. She has no idea. Perhaps she's good with a gun. A natural. The genius father and dead shot mother; what remarkable people they will be, Raj and the baby named Tajma, if they grow up.

The family went inside, work to be done, Jae and Skinner came here.

He misses carrying Jae. But she leans against him as they sit on a low step, just a step, leading to nothing, at the edge of the lane outside of an unopened shop with a front stained blue-green with mold. He looks at her leg, slight bend in the knee, red and swollen and bruised. Skinner looks up. The darkening sky. They are watched. So many pictures being taken right now.

He looks at the red-stained ground.

"By tomorrow night it will be impossible to get out."

Jae pokes her bandage, hisses with pain, pokes it again.

"Can you get them more time?"

He pulls her finger away before she can hurt herself again.

"If I have an asset, Jae, I have to keep it safe."

He looks at their hands.

"But I work for you. I can't end that contract myself. And I can't protect Raj if I stay here. It will need to be done from outside."

She nods.

"I'm staying."

She picks up a small sliver of wood from the step.

"Terrence. He promised me something. A front row seat where the future is being made. Every day will be different. The world will change because of what they do here. If they last past tomorrow. It opens up possibilities for me. I can feel them, inside my head. The possibility of the future. They need so much help. That reactor. I know something about that. And my robots. I can build things that will help them to be safer. I can help. I want to help. I don't want to look for dead bodies. I don't want to look at pictures. I want to do this. A world of lives to save."

She brings the sliver of wood to his thumb and uses it to scrape the dry blood from underneath his nail. Watching the delicate care with which she works, clever robot-building fingers, he wonders how much Terrence intended.

Did he see this, plan for it? Did he really need to hide the secret of what he was doing in a tangled configuration that only Jae could discover? Couldn't he just have told her, *Go there, see the future, and help.* Would anything less than living inside his bizarre scavenger hunt have brought her to this point? Her identity compromised by the shootout in Cologne, lover to a killer, perched on the verge of the most dangerous place in the world, and compelled to stay there. How far back did it begin? Did he usher Skinner into the world of protection knowing he would use him one day as a guardian to this mad experiment? How many of his choices have been his own since he met Terrence, and how many have been the result of Terrence's deft manipulation of the conditioning that was already in place when he first spoke to Skinner nearly twenty years ago? And, most of all, *this*. Did he plan *this?* Skinner and Jae, the murderer and the digger for the dead.

When she's done with both of his hands, cleaning the dry blood, he rises and helps her up. Standing on the step, she can look him in his eyes again, like in the train station at Cologne, but no one is waiting in the darkness with a gun this time.

"I'm canceling our contract. You have a new asset."

Kissing so immodestly, they draw a great deal of attention. Everything about them an alien curiosity in the glowing light. But these are strange times for everyone; kissing cannot be frowned upon overmuch. Skinner's eyes are closed. So that, though he feels it when Jae stops kissing him, and hears the tap of her cane until it fades into the sounds of the shopkeepers' lane, he does not see her walk away. He stands there for some time, eyes closed, letting himself be watched by the curious.

Strange American in a filthy suit, standing in the street with his eyes closed, in the lamp-lit dark.

horror

TWO NIGHTS LATER in a gated Maryland estate that showcases some of the finest security systems the free market has to offer, Cross is surprised to find an uninvited guest in his bedroom. All the more so because he has been sitting up in bed reading, with the door closed, for nearly fifteen minutes before he sees Skinner. The initial surprise done with, the shocking spike of adrenaline that literally made him bark beginning to fade, he becomes somewhat sensible, and realizes that he is about to die.

Skinner uncrosses his legs.

"It's a nightmare. Being afraid. Unable to scream."

Skinner points at Cross's neck.

"I can see your throat moving. But it's like someone has frozen the muscles. Glued your lips together."

Skinner rises from the chair next to Cross's writing table.

He's wearing a suit, charcoal, pressed oxford stripe shirt, dove-gray tie, brown belt, old boots. His hands are empty.

"When I was twelve, I became afraid."

He walks around the bed.

"I was afraid of the whole world. I was afraid of the sun."

He stands by the side of the bed, looking down at Cross.

"It was a terrible feeling. And it was very difficult to condition myself to feel otherwise."

He sits on the edge of the bed, picks up Cross's iPad, looks at the document he's been reading.

"I see here that there has been some discussion about how best to hit Dharavi."

He flicks his finger across the screen.

"I imagine commandos. A pinpoint attack on the reactor structure. An infinitely fast team of commandos who are able to kill everyone inside the reactor shed before any of the Naxalites can blow a hole in the side of the containment vessel. All of the commandos trained as nuclear engineers so that they are prepared to deal with a critical reactor if a breach occurs. All achieved while trained guerrilla fighters swarm the building from outside. Is it an op, or a scenario for a Hollywood pitch? Or both at the same time? Is it true that Kestrel has a new content division? Terrence would have been appalled."

He finds what he wants, stops flicking.

"You have an incoming email. Large. There are several images attached. It will take a few moments."

He sets the iPad on the nightstand, puts his hand on Cross's chest, and is silent for several seconds.

He lifts his hand.

"Your heart is very strong. Good."

A chime from the iPad.

"There it is."

He hands Cross the iPad, taps the screen for him, flicks to the first of dozens of photographs.

"I found these in Terrence's files. It is a comprehensive collection of my work. End results of my maxim."

Cross's hand moves, a spasmodic gesture, dragging each new image onto the screen, something he cannot seem to stop. Reflected in the lenses of his reading glasses, they look abstract, violently hued, chaotic. Shapes and colors not found in nature; not until nature is cut open and exposed to the light.

Skinner takes the iPad from his hands, sets it aside.

"I would like you to help me with something."

His hand slips inside his jacket.

"I want to plant an idea."

It comes out with a #28 blade X-Acto knife.

"I'd like for people to remember who I am. What I do. I'd like a simple and vivid thought to spread through your peers and confidants. Like *contraction*. Brilliant because it is so simple. Terrence was brilliant. And so are you. Quick to grasp the possibilities. Opportunities."

He takes Cross's eyeglasses from his face and rests them on the pillow next to his head.

"I find emotions difficult. Especially the strongest ones. Terror. Rage. I struggle with them."

He places the tip of the curved blade at the inside corner of Cross's right eye.

"Love."

Cross is not blinking.

"I am feeling all of those right now. And it is only with very practiced behaviors that I am controlling them. I will need to be very aware for the next little while so that I don't lose that control."

He looks into Cross's right eye, framed by the curve of razored steel.

"The idea that I want to plant is that if anything happens to my asset, I will appear. And I will do things to you."

It is a startling thing, to have your eye cut from your face, somewhere through the pain to feel it dangling against your cheek, and still, in the midst of this, to be unable to move or to scream. To be engulfed in a horror so deep and absolute that you would gladly die now for it to end.

With his remaining eye gaping, expecting the blade, Cross watches as Skinner wipes the X-Acto clean on a wad of tissues from the bedside box, before balling them to stanch the flow of blood from the empty eye socket.

"My asset is a child living in the Independent City-State of Dharavi. You must consider it, therefore, in your own best interests to protect the ICSD. However you want to go about that. Slow them down, Cross. Speak against action. Think about the child. So easy for him to get hurt if there's a raid. So easy for him to become a victim if the Indian government refuses to allow food aid and medical supplies into Dharavi. Do your best to help. And if nothing else works. Think about me."

He leans close to Cross's ear.

"It's a meme. The Skinner Meme. A potent and mutable idea. All you have to do is think it, and your imagination will do the rest."

He switches off the lamp.

"Goodnight."

Outside the house, Skinner feels the eyes in the night sky, searching the world, looking for secrets and fears. He turns his face to them then, and smiles, so that anyone peering close will see him and know that monsters still haunt the globe.

Then the screaming starts, and Skinner disappears.

EPILOGUES

SHE SPENDS MUCH of her time in the hut with Raj and the other kids. Minding the screens, searching the information. The ICSD is a constantly trending topic. There are independent city-states popping up around the world. Independent City-State of Mexico City, ICS Bronx, ICS Georgia, ICS Alabama, ICS Mogadishu, ICS Tiananmen Square, ICS Melbourne, ICS Stockholm. Mostly they are no more than a public park or a city block, and none has a reactor. It is being called the ICS Movement. There have been protests on both sides. Riots. Deaths. T-shirts. Songs. YouTube videos in support and condemnation. Here, they receive thousands of daily requests to emigrate, and as many threats of destruction by bomb, gun, germs, and/or various gods.

Sometimes she takes her father's knowledge into #1 Shed and helps with the work there. The work has no end. It is a race. Even if most of the people in the street don't know it, their days are numbered. But the new foundation has been poured, and they have reason to believe it will be strong enough to handle the torque of the generator when it begins to spin. The cooling tank is more difficult, and the towers. They have the advantage of no regulations or bureaucracy. One imperative, *Does it work?* Sadly, the Emerson software is another problem. The product itself is fine, but their computers are underpowered and can't run it properly. One of the electricity goons has found a breach in the army's perimeter. A captain who is very open to the possibility of bribes. If all goes well, some young men who used to work as IT wallahs in Bandra will go out tonight and buy what is needed and bring it back inside.

After that they might go out again and start finding materials she needs to start building her robots, a nest of spiders that she can set crawling along the perimeter.

Her leg hurts. She takes Tylenol. Or something labeled as Tylenol. That is what is available. It does little to help the pain.

She talks to Cross. She called him on her cell the first night, after Skinner left, told him that she'd seen the reactor. Told him it was real. Leverage to restrain any sudden preemptive attacks. They established an online contact protocol. Skype calls routed through the encoded Tor network. Anonymous communications like these are the best they can manage without scrambler technology on her end. They used the channel to communicate regularly in the first forty-eight hours. Feeding him disinformation along with just enough fact to give him the appearance of remarkable prescience as the community struggled to explain how they had missed something this big, and what they planned to do about it now. She knows Cross is far too smart to swallow everything she's told him, but uncertainty is the only real tool at her disposal. She told the lies and did what she could to get the ICSD through the first few days. Then something happened to Cross. She knows it was Skinner, but she doesn't ask what he did. Now she doesn't have to lie to get Cross's help. Now when Cross calls, it is usually at a very late hour in Maryland or DC or wherever his campaign to restrain action against the ICSD has taken him. He asks if he is safe, sometimes whispering; asking her, on one occasion, what he would see if he turned on the light. *Am I safe, Jae?*

Yes, she tells him, *you're safe.* And then she tells him what to do to remain safe.

But mostly she is with the kids, in the hut.

In the ICSD she has found the unpredictable edge of things. What will happen next? No one can say. There is no configuration, not here. Events have no precedent. Here is where the future is being manufactured; right next to tanneries and potting sheds and plastic recycling and open sewers. And there is a peace in it, not trying to find what comes next.

Until she is in front of the computers.

There she watches the feeds and the streams and the posts and the bulletins and reports, retweets and blogs and the digital walls. If they decide to come, this is where the signs will first appear. She will be the one to see it. If they discover the secret, that the reactor is not a danger at all, not yet, their relief and pique will show here, if only a moment before the guns come. And even after the reactor is online, if they can last these next few weeks, the guns will be looking for ways to come after them.

An affront has been offered.

They will not bear the insult, not if they have a choice.

Yet there have been some changes. Quantifiable reductions in the use of the term *contraction*. It seems to be a preparation for something. She suspects that Smith is getting ready to release the trove of Terrence's documents they sent to him from De Gaulle. They have their own darknet protocol, but Smith refuses almost entirely to use it. She knows that Skinner has been in contact with him as well. Smith did something for Skinner. Signals work, sent information to Cross. But Smith won't talk details. He just leaks documents from Terrence's trove. A trickle of incrimination so far; he's preparing to release the deluge. He remembers the burning body, men killed with the gun he made. Now he fires his own shots from the shadows.

So she works in the shed and she walks the streets and alleys and feels something easing in her head when she does. Disaster World is not the inevitability she saw at the end of every configuration. Not anymore. This may not last, but for now she can see a future with lives to save instead of bodies to dig from the troubled ground. Then she goes to the communications center in Raj's home, and she looks for the configuration of threat that means the world is coming to kill them after all.

And in between she looks at pictures. She waits for the most current Street Views on Google. She presses Cross and Smith for satellite imagery from obscure corners, on thin pretexts. She plunders photo-sharing services. Scanning crowds. Airports, a special interest. Looking for a tiny configuration. Defined by a single face. Looking for a sign of him.

Half hoping for danger here, to bring him back.

*   *   *

His father is always in #1 Shed.

And *he* is almost always in the media center. Even when he sleeps he is here. The other kids come and go, but he is here. At his computer. On the wall is the bloodstain.

His mom shot a man in the face there.

That thought will be his for the rest of his life. New world. Where Mom shoots a man in the face. Where he works all day and into the night, staring at the screens. Where Father never comes home. Where the army will let no one out of the slum.

David's family tried to leave. Fear ate them and they tried to leave. David's father came back alone. The army got David and his mom and his brothers and sisters. David's father ran. Now he drinks all day. Ashamed. No one knows what the army is doing with the people who try to leave. The TV says they are in a special camp. They have to stay there while the government decides who is a citizen and who is a terrorist. It looks like a refugee camp on the TV, but with big temporary buildings that look like jails; all of them say KESTREL on the roof.

Chiman has died.

His sister was alone at home in the morning while the rest of the family worked. Chiman came home for his cricket bat and found a young man from the neighborhood raping his sister. He had been doing it for years, but out of fear she had told no one. Chiman hit him with his cricket bat and the man took it from him and hit him in the head and Chiman died. The sister screamed and neighbors came and the man ran to the edge of the slum and the army got him and probably took him to the camp. Chiman's sister left the same night and also was taken by the army. She was ashamed that everyone knew what had been happening to her. So not everything has changed in Dharavi; these things are still happening.

Shitty people.

Raj does not like these shitty people.

But he does like Rani. And she likes him. She says she does. And they are tweeting with Kalki! Two days after Independence, she answered their question. *I have not come to Dharavi. But I want to see the ICSD.* And they talked for a very long time about how to answer and decided to invite her, when it was safer for her to come, and she could have dinner in their homes. And she answered again! Now she tells them to be careful. And asks how they are. Kalki! Jae says it could be someone else. Like when the man pretended to be Skinner and came to their home and his mom had to shoot him. But Raj and Rani don't believe it. And even if it is someone else, they don't tell her anything important. And it feels good to believe in this, even if it is a lie.

His friends are in the room with him, and his mom is making lunch to take to his father. His sister is on the cot getting ready to cry because she is tired and hungry. The ball is under his table, next to his feet.

There is no time for the ball now. But soon there will be. Work a little harder for a little longer and there will be time for them all to play soon.

Soon.

Maybe soon.

*   *   *

They didn't think he could last.

His pale skin would burn in the sun. His soft hands would be torn by the steel. His body, too big, would not bear the diet. Every mouthful must be wrung out, no energy wasted. His body when he came was an engine of waste. Required too much fuel. No. He couldn't last.

What the hell is he doing here anyway?

They were right. He could not last. He was burned. His hands tore. His body collapsed as he worked in the sun dragging sheets of rusted steel through the clutching wet sand. Then he got up. And dragged until he fell again. And again.

Repeat. Repeat. Repeat.

After months of it, the breakers can barely tell him from themselves.

On the polluted beaches of Chittagong, Bangladesh, where they drag the carcasses of dead ships to be riven for scrap, he has turned dark under the sun and his hands have become calluses and his body has stripped itself of all excess until his skin wraps bone and muscle and sinew like a withered hide.

He sleeps with them in the camp, taking a shift on a cot that he rents with five others. Four hours' sleep in rotations. There was a fight one night about whose turn it was, and when a drunken man threatened him with a knife he took the knife away from him and then put the drunk into the cot to sleep and threw the knife into the oil-scummed water of the bay.

Someone says he is a soldier who has renounced the wars.

Someone says he is a priest who made a woman pregnant.

Someone says he killed his brother and ran in shame.

Someone says he is secretly filming them.

Another fucking filmmaker, they say.

But he has no camera that they can see.

They break fucking ships here on the beach. If you can do the work, you can stay. It would kill most of the world, this work. But he works like a devil. He never gives anyone shit. And he pays his rent and for his food. So fuck it, he's okay.

But he is a strange fucker for sure.

White Western ship breaker. White skin. It's brown now. But still that's what they call him.

Skin.

Strange fucker.

Some nights he goes down to the beach and stands in the viscous tide, harsh reds and rainbow swirls rushing around his bare ankles.

And he looks up at the sky.

Months now.

There are TVs in town. All he has to do is walk a few miles. It's still the news. He doesn't know if the ICSD has lasted this long because they have the reactor online or because Cross has kept anyone from going in. He just knows that it's there. For now.

Safe. For now.

He thinks about her. Breaking the ships. Hidden here. He thinks about her.

As long as he's here, he can't be found. As long as he's here, Cross is afraid. The Skinner Meme in effect. He doesn't think about the thread dangling their lives. It is always there. Easy to cut.

Nothing new, this dangerous life.

He stands on the shore at night, the cameras whirling by overhead, shooting everything, looking at everything. And he pictures her, safe in a box he has constructed with the threat of himself, looking at her screens, camera lens views of the world at a distance. He knows he is watched then, and he imagines that it is her eyes that are watching him, making him real on this transient earth, and he looks up into the sky and he tells her his secret.

You are my asset, Jae. I protect you.

Everything else is just the world.

about the author

Charlie Huston is the author of the novels *Sleepless, The Mystic Arts of Erasing All Signs of Death,* and *The Shotgun Rule,* as well as the Henry Thompson trilogy, the Joe Pitt casebooks, and several titles for Marvel Comics. He lives with his family in Los Angeles.

charliehuston.com

MULHOLLAND BOOKS

You won't be able to put down these Mulholland Books.